Acclaim for Lee Vance's

RESTITUTION

"[A] relentlessly readable debut novel. . . . Vance plays his own excruciatingly complex game with great finesse, balancing the interior drama of Tyler's self-enlightenment with the spiraling complications of the financial crimes and the ripsnorting action of the chase scenes."
—*The New York Times Book Review*

"A tantalizing debut steeped in the world of high finance. . . . Vance shows a significant talent for action, plot twists and hair-raising near misses." —*Portland Tribune*

"An exceptional debut thriller, a brilliantly intricate page-turner. . . . As intelligent as it is intense, Vance's gripping debut marks the beginning of what should be a long and illustrious career as an adrenaline-inducing wordsmith."
—*Chicago Tribune*

"Readers will go from envying [Tyler] to despising him to rooting for him as his relentless quest brings him face-to-face with guys so bad and so tough they could use the Crips and the Bloods as their housemaids." —*The New York Sun*

"Vance thinks up a doozy of a double cross. . . . An impressive debut." —Bloomberg

LEE VANCE

RESTITUTION

Lee Vance is a graduate of Harvard Business School and a retired general partner of Goldman Sachs Group. He lives in New York City with his wife, Cynthia, and their three children.

RESTITUTION

RESTITUTION

LEE VANCE

ANCHOR BOOKS
A DIVISION OF RANDOM HOUSE, INC.
NEW YORK

FIRST ANCHOR BOOKS
MASS-MARKET EDITION, SEPTEMBER 2008

Copyright © 2007 by Lee Vance
Excerpt from The Garden of Betrayal
copyright © 2008 by Lee Vance

All rights reserved. Published in the United States by Anchor
Books, a division of Random House, Inc., New York, and in
Canada by Random House of Canada Limited, Toronto. Origi-
nally published in slightly different form in hardcover in the
United States by Alfred A. Knopf, a division of Random House,
Inc., New York, in 2007.

Anchor Books and colophon are registered trademarks of
Random House, Inc.

This book contains an excerpt from the forthcoming book *The
Garden of Betrayal* by Lee Vance. This excerpt has been set for this
edition only and may not reflect the final content of the forthcoming edition.

The Library of Congress has cataloged the Knopf edition
as follows:
Vance, Lee.
Restitution / by Lee Vance.—1st ed.
p. cm.
1. Murder—Investigation—Fiction. 2. Revenge—Fiction.
3. Wall Street (New York, N.Y.)—Fiction. I. Title.
PS3622.A58595R47 2007
813'.6—dc22 2007014673

Anchor ISBN: 978-0-307-27924-8

www.anchorbooks.com

Printed in the United States of America
10 9 8 7 6 5 4 3 2 1

For Cynthia, Zoe, Nikki, and Matthew

That which he labored for shall he give back,
and shall not swallow it down;
according to his wealth shall the restitution be,
and he shall not rejoice in it.

Job 20:18

FALL

1

"ELEVEN," Tigger crows triumphantly, his shot caroming off the plastic backboard into the hoop. "You got the yips big time today. That's eight hundred bucks you owe me."

"Double or nothing again," I say, rising to gather the Nerf balls scattered across my office floor. Glancing through the glass wall overlooking the trading desks, I notice several heads turn abruptly. The junior guys bet on our games. They can't see the basket hanging from the door, but it's common knowledge that the loser collects the balls. Having the guys on the trading floor see me drop four games in a row pisses me off almost as much as losing them.

"House rules," Tigger says. "Five-hundred-dollar game limit."

"House rules," I agree. "And whose house is it?"

"Bad form, Peter. Rules are the basis of civilization."

Tigger's Brooklyn vowels defeat his attempt at sounding cultured, marking him as an old-timer, one of the last guys to get a field promotion before Wall Street began recruiting professionals exclusively from the Ivy League. A small man in his early fifties, Tigger has a potbelly, fleshy cheeks, protuberant eyes, and an overly large head. He was my first boss, and still corrects me freely, despite the fact that I long since passed him in the corporate hierarchy.

"Eight hundred bucks," I say, grabbing a ball under his chair. "Big money. You could upgrade your entire wardrobe and use the other four hundred to have a HAZMAT team haul off the old stuff."

"Never buy anything that doesn't come in a three-pack. What'd you pay for that tie?"

"Hundred and ten maybe," I say, glancing down at the chain-link pattern. "In an airport. Retail's one forty."

"You're wearin' a hundred-and-ten-dollar tie that was made in China for fifty cents. You buy twenty-five-dollar hamburgers uptown and get hundred-dollar haircuts from guys with one name. I got a responsibility to take money off you because you're so fuckin' stupid with it."

Keisha opens the door while I'm on all fours, fumbling for a ball under the couch.

"Josh is on your personal line. He needs to speak to you *urgently*," she says, rolling her eyes.

Josh is my boss, the head of Klein and Klein, a former banker from the Rust Belt who's gradually taken on the grandeur of an Ottoman Empire pasha. Everything's urgent. It's just a matter of time until he begins referring to himself in the third person. I pick up the phone.

"Peter Tyler."

"Hold for Josh," his breathless secretary whispers.

"Hold for Josh," I say to Tigger, squeezing the mute button on the receiver. "What kind of asshole can't make his own phone calls?"

"Don't give him any money," Tigger warns. "Third quarter ends next Friday. We already made budget, and I want to go into bonus season with a tailwind."

"Peter," a bluff voice booms into the receiver, "how are we doing today?"

"Fine," I reply, thumbing down the volume. All the clients he used to cover must have been deaf. "Dollar's weaker, oil's higher, and bonds are soft. Generally good for us."

"Excellent," he says, not sounding particularly thrilled. "I'm a little concerned this morning, Peter. I've been looking at the firm-wide risk report."

"I'm sorry to hear that, Josh," I say, mentally appending the words *because you don't understand it.* "What seems to be the problem?"

"Controllers is suggesting that we've got our Japanese credit curve marked too wide. We're already under pressure to make numbers this quarter, and I don't want any unpleasant surprises."

"The curve is quoted as a yield spread over governments, Josh. We're long the underlying corporates and short the JGBs." I pause to let him get flustered. Josh has always been a relationship guy, his primary skill chatting up beefy CEOs on the links. His ignorance of basic market conventions is a source of constant amusement to the trading side of the firm.

"Your point being?" he asks warily.

"The value of the spread moves inversely to the value of our position. Controllers is accusing us of hiding profits, not losses."

Tigger's cracking up, both hands covering his mouth. I flash him a quick grin, but I have to credit Josh for asking questions. He's the one who will end up taking the heat if anything ever goes really bad, an all-too-common occurrence at financial firms like ours. Byzantine frauds brought massifs like Enron, Barings, and Daiwa Bank to their knees virtually overnight, their humiliated management's only defense that they were too dumb or inattentive to know what was going on. At least Josh is trying.

"We aren't supposed to be hiding anything," he says primly, glossing over his misunderstanding. "Which brings me to a second reason for my concern. Some of our banking fees have been unexpectedly pushed back to next month. We need to dig deep if we're going to meet the analysts' projections."

Right. On Wall Street, you're only as good as your most recent performance, and the bankers are busy playing the same game we are, trying to defer as much revenue as possible into the fourth quarter so they can look like heroes just before bonuses are decided.

"I'd love to lend a hand, Josh, but the cupboard's bare. We marked that Japanese credit spread wide because we have liquidity issues. We're long more than a hundred and twenty yards of corporates, and the market's only bid for about ten."

Tigger gives me two thumbs-up. Josh is silent.

"A yard's a billion yen," I add helpfully, knowing there's no chance that Josh can convert yen to dollars in his head.

"So you're saying it wouldn't be prudent to take profit at this point?" he asks after another brief pause.

"Exactly."

He sighs like a man carrying the weight of the world on his shoulders, but I'm not buying it. An ex-banker like Josh has to know that his former cohorts are sandbagging him, and there's no reason why my guys should pick up the slack. Whatever fees Josh needs from them to make the firm's numbers will miraculously rematerialize before Friday.

"One more thing, Peter," he says. "William Turndale called

this morning while I was at breakfast. Is there anything I should know before I get back to him?"

William Turndale is the CEO of Turndale and Company, an asset management firm that's one of our most important clients. He's generally agreed to be the biggest prick on Wall Street, which is a bit like having the largest shoe size in the NBA—it's not likely that he's calling Josh to tell him what a terrific job we're doing. Pasha or no, even the head of a Fortune 100 investment bank has to take shit from customers.

"Hang on a second." I press the mute button and look over at Tigger. "We got any problems with Turndale that you know about?"

"They're always bitchin' about something," he says, shrugging. "But I haven't heard about anythin' particular."

"We don't know why he's calling," I say into the phone.

"All right," Josh says wearily. "I'll give him a ring back and see what he wants."

"Let me know if there's a problem. And by the way, Tigger's sitting here with me, and he just passed me a note. He thinks we might be able to shake some cash loose from that Japanese corporate position. I'll look into it and get back to you."

Tigger jerks upright in his chair, sputtering a protest. I touch a finger to my lips.

"That's great, Peter," Josh says, sounding a bit more cheerful. "Thanks very much. Everything good at home?"

"Terrific. Thanks for asking."

"You be sure to send Jenna my best."

Josh has a three-by-five card in his Rolodex listing my birthday, my schools, and my wife's name. In season he congratulates me every time my old team wins, never missing the opportunity to add a personal touch.

"I will. And keep me posted on Turndale, please."

"Absolutely."

He hangs up. I smack the release button on my phone turret with the back of the receiver and drop the handset on the desk.

"He sends his best to Jenna," I say to Tigger.

"Douche bag," Tigger says, glaring.

"Be nice. You're talking about our fearful leader."

"The hell I am. I'm talkin' about you. What the fuck are you doin', tellin' him I said we could take profit on our Japanese position?"

"Sometimes you gotta go along to get along," I say, mimicking Tigger's accent. "Who used to tell me that?"

"You go along with guys that are gonna go along with you. Next time we got a problem here, Josh is gonna have trouble rememberin' your name. You know that."

"Maybe the next time is now. William Turndale's got to be calling about something."

Tigger stares into space for a second, thinking, and then gives a reluctant nod. "Good point," he says sourly. "I never met a guy that rich and that miserable. You gonna call Katya?"

I feel myself flush and hunch forward to recover an orange Nerf ball from underneath my desk. Katya's the number two at Turndale, an old friend who's helped us out of hot water with William in the past. I haven't gotten around to telling Tigger that she's probably not a friend anymore. Calling her wouldn't be a good idea.

"Let's wait and find out what's going on first," I reply, my face still hidden. "No reason to tee up a favor we might not need. Katya never does anything without demanding a quid pro quo."

"Sweet as pie and tough as nails," Tigger says approvingly.

"My kind of girl." He claps his hands together and sighs as I emerge with the ball. "I find out one of our guys hasn't told me about a screwup with Turndale and I'm gonna rip him a new one. You want me to drop the guys in Tokyo a note and tell them to re-mark that corporate position?"

"I'd rather talk it through with them first. Say nine o'clock. You mind setting it up?"

"Where you gonna be?"

"Here."

"Why?"

"I'm flying tomorrow, so I'm going to stay over at the Harvard Club."

"Flyin' where?"

"Frankfurt."

"And then where?"

"Helsinki and London, then back home Friday night."

"You just got back from Toronto," he says accusingly.

"So?"

"So what are you, on a fuckin' concert tour? How many customers we got in Helsinki?"

"Three."

"How many that've got two nickels to rub together?"

"One. We should ignore them?"

Tigger mutters under his breath.

"Don't start with the Yiddish," I say, feeling a dull pain throb behind my temples. "Please."

"You're spendin' half your time out of the country and the other half sleepin' in the city. Why? What's goin' on at home?"

"Things are bad," I say, looking out the window onto Battery Park. Glossy green leaves reflect morning sunshine in the treetops below, a light breeze creating the illusion of liquid motion. The line of sweating tourists waiting for the harbor ferries is half the size it was two weeks ago, a harbinger of the imminent change of season. Setting down the foam ball, I slip my watch off my wrist and begin toying with the metal band.

"Bad," he asks, "or every molecule in your body exploding at the speed of light bad?"

"More the latter," I say.

"You want my advice?"

Tigger and I have been friends a long time now, but I've always tried to keep my personal problems out of the office.

"I want you to mind your own fucking business."

"Tell her you're sorry."

"You've been studying to be a rabbi for what, ten years now? And that's your best shot? Tell her I'm sorry?"

"I've been married for thirty years. Take my advice. Say you're sorry, let her vent, say you're sorry again, let her vent some more, and keep goin' until you end up in the sack. Don't forget to nod a lot while she's talkin', and say stuff like 'You must have felt awful.'"

If only it were that simple. Jenna's been slipping away from me for years, her energy and attention increasingly focused on causes. I've never known what to say, afraid of sounding selfish. Anger and frustration led me to make mistakes. I tried apologizing when the big blow-up came, but it didn't do any good. Jenna asked me to leave last week. She said she couldn't stand to feel as alone as she did when we were together.

"You know what I like about work?" I ask Tigger, snapping my watch back onto my wrist.

"Ridin' on my back?"

"The fact that the rules never change. Me and you and the other guys work our butts off every day and the next morning we get a number that tells us how we did. Good numbers are good and bad numbers are bad, and as long as we make money, we don't have to give a shit how Josh or anyone else *feels* about it."

"Petey," Tigger says quietly. "Talk to me. What's wrong?"

Keisha opens the door again, saving me from the need to reply.

"I'm getting coffee," she says. "You guys want?" Keisha's smart, twenty-five, has honey brown skin the shade of buffed pear wood, and is wearing a little yellow dress that's driving half the guys on the floor crazy.

"My heart's already beatin' too fast," Tigger replies, clutching his chest theatrically. "You're gonna kill one of us old guys if you keep dressin' like that."

"I'm a little uncomfortable with that remark," Keisha says sternly, a smile playing at the corners of her mouth. "Peter?"

Tigger's only mouthing off to provoke me. Eve Lemonde, our head of Human Resources, leaned on me big-time a few years back with Josh's support, insisting I rein in the locker room chatter so prevalent on trading floors. I reluctantly agreed to start fining guys for remarks in violation of the employee conduct code, a wordy, gender-confused affirmation of political correctness that forbids expression of all human instincts save greed. The proceeds go to an employee-nominated charity, but every time I fine someone I feel like a corporate tool. Tigger's the number-one offender, happy to contribute all the money he saves on ties, hamburgers, and haircuts to the pot if it causes me a little angst. Eve's been urging me to fire him for years, a fact that only amuses him further.

"It's okay by me if your boyfriend beats the crap out of him," I say. Keisha's engaged to a guy at NYU Medical School who's built like a train.

"It's a thought," she says. "But I'd be happier if you socked him with a big fine. I designated the pot this month. The money's going to my grandfather. He runs an after-school program for kids at the public library up in Hell's Kitchen."

"Let's not make Peter the bad guy," Tigger says to Keisha, winking at her. "Tell you what: He owes me eight hundred bucks because he shoots hoops like a girl. I'll contribute that."

"Done," I say, feeling like I've been trick-bagged. "Print out a check please, Keisha. And I'd like an espresso."

"Make the check for fifteen hundred," Tigger says, "because he's gonna get the deduction. I'll contribute fifteen hundred also, as a credit against all the wrong things I'm plannin' to think about you later. And get me a latte. Spendin' money makes me tired."

"Good by you?" Keisha asks, looking at me.

"If Tigger buys the coffee."

"People call me a cheap bastard," he says, taking a twenty out of his wallet.

"You guys are the best," she says, starting to close the door. "Thanks." She sticks her head back in at the last moment, mock-glowers at Tigger, and whispers fiercely, "I'd kick your skinny butt at hoops any day of the week."

"Nice girl," Tigger says after she's gone. "She'd be good in a sales job."

"I've been working on it, but Lemonde has to approve, and she doesn't like the fact that Keisha went to a junior college. I'm trying to play a minority card."

"Shit," Tigger says, looking disgusted. "Don't let her find out."

I shrug. One reason this is my office instead of Tigger's is that I'm more willing to do what I need to do to get things done.

"You still owe me an answer," Tigger says. "Jenna. What's goin' on?"

I stare through the window onto the trading floor, sharing the quiet pleasure of watching Keisha walk to the elevator with about fifty other guys while I wrestle with the urge to confide in Tigger. Picking up the orange Nerf ball from my desk, I launch it toward the hoop.

"One more game," I say, watching the shot drop. "Loser buys lunch for the floor."

2

"WAIT A TICK," I say a few hours later, putting one of our economists on hold and punching the flashing intercom button. "What's up?"

"Josh on your rollover," Keisha says.

"Pick up line one and tell Kenny I'll get back to him, please. And ask Tigger to join me."

"The pizza came to three hundred and twenty dollars with the tip. I put it on your Visa card."

"Thanks." I got off cheap. If Tigger'd lost, I would have told Keisha to order sushi. Picking up my second line, I suffer through the "Hold for Josh" routine again.

"Peter," Josh says. "Are you familiar with an outfit called Fondation l'Etoile?"

He's in business mode, which is good. Beleaguered and solicitous are the emotional states to watch out for.

"Not particularly."

"You're listed as their internal contact in our system."

"L'Etoile's a charitable organization of some sort. A friend of mine is on the board. He said they might want to trade some cash bonds so I had the credit guys set them up. Is there a problem?"

"No. But William Turndale's interested in them for some reason. That's why he called. He'd like to know anything we can tell him."

Tigger slips in and I point to my handset, mouthing Josh's name. He frowns and settles on the edge of the couch.

"How did William find out we did business with l'Etoile?" I ask.

"He had one of his traders ask around."

I scribble a note on a yellow pad, reminding myself to find out which of my guys shot his mouth off.

"I thought firm policy was not to discuss one client with another."

Josh chews on my implied rebuke for a moment.

"I hardly think William's asking us to reveal anything confidential," he says stiffly.

"It doesn't particularly matter," I reply, figuring I've made my point. "My friend on l'Etoile's board works for Turndale. Andrei Zhilina. If William has any questions, it's better he speak to Andrei directly."

"Zhilina?" Josh repeats. "Related to Katya?"

"Her brother. He runs Turndale's Moscow office. He worked here, actually, about twenty years ago. We were analysts together."

It occurs to me that William's call to Josh might work in my favor, giving me an excuse to get in touch with Andrei. I haven't had the nerve to call him since my falling-out with Katya a few weeks ago, unsure what she might have told him, or how he'd react. Losing Katya as a friend was painful enough; losing Andrei as well would be devastating.

"Tell me," Josh begins, and then pauses. His secretary is saying something I can't quite make out in the background. She sounds upset. "Just a moment . . ." His voice trails off.

He puts me on hold, his secretary's voice looping in my head as I try to decipher her words. I could swear she said my name. Thirty seconds pass, a vague apprehension creeping over me. Tigger raises an inquisitive eyebrow.

"He's talking to someone else," I say. "Affairs of state maybe."

Tigger grins. A sharp click announces Josh's return.

"Something's come up," Josh says rapidly, his words running together. "I have to go now."

"Is everything okay?"

"I'm sorry," he gabbles. "I really am so sorry."

The line goes dead. I stare at my handset curiously and then toss it on the desk, my uneasiness growing.

"What was that about?" Tigger asks.

"No clue. Josh called to tell me Turndale was asking questions about a client I brought in last year, was interrupted by his secretary, and then said he had to go, sounding like his pants were on fire."

"Some journalist probably misspelled his name."

I smile automatically, a movement on the trading floor catching my attention. Eve Lemonde and a man and woman I've never seen before are walking toward Keisha's desk. The man looks like a bricklayer dressed to visit his bank manager, the woman as if she's playing the male lead in a sorority theatrical. Keisha glances up as they approach.

"Peter?" Tigger says.

I motion him silent, watching. Keisha listens for a few seconds and then turns to look at me, her expression a dagger to my heart.

"What's wrong?" Tigger asks.

"I don't know," I say, afraid that I might. I've lived this moment before, when I was fifteen. Time becomes syrupy as Keisha leads the others to my door, slowing enough for me to process the gold badges clipped to the strangers' waists, the tears already tracking Keisha's mascara, and Eve's practiced look of sympathy. They enter my office and tell me what's happened. My vision stutters and swims like low-bandwidth video. Keisha's a yellow blur outside the door; the two cops twitch awkwardly in my desk chairs; Eve vanishes and reappears like a Cheshire bureaucrat. Tigger stands beside me, his hand clutching mine, tears shining on his face. I sit as tall as I can behind my desk, holding the news at a remove, trying to stay in control. Words penetrate the static in my head like an AM radio signal bounced cross-country off thunderheads, fading in and out.

"Mr. Tyler," the male cop is saying. Eve introduced him, but I didn't catch his name. "It's important we move as quick as we can when we're investigating a murder. We need you to answer a couple of questions for us."

I nod, trying to focus my attention on him. His face is toadlike, pale jowls overflowing his collar beneath dark, hooded eyes.

"Our first take was that your wife just got unlucky. She surprised a burglar in your garage and he hit her with something metal, like a pry bar. There's a couple of things that don't add up, though. Her purse was still there, and her hair was pushed back from her face after she was down. It could have been someone that knew her. Can you think of anybody that might have wanted to hurt her?"

"No," I manage to say, an image of Jenna beaten and bloodied pulsing in my brain.

"An old boyfriend maybe? Some guy who had a crush on her?"

"Not that I know about."

"I see." He fishes a pen, a small spiral pad, and a pair of skinny black reading glasses from his jacket pockets. Slipping on the glasses, he opens the pad and begins turning pages with a moistened thumb. "The neighbor said she was doing public advocacy work. What kind of work was that?"

I open my mouth but can't seem to formulate a reply that puts Jenna in the past tense. A sudden vertigo makes me clutch the underside of my desk as Tigger answers.

"Jenna was a lawyer," Tigger says, his voice choked up. "She did pro bono stuff. The last couple of years, she's been workin' full-time on a lawsuit against New York State, because they underfund urban schools."

"Pro what?" the cop asks, taking notes.

"Bono," his female partner answers. "B-o-n-o. She was working for free."

The male cop swivels his entire upper body to stare at her from beneath his glasses, an expression of distaste on his face. "Detective Tilling's a *law student*," he sneers. "As if the world needs another—" He falls silent abruptly, Tigger's grip tightening on mine.

"If you have questions, ask them," Tigger says furiously.

"A few more things," the male cop says, straightening in his chair and glancing at Tigger expressionlessly. He flips some pages backward and looks at me again. "Did your wife travel much on her job?"

"Albany," I say, unsure how much longer I can hold it together.

"She spend many nights up there?"

"One or two every couple of months."

"Uh-huh," he says. "And what about you? You travel much?"

"Sometimes."

"You been traveling much recently?"

"Yes."

"When did you travel last?"

"I got back from Toronto on Friday. Up and back overnight."

"So where were you this past weekend?" he asks, pencil poised.

Some nosy fucking neighbor must've told him I wasn't home. My brain feels jammed, the seized cogs straining against one another. There's no way I'm going to drag my relationship with Jenna through the mud by telling some wannabe Columbo about our problems.

"Mr. Tyler," he says, lowering his voice as he leans toward me. "I know how you feel but I've got to ask. Were you having any marital difficulties?"

His name is Rommy, I suddenly recall. Detective Rommy.

"You know how I feel, Detective Rommy?" I ask, the pressure in my skull building as his words echo.

"Maybe you'd rather talk about this alone," he says, waving toward Tigger and Eve.

"*You* know how *I* feel?" I ask again.

"I been married," he says, giving me a quick man-to-man wink. "It's hazardous duty. Sometimes you take a bullet; sometimes you gotta cut loose for a little R and R. Either way, there's nothing to be ashamed of."

Rage propels me to my feet.

"You don't know a single fucking thing about how I feel," I shout, leaning over the desk and punching my finger toward him. "I loved my wife and I don't know anyone who would want to hurt her. Now get out of my office and go do your fucking job before I pick up the phone and figure out how to get hold of whoever your boss reports to. You too, Eve. I want you all out of here right fucking now."

"Jesus," Tigger says, dropping the window blinds after Eve and the cops have cleared out. Rommy made a fuss, but Eve smoothed things over. Tigger catches me by both shoulders and gazes into my face.

"Petey . . ."

"I'm going to need a few minutes here, Tigger," I say, interrupting him.

"You sure?"

"Yes."

"I'll be right outside."

He closes the door quietly. Tears flood from my eyes as I drop my head into my hands. Jenna.

3

TIGGER BACKS HIS VOLVO WAGON into a spot shaded by a spreading elm, nose pointed to the redbrick Catholic church on the hill above us. He cracks the windows before switching off the ignition, admitting a humid breeze. Cicadas chirp monotonously; a bedraggled monarch butterfly clings to the hood, orange-and-black wings beating listlessly. It's 11:30. We're half an hour early, the first to arrive. A dark blue Ford rigged with radio mast and spotlight creeps past and parks on the far side of the lot, sunlight flashing off a camera lens pointed through the open passenger window. Tigger uncaps a thermos, pours cool mint tea, and passes a cup to me. He nods toward the Ford.

"Fuckin' cops."

I don't respond, not wanting to get into it. Today's going to be hard enough without letting the police get to me. Either because of my outburst or because they haven't got any other leads, the cops have decided to play the odds, which means they've spent most of their time investigating me. The last ten days have been nightmare punctuated by low comedy, with Detective Rommy and his thuggish cohorts omnipresent in the role of threatening clowns, their ludicrous insinuations increasingly sinister. I've hired a lawyer to keep Rommy at bay, and a team of private investigators to double-check the cops and their investigation. The report I got on Rommy was exactly what I'd expected.

Tigger shifts uncomfortably in the seat next to me. Silence is hard for him. He's been trying to persuade me to open up, but I can't bear the thought of revisiting my mistakes with Jenna at this point. A third car pulls in and parks, and then two more. I drop the visor to make myself less visible. College friends, business school classmates, neighbors, and colleagues walk past as the lot fills. Quite a few of Jenna's colleagues, less of mine, but then, her firm shut down for the day so everyone could attend—the financial markets don't close for anyone except dead presidents.

Katya arrives without Andrei, and my heart sinks further. She sent a note, but I've been leery of getting back to her. Difficult as our relationship was before, it's unimaginably more confused now. Andrei's the person I need to speak with. He's the only one I could ever talk to about my problems with Jenna, and he's seen me through tough times before. When my father died, Andrei flew from London to Ohio for the funeral. The evening after the ceremony, we climbed the hill where my dad and I had gone to look at stars when I was a boy. We set up my father's telescope, built a fire, and spent the night drinking the remnants of his whiskey. A breeze rose toward dawn and I cast his ashes skyward, a gray plume streaming north toward the Great Lakes.

"Jenna's parents?" Tigger asks.

I glance in the direction he's looking and nod, not surprised he recognized them. Mary O'Brien's a three-quarter-scale version of Jenna, a woman who wore her age lightly until recently. Independent-minded and plainspoken to a fault, she's been excoriating the police in the press, chastising them for wasting time and energy investigating me when they should be focused on picking up other leads. We've met twice recently and talked on the phone a couple of times; it's evident Jenna hadn't confided our problems to her.

Careworn as Mary appears, the more dramatic change is in her husband. Ed's an old union stalwart, a blustering roustabout with a drinker's gut and a laborer's shoulders, who's insisted on arm wrestling every Christmas since I first began dating Jenna. My current record is 0 and 22. Today, his head hangs as he shuffles beside his wife like a punch-drunk fighter, rendered feeble by grief. Jenna was their only child.

I close my eyes, willing myself to calm down. Jenna inherited both her mother's outspokenness and her father's idealism. She took me to task for my conservative leanings the first time we met, approaching me at a pub night senior year and ridiculing a column I'd written for the college newspaper. We spent an hour arguing about Reagan and his Great Society budget cuts before I offered to walk her home.

Jenna walked me home instead, and I woke the next morning spooned naked against her, caught between two physiological urgencies. By the time I'd hurried back from the bathroom, she was already half-dressed, warm breasts just vanishing beneath a Toots and the Maytals T-shirt. She was tall and slim, long-muscled like a swimmer, with sandy blond hair that cascaded loosely around her face as she bent over to slip one bare foot into her jeans. She had a pale scar on her upper lip, and blue-gray eyes the color of soapstone. Seeing her in the morning light inflamed me, my lips and fingers burning with tactile memories.

"Don't go," I said, closing the bedroom door behind me.

"It's only seven. We can sleep another couple of hours, and then I'll make you breakfast."

"Sleep?" she asked, with a significant look at my tented boxer shorts.

"Whatever."

"'Whatever'? That's a new euphemism for me. Listen, last night was last night. It was fun." She tucked her hair back behind her ears and gave me a smile, top front teeth ever so slightly gapped. "Thanks."

"There's a party at the Deke house tonight. I could meet you there, or pick you up."

"I'm not big on frat parties."

"We could see a flick."

"I'm pretty busy with back-to-school stuff."

"You've got to eat. I'll cook you dinner."

"Are you going to make me hurt your feelings?" she asked quietly, eyes resting on mine.

"I guess so," I said, thoroughly confused, wishing I hadn't drunk so much the previous evening.

"You hang with a crowd. Everybody knows who you are. Captain of the basketball team, a big man on campus. I'm really not interested in getting involved in all that."

"Then what was last night about?"

"Poor impulse control."

"Ouch."

"Sorry," she said, grinning. "You've got that tall, dark, and handsome thing going on. I saw you across the room and was overwhelmed with lust."

"Now you're teasing me."

"A little. You mind if I move some of this stuff?" she asked, motioning toward the laundry piled on my desk chair. My room was a disaster. I hadn't been expecting company.

"Whatever," I said, wanting her to smile again. "But I'd appreciate the truth."

"The truth," she said, obliging me with another grin as she tossed dirty clothes on the bed and sat down. "I saw you play, last winter, just after I transferred in. I thought you were a good-looking guy, and I liked the way you moved. Then I started reading your rubbish in the school paper and found out you were on the Inter-Fraternity Council and head of the Young Republicans and Christ knows what else. I mean, really."

"So why last night?" I asked, ignoring her provocation.

"I'm kind of embarrassed about last night," she said, concentrating on her bootlaces. "It was a mistake."

"You make a lot of mistakes?" I asked, feeling a little pissed off.

"Everybody makes mistakes," she said, not smiling. "The trick is not to make the same one twice."

"I apologize," I said quickly. "You hurt my feelings. The Young Republicans is a quality organization."

"I warned you."

She got up to go.

"You still haven't answered my question properly."

"Why did I sleep with you?" she asked, meeting my eyes again. "I was working as a teacher's aide at the middle school last spring. You walked by the playground at recess and one of the kids recognized you and waved hello."

"I remember. His mom's in the Athletic Department."

"I figured that anyone who took forty minutes out of his day to teach a gang of eleven-year-olds how to run the pick and roll couldn't be a bad guy, regardless of his questionable extracurriculars and contemptible politics. So you had that going for you."

"So why leave?" I demanded. "You said it yourself—I'm a good guy. If you take your clothes off and get back in bed I'll go play ball with the kids again this afternoon."

"Sorry," she said, laughing. "I have to go to work."

"Give me your number. I'll dump all my friends and become a Democrat."

"I don't think so. Have you seen my bag?"

"No." I was lying. It was in the hall by the front door. She scanned the floor, eyes lighting on a pile of books.

"That's too perfect."

"What?"

"You have a copy of the Boy Scout manual by your bed."

"My dad gave it to me when I was a kid. It covers most situations. There's a good section on nocturnal emissions."

She laughed again, and I felt like I was making progress.

"He told me I wouldn't go wrong if I stuck to the Scout law."

"Be prepared?"

"That's the motto. There's a motto, a slogan, an oath, a code, and the law."

"I guess Scouts are prepared. So what's the law?"

I raised three fingers.

"A Scout is trustworthy, loyal, helpful, friendly, courteous, kind, obedient, cheerful, thrifty, brave, clean, and reverent."

"You're not doing so hot on clean."

"Some of the laws are more important than others."

"Tell me," she said, tipping her head sideways and folding her arms. "Which is the most important?"

"Loyal," I replied instantly. "No doubt about it."

"So you weren't planning to dump your friends?"

"Not right off," I said. "I'd appreciate it if you'd give them a chance."

She ripped a corner off an old newspaper lying on my desk and scrawled something on it with a pen.

"My number," she said, tucking the slip of paper into the waist of my shorts. She stood on tiptoe to kiss me chastely on the lips, ran a cool hand over my bare shoulder and down my arm. "Loyal was the right answer."

"Time," Tigger says.

We both get out, the car beeping as he locks it with the remote. He straightens my tie, flicks lint from my shoulders, and examines my pants critically. The waistband is bunched under my belt. I've lost about ten pounds. He buttons my coat and reaches into his pocket, pulling out a clean handkerchief.

"Wipe your face," he says.

I blot away tears and offer the handkerchief back.

"Keep it," he says. "I brought a couple."

"I've been thinking," I say.

"About what?"

"The guys I hired have got a good chance of figuring this thing out before the cops, because they aren't spinning their wheels on me."

"Yeah?"

"And when they do, I'm going to go after the fucker who murdered my wife and kill him myself."

Tigger glances down at his feet and then back up at me.

"We can talk about that tomorrow," he says quietly. "It's time to say good-bye to Jenna now."

I wipe my face again, square my shoulders, and walk toward the church.

4

A SMALL GROUP OF reporters and photographers are working the front entrance of the church from a police-barricaded
section of the street, and a television van is setting up in a
driveway opposite. Jenna's murder got a lot of local coverage
in our quiet corner of Westchester, but I'm unhappily surprised to see how much press has traveled to New Jersey for
her funeral. Maybe Rommy's leaked his suspicions of me—
the media always love a Wall Street defendant.

Shutters click as I approach, and a man with plastic credentials hanging around his neck rushes me from the side,
microphone extended as he calls my name. A uniformed cop
snarls at him, saying the press aren't allowed on church property. Ignoring them all, I follow Tigger through the heavy
wooden doorway into a dim vestibule. Jenna was confirmed
in this church, and she and I were married here sixteen years
ago. The organ groans as I retrace her steps down the aisle,
mourners rubbernecking. I concentrate on Tigger's back, keeping my face as impassive as possible.

Tigger hesitates as we approach the altar and then glances

back. Both front pews are empty, Jenna's parents nowhere
to be seen. I give a tiny shrug and tip my head to the right,
uncertain as to protocol. Mary planned the service, well
aware her daughter's religiosity had never rubbed off on me.
A polished mahogany coffin looms in my view as Tigger steps
to the side, an abrupt vision of Jenna's broken body within
making me flinch. I've been having nightmares, dreaming
Jenna's corpse lay in bed with me, and knowing with a
dreamer's certainty that my love could resurrect her. Night
after night I gather her cold limbs to mine, clear blood-
matted hair from her face, and breathe life desperately between
her waxen lips. Time and again her lungs empty lifelessly,
each chill exhalation finding me wanting.

Heart pounding, I edge into the pew after Tigger and lift
a program from the seat. The words swim into focus as my
breathing slows. Jenna's name is printed on the cover, and
beneath it the same claptrap I learned to mumble as a child,
save that the kingdom and the power and the glory are omit-
ted. More puzzling than Jenna's faith was her fidelity to a
church whose teachings so frequently infuriated her. Her
insistence on a Catholic wedding ceremony condemned me
to half a dozen basic religion classes and a solemn oath to raise
our children in the "One True Church." Jenna found ways to
compensate me for the pain of the educational sessions, but,
despite our best efforts, we never had any kids to raise. Would
it be better or worse to have a child of ours with me now? Better and worse maybe.

Father Winowski, Jenna's parish priest, emerges from the
sacristy clad in black-and-gold liturgical robes. I'm glad he's
saying the service; Jenna was fond of him. They used to trade
book suggestions, and Jenna stopped by his rectory every

couple of weeks to cook Polish dishes from his grandmother's recipes. A plump man with fussy manners, he had dinner at our house a handful of times, drinking neat vodka before, during, and after the meal, and giggling nervously as Jenna took him to task for Vatican lunacies such as the prohibition of condoms. He looks distressed today, eyes red-rimmed and shining with emotion. My heart warms to him for his grief.

"Peter," he says, approaching me. "I need a word."

"Of course," I reply, puzzled. Tigger starts to rise with me, but I put a hand on his shoulder.

Father Winowski leads me to the altar boys' vestiary, where a couple of black-cassocked teenagers are playing cards. He chases them out and closes the door.

"I'd like to take a moment to pray for guidance," he says, voice breaking. "You might want to pray also."

He bows his head and I follow suit, acutely uncomfortable as he murmurs to himself. Thirty seconds pass. He looks up.

"I have some things to tell you," he says, hands knitted together nervously. "I don't know if I've done right or wrong. I haven't been able to talk to my confessor yet."

"Please," I say, his demeanor unsettling.

"You know the church has had a lot of trouble with the civil authorities in the past few years. The bishop has us all on eggshells. None of us wants any more attention from the police."

"Tell me what happened," I say, my mouth dry.

"Detective Rommy and his partner came to see me yesterday afternoon, at my rectory. He asked if I'd been counseling Jenna and I said no, not in any formal way, and told him that we usually talked about books. Then he asked if it were fair to characterize the time I spent with her as social, and I said yes, that she and I were friends. And then he asked if she'd spoken to me about her relationship with you. I said I couldn't talk about that."

A tear skips down his pudgy cheek.

"What did Rommy say?" I ask, although I've already figured it out.

"He said I couldn't refuse to answer, that I'd already admitted we didn't have a privileged relationship, and that unless I were prepared to swear she'd never talked to me about you outside of the confessional, he'd arrest me for obstruction of justice. He said he'd call the local newspaper and get them to send a photographer over, and then take me out the front door of the rectory in handcuffs. I didn't know what to do."

He rocks back and forth in his distress, clasped hands pressed to his mouth. Some corner of my brain admires Rommy's ingenuity even as I resolve to hurt him.

"What did you tell him?" I ask, hoping Jenna kept to generalities.

He bows his head again, staring at my shirtfront.

"Jenna came over to cook a week and a half ago. We were playing Chinese checkers and talking after dinner. She said she'd asked you to leave."

"And?"

"And that she was struggling," he whispers. "She was considering a divorce."

I slump back against a wardrobe, feeling devastated despite my lack of surprise. It seems impossible that Jenna and I ended like this. The thought of Rommy gloating over Winowski's disclosures is a crowning blow.

"I loved her," I say bitterly. "Whatever problems we had

aren't important now. She would have wanted you to keep your mouth shut. This is only going to make things worse for her parents. I thought you were her friend."

His mouth works silently for a second, fresh tears starting.

"I loved her, too," he says.

"You loved her kielbasa," I snap, his moist, moonish face infuriating me. "It's not really the same thing."

He draws himself up stiffly, as if I'd slapped him.

"You're the one who was seeing another woman."

So Jenna told him. It's my turn to drop my eyes, rage giving way instantaneously to shame.

"You told Rommy I cheated?" I ask a few moments later, looking up to confirm my worst expectation.

He nods, stern-faced.

"Did Jenna tell you the other woman's name?"

"No."

I rub my forehead, a trickle of sweat running down my collar. This is going to be awful. Fucking Rommy. I stand up straight, pulling myself together.

"Okay," I say. "It's probably best that the O'Briens hear about this from me. I don't want to burden them any more today, but first thing tomorrow, I'll pay them a visit to apologize and explain. I'd guess they might want to call you afterward. Anything you see fit to tell them is fine by me."

"I don't think you understand," he says, sounding pained.

"Understand what?"

"The O'Briens are in the sacristy. Detective Rommy spoke to them last night. They're very upset. They've asked me to tell you that they don't want you to attend the funeral. If you insist on staying, Mrs. O'Brien says she'll denounce you from the altar."

I feel like I'm going to throw up.

"I've already emphasized to her that you have every right to be here," Father Winowski continues. "And I've told her that as a representative of the church, I'll strongly condemn any unauthorized statement she makes from our pulpit."

"What did she say?"

"She asked what I thought as Jenna's friend." He lifts one hand and covers his Roman collar, his eyes unexpectedly glacial. "I told her Detective Rommy made some persuasive arguments, and that I sympathized with her position."

A chill foreboding quivers in my chest, and it occurs to me for the first time just how damning Rommy might be able to make my sins and omissions seem. Maybe I haven't been thinking about things clearly. I walk to the door of the vestiary and peer through a small diamond-shaped window. The church is full, with mourners fidgeting in the side aisles and the back. There's no doubt in my mind that Jenna's mother will do exactly what she threatened. I try to imagine getting up in front of this congregation to admit my failings but profess my love. It's hard enough talking to Tigger. Defeated, I turn away.

"It's up to you," Father Winowski says. "I'm willing to speak to Mrs. O'Brien again if you want me to."

"Thanks for nothing," I say, anger surging through me. "But I'm leaving."

The vestiary has an exterior door. He tips his head toward it. "Do you want me to get your friend?"

"No," I say, determined not to slink away. "I'm going out the way I came in."

"I'll pray for you," he says in a conciliatory tone, extending a hand.

"You've done more than enough for me already," I reply, turning my back on him. "I wouldn't want you to put yourself out any further."

———

Tigger stares at me with a quizzical expression as I walk out of the vestiary.

"We're leaving," I whisper, leaning over the front of the pew.

"What?" he says, startled. "Why?"

"Later."

Standing upright, I turn toward the altar and approach the casket. Laying both hands on top, I close my eyes and summon an image of Jenna, the wood cool beneath my fingers. I see her cross-legged and barefoot on the ratty couch we had in our first New York City apartment, the one on the outskirts of Spanish Harlem that we took when she started law school. She's looking up at me with a smile, hair shining in a shaft of sunlight from the uncurtained window, an open newspaper in her lap. I bend from the waist and kiss the smooth lid gently. Jennifer Mary O'Brien Tyler. Good-bye.

Eyes dry, shoulders squared and tall, I walk back down the aisle, concentrating on swinging my arms normally. Tigger hustles ahead and pushes the interior doors open for me so I won't have to break stride. Cameras flash as we step outside, the light blinding me.

5

THE PRESS SCRUM OUTSIDE THE CHURCH has grown
by half in fifteen minutes. Three or four reporters shout questions at me.

"Mr. Tyler, why are you leaving your wife's funeral?"

"Is it true that your wife's parents insisted you leave, Mr.
Tyler?"

"Were you cheating on your wife, Mr. Tyler?"

And, finally: "Mr. Tyler, did you pay someone to murder
your wife?"

Incredible. Rommy only browbeat the fact of my infidelity from Father Winowski yesterday, but he's already
turned Jenna's parents against me and poisoned the press. I've
got to respect the guy for figuring out how to make the worst
day of my life so much more unspeakably dreadful. I'd love to
beat the son of a bitch to death with my bare hands.

The uniformed cop is still vigilant against the press setting foot on church property, so most of the reporters and
photographers jog down the street and around the adjacent
corner, keeping pace with Tigger and me as we descend the

long flight of stairs to the parking lot. Tigger's car comes into view. Rommy's leaning against the hood with his ankles crossed, talking on a cell phone. His female partner, Detective Tilling, stands stone-faced a few feet away. My hands clench involuntarily.

"Congratulations," Rommy says, snapping the phone shut as I approach. "That was the city editor from the *Post*. You're gonna make the front page."

"Excuse us," I say, way too angry to control myself in a confrontation with him right now. "We're leaving."

"Stay a minute." He bounces off the fender of the car toward me as Tilling drifts into Tigger's path, blocking access to the driver's door. "You've got time for a chat. Catholics do these things right. They'll be weeping and praying for another hour at least."

Rommy closes on me until we're only a foot apart. He's wearing a gray double-breasted suit over a navy shirt and a red raveled-silk tie. Gold links shine at his cuffs as he folds his arms, a lapsed weight lifter's sloppy bulk straining the seams of his jacket.

"I'm not in the mood for this," I rasp.

"Geez, I'm sorry," he says, feigning concern. "You having a tough day?"

"Fuck you," Tigger barks, glaring. Tilling lays a warning hand on his arm as he steps toward Rommy. He shakes it off angrily. "Let's go, Peter."

Rommy's grinning, nicotine stains on his teeth. He's balding, and three or four inches shorter than I am. A quick jerk of the head would break his nose on my forehead. I imagine Rommy doubled over, scarlet blood streaming through his hands onto the warm asphalt.

"Let me give you a news flash," he continues conversationally. "Tomorrow's not gonna be any better. The neighbors read the paper and they'll be nervous about letting their kids play outside. You're gonna start getting hate mail. Maybe some local hero tosses a brick through your front window or slashes your tires. Moving won't help. Something like this will follow you around wherever you go." He shakes his head from side to side and makes a tutting noise with his tongue. "The life you had is over, buddy. Everybody's gonna know you did it. You haven't gotten away with anything."

"Thanks for the heads-up," I say. My fists are cramping, fingernails gouging my palms.

"You're welcome. Much as I hate to say it, though, you got yourself a little window of opportunity here. The DA's gearing up to run for attorney general, and she wants your case closed before she starts campaigning. You come clean now and you might be able to get yourself sent to some country club prison in the Adirondacks. You could spend the next thirty years playing Ping-Pong and raking sand traps. That's not much worse than what your life's gonna be like on the outside. You might even meet up with some old friends. Those places are lousy with Wall Street scumbags."

"Sounds great," I say, forcing a tight smile. "Sign me up."

"You think that's funny," he says, nodding his head slightly. "Let me tell you something. I already gave you the best case. The worst is that we convict you of murder one and the jury sentences you to the needle. You spend ten years alone in a cinder-block cell waiting for your appeals to run out. Ping-Pong's gonna seem like a pretty good alternative when they strap you to a gurney." He leans forward, face inches from mine. "Are you that sure you didn't make any mistakes? That this girl you're banging won't get pissed off about something and give us a call? Or that the guy you hired isn't gonna get busted for whacking someone else and rat you out in exchange for a deal?"

Rommy's malice is almost hypnotic. I take a deep breath and exhale slowly.

"You should stick to shaking down priests," I tell him. "Guys who have guilty consciences."

"You're good," he snarls. "You always got a comeback. If you weren't some rich fuck, I'd drag you down to the station right now. I wonder how clever you'd be after a night in a holding cell with the homeboys?"

"Sorry to miss it. Are we done here?"

"You're done." Veins bulge on Rommy's forehead and sweat shines in his hairline. "Maybe if you hustle up, you can get to your girlfriend's place before the funeral's over. That'll be a rush, huh? Banging your girlfriend while they put your wife in the dirt."

Blood roars in my ears as I glance from side to side. The press photographers and a TV cameraman are set up across the street, too far away to hear our conversation. The two cops who arrived in the blue Ford are thirty feet away, observing intently. I'd be a fool to let Rommy provoke me with this kind of audience. To hell with it. Fool or no, I'm not about to let Rommy ride me this way. I lean forward until my nose almost touches his, compelling him to take a half step backward.

"Let's stop playing games," I say quietly. "You give me your version of what happened and I'll tell you why you're wrong."

"You already lawyered up," he replies contemptuously. "I'm not giving you shit if I can't use what you tell me."

"I'll waive my right to counsel," I say, determined to have it out with him. "Come on. What have you got to lose?"

Tigger objects, but I ignore him, my eyes locked on Rommy. Rommy flicks a glance at Tilling and then smiles.

"Okay." He rolls his shoulders, loosening up. "Why not. You're a hick from some shithole in Ohio. You shoot some good hoops, you get a free ride to an Ivy League school, you meet a nice Catholic girl and get married. She keeps house, gets a job with some fancy-pants do-gooder outfit, and shakes her ass for you in bed. Pretty soon you make a bunch of dough, because you're the kind of prick who does good in business. Everything's great. But you're bored. Maybe her tits are sagging. So you start fucking around."

He rests a hand on my shoulder like an old friend, smiling as he pinches my trapezius, conscious of the cameras.

"You're not careful enough, though. Jenna finds out, and suddenly she's talking divorce. You're gonna lose half your cash, your house, one of your nice cars. So you come up with a better plan. She's insured for a lot of dough. With her dead, you'll be even better off than you were before. Maybe you thought about doing it yourself, but you watch enough TV to know the cops always look hardest at the husband. So you arrange it. A guy like you, a million bucks is small change. Some parts of New York, you can get people offed for beer money. The place I'm going to send you, a pack of cigarettes is enough. Only the guy you hired is a chump. It's supposed to be a burglary gone to shit, but the scene's not right. I'm thinking the guy took a picture for you. That's why he pushed her hair back." Rommy purses his lips theatrically, wagging a finger in my face. "You fucked up."

"Finished?" I ask.

"No. I know it's you. Not because she was gonna divorce you, or because of the insurance, or because of this half-assed burglary." He pinches my shoulder again, thumb digging into my muscle. "I know because you got this big house, and this big car, and a wife that every guy on the block thinks about when he's banging the old bag he's married to. But you, you're never home. You're flying around all over the place, working weekends, spending nights in the city. Because it wasn't enough for you, was it? It's all about you getting more, and Jenna was in the way. Tell me," he says, leering. "What're you into? Black chicks? Schoolgirls? Drag queens?"

He turns his hip to the press and pumps a hand at his crotch surreptitiously. Tilling stares at the ground expressionlessly. I wonder what she did wrong to get stuck with Rommy.

"Done?" I ask.

"For now." He releases me, fishes a cigarette from his shirt pocket, and takes another step back, eyeing me like a boxer waiting for the bell to ring again.

"I was married for sixteen years and I cheated once."

"Yeah, you must've had a great relationship. It took Jenna's parents about ten minutes to roll over on you."

"With your encouragement."

"Facts are facts," Rommy says flatly, striking a match. "Maybe you should've told us about your little piece on the side before the priest ratted you out."

"She's got nothing to do with it."

"I'm sure," Rommy says sarcastically. "Tell me her name. I promise I'll be nice to her."

"You going to figure out how to get her on the front page of the *Post,* too? Talk to all her friends and relatives, and insinuate that she's a criminal?"

"I do what I have to do to put guys like you where you belong. It's my job."

"Your job is to catch the guy who killed my wife, not to be

jerking me around because I worked hard and got all the things you always wanted, while you're a forty-seven-year-old cop who can't do better than detective sergeant."

Rommy flicks his lit cigarette at me with his middle finger. Tilling makes a warning noise, but he's too worked up to pay attention.

"I'll tell you why you don't want to give her up," he growls, neck bulging. "Because little Miss Candy Tits knows something you don't want her to tell us. You told her about killing Jenna, didn't you?"

I step forward again, narrowing the distance between us. One of the most important lessons my father taught me was never to show weakness.

"So you've got me pegged as a scumbag?"

"Fucking-A right."

"Fine. You met the private investigators my lawyer hired?"

"Yeah. I told those little prick rent-a-cops to get lost before I shoved my foot up their ass."

I deliberately put both hands in my pockets.

"Maybe they don't listen very well. One of them talked to your ex-wife. She's got a lot to say on the subject of scumbags. She says one of your kids has a speech problem, but that you're behind in your child support and there's no money for a therapist. The other kids make fun of him, call him a retard."

Rommy grabs me by the tie. He drives me backward, barking threats into my face. Shutters click across the street, autowinders sounding like a swarm of angry insects. The two cops from the Ford are running toward us. I raise my voice but don't shout.

"She says she dumped you because you came home drunk

every night and you couldn't get it up anymore. She got tired of waking up next to a guy who shit in the bed."

Rommy swings as the male cops grab him from behind, a clumsy right that glances off the side of my head. He's still got hold of my tie. I shake off his punch, keeping my hands in my pockets.

"You've got money in your brother's bar. You're taking dividends in cash, but there's nothing on your taxes. The IRS isn't going to like that."

"You fucking asshole." The other cops have succeeded in prying Rommy's grip loose. They're holding him by the arms. His hair is mussed, his shirt untucked, his tie askew. "You're fucking threatening me?"

Brushing ash from my jacket, I straighten my clothing and slick my hair back with a hand.

"Tigger and Tilling heard everything. I didn't threaten you. I asked my investigators to find out why the police weren't doing a better job of finding my wife's killer. They checked you out, Rommy. They told me you were the B team, too tangled up in your own shitty life to do a proper job. I'm thinking about filing a complaint with the DA. I hope no one leaks a copy to the press."

Rommy curses in the background as I walk to the car. Tigger opens the driver's door and gets in. A hand touches my shoulder as he starts the engine.

"Did that make you feel better?" Tilling asks quietly.

"A little," I say, turning to face her. She's tall, with crooked teeth and a forehead creased by worry lines. The report I got said she has a good reputation. "I figure it was the least he deserved."

She frowns.

"Do people usually get what they deserve?" There's no hint of sarcasm in her voice.

"I don't know," I say. It's a question I've been thinking about a lot recently. "I used to think so."

"Jennifer deserves justice," she says. "I need your help to get it for her."

I fold my arms to conceal a tremble, exhaustion enveloping me like a damp cloak.

"I'm not holding back on anything important."

"But you're holding back."

Her phone buzzes on her belt and she silences it without looking, tired brown eyes locked on mine.

"Jenna and I were arguing. I'm not going to talk about why. We'd been married for a long time. I was unhappy, and I made a mistake."

"I need the woman's name," Tilling says.

"You don't. She doesn't have anything to do with this. We were only together once, and it was all over between us before Jenna found out about it."

"Jennifer was ready to divorce you because of this other woman. We have to speak with her."

Tilling's wrong. I open my mouth to correct her and then close it again.

"Are you going to help?" she asks.

I shrug, turning back to the car and catching hold of the door handle.

"You don't get it," Tilling says behind me, sounding disappointed. "You fucked up and you're still fucking up. All the smart money's going to be on you now."

"What about you?" I ask, looking back at her. "Are you betting with the smart money?"

"You hurt her, Peter," Tilling says. "I know that much. You have to tell me the truth if you expect me to understand."

The truth. I open the car door and get in. Tilling stands motionless outside, staring in at me through the glass as Tigger puts the engine in gear and creeps past her. The truth is that I broke Jenna's heart long before I ever cheated on her.

WINTER

6

SLEET FALLS from the night sky, tapping irregularly against the bedroom windows. I stand motionless in the dark, looking out. A cone of sallow streetlight illuminates a blue Ford out front, the trunk deck and side panels crusted with ice. Moisture beads the windshield and hood; the wind whips a milky streamer of exhaust over the roof. Wipers flap intermittently. There are probably two cops inside the car—one napping, one half-awake. The police surveilled me occasionally in the weeks following Jenna's funeral, a tactic my lawyer said was mainly intended to intimidate me. This is the first time I've seen them in more than a month, though. Wondering if the cops are finally going to arrest me, I briefly debate calling my lawyer before deciding not to bother. The bedside clock reads 5:40; they aren't likely to move before dawn unless I show a light. I've got plenty of time.

Tidying the room takes only a few minutes despite the dark. Yesterday's clean bedding, now damp and knotted, goes in a laundry bag hanging from the door. I remake the bed with freshly ironed sheets, folding taut hospital corners and snugging the coverlet under the pillows. A few steps carry me to the bathroom. Years of traveling on business taught me to organize my toilet kit efficiently, toothbrush here, razor there. I lather my face without light and begin shaving by feel, relieved at least to be spared the pitiful sight of myself.

Toilet complete, I slip sweatpants over my boxers and pad downstairs, dragging the laundry bag behind me. All the rooms in the house save the kitchen and the guest bedroom I've been sleeping in are entirely empty. When the cops finally cleared out, I called the local St. Vincent de Paul and gave them the contents, contingent on their taking everything. It was easy enough to replace the essentials at Ikea. Tigger suggested I not move back in at all, but I didn't want to give the cops or the neighbors the satisfaction of seeing me gone.

The kitchen is in the back of the house, so the police can't see in unless they've got someone in the yard. Unlikely in this weather. I flip on the undercounter lights, start coffee, and pour myself a glass of juice. When the coffee's ready, I settle in at the kitchen table and turn on a reading light. Yesterday's mail is stacked next to my laptop. There are two letters from Klein and Klein, my former employer. One demands acknowledgment of previous "communications"; the other is a wheedling, disjointed diatribe from Josh. Ignoring the sentences that were obviously written by lawyers, I assume the rest conveys his meaning. Josh is disappointed. Josh is hurt. Josh is angry. Josh knows I understand. And he's right: I do. Klein didn't do anything I wouldn't have done myself.

The Monday after the funeral, I put on a suit and went to work early, desperate for something to distract myself with. It took me an hour to catch up on my e-mail. Tigger caught me by the arm as I was returning from the bathroom and backed me up against a pillar on the trading floor.

"Where you been?" he asked. "I left a dozen messages on your cell phone and at the hotel. They said you checked out."

"The press tracked me down at the hotel, so I moved."

"Why didn't you call me?"

I shrugged. The pictures and video of us leaving Jenna's funeral had been everywhere the preceding few days. I'd been too embarrassed to return his calls.

"You shouldn't be here," he said.

"What am I going to do, Tigger? Sit home?"

"You should be talkin' to someone."

"Talking to who?" I asked, beginning to get angry. "Some dickless therapist in a little room on the Upper West Side? A guy who's going to ask all about my bad dreams and tell me it's okay to cry?"

"Petey," Tigger said, squeezing my arm. "It is okay to cry."

"That's bullshit," I replied furiously. "My dad used to say there are people who do and people who don't."

"Do what?"

"Whatever. That's the point."

"Sometimes there's nothin' you can do."

"Wrong," I said loudly. "I can find the fucker who killed my wife and put a bullet in his head."

A few of the junior staff nearby gaped openly. Tigger bounced nervously on his toes. We both knew I was going to knock his hand away if he didn't back off, and we both knew he wasn't going to back off. His eyes slid over my shoulder and he scowled. Eve Lemonde was threading her way across the floor in my direction, a somber expression on her face.

"Listen," Tigger said urgently. "Don't lose your temper and don't agree to nothin' without having a lawyer look at it."

He scuttled back to his desk, dropping Eve a deep curtsy as she passed and eliciting a flinty glare in response.

Eve's my age, vanishingly thin, finely coiffed, devoid of humor, and as meticulously false as any professional flack. Josh hired her as much to do his dirty work as to run Human Resources. I'd always maintained a decent relationship with her because it was the politic thing to do, but she and Tigger openly loathed each other.

"I thought we'd take a walk, Peter," Eve said.

"Why not?" I replied, falsely nonchalant. "I'll grab my coat."

We walked down Broadway into Battery Park. Eve offered her condolences. She asked how I was holding up, and nodded sincerely at my evasions. We settled on a bench overlooking the harbor and she let me have it.

"You're on compassionate leave indefinitely. Full pay, full benefits. The firm won't comment publicly."

"This is from Josh?"

"Yes. You can call him if you really want to."

Her gratuitous suggestion was intended to warn me off. Josh had been as happy for me to line his pocket as I was for him to line mine, but, just as Tigger had warned me, he was going to have trouble remembering my name now that I was a liability.

"Indefinite until when?"

"December. You'll get a fair payout in exchange for a resignation letter and a release."

I'd been on Eve's side of this conversation a hundred times. Being on the other side didn't feel real. I made an effort to keep my voice light.

"What if things get straightened out?"

Eve twisted sideways to face me head-on, her plucked eyebrows and crimson lips miming disappointment.

"The damage is already done. Don't you see that? The police have been questioning employees, demanding to speak with clients, subpoenaing records. The funeral was the last straw. Josh doesn't want a picture of you walking into our office on the front page of the *New York Post*. We have to do what's best for the firm."

I gazed out over the water at a single sailboat jibing lazily downwind, unable to think of anything else to say. Realizing the conversation was over, I got up to go. There was nothing in my office that Keisha couldn't box and ship.

"We'll send the paperwork to your home," Eve said. "We want to be fair."

"Wrong line, Eve. You were supposed to say, 'It was nothing personal; it was just business.' "

She stared at me woodenly, uncertain as to the emotion she should feign. I turned and walked north purposefully, shoulders tall, not knowing where I was headed, or what I was going to do when I got there.

I rip Josh's letter in half, and then in half again. A few days after my chat with Eve, she sent me an express-mail envelope containing a release and a confidentiality agreement. Both were laughably onerous, the kicker being a provision in each that I accept an arbiter of Klein's choice in the event of any subsequent dispute between us. It's easier to get a fair decision from a North Korean court than it is from a Wall Street arbiter. I tossed both documents in the trash, exhausted by the thought of negotiating with her. Every third day's brought a fresh demand for my signature, the language increasingly insistent. Despite Eve's evident frustration at my silence, it surprises me that she troubled to have Josh write. Klein's lawyers must be worried about something. I drop the pieces of Josh's letter into the garbage can under the table, disappointed that I don't feel more pleasure at making him unhappy.

Tigger got fired a week after I did. It was no surprise to either of us. Lemonde used to speak of him as "aged inventory" at our annual personnel reviews, a trading-desk term of art that means roughly the same thing as three-day-old bread. We'd been getting together regularly to play golf before the weather changed, but it's been difficult since then. Without some kind of activity there's nothing to fill the gaps in our conversation, and the one time we got drunk together I broke down and made a fool of myself.

Mail dealt with, I open the drawer in the kitchen table and take out a worn kraft box containing my father's service pistol and a cloth-wrapped cleaning kit. I remove the magazine, double-check to make sure the chamber's empty, let the slide ride forward, and then press down on the recoil-spring plug, field-stripping the weapon exactly the way my father taught me years ago. It's soothing to clean the gun, all the pieces precisely machined. I haven't actually fired it in years, because I never bothered to get a New York permit, but I remember the thunderous roar it made when I shot it as a boy, my dad leaning over my shoulder and wrapping his large hand around my small one to help absorb the recoil.

Reassembled, the gun fits comfortably in my adult grip. It's better not to dry-fire a weapon without a dummy round in the chamber to protect the firing pin, so I unload the live rounds from the magazine and arrange them in a neat heptagon before replacing them with a handful of snap caps I keep in a Ziploc bag. Racking the slide, I sight down the barrel and imagine Jenna's killer on his knees before me, features smudged and dark eyes wide with terror. I pull the trigger. The metallic click echoes loudly off the hard kitchen surfaces, and I see the killer's head jerk backward as my bullet smashes into his face, brains spattering the wall behind him. He crumples sideways, a pool of blood forming beneath his cheek as life fades from his eyes like light from an old cathode-ray tube. I cycle the slide by hand, ejecting a faux round onto the kitchen floor, and picture the killer on his knees again. His head snaps back repeatedly as I pull the trigger again and again, dull metal cartridges cascading from the ejection port until the slide locks open. Tears of rage blur my vision as I smash the impotent gun down onto the table, adding to the deep gouges already there.

Minutes tick past as my breathing calms slowly. The refrigerator cycles on and then off again, the entire house preternaturally quiet. It's just before seven. Most mornings, I load and fire the gun until my finger aches too much to pull the trigger, consumed by my fantasy of revenge. Not this morning. Gathering the false ammunition from the floor, I seal it in the Ziploc bag. It's time to face the truth.

Jenna's murderer will likely never be caught. The ex-cops I hired as investigators turned out to be better at gathering dirt on their former brethren than they were at generating fresh leads. Tilling took over the investigation after the footage of Rommy attacking me in the parking lot became an instant Internet sensation, forcing him to resign. To the best of my knowledge, I'm still the only suspect, and she's been wasting most of her time on my financial records, trying to find some link to the killer she thinks I hired.

The small satisfaction I felt at Rommy's dismissal curdled when he landed a job with a society journalist who's writing a book about Jenna's murder. They published a teaser in *New York* magazine last month, twelve pages of lurid insinuations carefully crafted to skirt libel. Tigger wrote an outraged letter to the editor that never ran; the one letter published in my defense was from a Texas divorce lawyer, reminding readers that even scum like me deserve a fair trial. Rommy's been calling me regularly, usually late at night, to slur drunken imprecations. I was scrupulously polite at first, figuring that was the best way to piss him off, but recently I've just been hanging up, my interest in playing games with him having faded. And Rommy's aren't the only late-night calls I've been receiving—he was right about the neighbors.

Jenna's parents never gave me a chance to explain myself. Mary demanded I resign in her favor as Jenna's executor, and I complied, hoping to open a dialogue. She immediately filed a civil suit for wrongful death against me on behalf of the estate, and obtained a court order freezing all the assets Jenna and I had held jointly. My lawyer thinks she might win, despite the lack of hard evidence. Nobody likes rich guys who cheat on their wives and lie to the cops, he might say, if he were ever candid. If I lose, political pressure will probably force the Westchester DA to file criminal charges against me, and a jury trial is always a crapshoot. The insurance company is refusing to release any money to me without litigation, and legal fees are rapidly consuming my ready cash.

When I was a boy, a teacher who'd played minor-league ball slipped from a diving board. The news that he'd become a quadriplegic shocked me, intimating a chance vulnerability I'd never considered. I crept into my dad's bathroom one morning while he was shaving.

"What's up, Sherlock?" he said, meeting my eyes in the mirror.

"Mr. Jackson," I said. "What's he going to do?"

"I don't know. Everyone has to make their own decisions."

"What would you do?"

My dad looked away, staring at himself in the mirror for a moment before dragging his straight-edged razor up his throat with a long backhanded stroke.

"You're playing chess," he said, setting down the razor and picking up a lit cigarette from the edge of the sink. "You let the other guy fork your king and queen. You're nine points or more behind in material. What do you do?"

"Resign."

He took a deep drag and then exhaled, a cloud of white smoke obscuring his features in the glass. "There's no point to life without dignity," he said.

I wash the dishes and the coffeepot and set everything out to dry on a clean towel. Returning to the table, I pick up the gun, select a single brass jacked bullet from the rounds I unloaded earlier, and carefully feed it into the chamber. Cleaning solvent burns my tongue like a nine-volt battery as I put the gun in my mouth. The trigger requires a six-pound pull to fire. A half gallon of milk weighs four pounds. I pull, hard enough to lift a quart of milk, a half gallon, more. The gun shakes violently and I bite down on the barrel, trying to still my trembling. My ears are ringing, an odd repetitive note that takes me a moment to recognize. Someone's ringing my doorbell. I take the gun from my mouth and let it dangle from the trigger guard, leaning forward to rest my head on the scarred table. I wonder whether I should answer the door.

7

DETECTIVE TILLING'S on the front step. She's wearing an
olive surplus parka and has an orange knit longshoreman's
cap covering her hair. A scowling black woman stands a few
paces back and to one side, her right hand hidden behind an
unzipped brown leather coat. Tilling looks me over, taking in
my rumpled T-shirt and baggy sweatpants.

"Did we wake you?" she asks.

I shrug, feeling half-dazed. The black woman looks ready
for a confrontation, but I assume I'd already be handcuffed if
they were going to arrest me. I wonder if Tilling can smell
gun oil on me.

"My new partner," Tilling says, pointing with a thumb.
"Detective Ellis. We'd like to talk to you."

"I don't think so."

"We learned something interesting recently. It could be a
lead. We could use your help sorting it out."

The haze in my brain is dissipated by a rush of adrenaline.
I've got to be careful here. My lawyer was furious at me for talking to Tilling in the parking lot at the funeral, icily informing

me that while a judge would almost certainly have excluded Winowski's statements, my admission to Tilling that I'd cheated on Jenna gave the DA an irrefutable motive to work with.

"I'll have to call my lawyer," I say.

"You waived your right to counsel last time we spoke," Tilling says. "You're welcome to reassert it, but I got to tell you, I'm not in the mood for a seventeen-point negotiation this morning. This is a simple deal, and it hasn't got anything to do with your mystery girlfriend. I tell you what we've turned up, and you answer a couple of questions if you feel like it. No obligations."

I hesitate. It's a compelling offer. I'm anxious to know what she's learned and, truth be told, I despise the condescending little fucker who represents me.

"We've been waiting on your beauty sleep for an hour and a half. You're too busy to give us fifteen minutes?" Tilling asks, a mocking note to her voice. "You got a big day planned? Lots to do?"

I'm happier talking to her than to Rommy, but that's no reason for me to take her shit.

"Cops must spend a lot of time hanging out in their cars," I say. "Tell me, is it a professional disadvantage for you ladies, not being able to piss in a bottle?"

Tilling laughs, a staccato bark.

"Yes or no, Peter. Ellis is going to catch cold."

"You want to come in?"

"No. We haven't had breakfast yet. There's a coffee shop on Willow. You know it?"

"I know it. Give me ten minutes. I have to get dressed."

"Peter." She touches her ear and motions at me to do the same. "Shaving cream," she says.

———

The coffee shop is almost full, the morning rush under way. Tilling and Ellis are seated side by side on a banquette, their coats draped over their laps. Ellis has a heart-shaped face, short-cropped hair, and wide-set eyes. She looks about four-teen. I smile at her as I sit down opposite, and get a fresh glower back. A tired-looking waitress fills our water glasses and pours coffee, greeting both cops by name.

"You come here often?" I ask.

"Yeah," Tilling says, pushing a powdered doughnut toward me. "To use the bathroom. Ground rules, Peter. I tell you what we know, you promise to follow up through us. I don't want to hear that your rental cops are chasing our leads."

"I didn't agree to any ground rules."

Tilling lays a finger on my wrist as I'm lifting my coffee, preventing the cup from reaching my mouth.

"We're not wasting our time here, are we, Peter? Because Ellis and I really have got other things to do."

I shift the cup from one hand to the other, shaking her finger away.

"You do your job right and I won't have to ask anyone else to chase your leads."

She stares silently. I pick the doughnut up without think-ing and immediately set it back down again, revulsed. Thirty seconds pass. I sip coffee, determined to make her speak first. She slips a manila folder from an interior coat pocket and puts it on the table in front of her, one hand resting on top protectively. Jenna's name is written on the label.

"I'm listening," I say.

"You know a guy named Andrei Zhilina?"

"Sure," I reply uncomfortably. I e-mailed Andrei repeatedly after the funeral and left multiple messages on his voice mail, slow to realize he must be ducking me on purpose. It's hard to believe he'd blow me off at a time like this, regardless of what happened between me and his sister, but there's no other conclusion to be drawn. His silence has been one more thing dragging me down.

"How?"

"We met right out of college. We did a training program together at Klein and Klein, and then we were roommates at business school."

"What did he do after business school?"

"Worked for the World Bank in London for a long time and then took a job with Turndale and Company about eighteen months ago. Why?"

"When's the last time you spoke to him?" she asks, ignoring my question.

"It's been a few months," I say, trying not to sound defensive. "He's based out of Moscow, so we don't get a chance to catch up too much."

"Was he at the funeral?"

"I'm not sure. You may recall I left early."

"You know where he is right now?"

"I thought you were going to talk and I was going to listen," I say irritably.

Tilling taps the folder.

"FedEx delivered a package from Andrei to your home the day before Jenna was murdered. Your cleaning lady signed for it at four-seventeen in the afternoon. She said she left it on the kitchen counter. You know what was in it?"

"No. I never saw a package."

"When we went through the house together, you told us

nothing was missing. Did you notice anything new? The size of a toaster oven or smaller, weighing two pounds or less?"

I cast backward in my memory to the walk-through I'd done with the cops the day after Jenna's murder, every detail seared indelibly in my mind.

"No."

"Any guess what it might have been?"

"Andrei and Jenna were book buddies," I say. "Like her and Father Winowski, except they mainly read stuff about politics and art. I'd guess he sent her a book."

Ellis produces a pad from her coat and jots a note.

"They'd read books and then talk on the phone?" Tilling asks.

"Or exchange e-mail."

"Was that a problem for you?"

"Was what a problem for me?"

"That your wife and Andrei were so chummy."

"Never," I say emphatically, realizing that I've accidentally given them another false lead to chase. "We were all old friends."

Ellis scribbles away as Tilling frowns down at the table, likely formulating another clumsy insinuation. I can feel my anger rising. Close as Andrei and Jenna were, there wasn't ever a moment when I didn't trust them together.

"Why'd you give all the stuff in the house away?" Tilling asks unexpectedly.

Jenna kept a Murano glass dish that she'd bought on our honeymoon on the front hall table. It was the first thing I'd seen when I entered the house with the police. The cops had been using it as an ashtray. It was all I could do not to weep.

"None of your business."

"Maybe if you told me this one inconsequential thing,"

Tilling says wearily, looking up at me, "I could kid myself that you were going to help us."

The waitress stops to fill my coffee cup, giving me a few seconds to think. I'm going to have to make some good-faith gestures if I want Tilling on my side, regardless of how hard it is for me.

"Two reasons," I say haltingly, after the waitress has moved on. "First, I didn't know who'd handled things. The murderer, Rommy, other people who were in the house. Nothing was clean anymore. And second, it all reminded me of Jenna. I've been trying to draw a line. To not think about how things were before."

"Before she was murdered?"

"Before everything. When we were happy."

Tilling holds my gaze until my face gets hot. I'm going to walk out if she asks another question. She picks up a spoon and begins studying the bowl.

"Let's talk about the time line," she says. "The package Andrei sent Jennifer arrived at your place at four-seventeen in the afternoon on Monday. Jennifer worked late, and you were sleeping in the city. She disarmed your home alarm at ten-thirty-eight Monday evening, and reset it at seven-thirty the next morning. She drove to work, logged on to her computer at seven-fifty-three, and was in her office all morning, until she got a phone call around ten-fifteen. She told a colleague she had to run home for a few minutes but that she'd be back before eleven. You live thirteen to seventeen minutes from her office, depending on the lights. Figure an extra ten minutes for logistics and you're looking at thirty-six to forty-four minutes round-trip. She must have been planning to drive straight home and come right back."

"What's your point?"

"She didn't have time to drop the package off anywhere. It wasn't in her car or her office. None of the courier or overnight services picked anything up from her. If she'd opened it, we would have found the wrapping in the trash. The garbage wasn't collected at your house that morning, and we sealed her office before anyone cleaned it. We double-checked the evidence inventory against the crime-scene photos, just to make sure some light-fingered med tech or beat cop wasn't pocketing stuff off counters. Nothing's missing."

"You think the murderer took it?"

"Murderers. Plural."

"What do you mean?" I ask, my heart beating faster.

"The cylinder on your garage door lock was pulled with a slide hammer. The internal scoring indicates that whoever operated it was right-handed. But the angle of the blows that killed Jennifer suggests that the murderer was left-handed. There are some disparate shoe prints and a couple of other things. I'm pretty sure we're looking for two guys."

"Is it significant that they took the package?" I ask, hanging on her words. I hadn't realized how clueless my investigators actually were.

"Your house was a shitty target for a daytime burglary. You're in a cul-de-sac, you've got an alarm, and the neighborhood's patrolled regularly. Two guys enter through your garage, slip on latex gloves, disable the alarm siren, cut the phone line, and open the interior door with a locksmith's tool. These guys are pros. But they only search the downstairs. Burglars always search the bedroom first. People sleep near their valuables."

"Hang on," I say, struggling to process her implication. I feel light-headed. "You think these guys might actually have been there looking for the package?"

Tilling shakes her head from side to side slowly, lips pursed.

"The working theory of the Westchester County District Attorney's Office is that you paid two guys to fake a burglary and kill your wife. We think you had somebody call her at work and trick her into going home. But that's an interesting idea you've got. It wouldn't hurt to know what was in the package."

I settle back in the booth, my initial excitement waning. The notion that Jenna was murdered by a couple of guys looking for a package from Andrei is too far-fetched to credit.

"You want me to ask Andrei what he sent Jenna?"

"No," she says. "We want you to tell us how to get in touch with him."

I vacillate an instant, trying to decide whether it's smart to put Tilling together with Andrei. Andrei's careful. He'd never say anything to Katya's disadvantage.

"I've got his home number back at the house. Or you can call him at work. Turndale's New York office is at Forty-seventh and Sixth. Moscow's eight hours ahead, so if you call their New York operator anytime before nine, she should be able to connect you."

"We already tried his home number. And we checked with Turndale. They say he left the company back in September, eleven days before Jennifer was murdered. They haven't heard from him since."

"That can't be right," I say, wondering why Andrei would have left Turndale so abruptly. "He's got to be in contact with them. If nothing else, he'd still have money tied up there."

"They claim not, and they've declined to answer any follow-up questions on the grounds of 'employee confidentiality.'"

More HR bullshit.

"Can't you subpoena their records?"

"The DA says no. Andrei's tangential, Turndale's connected politically, and she wants us to stay focused on you."

"I'm at a loss," I say uneasily.

Tilling taps the spoon against her palm.

"Turndale gave us Andrei's emergency contact. Oksana Zhilina, his mother. You know her?"

"She's a real piece of work," I reply without thinking.

"What do you mean?" Tilling asks quickly.

"Just that the couple of times we met, she seemed very opinionated," I say, not wanting to get into all the stories I heard about Mrs. Zhilina over the years, or the friction she created between Andrei and Katya.

"Are she and Andrei close?"

"As far as I know."

"Then it must surprise you that she claims not to know how to get in touch with him, either."

I'm beginning to wonder if Tilling's toying with me. Mrs. Zhilina must have a number for Andrei, and if for some strange reason she doesn't, she would have suggested the police speak with Katya.

"That's right. It does."

"You're his friend," Tilling says, setting the spoon down and folding her hands. "So you tell me. What's the best way for me to find him?"

"Let me make a few calls." The prospect of speaking with Katya is almost too daunting to contemplate, but I can't risk giving her name to Tilling without warning her first. "I'll get back to you later today."

"Wrong," Tilling says gratingly, shaking her head. "Remember? That's how I said it wasn't going to work. We're going to do the police work, not you or your hired cops. You tell us who to talk to and we'll take it from there."

I look around, unwilling to meet her eye. A Mohawked teenager is arguing with the Greek manager, who's refusing to sell him cigarettes. I'm pretty much fucked here. Not mentioning Katya's name could be as revealing as mentioning it, if Tilling already knows who she is.

"The best I can do is call you later," I say.

"Bullshit," Tilling barks, angry pink blotches visible under her eyes. She jabs a finger toward me. "This is more rope-a-dope. I want to know who his old girlfriends are, where he likes to hang out, everything. Right now."

"What happened to no obligations?"

"That was before. You think I spent twenty minutes describing our investigation just to hear myself talk? I'm making nice here, Peter. I'm offering you another chance to get on board and start helping us out. The DA's got me on a short leash. You cooperate, and maybe I can persuade her to let me widen my investigation a little bit. If not, we're going to keep chipping away at you."

"Look," I say, anxious to grab hold of the lifeline she's offering me. "I am going to help. I just need some time."

Tilling stands abruptly, knocking against the table and overturning an empty water glass. She stuffs the manila folder back into her coat as the glass rolls slowly toward the edge of the table. Ellis has her eyes fixed on me, motionless. I catch the glass as it falls and set it gently back down on the table.

"You're making a big mistake here, Peter," Tilling says. "The DA is riding me hard about you. Ellis and I are the only people even considering the possibility that you didn't do it. We're your only friends, and we like you less and less all the time."

There's no doubt in my mind she's telling the truth.

"I'll phone you later," I say. "Promise."

Tilling pulls a business card from a pocket and drops it on the table.

"My cell number is on the back," she says. "I'm expecting to hear from you today."

8

WORSENING WEATHER made the train seem the best bet to
New York City, but the thermostats are all set for tropical, one
car hotter than the next, the windows hermetically sealed. My
shirt's already sticking to my back as I settle down in an
orange plastic seat, leaning my forehead against the cool window and watching the snow fall outside. A stream runs next
to the tracks, the projecting stones covered with a thin layer
of ice. I tried Andrei's home in Moscow yet again after I left
Tilling, but his phone rang endlessly, not even a machine
picking up. Absent other options, I called Katya, unsure what
to expect. She was curt, and insisted we meet in person. The
glass fogs as I exhale heavily. I haven't got the energy for a confrontation with her. It's important to me that I speak with
Andrei, though—not just to learn what he sent Jenna but also
to see that he's okay, and to try to make things up with him.
We've been friends for a long time.

Andrei and I started at Klein and Klein on the same day,
hired into a two-year training program intended to teach us
the rudiments of investment banking and prepare us for business school. The deal was pretty simple. The firm paid us

triple the money public school teachers made, and tacitly encouraged us to run up the corporate tab eating at Delmonico's and club hopping in hired cars. In return, we were expected to work eighty to one hundred hours a week, be on call constantly, and cheerfully endure actionable abuse. It seemed fair.

Andrei phoned me around midnight one evening, about a month after we'd started.

"You working on anything important?" he asked.

"Proofreading an equity pitch to an oil-services company. Why?"

I swung round in my swivel chair to stare at his back, eight feet away. He was hunched over his desk, cupping the receiver so the other two guys in our office couldn't hear him.

"Can you spare a few hours?"

"Sure."

I hadn't really gotten to know Andrei yet. He was tall and lean-faced, with an accent that wandered from Oxford University to Coney Island, depending on whom he was talking to. Blond hair and blue eyes made him appear less Russian than his name suggested. It was clear from day one that every woman in the office was lusting after him, but he didn't seem to be taking much advantage. He struck me as a decent guy, and I was happy to lend a hand if he needed help.

"You got your kit?" he asked.

"My what?"

"Kit. Gear. Workout clothes."

Regardless of accent, Andrei defaulted to British vocabulary.

"Yeah."

Klein had a nice gym. Most of the professional staff exercised regularly to burn stress or fend off exhaustion. A good workout gave you an extra few hours of clarity.

"Take the lift down to B three in ten minutes, and bring your kit."

He met me there, guiding me through the basement and onto the loading dock. The triple-height exterior doors were closed. Eight or nine guys were shooting balls at a hoop clamped to a lamppost while fifteen or twenty guys watched. Andrei introduced me to an older man in blue coveralls, who was holding a cigarette pinched between his thumb and first finger.

"Peter. This is Leo. He's the night maintenance manager."

"So, Peter," Leo said, stressing the first vowel in my name. "Andrei says you played college ball."

"Small-time college ball."

"You want to play with us?"

"Why not?"

Andrei explained the rules while we changed in a bathroom. Two on two, game to eleven baskets. The winning team stayed on court, no rest until they lost. Each team put up fifty dollars a game, with the winners taking the pot. The real action was in the side bets.

"Can these guys play?" I asked.

"I watched the other night. Some are good; some are bruisers. Leo refs, and he won't call anything that doesn't draw blood."

"Why the secrecy?"

"They're all union, mainly maintenance and security. Some from this building, some from other buildings. They don't want the tenants to learn how they're earning their time and a half. Leo's Russian, one of my people. We got to talking about Dinamo in the lift the other day and he invited me to play. I vouched for you."

"Dinamo?"

"One of Moscow's football teams."

I looked Andrei over while we dressed. He was wiry like a climber, and had a long zipperlike scar on his left shoulder. He caught me staring and tapped the wound with a finger.

"Rugby. I played hooker, the fellow in the middle of the scrum who's supposed to kick the ball back to the line. An opposing player bit our left prop on the neck and the scrum twisted. Ripped my humerus right out of the socket."

"Sounds like a great game."

"Biting's a bit frowned on, actually."

"You played much basketball?"

"Enough," he said. "I'll feed you the ball and set picks. We'll get by."

We played once or twice a week for the next two years, winning more than we lost from the first day. Andrei never sank much from outside the key, but he understood the game and was terrific under the boards. Sometimes there were a hundred spectators, and thousands of dollars changing hands. Leo was constantly scouting the neighborhood for new talent. We played firefighters, some Con Ed workers, a couple of porters from the fish market. The real competition were the guys who grew up playing Harlem street ball. They played a beautiful, jazzy game—intricate dribbling, seamless fakes, balletlike spins to the basket. Andrei and I weren't flashy, but we worked well as a team, each learning to anticipate what the other was going to do.

We went out for a couple of beers one night shortly after we started playing together. We were sitting on top of a picnic table outside a TriBeCa dive when I noticed a girl waiting to cross

Greenwich Street. She was wearing jeans, boots, and an open leather jacket over a Ramones T-shirt, her hair loose around her shoulders. She looked like a slumming Disney princess. I nudged Andrei with an elbow and nodded toward her.

"What?" he said.

"What do you mean, 'What?'" I said, nodding toward her again.

"Not my type."

"You're kidding, right?"

The girl darted across the street between cars and made for the entrance to the bar. She picked Andrei and me out of the shadows and walked toward us, smiling. He stood up and kissed her on the cheek.

"My twin sister, Katya," he said. "She's just started with Turndale, the asset-management firm."

Katya extended a hand for me to shake. She was small and finely boned, with jet hair and a round, elfin face.

"That's supposed to be a great outfit," I said. "There was a profile of William Turndale in the *Journal* a couple of years ago."

"Every new employee gets a copy of that article," she said, smiling wryly. "They called him a modern-day Medici. A patron of the arts and a prince of finance."

"What's he like to work for?"

"I don't really know yet. We only spoke once, and I was busy knuckling my forehead and groveling."

I laughed.

"But let's back up a second. You were reading the *Journal* in college?" she asked, letting her eyes go wide.

"Yeah," I said, amused by her show of incredulity. "Why? What were you reading?"

"The *Daily Worker* and *Mother Jones*. College is when you're supposed to get that social justice stuff out of your system. A guy like you is unreliable. You're going to have a delayed crisis of conscience some day, just when you could really make a killing by stepping on the neck of the proletariat."

"Whereas you'll have no scruples?"

"None," she said sweetly. "Been there, done that. Isn't one of you supposed to be buying me a beer about now?"

"My shy sister," Andrei said, putting his arm around her.

A couple of beers turned into half a dozen. Katya kept up in the same vein, drawing Andrei and me out about work and basketball, and then deftly satirizing us, pricking our vanities and mocking our ambitions. I thought Jenna would like her. Katya's English was unaccented, a contrast she scornfully explained as the result of Andrei having been shipped off to an English boarding school when he was eight to learn to be a leader of men, whereas she'd been kept home in New York to concentrate on domestic skills. Andrei went inside when it was his turn to buy another round, and she picked my hand up off the table, turning my palm to the light. My skin tingled to her touch.

"You tell fortunes?" I asked.

"Some."

"Another thing you learned in college while I was busy with the *Journal*?"

"One of the domestic skills I picked up. My mother's a witch and my father's a prince. I take after him, but I can work the odd magic when the spirit moves me."

I wasn't sure whether or not to laugh.

"Let me guess," I said. "You see a crisis of conscience in my future."

"That's just work stuff."

"So what else do you see?"

"A couple of kids and a house in the burbs. Peanut butter fingerprints on your suit pants."

"And?"

She studied my hand intently.

"A cat you don't like. Fluffy or Fuzzy. He's going to pee in your golf shoes."

"That's it?" I asked, feigning disappointment.

She traced a finger lightly across my life line, making me tremble. I leaned toward her, inhaling her scent, and realized I was drunk.

"Difficult," she said. "It might help if you crossed my palm with silver."

I worked a quarter out of my pocket and put it in her free hand. She balanced the coin on her thumb and flipped it deftly into the street.

"Alloy. It's got to be the real deal if you want to hear the good stuff."

"I've got some silver fillings," I said, my head swimming.

"You can give it a try."

I lifted her hand to my face and touched my lips to the hollow.

"Hmmm," she said. "I think that worked."

"So what's the good stuff?" I asked, my voice low.

She tapped my palm gently.

"A girl."

"What does she look like?"

"You tell me," Katya said, turning her face up.

I hesitated, confusion overtaking me. Katya waited a long moment and then stood up, letting my hand fall. She zipped her jacket.

"It's late," she said. "And I've had too much to drink. Tell Andrei good-bye for me."

———————

An arctic gust of air snaps me out of my reverie as the train doors open on the elevated platform at 125th Street. There's a thump against the window behind my head. A bunch of kids on a rooftop opposite the platform are throwing snowballs at the train. I suck my breath in sharply as a small boy runs forward, heaving a snowball mightily and skidding to a stop less than two feet from the edge of the roof. The doors to the train close and the kids dance around excitedly, giving each other high fives. It would be nice to be twelve years old again. I glance at my watch as we begin moving. Katya told me to come by at one. I'm going to be early.

As I'd expected, Jenna liked both Andrei and Katya at first meeting, although Katya's cheerfully unbridled ambition occasionally caught Jenna up short. "Maybe you'd be happier with a girl like Katya," she'd tease me sometimes, when I sat up late doing work at home. "*She'd* think your work was important. *She* wouldn't ask you to come to bed and give *her* a back rub." I made the mistake of alluding to Jenna's teasing in the presence of both women once, saying that Jenna thought Katya and I would be a good couple. There was a frosty lull in the conversation, and Jenna was furious when we got home.

Darkness falls as the train enters the tunnel under Park Avenue. Much as I know my meeting with Katya is going to be painful, I realize I'm looking forward to seeing her.

9

I KILL HALF AN HOUR weaving through midtown, stepping in and out of shops, reversing direction frequently, and generally feeling like a paranoid asshole. If Tilling has people following me, they're too good for me to spot. Katya's secretary, Debra, is waiting in Turndale's lobby when I arrive. A heavyset Staten Island girl who loves to flirt, Debra mumbles hello, escorts me wordlessly through security, and studies the floor indicator as we ride the elevator up. It isn't hard to guess what she thinks. If she were a neighbor, she'd probably be leaving her garbage on my lawn.

The fortieth floor is done up like an English country house museum—dark oak floors, expensively threadbare carpets, and old master paintings from William Turndale's renowned personal collection. I give my coat and hat to an anorexic receptionist, deposit my umbrella in a Chinese ceramic vase, and follow Debra through a succession of bright, gallerylike corridors. We walk past an empty boardroom into a large semi-open space dominated by two oversized glass offices. The near office is dark, the name William Turndale etched on a panel flanking the door.

Katya's visible in the far office, silhouetted against swirling snow in three-quarter profile as she stands with her back to the room, gazing west toward the Hudson. She's wearing a blue silk jacket over a white blouse, and a narrow black skirt. Her dark hair's pinned back, exposing the length of her pale neck and the sapphire studs in her ears. One hand massages the circles beneath her eyes, a habit I remember her being vigilant against in the past. A confusing mélange of grief, guilt, and longing tightens my chest as I look at her. Debra opens the office door and I swallow nervously, afraid of my voice betraying me.

"Hey."

I start toward Katya automatically as she looks over her shoulder, but she holds up a finger and frowns, gesturing toward the headset I hadn't seen her wearing. She turns away again as I nod awkwardly, feeling foolish.

Katya counsels someone on an investment strategy in a cool professional voice while I wander around her office, struggling to calm down. A collection of silver-framed pictures on top of the credenza catches my attention. The central photo ran on the cover of *Forbes* a few years back: William Turndale in his desk chair, Katya standing behind with one hand on the chair back, posed like the heir apparent. Talented as Katya is, it's nonetheless amazing that she's lasted twenty years with a boss as difficult as William, rising steadily through the ranks to become his second in command.

Tucked among the other shots of Katya with smug white guys in business suits or Ralph Lauren sporting gear is a small black-and-white photograph of her and Andrei, looking very much like twins at the age of five or six. They're seated either side of their mother on a park bench, barren branches visible behind them. All three are heavily bundled. Andrei and Mrs. Zhilina are holding hands and leaning toward each other;

Katya's face is half-turned from the camera, her expression pensive. Shortly after I first met Katya, Andrei told me the truth of their parentage. Their mother had been abandoned by their father before they were born, and she never spoke of him. She and Katya had been at odds for years, both too strong-willed to get along. One of the nicer things Katya had to say about her was that she was a witch.

"I was thinking about Cornwall earlier," Katya says, a change of tone catching my attention. I glance over to see she's off the phone, the headset held tight to her hip as she continues to stare out toward the river. "The night we drove home from the pub."

Ten years ago, Jenna and I spent a few days after Christmas with Katya and Andrei at a rented cottage on the southwestern tip of England. We were headed home from the pub late one wet evening in Andrei's ancient Land Rover, Katya driving, when we crested a rise and saw a cow ambling down the middle of the narrow country lane. Katya locked the brakes and spun the wheel. The rear end slid out parallel to the front, the tires bit, and the car rolled, every window exploding simultaneously. We came to rest upright, inches from the startled cow's flanks, the engine still running. A panicked, clamorous four-way exchange established that not one of us had been as much as scratched. Rain blew into the car as a shocked silence fell, gleaming fragments of safety glass adorning our hair and clothes like gemstones. I began to laugh. Katya joined me a moment later, and then Andrei and Jenna. We drove home singing, giddy to be alive.

"We were lucky," I say.

"I loved it that you laughed," she says. "It was the one time in my whole life that I really felt invincible. I wanted to roll the goddamned car again."

I recall feeling the same: that nothing could hurt us, and that we were all going to be young and healthy and happy forever. Katya turns to face me, the pain in her eyes a piercing semblance of what I see in the mirror each morning. I check my impulse to go to her, afraid of being rebuffed. Dropping my head, I pinch the bridge of my nose and surreptitiously wipe away a tear.

"So how are you?" she asks.

"A little run-down," I say, looking up again. "Otherwise fine."

"I'm sorry about Klein, and all this stuff in the press. It must be terrible for you."

"I'm surviving."

She takes a step toward me.

"I've been thinking about Jenna a lot. She once told me—"

"Can we not do this?" I say, my voice strained. I'm only just holding it together as is. Being consoled by Katya after everything that's passed between us would be too much to bear.

"Not do what?"

"Reminisce."

She stiffens for a moment and then her features soften. Embarrassment grips me as I see myself from her perspective—clothes hanging loose and face gray with exhaustion.

"I wish you'd come to see me sooner, Peter."

"How could I, Katya?"

"Because of the police?"

I shrug, unsure how to answer.

"You should have told them the truth about us. Why didn't you?"

"Listen," I say wearily. "You don't understand. The cops weren't conducting an investigation. The detective in charge was just looking for ways to put pressure on me. He would have done everything he could to drag your name through the mud."

"People have affairs all the time. No one would have cared. We're both consenting adults."

She's being kind. She only consented because I lied to her.

"I was trying to do the right thing, Katya. I didn't want to hurt you again."

Her eyes drop as her cheeks color, and it suddenly occurs to me that she's as afraid of my pity as I am of hers. A tap at the door interrupts the awkward silence. Debra enters, showing in a white-jacketed waiter wheeling a gray plastic trolley. He sets lunch on the coffee table, fussing over a bone china platter piled with tea sandwiches and half filling crystal glasses with Diet Coke. Katya reviews a sheaf of phone messages, her hands trembling. Ever since that first night outside the bar, I've wondered what would have happened if I'd met Katya before Jenna. Would it have been harder or easier to be with someone more like myself? And every time I wondered, I felt guilty about imagining a past that excluded Jenna.

"I've only got a few minutes," Katya says, motioning me to the sofa as Debra and the waiter leave. She settles into an overstuffed armchair to my left and folds her arms, the softness gone from her face. "I understand that you were trying to do the right thing, Peter, and I appreciate it. But your cover-up's put us both in a worse position. The *Post* ran your picture under the headline 'Murder Mistress Mystery.' You don't know what it's like to be a senior woman executive. If the truth comes out now, there's no way my career will survive."

"Come on, Katya," I say, feeling a little defensive. "William's notorious for not giving a damn what other people think."

"You must have given up reading the *Journal,* Peter," she says, an edge creeping into her voice.

"What do you mean?"

"William's decided to spend more time on his art collection. He's announced his retirement, and the board's put together a search committee."

"So?" I say, intrigued despite her evident anger. Guys like Turndale usually die at their desks. "William chairs the board, and he owns a control stake. It's still his decision."

"Today it is." She leans forward to lift her glass of Diet Coke and takes a minuscule sip. "There are rumors that he's shopping his shares. Supposedly, he's negotiating with one of the big Dutch universal banks."

"What do you mean, 'rumors'? He hasn't told you?"

"William isn't in the habit of sharing his plans," she says, finger tapping on the glass. "I may just read in the *Journal* that he's decided to sell to the Dutch or someone else and that I'm competing with God knows who for the top job. So you understand why this isn't the best time for it to come out that I'm the *New York Post*'s mystery mistress."

Katya's given her whole life to Turndale, a major source of the ongoing conflict between her and her mother; to lose the brass ring now, when it is almost in her grasp, would devastate her.

"Nobody knows anything about us except me and you," I say, trying to reassure her. "As long as we both keep quiet, everything will be fine."

"Really? Jenna figured it out."

"I don't know how."

"Maybe that's the point. Things happen that we can't control."

A few months ago, I might have argued with her. More

and more, though, I'm realizing the extent to which my life was built on illusions.

"I'm sorry," I say, feeling even more spent than when I arrived. "There are a lot of things I wish I could change."

Katya sighs and tucks her legs up beneath her, looking small and vulnerable in the oversized chair. I lean forward and reach toward her arm without thinking.

"Don't," she says sharply, jerking away. Then, softer: "Please."

Embarrassed again, I look around for something to keep my hands busy and see a carved wooden fish made of interlocking puzzle pieces on the end table. The tail weaves sinuously as I pick it up. I pop out a dowel and the fish falls to pieces.

"Can we talk about your brother?" I ask, disentangling the pieces. "I've been having trouble getting in touch with him. He hasn't returned my calls or e-mail."

"You said the police want to speak with him. Why?"

"The detectives investigating Jenna's death found out that Andrei sent a package to my house the afternoon before she was murdered. The police suspect the killers took it. They want to ask Andrei what was in it."

"Killers?"

"The cops think there were two of them."

"And they believe they can track these guys through whatever was in the package?"

"I guess," I say, not bothering to repeat Tilling's unlikely logic. "They've already talked to your mother. She said she couldn't help, that she didn't know where he is. Is it true he isn't working for Turndale anymore?"

Katya looks down at the table, not answering immediately. It's a straightforward question, and her hesitation makes me uneasy. I fit together a few pieces of the fish, figuring it's better not to press her.

"I got an e-mail three months back from the head of our London office, telling me that William had fired Andrei," Katya says, her expression unreadable.

"What?" I ask, startled. "Why? Was he losing money?"

"Not that I know about. He reported directly to William, but I saw his returns in the monthly management package. He had about two billion dollars invested, and was generating consistent returns in the high teens."

"So why'd he get canned?"

She takes another tiny sip of Diet Coke, her hand trembling again. There aren't many reasons why traders who make money get fired.

"Personnel bullshit? He was sleeping around the office?"

"Europeans still think sexual harassment's a perk," she replies, her contempt audible. "And anyway, Andrei's always been discreet. It wasn't that. His clerk got fired the same day."

It had to be business if Andrei and the clerk got fired together.

"What was William's explanation?" I ask.

"He hasn't offered one. He said I didn't want to know."

"Didn't *want* to know," I ask slowly, "or didn't *need* to know?"

"Want."

The word hangs in the air between us like a bad smell. You don't need to know things that don't concern you; you don't want to know things that might compromise you. William waved a corporate plague flag, warning Katya off. Eastern Europe doesn't have a lot of securities laws. The most likely explanation is that Andrei did something in Moscow that would embarrass or incriminate Turndale if it were reported back home. Petty kickbacks or a little insider trading perhaps. The only problem with this theory is that Andrei's the most ethical guy I've ever known.

"What does Andrei say?"

"Nothing," she replies flatly.

"He won't talk about it?"

"I haven't been able to get hold of him, either. The last time we spoke was in September, a few days before I heard from London that he'd been fired."

I feel a sharp stab of anxiety—something's very wrong here. It's impossible that Andrei wouldn't be in touch with Katya.

"Has your mother talked to him?"

"Apparently. She tells me that he's well, and that I shouldn't concern myself."

"If he's well, why hasn't he called you?"

"An excellent question."

"I'm not getting this, Katya," I say, confused by her terseness. "Aren't you worried?"

She sits forward, suddenly furious.

"Let's count the things I'm worried about. One: I'm worried your stupid cover-up may end up torpedoing my career. Two: I'm worried our old-boy board might persuade William that they need a CEO who can drive a golf ball two hundred and fifty yards and tell amusing stories in the men's locker room at the club. Three: I'm worried about who might take my job if William sells his shares. Four: I'm worried about my brother. And five . . ." Her eyes slip from mine as she trails off.

"What?"

She shrugs, and I wonder what she's holding back.

"So what are you doing to make sure Andrei's okay?" I ask.

"I'm open to suggestions."

"You could push your mother harder for a start. Demand to know when she last heard from him and then work from there."

"To hell with her," Katya snaps. "She's never told me the truth about anything."

"You're just going to sit around here, then, and hope for the best," I say incredulously. "Is that what you're telling me?"

Katya glares. I look away after a few seconds and begin disentangling the wooden puzzle pieces on the coffee table, determined to wait her out. I can see her watching from the corner of my eye.

"Give me the goddamn fish," she says.

I slide the pieces to her and she reassembles it, hands moving too quickly for me to follow. She carries the fish to her desk and returns with a red accordion file.

"The keys and alarm code to Andrei's Moscow apartment," she says, setting the file down on the coffee table in front of me. "The master lease is in Turndale's name. Andrei's the subtenant until February."

"Why give them to me?"

"So you can go take a look. See how Andrei's doing, and find out why he hasn't returned our calls. You can ask him about the package at the same time."

Moscow? Fuck. This is why she wanted to meet in person, so she could ask me to traipse off across the globe and snoop around for her. I'm surprised by how hurt I feel to discover her true purpose. Like a fool, I'd secretly been hoping for some kind of reconciliation.

"Why not you?" I ask, looking for an out. The sad fact is that traveling to New York this morning was about as much as I felt up to. Moscow might as well be the moon.

"Because I'm tied down here with business and because William warned me off. I'm worried, Peter. I need your help."

"I don't know that I can do this right now, Katya," I say, ashamed to admit my frailty.

"I think you can," she says curtly. "One thing we have in common is that we both do whatever we make our minds up to do. If I can make myself ask you for a favor, despite everything that's happened"—her voice falters momentarily before regaining strength—"I'm confident you can make yourself do it." She lifts the file and holds it out to me. "You owe me, Peter. Don't let me down."

The look on her face forestalls any further protest. I take the file reluctantly, realizing it's my best chance to catch up with Andrei but still dreading the trip.

"What makes you think he's even there?" I ask, playing my last card.

"Our head of security in London checked with the alarm company in Moscow for me. Somebody's coming and going regularly, usually late at night. Now go."

She gets to her feet, our conversation over. Rising slowly, I tuck the file beneath my arm and turn to the door. Her hand touches my shoulder lightly from behind, making me start.

"Give Andrei my love," she says.

10

THE NAME LA FORTUNA is barely legible on a battered red awning wedged between a plumbing-supply distributor and a storefront car service four blocks from City Hall in lower Manhattan. The interior's Korean War–vintage Italian—fishing nets tacked to yellowed acoustic ceiling tiles, paint-by-number scenes of the Bay of Naples, straw-wrapped Chianti bottles wired to the sconces. Every table's taken. A chubby Mediterranean blonde wearing a low-cut white dress smiles skeptically as I approach the hostess station.

"Do you have a lunch reservation?" she asks.

"I'm meeting a friend, thanks."

She takes my coat and hands me a plastic claim check while I scan the crowded room. Tigger's at a table in the far corner, sitting with an older guy in a scarlet blazer and a hairpiece that can't pass from fifty feet. He spots me and nods, pointing to the tiny bar. I jostle myself close enough to the bartender to order a San Pellegrino and then wait for Tigger to join me.

I tried Andrei again after speaking with Katya, hoping to get lucky. No response. Sitting at my kitchen table, I almost persuaded myself to let the whole thing drop—to tell Tilling that I hadn't been able to get a line on Andrei, and to simply duck Katya. The package is bound to be a wild-goose chase, and if Andrei were in any serious difficulty, surely he'd have enlisted Katya's help. Eventually, though, I realized I didn't have a choice. Katya's right that I owe her, and I'm concerned about Andrei. I booked a flight for the next evening and then called Tigger, hoping he might be able to track down the clerk Katya had mentioned, the one who'd been fired with Andrei. The clerk's bound to know what happened, and I'd rather know what Andrei's done—or what he's been accused of doing—before I knock on his door.

"Hey," Tigger says, settling one haunch on a just-vacated bar stool. "How you doin'?"

"Good. Thanks for finding this guy so quick."

"No problem. I used to play Catholic-league basketball with the head of Turndale's back office when I was a kid."

"The fathers recruited Jewish kids?"

"The fathers wanted to win," Tigger says deadpan. "Besides, it wasn't the kind of neighborhood where they could worry too much about who mighta killed who."

It's no surprise that Tigger knows the head of Turndale's back office. Thirty years ago, all the Wall Street firms staffed the skilled clerical jobs collectively referred to as "the back office" with Jews and Italians from Brooklyn high schools. Neighborhood ties transcended corporate rivalries, and back office staff up and down the Street quietly cooperated to make sure business flowed smoothly and everybody's cousins were employed. The smartest kids, like Tigger, occasionally got promoted to lucrative seats on the trading desks next to Yalies and Princetonians, thus achieving the American dream in a single generation. With the rise of professional managers like Eve Lemonde, though, all the firms instituted new hiring policies, ensuring that street-smart guys who never went to college couldn't get a foot in the door, and purging the residual Brooklyn staff because, among other sins, they'd resisted "professional" management. The goombah network isn't what it used to be, but Tigger still knows people to call at most of the big Wall Street houses.

"What's this guy's name again?" I ask Tigger, glancing over my shoulder. His table companion is mopping olive oil off a plate with a hunk of bread.

"Tony Pongo."

"Is he going to talk to me?"

"Turndale made him sign a confidentiality agreement when he got canned. But he's workin' on a water glass of grappa, and I told him you were a stand-up guy, so he'll probably talk if you ask right and promise not to blab."

"If he doesn't pass out first," I say, seeing Pongo take a big hit from his glass.

"Nah. Pongo's a *paisan*. He'll get a little weepy maybe, but he won't keel over."

"Thanks, Tigger. I appreciate the help."

"Anytime, Peter. You mind if I ask you a question?"

I'm not used to hearing Tigger sound tentative. I rest one elbow on a corner of the bar like a guy with all the time in the world, hoping the waiter doesn't fill Pongo's glass again.

"Shoot."

"Did you sign a confidentiality agreement?"

"No. Klein's been chasing me for one, but I've been tossing their mail just to piss them off. Why?"

"I was embarrassed to tell you," he says. "I got a lawyer. We filed suit against Klein for age discrimination about six weeks ago."

I can't help laughing. He looks hurt for a second and then smiles.

"You spent the last decade on double-secret probation for diversity violations and you turned out to be a minority yourself?" I say. "How's it feel?"

"Like the white man owes me reparations," Tigger booms in bass tones. We both crack up, the hostess frowning as heads turn in our direction.

"You want me to do a deposition?" I ask when I've caught my breath. Like every other senior manager on Wall Street, I've been involved in a number of legal wrangles with departing staff, learning a fair bit about employment law in the process.

"We haven't gotten that far. We've been tryin' to subpoena my file, but Lemonde's a lawyer, and they're claiming it's all privileged work product. You were on the Human Resources Committee."

"I didn't save any documents."

"What about e-mail?"

"Firm policy is to erase anything older than three months."

"Yeah, but you saved it, right?"

"Of course. I've got a couple of gig on my hard drive, going back three or four years."

"Is there anything that would help me?"

I take a sip of water, thinking. It's hard to separate my recollection of things Lemonde actually said or wrote and things she only intimated with her penciled brow.

"Probably," I say, "but getting the mail from me isn't going to help you with the privilege issue. You've got to get the court to admit it as evidence."

"My lawyer thinks we might persuade the judge if you waive your privilege."

"What privilege?"

"Lemonde says she was actin' as a lawyer, and she sent you mail, so that makes you her client. You can waive the client privilege."

Tigger starts bouncing a little on his stool, gleeful at the thought of outwitting Klein.

"Is that going to work?" I ask dubiously.

"Who knows?" Tigger says. "But suddenly they're arguin' why we shouldn't be able to use stuff we already got, instead of us arguin' they should give us stuff we've never seen. We'd be doin' even better if you signed on as a claimant. That would really confuse things. The law covers anyone over forty."

"It's going to take a lot of chutzpah to argue Klein fired me because of my age."

"We can always drop you later. It's just to get the documents admitted."

"Your lawyer's got big balls," I say, shaking my head admiringly. "Who's representing you?"

"My daughter, Rachel," he says, grinning.

"Mazel tov." I laugh again. Tigger's lawsuit is the reason Klein's been pressing me to sign their documents. Lemonde isn't stupid. She must've anticipated Tigger would turn to me for help. "Have Rachel draw up a retainer appointing her to represent me on this and you're welcome to do whatever helps your case."

Tigger slips an envelope and a pen from his blazer pocket and offers them to me. The envelope contains a retainer printed on his daughter's letterhead.

"I should've known," I say, shaking my head as I sign and hand the letter back. "My laptop's over at the Harvard Club.

I'll burn the mail to CDs after lunch and leave them at the front desk under your name."

"Thanks, Peter."

"Seriously, though. Have you thought about this? If you sue Klein, you'll never work on the Street again. I know you don't need the cash, so why bother?"

"You'll laugh."

"Probably."

Tigger smiles and then looks away.

"Tell me the truth, Petey. All the bullshit aside, did I ever not give anyone a fair shake?"

"Bullshit aside, you've always been square with everyone."

"And did I do a good job?"

"You made money every year, and you trained half the guys on the floor, including me. Frankly, with both of us gone, I think Klein's in deep shit."

"So why'd they can me?"

I'm not sure what to tell him.

"Because your ties are a fire hazard?"

"Because I'm old school," Tigger says bitterly. "That's why I'm suing them. Because being discriminated against sucks."

11

PONGO'S BABY-FACED, in his late fifties, and wearing a double-breasted gray suit and yellow tie over a pink shirt with white collar and cuffs, the top button undone to give his fleshy cheeks room to breathe. He's got a salt-and-pepper Valentino mustache and long, dark eyelashes. Up close, his rug looks like a hibernating squirrel. I settle into Tigger's empty chair, extending a hand and saying my name.

"Tony Pongo," he replies. "Tigger left?"

"He had some errands to run."

"Listen," Tony says, taking a sip of grappa. "He told me you was lookin' for Andrei. I don't know where he is, or how to get hold of him. Last time I seen him was three months ago."

"So tell me about Moscow."

"Whadda you care about Moscow?"

"I'm flying over tonight. I'd like to know more about Turndale's setup there. What Andrei was doing, who worked in the office. That kind of thing."

"Good luck in that fuckin' place." He shakes his head doubtfully. "Turndale finds out I'm talkin' to you and they're gonna fuck with my pension."

"Why should they care?"

His pinkie ring flashes as he taps pudgy fingers nervously on the white tablecloth, not answering. I need to get him started.

"How'd you end up in Moscow?" I ask.

Tony sighs, letting his shoulders slump. "I'm a fuckin' *babbo*," he says. "An idiot. Turndale moved some of the back office to Tampa. I figure the weather is better and I got nuthin keeping me here, so I put my hand up for a transfer. Big fuckin' mistake. What they teach you in the army is right: Don't volunteer for nuthin."

I laugh appreciatively and he smirks.

"You put in for Florida and they gave you Moscow? Somebody doesn't like you, Tony."

"They blew so much smoke up my ass. 'We need a guy that knows what's what. We'll give you more money. We'll pay for your house. It'll be good for your pension. It's only gonna be a coupla years.' Yada yada yada. Shit. Fuckin' winter every day, nuthin to drink but potato wine, and food like you get in jail. And the girls. The ones under twenty-five are younger than my daughters, and I got a rule about that. The problem is the ones over twenty-five look like they should be chasin' tin rabbits at the track." His hands fly as he speaks. Tony's an entertainer.

"What was your job?"

"Just the same as here in New York. I confirmed positions, checked out trades, instructed money, proofread confirms, all the usual shit."

"Did Andrei talk to you much about what he was doing?"

"Not for nuthin, but I didn't care. I'm just doin' my job and waitin' out the time. I can tell you what the paperwork said, but that's about it."

"Was the paperwork clean?"

"Always. We got no problems. Everybody in London is very happy with me, tellin' me I'm doin' a good job and all that shit."

"Was the paperwork telling the real story?"

Pongo hunches forward conspiratorially.

"You mean was Andrei takin' a skim or somethin'?"

"Right."

"The paperwork was tight, but Moscow's a wild place. Everybody's mobbed up. Fuckin' place makes Brooklyn look like the Upper East Side. Ya gotta do business to do business," he says, rubbing his thumb against his first two fingers, "but I don't know nuthin for sure."

An elderly waiter settles a shrimp cocktail in front of Tony and then looks at me questioningly.

"Nothing for me right now," I say as Tony tucks a corner of his oversized linen napkin into his collar. The waiter nods politely and vanishes.

"You're missin' out," Tony says, his mouth already full. "The food here is the best."

"I already ate. So tell me. What was going on that the firm didn't like? Why did everything get shut down?"

Tony shrugs, holding a half-eaten shrimp by its tail fastidiously. I let the silence develop, but he seems perfectly comfortable, concentrating on his food.

"Did Andrei seem worried about anything?" I ask, trying a different tack.

"No idea," Tony says, swallowing. "Fuckin' guy was a mystery wrapped in a riddle. Smiled and said hi and that was about it."

I'm positive Tony knows why William fired Andrei. It's just a matter of asking the right questions.

"Tell me about the office."

Tony wipes his hands and frowns.

"You couldn't park four cars in it. Andrei's got an office and there's a conference room. I got a desk and the fat Russian broad that answered the phones had a desk. An extra desk for people that might visit. Nuthin special."

"Did anyone visit?"

"Nah. Who in their right mind would go to that fucked-up place? The secretary had a kid that used to come in and do stuff sometimes. A real mook. Ya know what I mean?"

"What did the kid do?"

"He fooled around with the computers. Andrei had a car. Sometimes the kid drove him places. Other stuff maybe."

"What's the secretary's name?"

"Olga Guskof."

"And the kid's?"

"I dunno. He had a big metal ring through his face. Whadda I want to know about him?"

Tony's a little bit too loud. It doesn't feel right that he wouldn't know the kid's name in an office that small. I hesitate, wondering what I'm missing. He dips another shrimp in cocktail sauce.

"Did you hear Andrei talking on the phone much?"

"I didn't pay no attention. It was mostly Russian anyway."

"Tell me about the phone system."

"Whaddya mean? They were phones."

"You taped everything, right?"

"Yeah, of course."

"How long did you keep the tapes?"

"Coupla months maybe. Olga handled it."

"Where'd you keep the tapes?"

"I dunno. It wasn't my job."

"Tony."

He stares down into his empty bowl, cocktail sauce in his mustache. I know he's lying. I just have to figure out why.

"The office wasn't big enough for her to fart without you smelling it. Right? That's what you said. What do you mean you don't know where she kept the tapes?"

He shrugs again, not looking up.

"Didn't you ever have to listen to the tapes?"

"What kind of fuckin' questions are these?" he asks angrily, pulling the napkin from his collar and throwing it on the table. "What do I know where some fat-ass Russian broad I wouldn't fuck with your dick kept a bunch of goddamned tapes. This is bullshit."

"No, Tony," I say, catching his wrist firmly as he gets up from his chair. "What you're telling me is bullshit. What kind of fucking hump do you think I am? Tigger told you I was a stand-up guy, and he told me the same thing about you. I'm not going to make him a liar, so why are you?"

He glares at me, looking like the kind of guy who got beat up a lot as a kid.

"Listen," I say, releasing my grip and trying to sound conciliatory. "Andrei's a friend of mine. His sister and I are worried about him. I just need you to tell me what was going on. Nobody else has to know anything about it."

"Shit," Tony says, his mouth working unhappily. He turns away and stomps off toward the bathroom, leaving his coat check on the table. At least I know he's coming back. Frank sings "My Way" while I wait. I make it even money that Tony either spills his guts or tells me to fuck off.

Tony's face is damp and he smells of fresh cologne when he returns. "Okay," he says, sinking heavily into his chair. "I got my own reason for talkin' to you, but you gotta give me your word that everthin' I tell you is between you and me."

"Done," I say, shaking his hand again.

He takes a big slug of grappa and then leans toward me, speaking in a hoarse whisper, as if afraid Turndale might have spies in the restaurant.

"I never moved to Moscow."

"What?"

"I never moved to Moscow. I went over to check it out and stayed about two weeks. What I said before is the truth. The place is the pits. I'm staying in some dump apartment and freezin' my balls off. I can't eat nuthin, the food is *merda*. I go to Andrei's office and tell him I'm not gonna do it, that I'll put my papers in. We talked. He says we can work it out."

Tony pats his hairpiece with his hands. I sure as hell never expected this.

"He asks if maybe I'd like to spend some time in Italy. My mamma's in Salerno, an hour or so from Naples. He says, 'Go live in Salerno. We'll give you a computer and you can do your work from there. We'll cover for you here. It's no big deal,' he says."

Tony grins, feeling better with his secret out. Despite my apprehension, I force a smile to encourage him; this is serious evidence that Andrei was doing something bad.

"It was simple. Olga took the calls and put everybody in my voice mail. Somebody really needs me and she transfers them to my cell phone. The cell phones work real good over there. Nobody knew. Nobody called anyway. The paperwork was always clean, so they left me alone."

"How'd you get the work done?"

"Pff." He waves the question away. "No problem. I taught

Olga how to do the local phone stuff. Confirms and whatever. Most of the fucks don't speak English anyway. She faxed
me down tickets and reports and shit. I dial Moscow on the
computer and put everything in the system. I only had to go
there two, three times maybe. Olga sent me the weather every
day so I could bitch and moan to the guys in London."

"Does Turndale know this?"

"Nah. I don't think so. It woulda come up when they
fired me."

"Weren't you suspicious?"

"Look, Andrei wants to send me to Italy and make my life
happier, I'm okay with that. I don't break the devil's dishes.
Everything ties together, the numbers are okay, so there's no
problem. Like I said before, maybe he had to get a little
mobbed up to do business. Maybe he's steering business to
somebody's girlfriend, maybe he pays too much for office
supplies. Who the fuck knows. He was makin' money for
Turndale and takin' care of me, and that's all I cared about."

The old Brooklyn guys are renowned for their pragma-
tism, but I'm still blown away by Tony's apparent sangfroid. I
wonder if he's a lot smarter than I think or a lot dumber.

"Tell me how it ended."

"Olga calls and says get your ass up here now. I show up
the next morning and William fuckin' Turndale himself is sit-
tin' in Andrei's office. He calls me in and tells me I'm retirin'.
Olga has a plane ticket to New York. I should go see Human
Resources when I get home and they'll straighten me out.
Good-bye and fuck you. That's all it was."

"You didn't ask him what was going on?"

"Another thing they teach you in the army," he says, shaking his head at me. "Don't volunteer and don't ask questions.

All I wanted was to keep my head down and collect my pension."

It's not likely William would have told Tony anything even if he had asked.

"Did he have any questions for you?" I ask, hoping to get some idea of what William was thinking.

"Just one. He said somebody swiped Andrei's laptop, and he asked if I knew anythin' about it. He seemed real interested in the computer, askin' about it a bunch of different ways. I said I didn't know nuthin about it, which was the truth."

Tony gazes at me guilelessly, big brown eyes unclouded. I can't imagine what Andrei was involved in.

"You said you had a reason for talking to me."

"Yeah."

Pongo swigs another inch of grappa, then sets down the glass and folds his hands over his face, like he's praying. When he looks up again, his eyes are moist.

"The week after I come back, some big guy comes around to my place in Staten Island to see me. He's full of questions about Andrei. Asks if I know where he is, or if I know how to get in touch with him, that sort of thing. A real tough guy."

"What day was this?" I ask sharply.

Tony hesitates, thinking.

"I was gettin' dressed to go out to the Meadowlands when this guy showed up at my front door," he says. "My ex-brother-in-law had tickets to the Giants against Dallas on Monday night."

A surge of adrenaline cuts my breath short. I watched that game in my room at the Harvard Club the night before Jenna was murdered.

"What'd this guy look like?" I demand.

"Clark Kent kind of asshole. Short hair, stupid glasses, wore his watch turned in like a military fuck. He had a tattoo on his wrist, Felix the Cat, if you can believe that shit. Polite in the way that means fuck you. And he had an accent."

"What kind of accent?"

"Not Italian and not Russian. Somewhere in between."

"Somewhere in between is half of Europe, Tony. You can't narrow it down any more than that?"

He throws his hands up, looking wounded.

"Don't worry about it," I say quickly, giving his arm an encouraging pat. Offending Pongo isn't going to help. "Tell me what happened."

"I tell this guy to get lost and he warns me not to mess with him, like he's gonna scare me into talking. He tries to give me a card with his number on it, sayin' I should call him if I hear from Andrei, and that he'll make it worth my while." Tony chokes up for a moment. "I had a new Doberman pup," he continues brokenly, "only a couple of months old. The dog's gettin' excited, barking at this guy. He's only a puppy, but he wants to protect me."

He covers his face with his napkin, tears now streaming from his eyes.

"And then?"

"And then this guy caught my puppy by the collar and broke his neck."

12

THE HARVARD CLUB booked a car to the airport for me, the driver a quiet Rastaman in a Blues Brothers suit with an attaché case full of reggae tapes. He introduced himself as Curtis. We're driving east on the Grand Central, the sun just set, slush spattering the windshield while Peter Tosh chants "Johnny B. Goode." I've got my eyes closed, trying to relax, but I'm too wound up. Pongo's story changes everything. Impossible as it seems, Tilling might be right. Maybe Jenna was murdered by some guys looking for Andrei, guys who found out that he'd sent a package to my house and wanted to know what was in it, or where it had been sent from. I need to get to the bottom of whatever Andrei's involved in, and a trip to Moscow doesn't seem like such a big price anymore. My phone rings and Curtis turns down the tape obligingly.

"Peter Tyler," I say.

"Grace Tilling."

"Is there some better way to reach you?" I ask angrily. "I've called you four times in the last three hours."

"One better way would have been to call yesterday," she says. "When you promised to call."

"Yesterday I didn't have anything to tell you."

"And today you do?"

"I ran down a guy who knows Andrei. He said some goon turned up at his door the day before Jenna was murdered, looking for Andrei. This guy told him to get lost, and the goon killed his dog."

"How?"

"Picked it up and broke its neck."

"What's the guy's name?"

"He doesn't want me to tell you."

"It's always great talking to you, Peter."

The phone clicks and she's gone.

"Shit."

I heave the cell phone against the front seat, the phone, battery, and belt clip bouncing off in different directions. Curtis looks over his shoulder casually, eye hidden behind black shades.

"Problem, mon?"

I shake my head, annoyed by my lapse of control. My high school coach used to dress me down when I lost my temper. "Losers kick the watercooler when they're behind. Winners work harder." I reassemble the phone and dial Tilling's number, getting her voice mail for the fifth time.

"Grace. It's Peter again. The goon who snapped the dog's neck left a phone number behind. If you find him, I'm pretty sure I'll be able to persuade the guy I talked with to cooperate." I read her the number and repeat Pongo's physical description of the tough guy, wondering why I called her Grace. "I'm out of town for a couple of days, but I'll be checking messages."

I hesitate, tempted to apologize for not being more forth-coming, and then hang up. Curtis pops the completed Peter Tosh tape out of the player.

"Any more preferences, mon?"

"You got *Natty Dread*?"

He smacks in another tape and the car fills with the sound of Bob Marley wailing "Lively up Yourself." Our senior year, Jenna and I drove from Ithaca to Brunswick, Ohio, to spend the Thanksgiving holiday with my father, playing this tape over and over again on the car stereo. I rest my head against the seat, listening to the wipers carry a backbeat.

"You're frowning," Jenna said.

The wind was roaring off Lake Erie, buffeting the car with great gusts that threatened to push us into the next lane. We'd had dinner before we left, about three hours earlier.

"I thought you'd fallen asleep," I said, turning down the music.

"Just drifting."

"There's a good truck stop right off the expressway, but I can't remember which side of Dunkirk it's on. I was thinking about a cup of coffee, and maybe a slice of pie to go with it."

"Think about this," she said teasingly, reaching over to caress my leg. "You're twenty-one years old, you're driving a car down a dark highway through the middle of America, you've got the king of reggae on the tape deck and a willing blonde in the front seat, and you're distressed because you can't remember where some truck stop is."

I glanced to my right. She was lying cocooned in a red wool blanket on the reclined passenger seat, hair gathered in a makeshift ponytail with a rubber band, only the neck of her white Shetland sweater exposed. The sweater had been a birthday present from me, blowing a huge hole in my budget. Headlights reflected off the roof liner, partially illuminating her face. Looking at her took my breath away.

"They fresh-bake their pies," I said.

Pushing herself half-upright, she whacked me on the arm. "That's from me and Bob Marley both. Philistine."

"Ouch. Wrong response, I guess. Should I pull over?"

"You missed your chance," she said dismissively. "Anyway, car sex was more of a high school thing."

"For other girls, you mean. I was your first, right?"

"In third grade, a boy named Timmy Telljohan gave me a peck on the cheek and then stuck his tongue out and licked me. An older boy gave him directions and he got mixed up. It felt kind of nice, though."

"I'll find the fucker and kill him."

"So now you're not thinking about the truck stop anymore?" she said. "You only focus on me when you think your property rights are threatened, and otherwise you're consumed by pie lust?"

"The whole pie thing was just sublimation. You know you're the only one. Although your story about Timmy has me thinking. Would you like it if I rubbed pie on your body and licked it off?"

"Gross," she said, laughing. "Don't think I'm not seeing through you here. This is kind of a two-girl fantasy, isn't it? Me and the pie both in the sack at the same time. And then eventually it will be just you and the pie in bed, listening to me leave long weepy messages on your answering machine. No way."

"Fine," I said, pretending to pout. "Wait until you want to do something kinky. See what I say."

"You'll say yes in a heartbeat. Men are all pigs."

"True. Tell me one of your kinky fantasies, and then maybe I won't need to stop for coffee."

"Ha," she said scornfully. "You couldn't handle it. You'd get all hot and bothered, and I'd have to spend the next three hours slapping your hands off my firm white body." She rolled onto her side, facing me, and tucked one leg up. I was already all hot and bothered. "I'll tell you what, though," she said, suddenly serious. "I'll play truth or dare with you."

"Dare. You want me to take my clothes off now?"

"Not so quickly," she said, holding up a finger. "I wasn't finished. You have to go first, and you have to take truth."

"Only if you promise to take dare. And I'm warning you, car sex is a definite possibility."

"Agreed," she said. I took one hand off the wheel and we shook solemnly, her touch stirring me.

"So what's the question?" I asked, confident that I'd out-traded her.

"I want you to tell me your fantasy."

"This could get kind of graphic," I said, embarrassed and titillated. "You prefer to hear about Princess Leia or the Doublemint Twins?"

"Boring," she said dismissively. "I want to hear your real fantasy. Where you see yourself in fifteen or twenty or fifty years, and what you will have done or achieved that's important to you."

I glanced over again, but Jenna's expression was shadowed. I'd lied before when I told her why I was frowning. I'd been wondering why she'd agreed to come home with me. The past eight weeks had been an uphill struggle to insinuate myself into her life. She was spending one or two nights a week in my room, but she never left anything behind, and I couldn't figure out what she was thinking. The nights she wasn't there I lay awake until the small hours, tormenting myself with the thought that she might simply drift away. Her question struck a familiar chord: She was always emphasizing how different we were. She was right, but I couldn't see why it mattered. I was afraid she only wanted to hear me talk about my future to remind herself why she intended to be somewhere else.

"What makes you think I have any specific fantasy about the future?" I asked, hoping to draw her out.

"Sorry," she said gently. "No explanations. The rules say you have to answer my question as best you can. If you haven't got a fantasy about the future, that's your answer."

I turned the tape deck off, the Doppler wailing of an eastbound truck underscoring the abrupt silence. A memory surfaced, a recollection I'd normally have suppressed as a matter of course. I wanted to be with Jenna more than I'd ever wanted anything.

"This might not be what you're looking for," I said nervously. "It's more of a kid thing, something I used to think about before high school."

She didn't reply. I let a few seconds pass and then began to speak, my confidence faltering.

"I told you my mom died in an automobile accident when I was fifteen. I didn't tell you that she was an alcoholic. My dad traveled a lot on business, but when he was home, they were always fighting. Sometimes, after they had a big fight, my mom would lock herself in their bedroom to cry, and my dad would come up to my room and tell me to load his telescope into the car. He's interested in astronomy. We'd drive to a hill about twenty minutes from our house where it was darker, set up the telescope, and look at the stars. Some nights we'd stay out almost until dawn. The thing is, I loved being there with him, but I could never really enjoy it. I always felt like I'd betrayed my mom by leaving her."

It all flooded back with surprising vividness: the smell of my dad's cigarettes, the chirping of the crickets, and the hollow, sick feeling I used to get in my stomach.

"That wasn't the worst thing," I said, hearing my voice quaver. "The worst thing was that I never wanted to go home. I just wanted to stay on the hill with my dad, where it was dark and quiet and I didn't have to deal with my loud, drunk, awful mother. And I felt terrible about that. I felt terrible about not loving her."

I wiped my face with one hand and took a couple of deep breaths.

"So I used to fantasize when we were up there. I'd imagine myself coming to that same hill when I was a grown-up, accompanied by my own little boy. And we'd look at the stars just the way I did with my dad, and he'd love it just as much as I did, but it would be better, because at the end of the evening, we'd both really want to go home. We'd want to go home because his mother was there, and she wasn't a drunk, and we both loved her, and she loved us. That's it," I said, afraid to look at Jenna. "That's the fantasy I used to have about my future."

Jenna said nothing. I turned the tape deck back on low with a trembling hand.

"I'm not sure why that came to mind," I said, pretending to laugh. "And, you know, I'm not trying to say that it should be a son up there with me instead of a daughter, or that my wife shouldn't be up there with us. . . ."

"Shut up," Jenna said. "Just . . . shut up."

I looked over and saw she had the blanket drawn up

around her head like a cloak. I flipped the dome light on and saw tears on her cheeks.

"What's wrong?"

"Put the light out."

"Tell me what's wrong," I said, touching the switch again.

"You don't get a question," she said, voice thick in the darkness. "Remember? You insisted on a dare. Are we going to do this car sex thing or not?"

"I dare you to tell me why you're crying," I said, convinced I'd fucked everything up somehow.

"Not fair."

"Not fair?" I said, getting angry. "We're driving along in the middle of the night, kidding back and forth, and you suggest we play some children's game, and then all of a sudden— *bang*—you ask me some big life question, and I tell you something I never told anybody else before, and now you're crying, and I don't know what the fuck is going on, and you won't tell me. You won't tell me anything. I don't know why you've been sleeping with me, or why you're coming home with me, or what you're thinking about us. That's what's not fair."

She sobbed loudly.

"I'm giving this my best shot, Jenna," I said, desperate to understand her. "You've got to tell me how I'm doing."

"Dare me again," she said brokenly.

"I dare you to tell me why you're crying."

She took a moment to collect herself, drying her eyes with the edge of the blanket as I braced myself for her response.

"I've been sleeping with you because you're cute, and you're kind, and you're funny," she said in a low voice. "And I decided to come home with you because you're always talking about your dad and I could tell it was really important to you and I feel guilty about not having been nicer to you. But you're on an express train headed straight for corporate America and the suburbs and the Lion's Club and thirty-six holes of golf every weekend at the country club with the token black member, and that's not what I want. You're going to become the chairman of IBM or some other fascist organization and spend the rest of your life at meetings being an important man and that's not what I want, either. So if you weren't so goddamned nice to me all the time and so persistent, I would have already ended things between us, because everything about you is blindingly obvious and predestined and has crisp corners, and I just find that scary as hell."

I felt gutted.

"So why are you crying?" I asked a few moments later.

"Because I'm confused," she said. "And when you told me your fantasy about family life just now, about how you felt when you were little and your heart was breaking, it made everything worse for me. Because that is what I want. Way down deep, beneath all the things I want to do with my life, I want that kind of family and that kind of love more than anything. That's why I'm crying."

A wave of relief washed over me.

"Confused is okay. We can figure out confused together."

"How?" she snapped. "I've fallen in love with you and that's not what I want. How are you going to help me figure that out?"

"I don't know," I said, suddenly floating. "But I've got another fantasy. One I was too embarrassed to tell you."

"I don't want to hear it."

"It's simple. My fantasy is to make you happy."

"Goddamn it," she said, weeping again. "That's exactly what I'm talking about. That's exactly the kind of stuff that's messing me up."

We've driven into a tulle fog, the visibility zero. The steering wheel vanishes as I turn to look at her. The blanket's transformed into a bloodstained shroud, only her pale, lifeless face protruding.

"I'm sorry I let you down," I say.

"You knew what I wanted," Jenna says, receding as I reach for her. "You knew how important it was to me."

The fog swallows her up. I stumble forward, grasping for her, and hear a voice calling me.

"Yo."

Opening my eyes, I see Curtis looking at me in the rearview mirror.

"You doing all right, mon?"

"Yeah." I wipe my cheeks with the palm of a hand, angry at myself for losing it in front of a stranger. We're at the airport. "British Airways, okay?"

Curtis nods. My phone rings.

"Peter Tyler."

"Where are you going?" Tilling asks.

"Moscow."

"We seized your passport when we searched your home."

"I have two. The second one was in my briefcase."

Tilling doesn't respond.

"It's not that uncommon for guys who travel to the Middle East a lot," I say hesitantly. "Because you need to send your passport to the different embassies for visas and you never know when they're going to get it back to you. . . ." My voice trails off. "Grace?"

"You got in touch with Andrei?" she asks curtly.

"Not yet. But I think I know where he is."

"Moscow?"

"Right."

There's another long silence. I can hear her breathing.

"The guy with the Felix tattoo," I say, anxious for her take on Pongo's story. "You figure he's important, right? You think he somehow might be involved in Jenna's murder?"

"He was looking for Andrei the day before your wife was murdered and he's violent," she says. "So yes. An old cop I knew used to say that one coincidence is a lead and two coincidences are a lock. He also told me never to believe anyone who'd already lied to me once. So it's hard to get very excited about this guy if you aren't going to give me enough to check him out for myself."

"I would if I could," I say, realizing how evasive I sound. Even if I were willing to betray Pongo's confidence, doing so would lead Grace straight back to Turndale, and maybe to Katya. "We're on the same side here, Grace. I swear it. I'll get back to you just as soon as I speak with Andrei."

"I make one call to the airport and you're not getting on that plane."

"Then we might never know what was in the package," I say, wondering if she's bluffing.

Curtis pulls to the curb and pops the trunk while I wait for her response.

"I don't like a single thing about this," she says eventually. "You be sure to stay in touch with me."

The phone goes dead. Curtis hands me my bag as I get out of the car, then slips his shades up on top of his head to look me in the eye.

"You sure you're fine?" he says.

"Nah worry, mon," I reply, standing up straighter and slipping him a twenty.

"Jah bless."

13

PACKED SNOW crunches underfoot as I follow a dimly lit path through Patriarshy Pond Park. The concierge at the hotel disapproved of my decision to walk, an exaggerated moue suggesting that Americans who wander through Moscow at night end up in the river, or, more likely, that he'd missed a commission opportunity in getting me a car. I ignored him, needing the exercise. The flight over seemed interminable, hour after hour confined to a small seat while I tried to imagine what Andrei could possibly have gotten mixed up in that would account for everything I've learned these past few days. I wish he'd answered his phone when I called from the hotel, and that we were sitting in a warm bar right now, drinking beers and figuring things out together. "If wishes were horses," Tigger likes to say, "we'd all be drowning in horse shit."

The square enclosing the park is surrounded by low-rise stone apartment buildings, about a third of the windows illuminated. Andrei's street is on the northeastern edge. A gang of teenagers enjoying their Friday night are gathered around a bench nearby, smoking cigarettes and chattering in French, ice skates piled at their feet. Expats tend to cluster—I noticed an English hospital a few blocks away. I haul out the map the concierge gave me and double-check to make sure I'm still oriented. The map's labeled with transliterated English names, making navigation in the Cyrillic-signed city an exercise in orienteering. One of the French boys calls toward me in a singsong voice as the others laugh. I'm reminded of something Andrei once told me—that the only thing most Europeans have in common is a dislike of the French. Still, they're only kids.

Andrei's building is six stories high, with a classical façade. His apartment is number eleven. I hang around across the street for a few minutes, scanning the exterior in a futile attempt to identify his windows and get an early read on whether anyone's home. I'm feeling jittery. Two cops in a dented cruiser no bigger than a VW Beetle pass for the second time, the driver slowing so his partner can look me over. It's time to move. Nervous or not, I'd rather be here than home in my kitchen, dry-firing my father's gun. Crossing the street, I open the lobby door with one of the keys Katya gave me.

I climb the stairs, stopping briefly on each landing to check apartment numbers. High-gloss mahogany moldings frame beige-papered walls and brass-fitted doors, the finishes suggestive of a luxury Ramada. The halls are silent save for the click of an expanding pipe, the predominant smell wood polish. The entire building was probably purpose-fitted to accommodate Western executives on short-term assignments. I've stayed in similar places in London and Tokyo, the fridges stocked with calcified boxes of baking soda and desiccated limes. The hush adds to my nervousness.

Number eleven is on the fourth floor. I listen at the door

without hearing anything. There's no bell, so I bruise my knuckles briefly on hardwood and then listen some more. Nothing. I dig keys and a penlight out of my overcoat pocket. It's hard not to feel like a thief when you open someone else's door. The alarm peeps like a baby duck and I enter the code hurriedly, relieved when it falls silent and a green LED blinks on. The door closes behind me with a metallic click, the apartment dark.

The narrow beam of my penlight trips over a chaotic jumble of items: a wilted plant on a counter, an overturned chair, a stack of magazines collapsed across the floor. I call hello a couple of times, listening to my voice die in the stillness. I realize that my greatest fear was of finding Andrei's body, but there's no smell of death—just the stale, sour odor of fermenting trash. Scrabbling one hand along the wall behind me, I locate a bank of light switches and flip them all up.

The apartment's laid out like a loft, a long, high-ceilinged room apportioned into zones. To my right, dirty plates and glassware are stacked haphazardly around a stainless-steel sink in the kitchen, a number of the cabinet doors ajar. There's a dining room table immediately in front of me, the surface littered with fast-food containers. Newspapers weighted with congealed cheese and catsup spill from the table to the floor, rancid grease rendering patches translucent. Beer cans are scattered everywhere, the tops dusted with cigarette ash. I move slowly to my left, toward the seating area. A yellowing pillow and a brown woolen blanket lie bunched on a white leather couch; a water glass on the coffee table contains a used condom. I pick up a few magazines from the parquet floor next to the couch and flip through them. Soccer, rock stars, and gay porn. The porn's nasty, color photographs of tattooed men bound naked to benches, and worse. The captions are in

German. I don't know who's been staying here recently, but it sure as hell isn't Andrei.

Twin doors flank a wall unit surrounding a fireplace at the far end of the room. I try the left-hand door first, turning on a light and finding a filthy bath, porcelain fixtures crusted and wastebasket overflowing. Exiting quickly, I try the second door, opening it on a small, immaculate bedroom. There's a neatly made bed, a bare dresser, and a nightstand. I spot a cell phone in a charging cradle on top of the nightstand and pocket it. Checking the nightstand drawer, I find a Russian-language book, the pages extensively highlighted. I slip the book in my pocket as well and move to the dresser. The drawers are empty save for a few pairs of clean socks and some folded boxers.

The closet contains a gray suit, a blue suit, three white shirts hanging neatly, and a single pair of treed black dress shoes on the floor. A small wall safe sits open, the keys in the lock. Two ties and a black leather belt dangle from pegs; my throat catches as I recognize one of the ties. It's printed with a tourist map of Manhattan, prominent sites like Wollman Rink and the Empire State Building caricatured. Andrei had admired the tie on me over an Indian dinner in the King's Road some years back. I'd slipped it off late in the evening and marked the location of the apartment Jenna and I were living in at the time with a razor-point pen, four or five pints of Cobra making me sentimental.

"In case you ever get lost," I'd said. "You can hang the tie over the front seat of a cab and point."

Tears well in the corners of my eyes as I brush my finger over the small black dot I made so many years ago. I leak like a fucking canvas tent these days, starting at the least touch. If Andrei were here, he'd laugh at me.

A door in the bedroom opens to an antiseptic bathroom stocked with basic toilet items. Rummaging through the vanity, I find three shoe box–sized cardboard boxes stacked beneath the sink, the top box open. I reach in and pull out a handful of condoms in foil packets, puzzling briefly before replacing them.

Feeling exhausted, I close all the doors, turn off the lights, and unshutter a large window in the main room that overlooks the park. Lifting the sash to admit some cool fresh air, I hop up on the sill, taking Andrei's phone from my pocket and turning it on. I check my watch before dialing Katya's cell number. It's eight o'clock here in Moscow, noon back in New York. She answers on the fourth ring.

"Andrei?" she asks excitedly.

"No, Peter. I'm calling from his apartment."

"Is he there?"

"No." I turn sideways in the window frame, looking out over the treetops. "I think he's cleared out."

"What do you mean?"

"Most of his clothing's gone. He left behind a couple of suits and shirts, so he must have thought there was some chance he'd stop back, but he hasn't been living here."

"The alarm company said someone was coming and going."

"Not Andrei. The apartment's trashed. It looks like a gang of teenagers have been using this place for a rolling party. They left a bunch of magazines lying around, including some gay porn. Whoever they are, they've got Andrei's keys and alarm code. Any ideas?"

"None," she says, sounding crushed. "What are you going to do now?"

"Wait here. Talk to whoever shows up. See if I can get a line on Andrei, or find out anything about why he left."

"Are you sure that's safe?"

"I'm not sure of anything anymore," I say, resisting the urge to remind her that she was the one who asked me to do this. "But I'll be careful. Now listen. I need you to do a couple of things for me."

"What does that mean exactly, that you'll be careful?"

"It means I'm here and you're not and I'd appreciate your not second-guessing me over the telephone."

Silence.

"There's no point in my going home without answers," I add, trying to take the sting from my rebuff.

"I'm really scared, Peter," she says in a small voice. "Andrei's missing and you're alone. . . ."

I'd like to laugh away her fears, the way I laughed away our shock back when we rolled Andrei's car, but I don't seem to have it in me.

"I'm going to be fine," I say. "There's no reason to worry."

"What do you need me to do?"

"Talk to William. Press him on why he let Andrei go. There's got to be some connection between Andrei's getting fired and his disappearance."

"I'll try to get hold of him," she says resignedly. "He's supposed to be at an art auction in Paris, but I suspect he's actually off negotiating with the Dutch. What else?"

"Try your mother again," I say, anticipating an angry response.

"That's a waste of time," she says stiffly. "I've been trying to persuade her to tell me things for years. I haven't had any luck thus far."

"Will you try?"

"Yes. Is that it?"

"That's it. Call me back at this number when you can."

"I will. You take care of yourself," she says, sounding more like herself. "If you get hurt, I'll be furious with you."

"I wouldn't want that."

"Goddamned straight."

The phone clicks and she's gone. An arctic breeze rattles the open window as I fidget with the handset, and I button my coat higher, wondering how long I'm going to have to wait for Andrei's squatter—or squatters—to show up. Despite Katya's concern, I'm not too worried. Andrei's bedroom hasn't been touched, and his phone wasn't stolen, suggesting that whoever's been using this place has some sort of relationship with him.

I gaze skyward, seeing a full moon overhead. My dad traveled to a convention in Seattle when I was thirteen, and he called home late one night, waking me. His hotel had a telescope on the lobby terrace. We synchronized our watches and took simultaneous measurements of the angle between the moon and some familiar stars. He explained the parallax principle when he got home, telling me I could estimate the distance to a near object like the moon by assuming our dual observation points were fixed relative to the distant stars, and using the differences we'd measured in the position of the moon to triangulate on it. It took me a couple of days to get the math straight, my first result wrong because I'd forgotten to adjust for the curvature of the earth between Seattle and Brunswick. My final answer was within 10 percent of the distance I'd looked up in the encyclopedia. "Good," my father said. "It's like Archimedes and the lever. You can triangulate on anything with enough perspective."

The breeze continues to freshen, whistling through the leafless trees across the street. Moscow's quieter at night than New York. I can hear the wind, and the French teenagers still horsing around in the park, and something else—a low, familiar clicking I haven't been paying attention to. A computer.

Getting to my feet, I begin searching the cabinets surrounding the fireplace. Sure enough, one of them is stuffed with electronic gear and a rat's nest of cables. The cabinet door drops vertically to form a cantilevered desktop, revealing a laptop, modem, scanner, desk light, and a spindle of writable CDs. Tiny green network lights blink furiously, the hard drive chattering nonstop. Pulling up a chair, I turn the light on and slide the laptop forward, feeling the warmth in my hands as I rotate the case carefully, examining it. A silver sticker on the bottom is printed with a bar code and the words *Turndale and Company.* Taped directly above is Andrei's business card. Pongo said William had asked several times about Andrei's missing laptop. This must be it.

The computer opens to a standard Microsoft splash screen, but the language option is set to Russian, the familiar icons frustratingly cryptic. It takes me ten minutes to cajole the interface back to English. I'm relieved not to have to reboot, nervous the machine might demand a password.

The hard drive contains folders named in both English and Russian, the Russian folders all created within the last few months. I click a few of these at random. They're HTML pages and associated data files, the data mainly digital pictures of naked guys doing stuff that makes me slightly queasy. Someone's using Andrei's computer as a Web server, uploading gay porn to God knows where. I unplug the network cord and the drive falls silent. Hopefully, the Web master, wherever he is, will notice his site's down and stop by to fix it.

The English folders contain a random collection of documents and spreadsheets, most routine. There's a letter to the New York Department of Motor Vehicles concerning the renewal of Andrei's driver's license, one to his prep school, pledging a one-thousand-pound gift, and another to his tailor, placing an order for new shirts. Nothing and more nothing. A folder labeled "Records" contains an Excel spreadsheet. I click on it and a dialogue box pops up, demanding a password. Shit. I've seen advertisements on the Internet from companies that claim to be able to recover lost passwords. Lifting a blank CD from the spindle, I pop it into the computer and drag the Excel file to it. A second dialogue box asks if I want to wipe the original file from the hard drive. I hesitate a moment and then click on "OK," figuring Andrei wouldn't want a file he'd bothered to protect on a computer being used as a Web server.

It takes another ninety minutes to persuade myself that there's nothing else interesting on the computer, unless Andrei's hidden information in a system file, in which case I'll never find it anyway. The apartment's freezing, but I don't want to close the window. I turn the light out, close the laptop, and flip it over, leaning forward in my chair to rest my hands and cheek on the warm case. The fan hums soothingly. An image of Jenna comes to mind, huddled in bed in some frigid Scottish hotel, laughing as I blew warm air under the covers with a hair dryer. I push the memory away, trying to remember exactly how I calculated the distance to the moon, and what it felt like to be so confident of my perspective.

14

I WAKE to the sound of a key in a lock. Someone rattles Andrei's doorknob as I rub my face with my hands, recalling where I am. Muffled thumps sound from the hall, a hand or foot striking the door repeatedly. I left the dead bolt unlocked; whoever's trying to get in must have turned the key the wrong way. It's just past two. Waiting in the dark as a stranger assaults the door, I wonder if I was wrong to dismiss Katya's fears so lightly. I wish I'd brought my father's gun with me.

The door eventually opens, revealing a man in a baseball cap backlit from the hall. He coughs an angry word in the direction of the open window before turning to the alarm panel. My chair squeaks as I stand up, prompting him to spin toward me.

"Andrei?" he says.

"No, a friend."

He snaps on the overhead lights. I raise a hand against the glare, startling him into jumping back toward the door. Realizing his error, he steps forward again and erupts in vitriolic Russian, his meaning clear despite the language barrier. He wants to know who I am and what the fuck I'm doing here. The volume rises as he begins shaking a finger. He must be threatening to beat the crap out of me. He's too small to be much of a threat, a skinny twenty-year-old in an Oakland Raiders cap, wearing low-slung jeans, a leather bomber jacket over a hooded sweatshirt, and black high-top sneakers that look like the Keds I wore when I was twelve. I'm about to tell him I don't speak Russian when I realize he's switched languages.

"So who the fuck are you?" he says, doing an adenoidal De Niro.

"I work for Turndale," I say, improvising. "This is our apartment." Lifting the computer behind me, I turn it so the silver sticker on the bottom is visible. "And this is our computer. So the question really is, Who the fuck are you?"

"Fucking liar. I never see you at the office."

The cap's brim shadows his eyes, but I can see a gray metal ring piercing his lower lip. Pongo said the secretary had a son, a mook with a metal ring in his face.

"I work with Katya Zhilina in New York. You're Olga's kid, aren't you?"

Surprise flashes across his features, giving way almost immediately to sullen watchfulness. He's staring at the computer. I sit down again, my forearm resting on top of the machine, and smile reassuringly.

"I'm not here to hassle you. You answer a couple of questions and I'll get going."

I wait patiently while he gives me the flat stare tough guys use in the movies. After about thirty seconds, he crosses to the open window, slamming it shut so hard that I can hear the counterweights bang against the pulleys.

"What fucking asshole opens the window at winter?" he says.

"Your English is lovely. You learned in school?"

"MTV," he sneers. "From *Beavis and Butt-Head.*"

Dragging a dining room chair over, he straddles it backward, pulling Marlboros and matches out of a jacket pocket. Cigarette lit, he leans sideways to drop the match into the glass containing the used condom, doing the tough-guy stare again through the smoke.

"What's your name?" I ask.

"Dmitri."

"I'm Peter. The sooner you tell me what I want to know, Dmitri, the sooner I'm out of here. *Capisce?*"

"Li sento," he says, affecting a yawn.

"Where's Andrei?"

He shrugs.

"Do you know how to get in touch with him?"

"No."

"Does your mother?"

He doesn't even bother to shrug, a twist of his lips suggesting contempt at the notion that he talks to his mother.

"Andrei's going to be pretty unhappy if he learns you trashed his apartment."

"So I'm sorry. No big deal."

"Is it a big deal that you stole his computer?" I ask, guessing that he was responsible for the machine's disappearance.

"Andrei's computer is stole?" His eyes widen in feigned amazement. "You found it here, yes? In his apartment? This is a very strange stealing."

"I found it uploading pictures of guys with nine-inch dicks getting to know each other better."

"You like the pictures?" he asks mockingly. "You want to meet one of those boys?"

I take Andrei's phone out of my pocket.

"What are you doing?" he asks.

"Calling your mother," I say, bluffing him. "This is Andrei's phone. She's on his speed dial. I'm going to ask her to come over. She knows you're using Andrei's apartment, right?"

"Wait." He shakes his head, eyes skittering nervously around the room. "Don't call her. She'd have a fucking cow."

"So talk to me. When did you last see Andrei?"

He takes a deep drag on his cigarette, looking painfully put-upon, and then flicks ashes morosely in the direction of the water glass.

"The day he flied out. He called me in the morning and said to pick him up in the car."

"Where did he fly to?"

"I don't know. He says take him to the airport and I take him to the airport."

"You always drove him?"

"For a year almost. My uncle drove, but he makes a crash from too much vodka, so my mother makes me drive."

"How did Andrei seem that day?"

"Like he is thinking somewhere else."

"Distracted?"

"Right." Dmitri nods. "He is distracted. He gets in the car and says he is leaving, and that he might not come back. He says my mother has money for me." Dmitri clucks derisively, shaking his head.

"What?"

"That fucking bitch never gives me money. She keeps

everything I am to be paid. For the rent, she says, and the food. Her cabbage is very fucking expensive."

"You were working for nothing?"

"Nobody is working for nothing," he says, giving me a cool glance.

I take my wallet from my jacket, remove a hundred-dollar bill, and crease it neatly down the middle.

"Tell me," I say, putting the bill on the coffee table between us. He picks the money up and pockets it.

"Andrei isn't using the car very much."

"Ah. And when he wasn't using the car, you were."

"A car can make a lot of money in Moscow," he says with a shrug. "Enough to get my own flat maybe. If Andrei goes, I must give the car back. Turndale is only leasing it."

"Which was a big financial hit for you."

The kid nods emphatically.

"Is that why you stole his computer?"

Dmitri objects strenuously to the notion that he swiped the computer, and we agree to settle on the word *borrowed*. He explains that Andrei's files were automatically backed up to an external hard drive every day in the office, ensuring he never lost data.

"Which is why you thought it was okay to borrow the laptop," I say.

"Right. Who will care? Andrei leaves the computer on the backseat. I check to make sure it is backed up and put it under a blanket in the boot. I go for coffee and say I forgot to lock the door. No big deal. The computer is here; nothing is stolen."

Dmitri flaps a hand casually but sounds a little embarrassed.

"Where's the external drive that Andrei backed up to?"

"He took it with him."

Sitting up straight to unkink my back, I run my hands over the top of my head, trying to think.

"You look like shit," Dmitri says matter-of-factly.

"Thanks for the feedback."

"Here." He reaches into a pocket and pulls out a small yellow box. "Rub a little under the eyes," he says, offering it to me. "Is very good when you are getting no sleep."

I flip the box over, recognize the logo, and toss it back at him disgustedly.

"I don't want your fucking hemorrhoid cream."

He catches the box in midair, surprisingly quick.

"This box is only for the face," he says, sounding offended. "All the boys use it."

"What boys?"

He produces a pink business card from another pocket with a theatrical flourish and then snaps his wrist, flipping it at my chest. I grab at it but miss, then pick it up off the floor while he smirks at me. The card reads "www.russianboys.net" in fancy gold script on one side and has a phone number on the other.

"You're a pimp?"

"I have friends," he says coldly.

"Tell me about your 'friends.'"

"You are too nice to be hearing about my 'friends,'" he says, mimicking my inflection. "Probably you should fuck off now before you are hearing something bad."

I wonder whether I shouldn't just smack him. "Maybe your Web site is more like a dating service? Where friendly people can meet each other?"

Ten minutes later, I understand the rudiments. Dmitri's

stock-in-trade is knowing people—mainly young gay Russian men. He makes introductions, arranges parties at clubs, and moonlights as a car service. Some of his friends like to meet foreign businessmen. The better hotels won't let his friends hang around, preferring to fill up their lobbies with "peasant girls in cheap shoes, showing off plastic tits." So Dmitri's friends pay him a small fee to be listed on his Web site, and he pays barmen and bellboys in the hotels to hand the cards out discreetly.

"You're using Andrei's computer as a graphics server," I say.

"The Web site is getting more hits with more pictures. Other people link to good content. Google 'gay Russian boys,' " he says pridefully. "I'm number one."

"It must be nice to have Turndale paying for your bandwidth."

He leans back, eyeing me suspiciously.

"Listen. I don't give a shit about anything except finding Andrei. Whatever you're doing here is fine by me."

He lights another cigarette from the butt of the previous one and shrugs.

"Fucking bandwidth will kill you."

We sit quietly for a minute while I try to figure out how Dmitri fits into Andrei's disappearance and Jenna's death.

"How'd you get the keys and alarm code to Andrei's apartment?"

"My mother has keys."

"And the alarm code?"

"The same as his network password at work," he says disapprovingly. "Except the letters turned into numbers. Is very bad security."

"You hacked Andrei's network password?" I ask, a

suspicion beginning to form. Maybe Dmitri's responsible for some of Andrei's problems. "Did you ever do anything on-line using Andrei's identity?"

"I am network administrator," he says, shaking his head vehemently. "I don't hack and I don't phish. Business is about your reputation. Everything I do is on the up-and-down."

"You tell me the truth now and there's no problem," I say, hoping to encourage some admission from him. "But if I waste a bunch of time chasing Andrei's credit card charges or his phone bill and discover I'm investigating stuff you did, I'm going to be very pissed off. You and your mother will both hear from Turndale."

He smokes some more, considering.

"You don't care about small things."

"Right."

"Maybe somebody made an extension on the car," he says, examining his cigarette. "Maybe somebody made an upgrade on the Internet service."

"What else?"

"Nothing," he says, still not looking at me. "Nobody wants to go to jail. Andrei signed up the car and the T1 line. Maybe somebody just made changes. Changes are a small thing."

I take a moment to regroup, trying to intuit whether he's holding something back. Pongo I could read like a book. This kid's a little outside my experience, but he doesn't seem particularly criminal.

"Tell me about the day Andrei flew out," I say, deciding to move along. "Before you took him to the airport. Where were you when he got out of the car and left his computer on the backseat?"

"To the clinic."

"What clinic?"

"Moscow Free Clinic. Andrei is knowing the doctor who runs it, Dr. Anderson. She takes care of boys and girls who get sick."

"Where is it?"

He removes yet another item from his coat pocket and offers it to me. It's a foil-wrapped condom, identical to the ones under Andrei's bathroom sink. I tilt it to the light, noticing Russian numbers and letters on the wrapper.

"It is the address of the clinic. The address is also on the condom, so it can be read when you are wearing it. Sometimes it is a big clinic and sometimes it is a small clinic," he says, leering.

"What's Andrei's connection to it?"

"Andrei is helping. He knows I have many friends, so he makes me meet Dr. Anderson. She gives me condoms to give to my friends."

"To give or to sell?"

"She makes me promise not to take money."

"And do you?"

"No." He looks offended. "Not from my friends. Also I give them away with my card. The girls pay small money sometimes," he says, grinning. "You know, a handling fee."

There's a piece missing. How the hell did Andrei get involved with a Russian AIDS clinic?

"Is Dr. Anderson young?"

"Old," Dmitri says. "Maybe your age."

"Is she attractive?"

"She might be cute. She should wear lipstick, and buy new shoes."

"Was Andrei seeing her?"

"I told you. He is seeing her that day."

"No. I mean was he sleeping with her?"

Dmitri frowns uncomprehendingly.

"He was sleeping here."

"Was Andrei fucking her?" I ask, irritated.

Dmitri looks at me curiously and then his face lights up with amusement.

"You are very confused," he says.

The desire to smack him is stronger, but he's right. I'm confused, and I'm tired. The smart thing is to get some sleep. I can speak with this Dr. Anderson myself tomorrow. Dmitri shrinks back warily on his chair as I get to my feet, but he's still grinning.

"I'll be back in the morning," I say. "You get this place cleaned up before then or the car and the T1 line are gone."

His face falls comically as he looks around.

"Cleaning up after yourself is a small thing," I tell him. "And nobody gets anything for nothing."

15

IT'S WELL PAST THREE by the time I get back to my hotel. I brush my teeth and crawl into bed, exhausted, but my brain's spinning too fast for me to fall asleep. Dmitri raised more questions than he answered. I can't imagine why Andrei fled or what his involvement was with this clinic, and I still don't have any idea who was looking for him or what he might have sent Jenna. Frustrated, I sit up and turn on the light. Grabbing the phone from the bedside table, I dial Tilling's number. I want to know what she's learned about the guy with the Felix tattoo.

My call gets kicked into her voice mail. I hang up unhappily and dial my own number, hoping perhaps she called me. I've got one new message.

"Hey, Peter. It's your old pal Rommy here. What's the matter? You not taking my calls anymore?"

He sounds as if he's talking with his mouth full. I take the phone from my ear, intending to delete his message, when a half-heard phrase catches my attention: "Brunswick, Ohio." He's in mid-sentence as I lift the phone to listen again.

". . . a real nice place you grew up in. A lot of cute

forty-year-old blondes drivin' minivans full of kids. I'm won-
derin' how many of these soccer moms you banged back
when they were juicy little cheerleaders. Might have been better for everybody if you'd never left this place."

Rommy pauses, a rustling noise filling the silence. It's
hard to imagine him in my old hometown.

"Sorry," he mumbles, chewing loudly. "I'm eatin' my dinner here. A Double Whopper with cheese, the best burger in
town. Anyway, I'm doin' a little research for the book. I
stopped by the local cop shop and got them to extend me
some professional courtesy. Imagine my surprise when I
found they had a file on your mom. They must have had a
real good police photographer back then. Great pictures.
They're gonna make nice art for the book. There's one of your
mom here in the front seat of her car, with a couple of firemen
workin' one of those Jaws of Life things. . . ."

I punch the off button and leap to my feet, fighting an
urge to put my fist through the wall. I'm halfway across
the world, getting jerked around by teenage pimps, while
Rommy's being spoon-fed photographs of my dying mother.
If I could get my hands on him right now, I'd beat him to a
pulp, regardless of who might see me or what the consequences might be. Sweat drenches my T-shirt as I begin pacing, memories of my mother's death pulsing in my head.

It was lunchtime. We were playing a full-court pickup game
in the main gym, five a side, wearing street clothes. I'd just
scored on a fast break when I heard Coach call my name. I
was surprised to see him walking toward me with Miss Jones,
the school nurse, and discomfited by the expression on his
face. Coach had only one look, a fierce, half-bored glare that

suggested he'd be happy to kick your ass if you weren't so pitiful. A scrub named Irwin did a brilliant imitation of Coach
fucking his wife, sixty seconds of wild, deadpan hip thrusts,
culminating in a single laconic grunt. When someone wasn't
playing aggressively enough, Coach announced contemptuously that the offender had run out of mean, and he sent him
outside to take laps. Walking toward me that day, Coach
looked like he'd run out of mean. My eyes slid to Miss Jones
and I noticed she was wearing her heels on Coach's high-gloss
maple floor. I knew something bad had happened, but the
words Coach mumbled were worse than anything I'd let
myself imagine.

Miss Jones rode shotgun in Coach's car while I sat in the
back. She was a mousy brunette scarcely older looking than
some of the seniors, with perfect breasts that strained against
her tight white office coat, embarrassing more than one boy
during team physicals. Undeterred by my refusal to make eye
contact, she glanced over her shoulder frequently while carrying on a nervous monologue about Jesus and lambs and
God's mysterious plan, seemingly unable to shut up. Coach's
glance caught mine in the rearview mirror, and I saw the corner of his mouth turn up for a second before he remembered
himself. The smile made me feel better, and lessened the
shame glazing my grief.

One look at the spare hospital chapel was all it took for
Coach to bail, Miss Jones assuring him she could take the bus
back to school. He gave me a bone-crunching handshake and
whispered, "Winners never quit," as if he were afraid that
God or Miss Jones would hear him. Declining her repeated
suggestion that we pray together, I spent the next forty minutes watching her shift uncomfortably on a thinly padded
kneeler, her suffering doubtless a sacrifice to the Lord and a

lesson to me. I wondered when my father would arrive, and whether it would be appropriate to tell him about Miss Jones's aching knees on the car ride home. Stories about vanity or pretension always made him laugh. I heard a door open behind me.

"Peter."

I rose and walked toward my father, studying his manner for cues. Cheeks pinked with emotion, Miss Jones fluttered past me, one hand smoothing her crushed dress.

"Mr. Tyler," she said. "I'm Miss Jones, the school nurse. I just want to tell you how terribly sorry I am for your loss."

"Thank you," my father said.

"I lost my mother six months ago, and I know it's not the same thing, losing a parent and losing a spouse, but losing any loved one is a terrible trial. I know just how you feel, I really do, and the only thing that helped me get through it was prayer. I tried to persuade your son to pray with me, but he wasn't ready yet. We have a prayer circle at St. Michael and All Angels every Monday night for anyone who wants to attend. Evenings can be terribly difficult when you're grieving. You'd both be welcome to join us tonight."

"You know how I feel?" my father asked politely.

"I do. The terrible thing about losing a loved one is that it makes you doubt God's goodness just when you most need His love. Praying with other people helps, it really does, because it reminds you that you're not alone, and that whatever suffering we experience in this life is only a small measure of the suffering God's son undertook for our salvation, and that we'll all be reunited forever in God's kingdom in the next world, and comforted by His love eternally."

"*You* know how *I* feel?" my father asked again, inflecting the pronouns just enough to make the emphasis audible.

"Do you belong to a church?" Miss Jones asked, pinking some more.

He opened the door for her and held it, inclining his head toward the hall courteously.

"You've been very kind," he said. "Thank you for everything."

Miss Jones rushed out, her cheeks blazing.

"We'll give her a few minutes," my father said after he'd closed the door. "Riding an elevator together would be uncomfortable."

He didn't say much until we'd pulled into our garage at home. Turning off the car, he closed the overhead door with the remote, not making any move to get out. His car was his office, a Chevy Caprice with a police package that he captained on weekly thousand-mile loops through a territory bounded roughly by Grand Rapids, Indianapolis, Uniontown, and West Seneca, selling specialty machine tools. He liked to do business in his car.

"Take notes," he said.

I took a pencil and pad from the plastic caddy between the front seats and opened to a blank page.

"Short-term: No school tomorrow or Wednesday. There'll be visiting hours both nights at the funeral home. You'll need a navy blazer, blue shirt, clean khakis, brown belt, and a pair of decent brown shoes. You need to buy any of that?"

"No."

"I want to see everything before you go to bed, washed, ironed, or polished."

"Okay."

"First thing tomorrow, you go to Clark's. You're going to need a new navy suit, a white shirt, a dark tie, a black belt, and black shoes."

"I've already got some of that."

"Doesn't matter. You're not going to your mother's funeral in worn clothing. Ask for Mr. Sherman and tell him you need everything by Wednesday lunch. His wife should be able to get any alterations done. Thursday's the funeral. After the funeral, some folks are going to want to come back to the house. I'll take care of liquor and food. Your job will be to bus dishes and make sure we don't run out of glasses or plates."

"Fine."

"Friday, you're going back to school. Friday night, you've got your first varsity game. I plan to be there. This weekend, we'll clean out the house and box everything we don't need for the Salvation Army. I'll go through your mother's things. You've probably got a lot of kid stuff we should've gotten rid of years ago. After that, we'll divvy up chores and discuss the medium term. Food shopping's going to be a problem until you get your license, but we'll figure it out. You know how to cook some, right?"

"Yes."

"Of course," he said, rubbing his forehead. "You know how to do all the things a boy's mother usually does for him."

The garage light went out automatically and I reached up to switch on the ceiling dome. He caught my hand and pushed it away gently.

"Let's talk, Sherlock," he said, resurrecting my childhood nickname. "They tell you what happened?"

"Only that there was an accident."

"She hit a light pole at the intersection of Pearl and Miner. She wasn't wearing a seat belt."

"Was she drunk?"

"Yes," my father said, not bothering to point out that she

was drunk pretty much all the time. We sat silently for a minute, listening to the engine tick as it cooled.

"I know you've got more questions," he said. "Now's the time to get them out—you don't want to be living your life with one eye to the past."

"Why'd she drink so much?"

"That school nurse of yours, the one with the big rack."

"Miss Jones."

"Why'd I get pissed off at her?"

"She doesn't know anything about you. It's insulting for her to say she knows how you feel."

"Exactly."

My father pushed in the lighter and took a cigarette from a pack in the caddy, tapping it against the dash. The lighter popped and he lit up, taking a deep drag and blowing smoke out slowly.

"Half the time," he said, "women think they know what you're feeling. And the other half, they're trying to figure it out. Every time you do or say something, they've got a little process running in their brains, trying to decide what you meant by it. And what they want, more than anything else, is to know what you're thinking and feeling all the time. But there's a catch. They only want you to be thinking and feeling the things they want you to be thinking and feeling. And there's no guy in the world who thinks and feels the way a woman wants him to except when he's rutting. That's just a fact. So either men lie to women or women end up feeling disappointed."

He drew on the cigarette again and exhaled, a gray haze settling between us.

"No one can control their feelings, and it's a waste of time feeling bad about them. A boy can love his mother and be embarrassed by her at the same time, maybe even wish she was dead sometimes. And if she did die, his grief would be mixed up with all kinds of bad feelings about himself for thinking ill of her. Happens all the time, and not just to boys."

I turned my head so my father wouldn't see my tears.

"Now listen," my father said, "because this is important. Nobody ever knows how someone else really feels. We're all alone in this world. But that doesn't matter. What matters is behavior. Men understand that. You give a guy your word and you keep it, no matter what. Friendship means you can trust another guy to watch your back, regardless of how he feels that day. A couple of good friends will carry you a long way in life. But if you start worrying about how people feel all the time, sooner or later you're going to end up driving around town with an open fifth of vodka in the front seat."

"You think that's why Mom drank?" I asked, unable to conceal my bitterness.

"I don't know why she drank. That's what I've been telling you. No one ever really knows why somebody else does something. The only thing I know is that she did."

I opened the car door. My father caught me roughly by the shirt.

"Close that door," he said. "Maybe you didn't take my point before. When we get out of the car, we're drawing a line. This is all going to be in the past. So unless you want to be pacing around your bedroom at four in the morning twenty years from today, I suggest you get everything off your chest right now."

Shutting the door, I took a deep breath and let fly.

"She said she drank because you didn't love her."

"And?"

"And that you were cheating on her. That you had a girlfriend in Michigan and another one in Pennsylvania. She said you spent a lot more nights away from home than you had to because you didn't want to be with us."

"Cause and effect," he said. "Always difficult to sort out. Was she miserable because I was cheating on her, or was I cheating on her because she was miserable? Maybe Miss Jones can get an answer from the Almighty."

"You were cheating."

"That's true."

"You said behavior mattered," I shouted, anger overwhelming me, "that being a man meant doing the right thing. Were you doing the right thing?"

"Would the right thing have been for me to lie to your mother about how I felt? Or to spend more time fighting with her?"

"Is it right to cheat?" I demanded.

"Men are men," he said, shaking his head. "And a man can't let himself be held hostage to a woman's disappointment." He tapped the butt of his cigarette with his thumb, flicking ashes into the ashtray. "Maybe you wonder why I never moved out."

I glared into my lap, unwilling to answer him.

"I stayed because of you."

My father never declined an invitation to shoot hoops in the driveway when he was home. We launched cameras and mice on model rockets, and won the local soap box derby with a home-built car when I was twelve. He'd driven two hundred miles on a Wednesday afternoon three years back to see my team try for the Pop Warner title. And we'd spent untold hours together with the telescope.

"I hate you," I said, tears spilling from my eyes again.

"I don't doubt you feel some hate," he said. "That's normal.

I thought I hated my dad when I was your age. As I got older, I judged him differently. He did the best he could by his own lights. And regardless of what your mother and I went through, I've tried to do the best I could for you by mine."

He reached out and touched my shoulder. I was sobbing.

"Your mother couldn't bear anything that wasn't perfect," he said, "and nothing is. Everyone's got problems, and there isn't a damn thing you can do about most of them. You're only responsible for yourself. If you need to roll a rock up a hill a hundred times in a row to achieve some objective, then roll it up the hill. But don't go rolling someone else's rock up a hill if they keep letting it roll back down on top of you. You understand?"

I nodded. He gave me his handkerchief and I dried my eyes.

"Will you be home more now?" I asked.

"You're fifteen years old," he said. "You've outgrown the soap box derby. Next year, you'll be driving. You're not going to need me around as much as you might think."

He touched a finger to the clock.

"It's almost three. I've got to call the funeral home. Are we about done here?"

"I don't want to get out of the car," I said, a fresh sob constricting my throat.

"That's how you feel. Maybe I feel the same way. But we're going to get out of the car and we're going to get squared away and we're going to do the right things. I've got your back and you've got mine. It can be that simple between us."

He extended his hand and I took it.

"Friends," he said. "Now open the door."

16

THE CONCIERGE GRIMACES as he reads the address printed on the foil condom packet I've placed on his honed granite counter. He clicks his ceramic ballpoint rapidly eight or ten times, marks the Russian-language map I bought in the gift shop with a dismissive flourish, and then flicks the condom away with a buffed nail. It slides off the counter, falling to the floor.

"Sorry," he says snidely.

I paced for hours last night, collapsing into a fitful sleep only after the sun rose. Dreams of my boyhood were peopled by odd characters—Rommy at the wheel of my father's car, Pongo running a varsity basketball practice, Andrei as the brother I never had, sitting next to me silently at the dinner table while our mother drank and wept. Waking exhausted shortly before noon, I dressed hurriedly, needing to escape the room.

I smile politely at the concierge and put a ten-ruble bill, worth about thirty American cents, on the counter in front of him.

"You've been very helpful," I say.

I wait until he picks the bill up, and then continue staring at him until he says a sullen thank-you. I may feel beat, but I'll be goddamned if I'm going to act it.

The clinic is near the Lubyanka, in the basement of a massive limestone building whose Beaux-Arts façade and tattered vinyl shades suggest government offices. I walk down a flight of stairs, pull open a heavy metal door, and step into a wide stone corridor. Battered pilasters support a vaulted ceiling, capitals adorned with paint-crusted imperial eagles, twin heads facing in opposite directions. It's cold enough to see my breath.

A large man wearing a black knit ski cap and an American army jacket is seated at a folding table, a line of people waiting patiently for his attention. He scrawls something on a piece of paper, hands it to the young woman at the head of the line, and points to his right. The woman shuffles away, a toddler sleeping on her hip. I join the line and wait my turn.

Ten minutes later, he addresses me in Russian.

"I'm sorry," I say. "I only speak English."

"You are here to see who?" he asks with a thick accent.

"Dr. Anderson."

"You have an appointment?"

"No."

"She will not see you. You must phone first." Motioning toward the door dismissively, he turns his body a fraction to signal that he's now addressing the person behind me.

"I think she'll want to see me."

The muscles in his neck bulge as he cocks his head, looking back to me. He has a prizefighter's nose, flattened and skewed, with a jagged vertical scar on the oblique side, where his face was inexpertly sewn together. He must be the receptionist and the bouncer.

"She will not. You must phone first."

"I'm only in Moscow today. A friend of mine asked me to call on her. Andrei Zhilina. I'm here to make a contribution. To give money."

He gazes at me unblinking and then bends forward slightly, scrutinizing me from the floor up. I'm wearing Timberlands, jeans, and a Burberry all-weather coat. Hopefully, my clothing's more presentable than my face.

"You have a business card?"

I dig one of my old cards from Klein out of my wallet and hand it to him. He examines it carefully and then dials a cell phone, conducting a quick, mumbled conversation in Russian. I hear him speak both my name and Andrei's.

"Come," he says, standing up.

He snaps his fingers at a man I hadn't noticed, who's leaning against the wall behind me. The second man walks over and sits at the reception table. The bouncer escorts me down the corridor, past a crowded waiting area, and into a small examination room.

"Lift arms, please."

"Why?"

"You want to see Dr. Anderson, yes?"

"Yes."

"Lift arms."

I raise my arms and he pats me down carefully, fingers lingering on the CD I made at Andrei's apartment and the book I took from the nightstand. His breath smells like yesterday's fish dinner.

"You have a lot of trouble here?" I ask, puzzled by all the security.

"Wait," he says, ignoring my question. "Dr. Anderson will come."

He exits, leaving me alone. The examination room contains a wooden table, a locked metal supply cabinet, and a rolling stool with a white vinyl top. A brightly colored Russian-language poster hangs on one wall, somber Sesame Street–like characters displaying genital rashes. I sit down on the stool and close my eyes, struggling with a sense of unreality. Three months ago, Jenna was alive, and Tigger and I were shooting hoops in my office. How the hell did I ever end up here?

The door opens fifteen minutes later, admitting a tall ash-blond woman wearing a long white coat over a black cable-knit sweater and pale blue corduroys, half glasses perched on the tip of her nose. She extends a hand.

"Emily Anderson."

"Peter Tyler."

Emily has short-cut nails and a firm grip. Her accent is Kansas, or somewhere thereabouts, and I'd guess she was voted queen of her hometown agricultural pageant about twenty years ago.

"You're a friend of Andrei's?" she asks.

"Yes. We started work at the same company, and roomed together at business school, a long time ago."

"Peter," she says, smiling. "You and Andrei played basketball together."

"Yes."

"Andrei told me stories. He's very fond of you and your wife."

I smile back, glad she knows who I am but uncomfortable meeting someone who doesn't know about Jenna.

"I'm having some difficulty catching up with him. One

reason I stopped by was to see if you had a number or an e-mail address where I could reach him."

"I'm afraid not," she says, her smile fading.

"He isn't staying in his apartment. Do you know if he's still in Moscow?"

"I haven't seen him recently."

"He left his job. His sister, Katya, doesn't know where he is." She purses her lips, frowning.

"I don't think I can help you."

"Maybe we could discuss it over coffee," I say, realizing she's about to blow me off. "I'd like to learn more about your work here. And I do want to make a contribution."

She glances at her watch, shaking her head negatively.

"I'm sorry. I've got to get on a plane later, and there's a stack of paperwork I need to finish."

"Please," I say, abandoning any pretense. "I really need to speak with Andrei. Both his sister and I are worried about him. Anything you can tell me about his life here might help me figure out how to get in touch with him."

"Why do you need to talk to him so urgently?"

"It's complicated," I say, knowing how lame I must sound. "If you give me a few minutes, I can explain."

She lifts her chin slightly to study me through her glasses.

"There's a place across the street that makes good coffee. It's smoky, but they have heat. Let me just tell Vladimir where I'm going."

Vladimir is the broken-nosed man, and he's waiting right outside the door. Emily speaks a few quick sentences in Russian to him. He replies at length, handing her a thin sheaf of paper. She looks concerned.

"Problem?" I ask, hoping she isn't going to change her mind about coffee.

"I have to deal with something quickly," she replies, not looking at me. "I'll meet you by the front entrance in a few minutes."

She hurries away, white clogs slapping on the stone floor, her ponytail swaying. A rancid odor makes me turn. Vladimir's crowding me from behind.

"You boxed?" I ask, tapping my nose.

"Boxed?"

"Fought."

"Fought," he repeats. "Yes. Mussulmans, in Afghanistan. There is trouble. Here," he says, tapping me on the chest lightly, "is no trouble. Understand?"

I inhale as shallowly as possible, wondering how a thug like Vladimir ended up working in an AIDS clinic. He cups one hand behind his ear, miming someone trying to hear better.

"Understand," I say.

Emily ignores my attempts at conversation as we cross the road and enter a dimly lit café. The only other customers are two young men in working clothes, smoking cigarettes and drinking from glass tumblers at the bar. The bartender sings out a greeting, but Emily barely acknowledges him, ordering coffee with a single word and leading me to a corner table. She edges her chair away from me as she sits, eyes not meeting mine.

"Vladimir told you something," I say, guessing at the reason for her abrupt change of attitude.

"He looked you up on the Internet. He printed out some news stories about your wife's murder."

"And you read that the police suspect me."

She looks up at me and nods, blue eyes magnified by her glasses.

"The cops are wrong," I say, anxious to convey my sincerity. "I'm here because I'm trying to find out who murdered her. I'm looking for Andrei because I need his help."

The bartender walks over, setting down two white earthenware cups and a lidless metal pot, black coffee grounds visible on a cushion of brown foam. He scoops a spoonful of foam into both cups before filling them with viscous coffee. Emily cradles her cup in both hands, eyes still locked on mine.

"How can Andrei help you?"

"It's a long story."

"A little while ago you said it was complicated. Why don't you just explain as best you can and I'll try to follow along."

Ignoring her sarcasm with an effort, I stitch together an abbreviated version of recent events, covering the package, Andrei's firing and subsequent disappearance, and Pongo's visitor.

"Andrei's in the middle of everything somehow," I conclude. "I've got to find him to understand what's going on."

Emily hasn't moved except to lift her cup to her lips, not giving me any hint as to her reaction.

"I can try to get a message to him," she says quietly.

"You know where he is?" I ask excitedly.

"I know some people to call. One of them might be able to get hold of him."

"Can you give me their names?"

"I can't. Not without speaking to them first."

"Why?"

"I have to be careful," she says firmly. "The politics here

are complicated. My primary concerns are the clinic and my patients."

I slump back despondently, frustrated that she won't divulge anything more substantial. Glancing around the café, I see Vladimir at the bar, a glass tumbler in his hand. He must have followed us, afraid I might beat his employer to death with a coffee cup.

"Why does the clinic need so much security?" I ask, trying a different tack.

"Moscow's a difficult environment. The WHO team I was with had all sorts of problems—theft, extortion, embezzlement, you name it. Vladimir and his boys have been a godsend. We haven't had a single incident of any kind."

"WHO?"

"The World Health Organization. I was working for them when I first came to Moscow, studying drug resistance in tuberculosis patients."

"I came across one of the clinic's advertisements," I say, hauling the condom Dmitri gave me out of my pocket. "I assumed you were focused on AIDS."

"Who would have guessed that a girl from Omaha would become the condom queen of Moscow," she replies, a smile flitting across her face. "We're focused on AIDS and TB. Tuberculosis is the number-one killer of AIDS patients in the Third World. WHO finally woke up to the link a couple of years ago and started advocating that the diseases be treated in tandem."

"TB's curable though, right?" I ask, trying to draw her out.

"Today. Maybe not tomorrow. A full-blown TB course lasts six to eight months, and the pills are expensive. What do you think most people in the Third World do when they start feeling better? Continue taking pills they don't think they need, or stop treatment early? An abbreviated drug course kills off the weak bacilli and lets the strong survive. It's the best-possible way to breed drug resistance. We've seen some superstrains recently that are virtually untreatable, and the mortality's frightening."

She's becoming more animated as she discusses her work, leaning toward me and using her hands to emphasize her words.

"Drug development isn't keeping up?" I ask, pouring more coffee for both of us.

"TB will kill two million people this year, and the pharmaceutical companies are doing zero work on it," she says contemptuously. "There hasn't been a new TB drug in forty years. The big pharmas are all working on hair loss and impotence."

"Why?"

"You're a businessman," she says, making the word sound like an epithet. "You tell me."

"TB's a Third World disease," I say, catching her implication. "There's no money to pay for drugs."

"Correct. Wait a few years, though. When resistant strains begin spreading to Europe and America, the pharmas will fall all over themselves researching treatments. A lethal disease that can be spread by coughing or sneezing? The First World will spend trillions."

"So how was Andrei involved in the clinic?" I ask, steering her back to the subject.

"It was his idea. He dealt with the politics, found the space, raised the money, and recruited me to run it."

It's startling to learn that Andrei was involved in so many things I know nothing about.

"That's a lot for him to have accomplished."

"Andrei knows people," she says matter-of-factly. "Local businessmen, politicians, some senior army officers. One of the political guys is a deputy mayor. That's how Andrei got our space."

"And why do all these important people support your clinic?" I ask, digging for any snippet of information that might shed light on Andrei's activities.

"Because we treat their children," she says, sounding perplexed by my question. She checks her watch. "I've really got to leave soon."

"Just a few more minutes," I protest, still suspecting there's a clue in Andrei's connections. "Do you ever speak with any of these influential people directly?"

"Almost never. I give the occasional tour."

"So who's handling the external stuff now that Andrei's gone?"

"Vladimir. He took over when Andrei left."

I look toward the bar again doubtfully. Vladimir's chatting with the bartender, his army jacket draped over a stool. A tightly stretched knit turtleneck emphasizes the breadth of his shoulders. It doesn't make sense that Andrei assigned a bruiser like Vladimir the task of representing the clinic to Moscow's business and political elite.

"Vladimir doesn't seem like the administrative type."

"He and Andrei had a prior relationship," she replies, shrugging. "They'd worked together before."

"Worked together on what?"

"I don't know," she says evenly. "Andrei kept me out of things, and I made a point of not asking questions. It was the only way I could be involved."

"What do you mean?"

"This is Moscow, Peter. Nothing's ever straightforward. The deal I made with Andrei is that I'd do the medicine and he'd handle everything else."

So Andrei was involved in something shady. And Emily either doesn't know the details or isn't willing to tell me. I gulp the rest of my coffee glumly, my eyes drifting back to Vladimir. Maybe he and Andrei had a falling-out over this other business of theirs. He's the one I really need to speak with, but he doesn't seem like the chatty type. I look back to Emily. Vladimir aside, there's still something fundamental that I'm missing here. I can feel it.

"Of all the things Andrei could have given time and money to, what made him get interested in AIDS and TB?"

A surprised expression flashes across her face, echoing the look Dmitri gave me when I asked if she and Andrei had been having sex.

"He was concerned."

"There are lots of things to be concerned about," I say, a half-formed thought hovering just beyond my reach. Dmitri smirked when he said I was confused, amused by my ignorance. Ignorance of what?

Emily takes her glasses off, closes her eyes, and massages the pink indentations on either side of her nose.

"What are you asking me?" she demands tiredly.

The elusive thought clicks, shock rendering me speechless. Could I really be so clueless as never to have suspected that Andrei might be gay? Emily reads the surprise on my face and sighs. Taking a pen from her pocket, she scrawls something on a napkin.

"My cell phone number. Assuming I reach someone who can help you, how should they get in touch with you?"

I take her pen with numb fingers and scribble my details on a second napkin.

"Can't you tell me what's going on?" I ask, recovering enough to make a final appeal. "Where Andrei is, or why he disappeared?"

"I told you before," she says, getting to her feet. "I don't know anything. The best I can do is talk to some people for you."

She walks away and doesn't look back.

17

I BUTTON MY COAT dazedly as I walk away from the café. The sun's already set, despite the fact that it's just past four, and the wind is rising. Triheaded streetlamps gleam high overhead, reflected light casting a pinkish moiré in swirling crystalline spindrift. I should be glad Emily offered to try to get a message to Andrei, but I'm feeling at sea.

Andrei dated any number of girls over the years, inclining toward willowy European grad students working on esoteric political dissertations. I took to calling them all Giselle, after a flaxen-haired German feminist historian he brought to a dinner party in New York some years ago. She took a book from her backpack midway through the meal, shrugged her blouse down below her bare breasts, and announced loudly that the men seated to either side were welcome to continue conversing with her tits while she caught up on her reading. I'd asked Andrei about settling down once, curious about his serial relationships, and he said he couldn't imagine domesticity with the kind of girls he found interesting enough to date. I'd laughed, surprised that the desire for family didn't tug at him more strongly, but taking his point about the Giselles.

An arctic gust penetrates my coat, evaporating the caffeine sweat slicking my skin and seeming to carry my illusions with it. Andrei lied to me about who he was. Incredulity at not having figured it out gives way to other equally disturbing thoughts. Does Katya know? Did Jenna? And why would Andrei have felt that he couldn't tell me? More than anything else at this moment, I feel alone.

Turning my collar up against the chill, I hustle through Lubyanskaya Square toward GUM, the old Soviet department store. The tourist map I navigated by last night touted it as a shopping destination. I need to buy another warm layer or I'm going to freeze to death.

Foot traffic exits the square by way of a cellarlike pedestrian underpass, the curved concrete walls faced with thickly veined stone panels. An olive-skinned preteen wrapped in layers of ragged shawls approaches as I pass, begging for coins in a multilingual patois. I wave her off, but she darts in front of me and begins clapping loudly in my face, chanting something. I've lived in cities for a long time. Reaching to protect my pockets, I catch hold of a skinny wrist protruding from my coat. I haul the owner's hand out of my pocket and jerk him forward. A fourteen- or fifteen-year-old boy smirks at me, feral features lined with grime. He doesn't even bother to try to pull away, probably figuring the most I'll do is yell at him. Frustration boiling over into rage, I twist the boy's arm so his elbow points skyward, then lean forward, using my weight to force him to one knee. Having chased phantoms for months, the urge to break the arm held solidly in my grip is almost irresistible. He moans, struggling feebly, as the girl shrieks and kicks out at me. An embroidered slipper flies off her foot, striking me in the chest. A hand touches my forearm as I ward her off. Looking sideways, I see an older woman in a fur hat staring at me, shock and disgust written on her face. What the hell am I doing? I let go of his wrist and back unsteadily toward the underpass steps. Bent over a few blocks away, hands on my knees, I try to contain the fury still coursing within me. I can't believe I almost hurt a child. I've got to stay focused and hold it together. The only thing that matters now is my doing right by Jenna.

GUM is about two hundred yards long, a cross between a modern mall and a Victorian greenhouse. Three wide, parallel, glass-roofed halls run the length of the building, each containing three stories of shops. Stone bridges with ornate iron rails connect the upper levels. The crowded stores have familiar Western names. I buy a sweater and knit hat at Benetton, wearing both purchases out.

Removing Andrei's phone from my pocket, I turn it on and call Dmitri. I promised him another hundred bucks to persuade his mother to meet with me. He answers on the first ring.

"Allo."

"Dmitri? It's Peter."

"My mother wants your family name."

Shit. I told him that I worked for Turndale—she's going to look me up in the company directory.

"Brown," I say. There's got to be a Peter Brown in an organization as big as Turndale.

"She will meet now. At your hotel."

Dmitri sounds like he's been drinking.

"No," I reply, figuring my false name will create some kind of problem at the hotel. "At GUM. I'm there now."

Dmitri covers his mouthpiece, a harsh rasp obscuring a whispered exchange.

"There is a café," he says. "Bosco."

"I saw it."

"We will meet at Bosco. Thirty minutes."

A clock in a store window reads 4:30.

"Five o'clock."

"Five o'clock," he confirms, hanging up.

I wander through GUM aimlessly, depressed by the Christmas decorations, gravitating to the third floor because it's less busy. Dmitri's mother is bound to know more about what Andrei was doing, and might even have a contact number for him. At a minimum, she should be able to tell me who else he was close to in Moscow. Leaning against the metal balustrade edging a stone bridge, I shoot my cuff to check the time and realize the punk in the tunnel stole my watch. My rage rises again instantly. Jenna gave me the watch for my thirty-fifth birthday; it was the only keepsake of her I carried. Covering my face with my hands, I see Jenna before me, a strained smile on her face.

"It wasn't the gift I wanted to give you," she said.

I turned the watch over, reading the inscription while I decided how to answer. *Peter from Jenna, my love always.* A waiter cleared our dessert plates and poured the last of the wine. The lights of lower Manhattan shone across the East River outside the restaurant windows, and I could hear the hum of traffic on the Brooklyn Bridge high overhead.

"I love it," I said, bending forward to kiss her. "And I love you. Always. Thanks."

"You're welcome," she replied in a small voice.

I snapped the watch onto my wrist and reached across the table for her hands.

"Did you speak to Dr. Kim today?"

"I did. She agrees that it's time to do more tests."

"Both of us?"

"Only me this time."

Candlelight cast nervous shadows on her face. We'd been trying to get pregnant for a year, and Jenna was just a few months shy of her own thirty-fifth birthday. I knew she was thinking the same thing I was: that it had been a mistake for her to wait so long. I'd suggested we try earlier, but she hadn't wanted to set aside her work and I hadn't pressed, mindful of her early concerns about our incompatibility. Now we were suffering the consequences.

"I'm feeling lucky tonight," I said, pressing my leg to hers beneath the table. "Maybe we should head home and try to cheat Dr. Kim out of a patient."

"That's an excellent idea," Jenna said, a small grin flickering. "But let's sit for another minute. Dr. Kim also suggested we talk. We need to start thinking about what we're going to do if I have a serious problem."

"That's easy." I lifted her hands to kiss them. "I want a family with you. I always have. I know the whole in vitro thing is supposed to be an ordeal, but I promise I'll be there with you every step of the way. As far as I'm concerned, the sooner we get started the better."

"IVF's an option, Peter, but it's not the only possibility."

I felt my smile slip as I recognized the earnest look on her face. I'd thought about adoption, but only as a last resort. No matter how careful we were, we'd never know exactly what problems someone else's child might have.

"Oh?" I said, trying to keep my voice neutral.

"There are a lot of kids out there who need good homes. I've been doing some research, and the literature is heartbreaking.

Special-needs children almost never get adopted. We've been fortunate in so many different ways. It would be great to give something back."

I let go of her hands and unsnapped my new watch. Special needs. Unbelievable. Jenna donated a third of her time to Legal Aid's Juvenile Offender Project, and spent most of our limited time together agonizing over the teenage thieves, drug pushers, and scam artists she represented. I should have anticipated she'd want to go the final step, and make our family one of her vocations as well.

"You've been pro bono full-time for eight years now, Jenna. You give back plenty."

She looked at me searchingly.

"You don't like the idea of adoption?"

The waiter interrupted with the check and I searched my wallet for a credit card, feeling the weight of her gaze. When I was a boy, some childless neighbors of ours named Donnelli tried a stint as foster parents. I remembered looking through the front window with my father when I was about twelve, watching a pair of uniformed cops lead the Donnellis' teenage ward out of the house in handcuffs. I gave the waiter my credit card, thinking the smart response to Jenna would be to equivocate. I was too pissed off to do the smart thing.

"My dad told me a story once," I said.

Her face tightened.

"Your dad told you lots of stories."

"This one was about the cuckoo bird. It lays its egg in other birds' nests. After the baby cuckoo's born, it pushes the natural hatchlings out so it can have all the food. The adult birds don't notice. They go right on feeding the baby cuckoo as if it were their own."

"I'm not seeing the relevance," she said coldly.

"Adult birds want baby birds," I said, hearing my father speak the words as the Donellis wept in their driveway. "A baby cuckoo might seem better than an empty nest. But all the care and feeding in the world isn't going to make a cuckoo a songbird. Nature always trumps nurture in the end."

"The apple falls close to the tree," she said, biting her words off furiously. "Is that your point? If so, we disagree. One reason I married you is that I believe people can overcome ugly influences."

It took a moment for her implication to register.

"Don't think you can judge my father," I said heatedly. "You don't know what it was like between us."

"Arguable. But I'm not interested in his opinions. I'm interested in yours."

We glared at each other. My temples were throbbing and it was all I could do not to remind her that it was her decisions that had put us in this situation. Glancing down, I saw the watch in my hands, the inscription gleaming. I took a deep breath, reminding myself how much I loved her. Snapping the watch back on my wrist, I laid my hands palm up on the table between us.

"My opinions are changeable," I said. "My ambitions aren't. Years ago, I told you my ambition was to make you happy. That's still true."

A tear formed at the corner of her eye and trickled down her face. She put her hands in mine.

"You know how important family is to me, Peter. But we're a couple. Any decision we make has to be right for both of us."

I leaned forward and she kissed me. The waiter approached with my receipt. Jenna dabbed her face with her napkin and stood up.

"I'll be right back," she said.

I signed the receipt and sat alone at our table, gazing at the guttering candle. Dr. Kim had said the odds were in our favor if we started fertility treatment soon and kept at it. And if worst came to worst, and Jenna wasn't able to bear children, I was prepared to do the legwork necessary to try and make sure we ended up with a kid we could both be proud of. The one thing I wouldn't do was to take someone else's flotsam in as my family. I wouldn't be held hostage to Jenna's disappointment. My father had warned me about that.

18

I'M SEARCHING FOR A CLOCK when I notice Dmitri enter the building forty feet below me, three men in dark overcoats and hats accompanying him. He's wearing the same clothes he wore last night, but now he has a bandage on his face. One of the men is holding his arm. I step quickly off the bridge into a shadow, wondering what the hell is going on. Pressing the redial button on Andrei's phone, I see Dmitri and his escorts pause. The man holding Dmitri hands him something.

"Allo," he says, raising the phone to his mouth.

"Which one of those guys is your mother, Dmitri?"

Dmitri presses the mouthpiece to his coat and speaks to the man holding him. All three of his companions immediately begin scanning the crowd. I step back farther into the shadows, watching. The man holding Dmitri says something to him, shaking his arm for emphasis.

"They are *menti*," Dmitri says, talking into the phone again. "Police. You will be meeting them now or have big trouble."

The little prick. Punching the disconnect button, I walk

toward the nearest stairwell, forcing myself not to run. I don't know why a bunch of Russian cops are interested in talking to me, but the bandage on Dmitri's face persuades me that these aren't guys I want to meet. Maybe they aren't even really cops. Either way, I have to get out of here right now. Tugging my hat down over my ears, I fall into step next to a bag-laden woman on the ground floor and ask directions to the Metro. She's Italian, her English uncertain, and we exit GUM together, conversing as we cross Red Square. My heart hammers as I listen for footsteps or shouting behind me. I turn left randomly as we pass the Historical Museum, ignoring my companion's admonition that I'm going the wrong way.

The good news is that Dmitri doesn't know my real name. The bad news occurs to me a split second later: He knows I was going to see Emily, who does know my name. Pulling Andrei's cell phone from my pocket, I start to dial Emily's number and then stop. I used the phone to call Dmitri; if the guys with him are cops, they might be able to track the cellular signal. Reluctantly dumping the phone in a nearby garbage can, I look around for a pay phone. There's an enormous stained-glass dome to my left, the apex crowned by a spotlit statue of Saint George slaying the dragon. The dome was on the cover of the hotel magazine; it's the cupola of an underground shopping mall. Descending a flight of stairs, I locate a newsstand that can sell me a phone card, then waste five minutes trying to figure out which digits of Emily's number to dial or omit.

"Dr. Anderson," she says when she answers.

"It's Peter," I say, relieved to reach her. "Can you talk?"

"I don't have anything else to tell you right now."

"Just listen for a second," I say rapidly. "Dmitri and I were supposed to meet. He brought along a bunch of guys. They might have been cops, and they tried to grab me. Dmitri doesn't know my last name, but he knows I was going to see you. I don't want these guys to find out who I am before I've figured out what they want."

"Are you okay right now?" she asks calmly.

"As far as I know," I reply, registering her lack of surprise.

"Go to the U.S. Embassy. If the police want to interview you, the embassy will arrange it. There's nothing for you to be concerned about. You don't know anything."

"And what about you?"

"I'm on my way to the airport. Anyway, it doesn't matter. They can use the local cops to hassle you, but the clinic's protected. They can't touch me."

" 'They'?"

Ten seconds tick by. She lied to me. She knows exactly who these guys are and why they're trying to grab me. I was a fool to fall for her down-home innocent act.

"I can't talk about it, Peter," she says quietly.

"You told me you didn't know anything," I reply coldly. "The 'they' you mentioned might be the same people who murdered my wife. I'd appreciate it if you did talk about it."

"I made a call for you. I might have something to tell you after I land."

I struggle silently against my temper, realizing I'm not going to get anywhere by shouting at her on the phone. The Bakelite receiver I'm holding feels like it weighs fifty pounds. I wipe sweat from it onto my coat and put it back to my ear.

"Where are you going?"

"New York. I should be able to call you in about twelve hours."

I glance at my wrist automatically, then curse the little

fuck who took my watch. "What about Vladimir?" I ask. "What will he tell the cops?"

"Nothing. No one at the clinic will talk to the police without my okay. You should go to the embassy right now. You'll be safe there."

The advice Tilling received from the old cop pops into my head. Never trust anyone who's already lied to you once.

"Fine," I say. "I'll go to the embassy. Will I be able to call you in New York?"

"Yes. My cell phone works there."

"We'll talk soon."

I hang up. To hell with the embassy. I haven't got any friends in Moscow, and I'm not about to throw myself on the mercy of some junior diplomat. I tap my pockets, reassuring myself that I've got my passport. My hand brushes against the data CD I made at Andrei's apartment and I swear silently. I can't risk losing Andrei's files.

I trot down a central circular staircase, checking out the shops. There's an Internet café on the lowest floor. A long-haired boy with a plastic spider hanging from his earlobe sets me up at a workstation in a Lucite-winged cubicle, cheerfully changing the operating language to English in exchange for a hundred-ruble tip.

Opening a browser window, I create a new e-mail account on Yahoo, insert the CD into the workstation's optical drive, and mail the files to myself at the new address. After confirming the files are in my in-box, I remove the CD, scratch the entire readable surface with a coin, and then bend it in half. The CD snaps with a bang, projecting a flurry of silver foil skyward. Neighboring customers look over curiously. I sweep most of the foil off the floor and dump it in a trash can as I leave.

The Moskova Hotel is just opposite the mall. Finding a pay phone in the lobby, I call Dmitri. It's been about forty minutes since I saw him at GUM.

"Allo."

"Can you talk?"

"Fuck your mother," he says, sounding exhausted.

"Is that a yes or a no?"

"You bringed the fucking *menti* to Andrei's flat."

"You didn't call them?"

"Fuck no, you stupid fuckhead fuck. You used Andrei's phone. They were listening."

Shit. What did I say to Katya? That I was in Andrei's apartment, and that I thought Andrei's disappearance might be linked to Jenna's murder.

"Did you hear them say anything else?"

"Fuck off, you." He hangs up. It's time for me to leave Moscow.

The bellman out front flags a taxi for me. The cabbie doesn't speak any English, but he recognizes the phrase "Domodedovo Airport." If I hustle, I might be able to catch Emily's flight.

19

THE ONLY FLIGHT TO NEW YORK without an overnight layover was British Airways connecting through London. I walk the length of the plane twice after we've taken off. Emily isn't on board. She might have flown out of Sheremetyevo, the other airport. I settle into my seat, disappointed and exhausted, and ring the call button for an attendant.

An aproned steward with a clipped mustache brings me two Laphroaig miniatures, a glass smelling of his cologne, and a dish of cashews. I rinse the glass in the lavatory sink, shoot the minis, and press the call button again, ordering two more. The alcohol hits me instantly, my head buzzing and stomach lurching. I can't remember when I last ate, and I spent the dregs of my adrenaline in the passport-control line, attempting to look bored while a pimply teenage officer tapped my details into his computer. I've started trembling so badly that I have to brace my forearms against the tray table to pour the third and fourth minis without spilling them. Downing the liquor, I settle back in my seat and try to think.

Even setting aside the possibility that Emily will put me in touch with Andrei, I've got three solid leads. First, she knows who was chasing me and, once we're in New York, I can probably get Tilling to persuade her to be more forthcoming. Second, there's the man with the Felix the Cat tattoo. Tilling's likely identified him by now. And third, I may well get some answers from Andrei's files after I've had them decrypted. My one regret is not having at least attempted to question Vladimir. If Andrei really did do something wrong, my guess is that Vladimir's involved right up to his thick neck.

I should be energized by the prospect of so much to follow up on, but I feel just as desperate and confused as I did when I had my father's gun in my mouth. The more I learn, the more I'm forced to confront questions I don't want to approach. Why would Andrei have lied to me? What secrets has he been keeping? And is it really possible that he's somehow responsible for Jenna's murder? I ring the call button and order another couple of drinks. I always thought all a guy needed to get through life was a few good friends. Jenna's dead, Katya's written me off, and I don't know what to think about Andrei. Tigger's all I have left.

Glancing sideways, I see a small brown hand snatch a cashew from my bowl. The seat next to me is occupied by a dark Asian girl flying as an unaccompanied minor, a ward of the cabin staff, all of whom seem to be ignoring her. She looks to be about eight, and has a plastic packet of paperwork hanging from a string around her neck. Realizing I've busted her, she tucks her chin to her chest, staring fixedly at her bright yellow sneakers. I nudge the bowl toward her and she squeezes her eyes shut, making herself invisible. I turn my head to look out the window, watching her reflection in the filmy plastic panel. A minute passes. Fingers darting, she steals another nut.

The steward brings me a single mini, telling me apologetically that they've run out of Laphroaig. More likely he's cutting me off. I ask for a refill of the cashews, gulp the scotch, and glance at my wrist yet again, too slow to catch myself. I wonder what Jenna would have said about the Gypsy boy who stole her gift to me. That he was only a thief because no one like us ever took him in and cosseted him? That with a little loving attention he could have become the child we were never able to have—captain of the swim team, president of the Environmental Awareness club, and an Ivy League legacy?

Leaning my head against the window, I close my eyes. The infertility treatments were tough on my relationship with Jenna, a multiyear cycle of false hopes and cruel disappointments. She threw herself into work after each failure, spending progressively less time at home. The technology kept getting better, though, and we only needed to be lucky once. This past spring, we made it as far as the fourth month. I was in Singapore when she miscarried, blood soaking her dress during a court appearance. It took me a full day to get home to her. I held Jenna while she cried, and swore not to leave the country after her next round of implantations.

True to pattern, Jenna kept so busy preparing for a major lawsuit during the next few months that I barely saw her. I was almost relieved when she suggested counseling one night. I could live without children, but not without her. The candidates she proposed were Father Winowski or the shrink she'd begun seeing recently, an Indian woman named Subrahmanyan. I opted for the shrink as the lesser of two evils, the notion of discussing my marriage with a religious celibate too ludicrous to contemplate. All the same, when the time for our first appointment rolled around, my resentment at airing our shortcomings to a third party was barely containable.

Subrahmanyan's office was two small rooms on the ground floor of an Upper West Side apartment building, with a view onto a barren interior courtyard. A short, energetic woman, she had a prominent mole on her chin.

"This is Dr. S., Peter," Jenna said, introducing us.

"Peter," she said liltingly. "It is very nice to meet you."

"Likewise," I replied, scanning the diplomas on her office wall. "Tell me, are you a medical doctor, or do you have a Ph.D.?"

"Please don't," Jenna said quietly.

"No, no, it is an appropriate question," Subrahmanyan said. "I am not a medical doctor or a Ph.D. My highest degree is a master's in counseling psychology from NYU. Patients find my names difficult to pronounce, so I let them decide how to address me. Jenna chose to call me Dr. S. My given name is Tripurasundari. Please address me as you wish."

I smiled politely and we began. Subrahmanyan asked me about myself and listened actively as I gave her a capsule biography. Her sympathetic murmurs were like nails on a blackboard, but I kept myself in check for Jenna's sake. Jenna fidgeted with the hem of her dress as I spoke, fingers bunching and crushing the material. When I eventually ground to a halt, Subrahmanyan thanked me for sharing.

"Jenna," she said. "You have some things to tell Peter, don't you?"

"I'm done with the IVF," Jenna said tremulously. "I want to adopt, and I need to know whether you're going to be there for me."

I flicked some lint from my suit pants and nodded, reeling internally. This wasn't about us at all. This was about Jenna wanting to bring her work home.

"So this is really a workout," I said.

"'A workout'?" Subrahmanyan repeated doubtfully.

"It's a bankruptcy term. When a big company borrows money from a bank, it has to commit to meet certain financial targets. And if it violates those covenants, the bank calls in the poor son of a bitch who runs the company and presents him with an ultimatum. They tell him exactly how he's going to run his business from that time forward, and if he doesn't like it, they tell him to fuck off. Tell me," I said, looking at Jenna. "Which of our covenants have I violated?"

"None," Jenna said, choking on the word as her tears fell. "But every time I bring up adoption, you come up with some new clinic or procedure and make me feel like I'd be letting you down if I didn't try it. I can't keep doing it. I'm not strong enough."

"Peter," said Subrahmanyan, interrupting as she offered Jenna a box of tissues. "This is not a time for argument. Jenna asked you here because she feels that she can't talk to you about this terribly important subject. Her feelings are not right or wrong, and they are not an accusation. They are simply her experience of your relationship. Now we need to know how you are feeling."

"That's easy, Dr. S.," I said, getting to my feet. "I feel like leaving."

Jenna caught up with me out front a few minutes later. I didn't trust myself to speak. The car I'd called wasn't due for twenty minutes yet, so we sheltered silently beneath the building's narrow awning as a pounding summer rain splashed off the sidewalk and onto our legs. Jenna's dress was getting wet. I offered her my raincoat and she threw it into the street.

"You gave me that coat for Christmas," I said. "I hope it wasn't too expensive."

"I never thought I'd be this disappointed by you, Peter."

"Maybe not this disappointed," I said, turning toward her. Mist shone in her hair, and her cheeks were damp. "But you've been a little disappointed for a long time, haven't you? I was never the guy you wanted to marry."

"That's not true."

"It is," I said furiously. "You only fell in love with me because you thought I had this sad, miserable little kid inside me. You don't like the fact that I'm strong enough to deal with my own problems."

"It's hard never to feel needed," she said.

Her words took me aback. My mother had said almost the same thing once when I'd pleaded with her to stop drinking. I hadn't known what she meant, and she never explained.

"I'm sorry, then," I said tentatively. "I can't be something I'm not."

"I knew who you were when I married you," she said, touching my lapel. "And I knew there were things about you that were going to be difficult for me. You have to understand. I don't expect you to be that sad little boy, Peter, but I need to know that you could love some sad little boy with me. It can't just be about us."

"It can," I said, desperate to get through to her. "That's what it was like for my father and me."

She drew back, her lips compressing scornfully.

"Bullshit. It was only ever about him. When are you going to wake up to the fact that your father was a selfish jerk and free yourself of his prejudices?"

I watched my arms lift, left hand catching hold of the front of her dress and right hand bunching into a fist. I hauled her forward onto her toes, her face inches from mine.

She looked frightened for a moment before her expression hardened into contempt.

"Use your words, Peter," she said, taunting me with a nursery phrase.

"My words," I said, incandescent with rage. "It's not my fault we're in this situation. I'm not the one who decided to wait, and I'm not the one with a fertility problem. And yet you blame me because I won't let you compound your mistake. So once and for all, here are my views on adoption: I don't want a three-year-old with fetal alcohol syndrome. I don't want a baby who was shaken, or born addicted to crack, or has HIV. I don't want a kid some Chinese farmworker threw away like a bad melon, or to go to sensitivity training so I can learn how difficult it is for our black child to grow up in a privileged white family. I don't want a kid whose parents were fundamentalist Christian hypocrites, or a fifteen-year-old checkout girl at the local supermarket and her bald forty-eight-year-old manager. I don't want a kid who's a fucking loser. Are those enough words? Do you understand me now?"

"Perfectly," she said, tears starting down her face again. "I understand you perfectly now."

I open my eyes again some time later, mouth dry as dust and a headache banging behind my temples. The child next to me is sleeping, goose bumps covering her bare arms. My cashew bowl's empty. Ringing for the steward, I request a bottle of water and a blanket. I gulp some water, unfold the blanket, and spread it gently over the sleeping child, careful not to wake her. I start to look for my watch and catch myself just in time. It isn't easy to unlearn behavior at my age, but it can be done.

20

THE IMMIGRATION OFFICER AT KENNEDY apologizes because my passport won't scan correctly, frowns at her screen, and begins typing with one finger. I rub the wrist where I used to wear my watch, annoyed by the delay. My U.S. cell phone and computer are in the luggage I left behind, so I'll either have to hustle up some change and find a working pay phone in the terminal or wait until I get to the Harvard Club to call Emily. A digital clock on the wall displays military time and the day of the week: 23:15, Saturday. If there are cabs waiting and I don't hit any late-night traffic, I should be in my room before midnight. Despite my impatience, it's probably better to wait. I shift restlessly from foot to foot, craving an ice-cold Coke and a handful of ibuprofen. I had a few more Laphroaigs after changing planes at Heathrow, and my head feels as if I've got a spiked metal ball rolling around in it. The officer is still tapping away at her computer, squinting at my passport myopically. It would be nice if the government hired people who knew how to type.

"Peter Tyler?"

Two white-shirted policemen are standing behind me,

gold badges painfully bright and holstered guns prominent. The one to my left has a hand resting casually on the butt of a black metal baton hanging from his belt.

"Yes?" I say apprehensively.

"Would you step that way please, sir?" the cop to my right says, pointing to a beige door fifteen yards away. He's older, with a gray fringe around a bald pate and a beer gut hanging over his belt.

"Why?" I ask, wondering if Tilling's arranged this reception for me, or if it has something to do with Moscow. Either way, this isn't good.

"We have some questions for you," he says, taking my passport from the woman who'd been examining it. He gives it a cursory glance before slipping it into his pocket.

"About what?"

"Please don't make this difficult, sir."

People in other lines stare curiously as the police lead me away, my stomach knotted with anxiety. The beige door opens to a wide cement-floored corridor with pale green walls, the plasterboard immediately opposite dented at head height, a streak of dried blood visible.

"Face the wall, arms extended, and lean forward," the older cop says.

"Are you arresting me?"

"We're detaining you."

"You can't detain me without arresting me, and you can't arrest me without telling me why. So either tell me why I'm under arrest or let me go."

"Are you going to make us do this the hard way?" he asks in a bored voice.

The younger cop steps forward smartly, the billy club in his hand.

"No," I say quickly, turning to the wall and leaning forward spread-eagled. "I'll cooperate. But I want to call my lawyer."

"We'll pass the message along, sir," the older cop says. He frisks and handcuffs me, the pressure on my wrists immediately uncomfortable. I wish to Christ I weren't so hungover. I can't help feeling scared.

The two police catch hold of my biceps and steer me to an elevator. We descend, walk through more pale green corridors, and enter a white-tiled room. The room's empty save for a folding table with a box of surgical gloves, a flashlight, and a couple of wire baskets sitting on top of it.

"I'm going to uncuff you now," the older cop says. "You're going to empty your pockets onto the table and take all your clothing off. You understand?"

"When will I be able to call—"

He twists the cuffs hard, so they bite into my wrists, and jerks up, forcing me to stagger toward the table with my head dropped to belt level.

"And keep your fucking yap shut please, sir," he says. "Nobody wants to listen to your bullshit."

I wake in a cell hours later. It's got to be Sunday morning by now. My body's drenched with sweat and my head hurts even more than it did earlier. After the police shined their flashlight up my ass and made me lift my balls, they gave me a blue paper jumpsuit and escorted me to a windowless six-by-eight cell smelling of ammonia, the ballast in the overhead light humming loudly. I spent a few hours pacing, claustrophobia sucking at me like an undertow. Not knowing why I've been detained makes everything more oppressive. I tried telling myself it was just bad luck to get picked up on a Saturday night, when every cop over the rank of thug is home watching NASCAR highlights on cable, and that I'll be able to talk to someone responsible in the morning, find out what's going on and get my lawyer working on my release. It didn't help.

I swing my legs off the metal cot bolted to the floor and try not to groan as the pain in my head pulses harder. The ammonia smell is stronger near the sink. Cupping my hands, I rinse my face and slurp a mouthful of tepid water. A mounting sense of fear makes it difficult for me to swallow. I've got to get out of here. I press the call button next to the door, wait twenty minutes for a guard, and demand a phone call again when one finally shows up. He drops the flap over the judas hole and walks away without responding.

I sit back down on the cot and hunch forward, drawing deep breaths. If the Westchester DA has her way, this could be my future, held helpless in a cage and overseen by sullen keepers. A former scoutmaster of mine talked to our Webelo den before our first big overnight camping trip. He told us that when he was a boy, he'd played in an abandoned field forbidden to him and had fallen down a well. An entire night passed as he floated in the icy water, clinging to a protruding stone overhead with a death grip. He kept his panic at bay by imagining every detail of the rescue party he knew his father would have mustered. He knew the names of the men who would be looking for him, and the names of their dogs, and—most reassuringly—he knew that they were the kind of men who wouldn't give up. If any of us ever got lost in the woods, he said, or fell down a well, or had any kind of trouble we thought we couldn't get out of, the important thing was that we stay put and not panic, because men like him and our dads would always come looking for us.

There's no one looking for me now, and I can feel my strength ebbing away as surely as if I were floating in that cold, cold water. Tears of self-pity sting my eyes. The worst thing is that I thought I'd grown up to be that kind of man, the kind who doesn't ever give up when someone he loves needs help. I let Jenna down when she needed me, and I'm letting her down again now. Hauling myself to my feet, I resume pacing. I never thought I'd be glad my father was gone, but I couldn't bear to have him see me like this.

"Tyler," a voice says through the door. "We're going to open up. Step out of your cell, face the wall, and put your hands on your head."

Two guards I haven't seen before handcuff me and lead me through more corridors to a room where three men in business suits sit behind a metal table. A low stool is bolted to the floor, and a large mirror's set into the wall opposite. There's a second door in the wall to my right. The guards manacle my ankle to one leg of the stool, uncuff my wrists, and leave. I examine myself carefully in the mirror. I look pale and sweaty, but there's no sign of my tears.

"I want to call my lawyer," I say.

The guy in the middle leans forward, fingers interlaced. His florid, chubby face reminds me of a broker I knew who died of a heart attack on the seventeenth green at Van Cortland Park.

"We can handle this one of two ways, Mr. Tyler," he says. "If you cooperate with us, we'll keep you on the books. That means due process. You'll see your lawyer and get a chance to explain things in front of a judge, if things go that far. If you don't cooperate, we'll make you a special-category detainee. Your legal status will become problematic. Even if you're innocent, it could take months to sort things out."

"Innocent of what?" I demand disbelievingly.

"That remains to be seen."

"You're full of shit."

"Happily not, Mr. Tyler. We have quite a bit of latitude these days when it comes to dealing with people like you."

"'People like me'? What the hell are you talking about?"

"What the hell are we talking about?" the man to his right says. He's clearly the bad cop. He's got the mean, beady-eyed expression of a guy who had trouble learning to read as a kid, and anabolic acne on his cheeks. "We're talking about Gitmo. We're talking about an all-expenses-paid holiday courtesy of the U.S. Marines. That's what we're talking about."

"Get fucked," I say, certain they're just trying to scare me. "I'm an American citizen. Save your act for somebody who doesn't know any better. You take me to a phone right now and let me call my lawyer, or you cut me loose. Otherwise, I'm going to make a huge amount of trouble for you guys when I get out of here."

The chubby cop smiles pleasantly.

"I haven't introduced us," he says. "I'm Inspector Davis and my colleague here is Inspector De Nunzio." He tips his head toward the bad cop. "We're with the Department of Homeland Security, Strategic Investigations Branch. I assume you've heard of the Patriot Act?"

I nod tentatively, apprehension beginning to wash over my anger.

"Well, we're the patriots," he says smugly. He points to the third man. "Mr. Lyman is a consultant."

"I'm an American citizen," I repeat, my voice sounding weaker. "You can't fuck with me."

"You'd be surprised what we can do," Davis says. "Mr. Lyman?"

Lyman takes a miniature tape recorder from his pocket and puts it on the table. His suit's a little too shiny, his wire-rimmed glasses more oval than normal, and he's got a styled military haircut with mousse in it. He looks European.

"You're an American citizen with serious legal problems," Davis says. "Those problems could get worse."

Lyman touches the play button. I hear a woman crying, and then recognize Andrei's voice as he speaks Jenna's name, comforting her.

> "Jenna. Come on. Don't cry, sweetheart. Tell me what it is."
> "We had a fight. Peter grabbed me. For a second, I thought he was going to hit me."
> "Jesus."
> "I'm so scared, Andrei. I think it might be over."

Lyman pushes the off button as Jenna's voice trails into sobs. I feel sick with self-loathing. It's hard enough to live with myself without being forced to confront my failings in front of hostile strangers.

"We haven't shared this tape with the police yet," Davis says. "Or any of the other tapes in our possession. Your wife's murder isn't of interest to us. What we eventually decide to release, and to whom, depends largely on your cooperation right now."

My brain's slowly beginning to work again. This is about

Andrei. I feel disoriented, unable to imagine what he might have done that's attracted the attention of the Department of Homeland Security.

"I don't know anything," I say, struggling to sound composed.

"Enough of this shit," De Nunzio announces. "Listen, Tyler, I got a couple of Cuban hookers in the cell next door, and I know I'd have more fun with them. You don't want to answer questions for us now, we can give you a week to think about it, let you get used to eating instant oatmeal that the cook pissed in. So you tell me, we gonna talk now, or later?"

"What do you want me to tell you?"

Two hours later, we're going through my trip to Moscow for the third time, Davis asking all the questions. Lyman's taking notes, and De Nunzio's hanging his head, picking his zits, and looking bored. The repetition's given me a chance to pull myself together. I've been forthcoming on all fronts save that I haven't mentioned Pongo, the files I took from Andrei's computer, or Emily's implied admission that she knew who was after me in Moscow. Davis said he didn't care about Jenna's murder. I'm not going to give up any of my leads to him willingly.

"So that's everything, Mr. Tyler? Nothing you've forgotten to tell us about?" Davis asks.

"Not that I recall."

De Nunzio sits straighter in his chair as Lyman looks up, pen tapping against his teeth. I brace myself, sensing Davis is finally going to get to the point.

"Perhaps we can refresh your recollection," he says.

"Perhaps."

"Do you know what a log file is, Mr. Tyler?"

"Yes," I say with a sinking feeling.

"Please tell me," Davis says. "I'm not very good with computers."

"A log file records activity on a computer."

"Would a log file record the fact that someone transferred information from a computer to a CD?"

"It's possible."

"And would a log file record the fact that someone erased information from that computer?"

"Also possible."

"And would a log file record when those things happened?"

"It might."

"Would you like to tell us about it, Mr. Tyler?"

I stare at myself in the mirror, trying to figure out how Davis knew about the file. The Russian cops who picked up Dmitri could have found Andrei's computer. Even if they had the technological savvy to go poking around in log files, it's difficult to believe they'd be feeding information to the U.S. government in real time. My eyes slide to Lyman. Davis said he was a consultant, which could mean anything, and he's the one who has the recording of Andrei and Jenna.

"We're waiting, Mr. Tyler," Davis says, a bullying sneer on his fat face.

My mouth opens. I have absolutely no idea what I'm going to say.

"I found an encrypted file on Andrei's computer."

All three men lean toward me.

"And?"

"The password was the same as his alarm code," I say, recalling Dmitri's stratagem. "It was all porn, digital pictures of men doing stuff to each other that would make you want to puke."

"There were many files on that computer," Lyman says harshly, speaking for the first time. "Why copy that one? And why erase it from the hard drive?"

He's got an accent—Germanic, with a nasal intonation. Dutch perhaps, or Swiss. He knows what was on Andrei's computer. Maybe he was in Moscow yesterday, too.

"I was in a hurry," I say. "There were hundreds of folders in the file. I figured I'd go through them more carefully when I had a chance, see if there was anything that might help me figure out how to get in touch with Andrei. I erased it because Andrei was in some of the pictures." I shrug, trying to look embarrassed on Andrei's behalf. "I didn't think he'd want pictures of himself doing stuff like that on a computer serving information to the Web, even if they were encrypted."

"And where's the CD you copied the file to?" Davis demands silkily.

"I broke it in half and dumped it in a garbage can outside Manezh Square mall. The cops were chasing me. I didn't want to get picked up in Russia with a bunch of gay porn in my pocket. I have no idea what kind of laws they've got over there."

There's a long silence. De Nunzio's shaking his head back and forth, looking disgusted. Davis is staring at Lyman. Lyman is staring at me. I sit forward, making an effort to look earnest.

"I could draw you a map," I say. "Show you exactly where the garbage can was. Would that help?"

21

DAVIS ANNOUNCED A BREAK after another half hour of repetitive questions. I asked for a cup of coffee politely as he and the others exited through the side door, and a guard brought me a helping of lukewarm chemical sludge in a waxed-paper cup. I'm hoping the courtesy means they bought my story. My hand shakes as I sip, and I can see fresh crescents of sweat staining the jumpsuit beneath my arms in the mirror. I want to talk to Emily. Lyman might represent the "they" she mentioned, the people she said could use the Russian police to question me. If so, he's got both the Russians and the Americans working for him. Which means what? That he's Interpol or some other kind of international cop? Everything I learn only confuses me more. What's Andrei involved in?

I rest my elbows on my knees, staring down at the scuffed linoleum floor and wishing Andrei had confided in me. The last time I saw him was in Rome, shortly after Jenna and I had the scene in the street outside Subrahmanyan's office. Some Italian clients had called on short notice and asked me to make a breakfast presentation to their investment committee.

Jenna and I weren't speaking, so I left a note on her vanity and headed for the airport. I started drinking as soon as the plane took off. When the phone rang in my hotel room the next morning, I felt like death.

"Hello?" I croaked.

"It's six a.m.," a voice said. "The best hour of the day for a run."

"Andrei?"

"I'm in the lobby," he said. "Get down here now. We need to get going before the smog builds up."

I sat up too abruptly, the room swimming.

"Keisha sent you my itinerary," I said, trying to get my brain working.

"As usual."

Keisha had standing instructions to copy my itinerary to Andrei whenever I traveled to Europe. He was on the road as much as I was, and we'd managed to connect in a number of different cities.

"I didn't bring any running shoes."

"I shopped for you at Heathrow. You're an American eleven, right?"

"How the hell do you know that?"

"Omniscience."

"I'm not up to repartee this morning," I said testily. "I'm kind of hungover."

"All the more reason for a run. Come on. It's a beautiful day."

We ran out the front of the hotel and into the Borghese Gardens. The sun was still low and the gardens were cool and lovely in the half-light. Ten minutes later, I was puking my guts out into an ornamental iron garbage can. Andrei jogged in place a few steps away, waiting for me to finish.

"I need water," I said.

"I saw a drinking fountain back by the Villa Giulia," he said, taking off down the gravel path at full speed. I followed as best I could, too parched and winded to curse him.

We did laps around the garden for another forty minutes, dog walkers appearing as the sun climbed higher and the air warmed. I burned through the alcohol and started feeling pretty good. Andrei was the one lagging by the time we finished, and I gave him shit while he sucked wind, his hands on his knees.

"I've been a little under the weather recently," he said.

"A likely story. You're just old and tired."

We bought a dozen dwarf oranges in a mesh bag from a cart near the top of the Spanish Steps and sat on the edge of the central fountain in the Piazza di Spagna, popping peeled orange quarters and talking about the markets. Sweat puddled beneath us as we cooled down.

"When'd you get in?" I asked.

"Same as you," he said. "Late last night."

"You free for dinner?"

"Sorry. I've got to fly down to Naples for a lunch meeting and then catch a plane to Luxembourg."

"That doesn't give you a lot of time on the ground here."

"Just long enough for a run with you and some of this delicious but annoyingly small fruit."

I suddenly realized how Andrei'd known my shoe size.

"Jenna called you."

He glanced up from his partially peeled orange.

"She sounded pretty upset."

I couldn't decide whether to be angry or not. I'd told Andrei about our problems myself, but not how bad things had gotten recently.

"Did she ask you to talk to me?"

"No."

"You here to tell me I'm an asshole?"

"Wouldn't dream of it."

"Then what?"

The sun cleared the roof of a building and caught the side of Andrei's face. He looked tired.

"I gathered you were going through a rough patch, so I decided to fly down and say hello."

"You have some words of wisdom for me?" I said acerbically. "A quote from Schopenhauer or Nietzsche maybe?"

"None that come to mind."

"An opinion of your own, then?"

"Sure," he said. "I think you're an asshole."

I laughed and felt my irritation dissipate.

"Seriously?" I asked uncomfortably.

"Jenna's unhappy and you're drinking too much. My only opinion is that whatever you and she are doing isn't working."

"I don't know how to talk to her," I admitted. "She has her heart set on adopting some kid with problems."

"And you don't want to?"

"It's hard to explain," I said, wiping my face with my shirt. "My dad and I used to do a lot of things together when I was a kid. I always kind of figured I'd do the same things with my child."

"And you're afraid you won't know how to relate to a kid who can't do those things with you?"

"Pretty much," I said, dissembling slightly. The real truth was that I was afraid I couldn't love a kid who didn't meet my expectations.

Andrei finished the last orange and began stuffing the peels into the mesh bag.

"Let me ask you something," he said. "Suppose Jenna got pregnant and the two of you had a healthy child. Would that make everything better between you?"

I gave his question some thought, watching a young couple ride past on a shiny red Vespa. The man was wearing a sharply tailored business suit and had a cigarette hanging from his mouth; the woman's hair blew loose as she clutched his waist.

"I'm not sure," I said. "What's your point?"

"Only that you need to figure out what your real issues with Jenna are. I love you like a brother, Peter, but you've got such a rigid worldview that you don't always see things—or people—the way they really are."

A church bell rang while I was working on an answer. I checked my watch.

"I wish I'd known you were coming," I said. "I've got a meeting that I can't cancel."

"I could shuffle a few things around and meet you in London tomorrow night," Andrei said. "I'd be happy to stand you a nice curry."

"Another time," I said. "I'm booked solid tomorrow, and then I've got to be back in New York for a committee meeting."

"Another time, then," he said, getting to his feet.

I squinted into the sun, looking up at him.

"I'm glad you came by," I said. "I really am. I needed the exercise. But you don't have to worry about me."

"I do, though," he said. "I worry about you and Jenna both."

22

THE CHEMICAL SLUDGE IN MY CUP is ice-cold when the side door opens again, a pale layer of scum congealing on top. Davis and Lyman file back in, resuming their previous seats. De Nunzio's absence has to be a positive development.

"Mr. Tyler," Davis says, a solemn expression on his face. "I'm going to tell you some things that have the United States government very concerned. I think these things will concern you as well. I'd like you to understand why your cooperation is so important to us."

"Okay," I say, hoping I'm about to get some answers. I watch Lyman covertly as Davis speaks. He's paging through his notebook.

"Several months ago, a Swiss pharmaceutical firm reported the theft of a superstrain of tuberculosis they'd isolated for vaccine-research purposes. We believe this strain has the potential to be utilized as a biological weapon, with devastating consequences. We further believe Mr. Zhilina may be able to help us locate the people responsible for this theft."

I stare at Davis incredulously, wondering if he seriously thinks I'm going to fall for this line of shit. Andrei's a financial guy. I've come around to the idea that he might have crossed a few lines, but this is way beyond the bounds of any impropriety I can imagine him involved with.

"That's ridiculous. You've got a wire crossed somewhere in your organization. You're confused because Andrei's involved with a tuberculosis clinic in Moscow."

"Do you know what a genetic marker is, Mr. Tyler?" Davis asks.

"Roughly."

"Enlighten me, please."

"A bit of a gene or chromosome that's easily identifiable."

"The strain stolen from the Swiss had several distinctive genetic markers. The clinic Mr. Zhilina's affiliated with reported a number of TB deaths in recent months. Autopsies established that three of those individuals died from the stolen Swiss strain."

"What are you saying?" I ask, completely bewildered. "That the clinic is killing people on purpose?"

"No. We think the clinic's being used by someone with an ulterior motive."

" 'An ulterior motive'?" I fight back a nervous laugh. Davis sounds like one of the Hardy Boys.

"Weapons, Mr. Tyler, need to be tested in the field against competent adversaries. The best place to test a biological weapon would be in a clinic dedicated to defeating it."

"You think that Andrei's involved with terrorists?" I ask disbelievingly.

"No, Mr. Tyler. We don't think it; we know it. And if you know anything about Mr. Zhilina's activities or whereabouts, now is the time to tell us."

He looks dead serious, but I'm not buying it. This must be a ruse of some sort.

"I'd help you if I could," I say, concentrating all my energy on sounding sincere. "But I already told you everything I know."

"Perhaps you need more time to think," he says with a frown, touching a button on the table.

"Wait," I protest loudly as the door opens and a pair of guards enter the room. "I don't know anything else. There's no reason to hold me."

Davis doesn't respond. The guards refasten my hands, unchain my ankle, and pull me to my feet. I turn my head as I reach the door, determined to make another appeal. Lyman's chin is resting on his right hand, two fingers splayed against his cheek as he studies his notes. His shirtsleeve sags, exposing his wrist, and a tattoo: Felix the Cat.

23

AS WE LEAVE THE INTERROGATION ROOM and march back to the cell block, it's all I can do to contain myself. Lyman is Felix. Cop or not, this might be the guy who murdered my wife. I see Lyman in my mind's eye as the guard uncuffs me outside my cell. Tilling said two men broke into my house, one right-handed and one left-handed. The right-hander picked the lock; the other attacked Jenna. Lyman was taking notes with his left hand. The guard shoves me roughly into the cell and slams the door. I heave myself against the door as he turns the key, wild with rage and frustration. I'm starting to hyperventilate, black spots swimming in front of my eyes, my chest heaving. I've got to tell Tilling about Lyman before he can leave the country.

I begin pacing frantically. Rage gives way to despair as I walk mile after mile. Hours have passed. Food trays come and go twice, making it Sunday night. Lyman could be halfway back to Europe already. I'm collapsed on the edge of my bunk, completely exhausted, when I hear footsteps stop outside my door.

"We're opening up, Tyler. You know the drill."

An effort of will gets me to my feet. I'm expecting a return to the interrogation room, but the guards escort me to the elevator, my spirits rising as we ascend. Our destination is the white-tiled room. My stuff is on the table.

"Get dressed," one of the guards says.

"I'm being released?"

"You're being transferred. Get dressed."

I change as quickly as I can, telling myself firmly that anything that gets me back into street clothes has to be good. We ride the elevator higher, handcuffs biting my wrists. The guards open a succession of doors, and suddenly we're outside, in front of the British Airways terminal. It's nighttime, the cold air smelling of taxi exhaust and salt water, an indescribably rejuvenating New York aroma. Tilling and Ellis are leaning against an unmarked sedan at the curb, Tilling still in her surplus jacket, Ellis in a slick black Patagonia outfit. I never thought I'd be so happy to see them.

"You want him cuffed?" one of the guards asks after Tilling displays her badge and identification.

"I've been through this with your boss already," she says, an edge to her voice. "We only put a flag on him. You decided to hold him, that's your business."

"So you don't want him cuffed?" the guard says.

Tilling stares at him. The guard salutes her with a finger, looses my hands, and disappears back into the terminal with his cohort, laughing. I leap forward and grab Tilling by the shoulder.

"He was here. The guy with the Felix tattoo. He questioned me with a couple of other guys, federal officers. His name is Lyman, and I think he was in Moscow with me yesterday. He's a European. He might still be here. We've got to catch him before he can get on a plane."

She knocks my hand away, looking at me as if I'm crazy.

"Who questioned you?"

"Homeland Security," I say urgently. "Two officers named Davis and De Nunzio, and this guy Lyman. He may be a cop also, Interpol or something. I don't know."

"What did they want to know?"

"About Andrei, and my trip to Russia. We're wasting time, Grace. Lyman's the guy who killed the dog."

She seizes my biceps and gives me a shake.

"Calm down," she says. "Nothing's going to happen until I understand what's going on. Get in the car and we'll talk. And this time, I want the whole story."

Ellis double-parks near the mouth of an access road leading to the tarmac, a few hundred yards beyond the terminal. Tilling sits sideways in the front seat as she questions me, a dashboard-mounted work light reflecting off her notepad, uplighting her features. She curses steadily under her breath as I describe my interview with Lyman and the two "patriots," trying to explain everything as succinctly as possible.

"I'm going to need the name of the guy whose dog got killed," she says.

"Tony Pongo," I reply instantly. This is too important to worry about my promise to him. "He lives in Annadale, on Staten Island. He was Andrei's clerk in Moscow. That's everything, Grace. You've got to move on Lyman now, before it's too late."

"Listen," she says, snapping her notebook shut. "Stop telling me what to do. I haven't got a shred of jurisdiction here, and there hasn't been a fed born yet who will cooperate with the local cops unless there's something in it for them."

"Then what the fuck are we doing?"

"*We're* not doing a goddamned thing. You're going to sit in the car while Ellis and I work the phones, see if we can figure this thing out."

"And how long is that going to take?"

"You'll know when we're done."

Time passes. I fret in the back of the car, feeling completely helpless as Tilling and Ellis pace outside, making calls. Tilling hands me the phone once, asking me to confirm her identity to an unhappy Pongo. More time passes. Tilling gesticulates vehemently as she argues with someone. It's after ten when both women get back in the car. Ellis starts the engine and begins driving.

"Where are we going?" I ask.

"Manhattan," Tilling says.

"Why?"

"Lyman's registered at the Marriott Marquis, in Times Square."

"Davis and De Nunzio gave him up?" I ask, amazed.

"That'll be the day," Tilling says. "The DA agreed it was a waste of time to talk to the feds before we had something to trade. I called the duty officer at Kennedy and told him I mislaid Lyman's phone number. He checked their sign-out sheet for me. Lyman left the Marriott as his contact number. We'll chat with the feds after we've got their boy."

The ride into Manhattan seems to take forever. At the corner of Forty-ninth and Broadway, Ellis pulls up behind a parked blue-and-white New York City patrol car. She and Tilling get out and confer with the city cops on the sidewalk for a few minutes before getting back in the car. Tilling briefs me over her shoulder as the patrol car pulls out slowly from the curb, Ellis following.

"Here's the deal. Ellis and I are going to go upstairs with the uniforms and talk to Lyman. We'll tell him you've had a change of heart. You're saying you want to give Andrei up, and we don't know what to make of it. We'll ask him to go to the local precinct house with us. Your job is to sit in the car and identify him when we bring him out, make sure we got the right guy."

"And what happens when he gets there?"

"Pongo's cooperating. We've got another set of uniforms driving him in from Staten Island. If Pongo makes Lyman as the guy who killed his dog, we'll book him on some bullshit animal cruelty charge. It's late enough that he won't get a bail hearing before morning. We'll take his prints and search his person, figure out exactly who he really is and whether he's got any kind of record. With a little luck, we might even tie him to your house. We've got the shoe prints from the crime scene, and some hair and fiber. If we get any kind of match, a judge will issue a warrant for his hotel room. It's a start."

It's a lot more than a start. It's the moment I've been living for. I'm looking forward to seeing Lyman on the wrong side of an interrogation table, his ankle cuffed to a chair.

The city cops drive beneath a cement porte cochere extending from the Marquis's front entrance and pull to the curb. Ellis parks about thirty feet behind them. All four cops get out and confer again by the bellman's station. Tilling walks back and speaks to me through the open window.

"We're going to bring Lyman out that door there," she says, pointing. "You stay in the car and give me a thumbs-up when you recognize him. If he looks toward you, just turn your head the other way. You got it?"

"Yes."

"You can see okay, right? You don't need glasses or anything, do you?"

"I can see fine. Just please go get him, Grace."

She nods and walks away, leaving me on my own. I clench my hands between my knees, rocking slightly with anticipation. For the first time in months, I'm playing offense instead of defense: If Lyman's the guy, I'll learn the truth. And then I'll find some opportunity to blow his fucking brains out.

Five minutes later, Tilling and one of the city cops come hustling through the door, double-timing toward the parked patrol car. She beckons to me urgently, her phone to her ear. I throw my door open and step into the path of an oncoming taxi. The driver honks and swears as I jump out of the way. Tilling's standing next to the patrol car, one foot propped on the driver's doorsill while the cop behind the wheel talks on his radio.

"Wait one," she says into her phone as I approach, smothering it against her coat. "It looks like someone grabbed Lyman. His door was forced, there's blood on the carpet, and his stuff is scattered everywhere. This is going to be a huge cluster fuck. I don't even want to think about how many agencies will be involved. I want you in New York, where I can get hold of you. Where are you going to be?"

I feel stunned, as if I'd walked into a glass door.

"The Harvard Club, I guess," I say. "What do you think—"

"Just stay put until I call you."

She's already talking into her phone again. I hover nearby, trying to eavesdrop. She lowers the phone and glares at me.

"I want you out of here," she says. "I'll call you."

I start to protest, but the uniformed cop climbs out of his

car and catches hold of my upper arm, walking me forcibly toward Broadway. Two more police cars turn into the Marriott's entrance and I stop to see what's happening behind me. The cop gives me a small shove and points south.

"I believe the Haaavard Club is in that direction, old sport," he says in an affected drawl. "Now get the fuck out of here."

24

A SHUDDERING BANG startles me awake, a shaft of light from the hall penetrating my darkened bedroom. Someone's opened the door, catching it against the security chain. I bolt out of bed and trip over the desk chair, hitting my face hard as I fall.

"*Señor, señor.*"

I groan, knocked semiconscious. Opening my eyes, I find myself beneath the chair, my nose and cheek throbbing. A round-faced maid is peering anxiously through the narrow gap between the chained bedroom door and the jamb.

"*Dispénsame, señor. ¿Está bien?*"

I touch my face and turn my hand toward the light from the hall, relieved not to see any blood.

"Yeah, I think so."

Pushing the chair aside, I stagger to my feet, trying to get oriented. I'm in a small white-plaster bedroom at the Harvard Club, the draperies drawn, my dirty clothing in a heap on the floor next to the upended chair. Glancing into the framed mirror over the desk, I see myself naked and emaciated in the dim light, hair wild. Crimson letters emblazoned on the glass spell out *VERITAS*.

"What time is it?" I ask.

"No speak," the maid says, her eyes averted.

"*¿Qué hora es?*"

"*Once y media.*"

"*Bueno. Gracias.* Come back later, please."

She closes the door, muttering to herself. It can't be 11:30. I fumble for the clock radio that fell from the bedside table. It reads 11:34. Turning on the light, I check the room phone for messages and call my voice mail. The only message is from Katya, informing me that she has a call in to William about Andrei, and that she spoke to her mother, who didn't have anything to add. I dial zero.

"Harvard Club," the operator says.

"This is Peter Tyler in five twenty-one." My cheek aches as I speak. "Do you have any messages for me?"

"No, sir."

"Do you mind calling me back? I want to make sure my phone's working."

The phone rings a second later. I thank the operator and ask him to send up a bucket of ice and some ibuprofen.

I left messages for Emily and Grace before going to sleep, leaving the Harvard Club's number. Dialing both again, I get voice mail twice more. Shit. I slam the phone down. I can't believe Lyman vanished when we were so close to picking him up. Sitting on the edge of the bed with my head in my hands, I try to conjure next steps, figure out what I can do other than simply waiting for my phone to ring. I've still got Andrei's file, and Dmitri may have given me the clue I need to decrypt it. First things first, though: I've got to get cleaned up, buy some fresh clothes, and clear the cobwebs from my head with a large cup of coffee. Standing, I catch sight of the crimson letters on the mirror again. *VERITAS*. I wonder what the Latin is for *vengeance*.

I'm sitting on a stool in a tiny haberdashery on Forty-sixth Street an hour later, wearing my Burberry coat over fresh underwear while an efficient Hasidic man hand-hems a pair of charcoal slacks for me. I've got a new cell phone in my pocket and a new plastic watch on my wrist. My face throbs as I sip coffee from a thirty-two-ounce cup. I shouldn't have left the impromptu ice pack I made in my bathroom sink, no matter how self-conscious it made me feel. I notice my coat sagging on one side and check the pocket, finding the paperback I took from Andrei's bedside table. The binding's been replaced with a piece of duct tape; the immigration cops must have ripped it open, searching for contraband. I flip through the inscrutable pages, noticing a sentence that's both highlighted and underlined, an ink star penned into the margin. An idea occurs to me as I wonder what Andrei was reading.

"There's a public library around here, isn't there?" I ask.

"Forty-seventh, west of Tenth," the shopkeeper says, talking through a mouthful of pins. "On the north side. My nephew owns the kosher Chinese on the corner—Shalom Hunan. Tell him I sent you. You should eat something so your pants don't fall down."

A sign identifies the library as the Clinton Branch. It's only two narrow brownstones joined together, but the interior is surprisingly busy, twenty or thirty people of all ages working at long tables, about half seated in front of IBM workstations or laptops. A uniformed security guard stops me as I enter, informing me gruffly that I can't take my coffee inside.

"I'm here to see Mr. Rozier," I say.

"Your name?" he asks, picking up a phone.

"Peter Tyler. Tell him I worked with his granddaughter, Keisha."

An elderly black man in a navy sweater vest approaches moments later, bushy-browed eyes framed by tortoiseshell glasses.

"Mr. Tyler," he says, offering me his hand. His palm is as calloused as a mason's, an unexpected contrast to his bookish appearance. "It's a pleasure to meet you."

"Likewise," I say. He has a trace of an accent that I can't place.

"I want to thank you again on behalf of the children, and to tell you how grieved my family was by your tragedy. It was kind of you to remember us during a time of such tribulation."

"Thank you," I say. I'd sent him the fifteen hundred dollars a few weeks after the funeral, my hoops game with Tigger seeming as distant as Little League. "I got the card the kids made. Keisha's well?"

"Very. She got a big new promotion she's all excited about."

"Good," I say, glad to learn my intervention on her behalf eventually bore fruit. "She deserved it."

"What can I do for you today?"

"Two things. First, I was hoping you might have someplace private where I can use a computer connected to the Internet."

"Of course," he says. "And second?"

I shift my coffee from one hand to the other and dig Andrei's paperback out of my pocket.

"This book belongs to a friend of mine. It's in Russian. I'm wondering if you can tell me what it is, and whether you might have an English copy."

He lifts an eyebrow quizzically as he takes the book from me, flipping it over to look at the photograph on the back.

"Tolstoy," he says immediately. He opens it carefully, knobby dark fingers caressing the pages. "Too short for a novel, too long for a short story. Probably one of the religious essays he wrote. Come with me. This shouldn't take long."

"Is there somewhere I can get rid of this?" I ask, holding up my coffee.

"You can take it upstairs if you're careful," he says, smiling. "We try to accommodate friends of the library."

Mr. Rozier settles me in a battered armchair in his windowless second-floor office, excusing himself to gather some reference works. An ancient Apple laptop on his desk is surrounded by neatly stacked correspondence and periodicals, a blizzard of yellow Post-its stuck to every surface. Plastic-framed family photos cover the walls. I pick out Keisha as a tall teen on a pony, in her confirmation gown, and on the arm of her fiancé. There's a holly-bordered photo of Mr. Rozier in a Santa hat, a baby in each arm. Jenna always saved the Christmas pictures people sent us of their families. She used to enclose vacation photos of us in our cards when we were first married, but she gave it up some years ago. I never asked why.

"You have a lovely family," I say as Mr. Rozier reenters the room, a couple of large books under his arm.

"Four children, eleven grandchildren, and three great-grandchildren. I've been very blessed. Here." He offers me a Styrofoam cup filled with ice cubes and a small stack of paper towels. "You should ice that bruise on your face. You're going to have a shiner."

"What have you got?" I ask, helping him clear space on the desk for two hefty volumes.

"A Russian-English dictionary and Tolstoy's collected essays. I'll need a minute to figure out the Cyrillic alphabetization."

"You want some help with that?"

"No," he says. "I enjoy puzzles. I do a unit on code breaking with the kids. Mainly just number substitution, but we have fun with it."

I fold ice cubes into a paper towel as he pores over the dictionary, jotting notes in a cramped hand on a piece of scrap paper.

"I thought so," he says, looking up. "The title's 'A Confession.' Tolstoy wrote it in—let me see." He opens the collected essays and runs a finger down the title page. "Eighteen eighty-two."

"Have you read it?"

"Years ago. Do you know anything about Tolstoy?"

"Not really."

He steeples his hands against his mouth and thinks for a moment.

"Tolstoy was born a Russian aristocrat sometime around 1825. He served in the military before becoming a novelist, and was known as a playboy in his youth, but then he became depressed as he entered his middle years. The first half of 'A Confession' is about his struggle not to commit suicide. The second describes his discovery of a personal faith in God outside the ritual of the Orthodox Church."

I never knew Andrei to be religious. Picking up the book, I turn pages until I find the sentence he underlined and starred.

"Any chance you can tell me what that says?"

Mr. Rozier flips through the English and Russian texts simultaneously, comparing chapter headings and counting down paragraphs. He refers back to his dictionary and then turns the English copy toward me, indicating a sentence with his finger.

" 'What meaning has life that death does not destroy?' "

A chill runs down my spine, the ominous words somehow calling to mind Davis's wild accusations of biological terrorism.

"What was Tolstoy's answer?"

"Love of mankind. Tolstoy renounced his wealth, spoke out against social inequities, and became a prominent pacifist. Gandhi was influenced by Tolstoy's writings."

I nod solemnly, suspecting it might alienate Mr. Rozier to tell him it all sounds like crap to me. Everyone's responsible for themselves. Utopianism is a philosophy for losers.

"Perhaps you'd like to borrow this," Mr. Rozier says, nudging the book toward me.

"Thanks for the help, but no, I'm not much interested in religious texts," I say. Tolstoy isn't going to help me solve Jenna's murder. My time's better spent on Andrei's files.

"A secular spin might have it that life can be made meaningful only by helping others," Mr. Rozier says. "Maybe by doing things like donating money to library programs for kids you don't know."

"It's a thought," I say, impatient to get on with my research. "I'd be grateful if you could show me where I can get on-line."

"Of course," he says, standing. "I'm here to help."

25

MR. ROZIER walks me down two flights of stairs and into a dim basement filled with racks of books. It's musty but dry, and comfortably cool. A scarred wooden desk sits beneath a high barred window at the far end of the basement, a computer and a banker's lamp with a cracked green shade resting on top of it. He turns on the lamp, a rhomboid of yellowish light illuminating the desktop.

"Anything else you need?"

"A pen or pencil and some paper?"

He slides open the desk drawer, revealing some chewed pens and a few pieces of cheap stationery with the letterhead of a marine-supply store.

"People leave all sorts of stuff behind," he says. "Funding's tight. We try to live off the land as much as possible." His laugh is a creaky chuckle.

"Thanks," I say. "I really appreciate this."

"My pleasure. I'll check back in on you later."

He climbs the stairs slowly as I take my new cell phone out and check for reception. Weak but serviceable. I dial the Harvard Club and my voice mail. Still nothing. Frustrated, I turn on the computer, log in to the mail account I created on Yahoo, and download Andrei's file. I click on it and get the dialogue box demanding a password.

Dmitri said that Andrei's alarm code was the same as his network password, except that he'd changed the letters to numbers. If he used the same password to protect this file, I might be able to figure it out. I enter the numeric alarm code first—8657869—thinking I might get lucky. Nothing. Using my cell phone as a reference, I write the letter groups associated with each number on a piece of marine-store stationery and then stare at it. TUV-MNO-JKL-PQRS-TUV-MNO-WXYZ. Hopefully, Andrei's underlying password is English, and not Russian or German. While there are thousands of potential letter permutations, only a limited number of vowel, prefix, and suffix combinations make sense. I mouth fragments silently, determined to be patient. A recognizable combination suddenly rolls off my tongue and I sit bolt upright. T-O-L-S-T-O-Y. My heart thumps with excitement as I tap the name into the computer and press enter. An Excel spreadsheet opens on the screen in front of me. The spreadsheet contains dozens of interlinked pages, with hundreds of entries in each. They look like financial statements. Excited to have discovered something I understand, I pick up a pen and begin taking notes. Maybe Tolstoy's going to help me solve Jenna's murder after all.

Thirty minutes of tedious cross-referencing establishes the basics. The pages are trade records, from the perspective of Turndale and five clients. About half the purchase and sale activity is in ruble-denominated Russian securities, and the other half consists of foreign-exchange trades, mainly euros against the dollar. I set the foreign-exchange trades aside for the moment, deciding to concentrate on the securities first. A separate page identifies the traded securities by ISIN and lists daily settlement prices over a fourteen-month period, ending in August. The trade and price records link to running position and portfolio value reports aggregated by client. There's too much going on for me to immediately discern anything beyond the basic fact that Turndale seemed to be making money. Fortunately, Andrei also linked all the trading activity to a series of pages detailing the underlying money movements. A frenetic Australian professor taught me the rudiments of forensic accounting at business school, his first and foremost rule to always follow the cash.

I've barely begun on the cash when I notice an odd and ominous inconsistency. The trading records cover Turndale and five clients. Hence, money should be moving among six bank accounts. I count a second time, knowing I haven't made a mistake. There's cash flowing among seven accounts. My accounting professor taught us a unit on fraud, opening with the story of a supermarket chain that was consistently losing 10 percent of their sales in a particular store to theft. Only after wasting significant time and money on detectives and security cameras did they turn to their accountant for help. The accountant toured the premises and immediately noticed that while the manager had been submitting receipts for nine cash registers every day, there were ten registers in the store. The moral, according to my former professor, was that all fraud is obvious once you've admitted the possibility. I lift my pen again with a sense of dread, fearful of what I'm about to learn.

A muted cough from the dark stacks to my rear startles me out of grim reverie some hours later. Turning my head, I see Mr. Rozier approaching with a white ceramic mug in his hand.

"You've been down here quite a while," he says, setting the mug in front of me. Faded gold letters on the side spell out *World's Greatest Grandfather*. "I thought you might like some fresh coffee."

"Thanks."

I lean back in my chair and rub my face with both hands, careful to avoid my bruise. It's dusk already, a flickering streetlight visible through the ground-level window overhead. My neck aches as I twist my head from side to side, trying to work some of the tension out of my back and shoulders.

"You look tired," he says, sounding concerned. "Maybe you should take a break, get something to eat."

"I'm almost done here. I've just got to figure out one more thing."

"Anything I can help with?"

"Maybe," I reply, looking up at him. "Was Tolstoy or anyone from his school of thought ever known as the 'good father'?"

"Not that I know of," he says, his eyebrows lifting. "Why?"

"I'm trying to log in to an account on a French-language Web site, but the system's demanding the answer to a secondary security question." I tilt the computer monitor upward so he can see it, touching the screen with a finger. "Here. This phrase translates as 'Enter your private word,' and then when you click on the button next to it, the system gives you a hint."

"'*Bon papa*,'" he says, the accent I noticed earlier more pronounced as he reads from the screen.

"You speak French?"

"After a fashion," he says, still studying the monitor. "I was born in Haiti and grew up speaking Creole. When real

French people hear me speak, they cover their ears and moan." He raises his hands and mimes a grimace of cultural pain. I give him a tired grin, but the mirth's already fading from his expression. "You're trying to log in to an account at a Luxembourg bank. Why?"

It's the seventh account, the one that's destroyed my faith in Andrei. Turndale and their counterparts were buying and selling securities furiously, but somehow all the cash ended up in Luxembourg. Andrei had pasted in the electronic statements for the account through August, and it was clear who the beneficiary was. The trip he'd taken to Rome, the last time we saw each other, had been paid for with a debit card linked to the Luxembourg account.

"I'm looking for an old friend," I reply, choosing my words carefully. "The fellow who owns the Tolstoy book. If I can access the account on-line, I might be able to see where he's been spending money recently, and track him down that way. I know the account number and password, but I'm getting tripped up by the security question."

"Your friend told you the password to his bank account?"

"I guessed it."

Mr. Rozier frowns for a second and then turns his back to the desk, gripping the edge with his hands and easing himself to a seated position on top of it. His knees crack loudly as they bend and he sighs.

"Some mornings I get out of bed and it sounds like those cartoon characters from the cereal commercials on TV— Snap, Crackle, and Pop. You mind if I call you Peter?"

"Please."

"My name's Rupert," he says. "Kind of old-fashioned, like me. I take it this friend of yours has gone missing."

"Yes."

"Any special reason?"

"He did something bad," I say flatly, my newly acquired knowledge eliminating any doubt. I know why William Turndale fired Andrei.

"Mmm," Mr. Rozier says. "Are the police looking for him?"

"If they aren't, they will be soon."

"And what do you plan to do if you find this friend?"

"That depends on what he has to say for himself."

Mr. Rozier stares at his shoes, feet kicking gently. I can hear running footsteps and high-pitched laughter overhead.

"It sounds like your after-school group is here."

"Yes. I've got to get back upstairs before they tear the place down." He slaps his hands on his thighs and looks up, meeting my eyes. "*Bon papa* translates as 'good father,' but it's a colloquial expression in French. It pretty much meant grandpop when I was a boy, but more recently it's also been used to mean father-in-law, or maybe even some other older person who's particularly close to a youngster—a favorite neighbor perhaps, or a mentor of some sort. Do you know anyone else in your friend's family? Because that's whom I'd ask."

"I do," I say, taking my phone from my pocket.

"Keisha told me you were a good man, Peter." Mr. Rozier leans forward and puts a hand on my shoulder. "She was angry about those stories in the paper. She said you'd never hurt anyone."

"I'm grateful for her confidence," I say, meeting his gaze. And sorry that she's wrong.

"Well," he says, standing up stiffly, "I've got to go round up those kids. Is there anything else I can help you with?"

"One thing, maybe." I hunt through my notes. "More of

a loose end. I can reconcile all the cash flowing in and out of my friend's account except for the opening deposit. The account was originally funded eighteen months ago with a wire transfer of four point one six million Swiss francs from something or somebody called GPICCARDAG. I assume it's another bank, but I haven't been able to nail it down on the Internet. Do you have access to any kind of directory that might be able to help?"

"Maybe." He reaches out to take the note from me. "I'll do a little research after I get the kids settled."

"I'd appreciate it," I say. "You've been a big help already."

"You can do me a favor back."

"What's that?"

"God will speak from your heart if you take the time to listen," he says, touching a finger to my chest. "Slow down a little bit. Don't do anything you're going to regret later."

"I'll try to do the right thing," I reply, resisting the urge to ask him if he's talking about the same God that denied Jenna children and then let two thugs murder her in our garage.

"Good," he says, turning away. "That's the best any of us can do." He starts off toward the stairs, joints cracking loudly. "And drink that coffee before it gets cold. The Lord abhors waste."

I can hear him chuckling as I dial Katya's office number on my cell phone. I pick the mug up and take a sip. The coffee's hot and excellent.

"Katya Zhilina's office," Debra says when she picks up.

"It's Peter Tyler," I say, setting the mug down. "I need to speak with Katya urgently."

"She's not available."

"Where is she?"

"I'm not at liberty to say."

"Fine," I say, trying not to sound irritated. "I guess I'll just call her on her cell, then."

"Be my guest." Debra hangs up.

Katya's cell number rolls into voice mail. The whole god-damned world is on voice mail.

"Katya. It's Peter." I hesitate, unsure what message to leave. "I found out what Andrei did. We need to talk as soon as possible. Call me when you can."

I read her the new number, hang up, and then tap the phone against my forehead impatiently. It occurs to me that there's someone else I can try, someone who might be able to tell me about Andrei's *bon papa,* or even more. Dialing information, I ask for the number of the Metropolitan Museum of Art.

26

THE MET'S CLOSED to the public on Mondays, the cavernous entrance hall seeming haunted without crowds. I'm standing in a small room just inside the main doors, a gore-spattered saint staring at me from a poster on the wall while a guard talks into a phone. I check my new watch and see that it's a few minutes past five.

"Mrs. Zhilina's finishing some work," the guard says. "One of my colleagues will escort you upstairs in a moment."

"Thanks."

I sit down on an uncomfortably architectural bench and lean all the way forward, locking my hands under my knees to stretch my lower back. Katya insisted it would be a waste of time for me to ask her mother questions, but that was before I learned what Andrei'd done. Once Mrs. Zhilina understands how Andrei's actions have placed Katya in jeopardy, I should be able to persuade her to help me. And if she tells me where Andrei is, I won't have to bother fooling around with his bank records.

"Sir?"

A slender Asian woman wearing a white shirt and a red

museum ascot beckons to me. We climb two flights of fire stairs and pass through several long hallways before reaching a white door labeled A32: CONSERVATION. She taps, waits for a hail from within, and then opens the door with a key card.

A windowless rectangular room extends to my right. Glass-fronted cabinets line the long walls, displaying brown sample bottles and geometrically shaped glassware; unfamiliar electronic equipment rests on counters beneath. A semicircular bank of work lights shine brilliantly at the far end of the room, casting eerie horizontal shadows. Shading my eyes with both hands, I see an easel at the focal point of the arc, a haloed figure half-hidden behind it.

"Sit please," Mrs. Zhilina says, pointing some sort of tool at me. "Or stand. I'm almost done here."

"You mind if I take a look?" I ask, walking toward her.

"I do," she says firmly, waving me back. "And be quiet, please."

A good beginning. Her throaty accent carries me back in time. Our first meeting pretty much set the tone of our relationship. She'd thrown a dinner party to celebrate Andrei's graduation from business school, the guests Katya, Jenna, me, and a handful of older Euro types, the conversation exclusively about art. My one contribution was the admission that the only museum I'd ever visited in New York City was the Museum of Natural History. Nobody seemed interested in hearing about the dinosaurs.

I take a seat on a stool at a high worktable and reach for a binocular microscope, pulling my hand back before she can tell me not to touch anything. Glancing over my shoulder, I notice a hinged wooden diptych hanging on the short wall adjacent to the door, twinned portraits of pale young women in three-quarter profile, ink black hair pulled back severely.

Bare shoulders and lowered eyes convey an impression of sad vulnerability. The nearer face is Katya's, the farther like enough to be her sister. A cousin perhaps.

The work lamps extinguish abruptly, plunging the room into darkness. Undercounter lights come up a moment later, harsh shadows exchanged for soft. I can see Mrs. Zhilina more clearly now. Her hair's grayer than I remember, but she doesn't look much different otherwise, a slight woman with stern dark eyes and a skeptical cast to her features.

"So," she says, peeling off surgical gloves. "Peter Tyler. It's been six years, no?"

"About," I reply, not recalling when we last met. "I was just admiring Katya's portrait. Who's the woman on the right?"

"Me, a very long time ago," Mrs. Zhilina says, draping the easel.

"They're remarkable," I say, embarrassed at not having guessed. It was the expression that fooled me. It's hard to imagine Mrs. Zhilina looking vulnerable. "Did you paint them?"

"Yes."

"I didn't know you were so accomplished."

"I painted what I saw," she says dismissively. "Great art is painting more than you see. Would you like some tea?"

"No, thanks."

She limps toward me, leaning heavily on a cane and carrying a tray laden with metal implements that look like dental tools.

"Can I help?" I ask, standing up.

"No," she says, gesturing me back to my seat with the tray. "I'm not a cripple. Some fool tripped me with his umbrella in the street a few months ago and I broke my hip. It hasn't healed properly, but I've gotten used to it."

She hooks the cane over the edge of a sink and fills an electric kettle before meticulously cleaning her tools and placing them in a rack to dry. She's tiny from the back, certainly not five feet, and is wearing a white lab coat that falls to her ankles. Turning from the sink, she seats herself on a stool opposite me, carefully lifting her bad leg with both hands and resting both red-slippered feet on a rung.

"So," she says again. "Permit me to tell you how grieved I was to learn of your wife's death."

"Thank you."

Her smock-covered knees are slightly higher than her waist, giving her the look of a gnome on a toadstool. The intensity of her gaze belies any comic impression, obsidian eyes boring into me.

"Katya told me that you were looking for Andrei, and why."

"I know. I asked her to call you."

"I'd hoped not to hear your name from her again. Your recent liaison was very painful for her."

Christ. I can feel my face reddening. It never occurred to me that Katya might confide in her mother.

"You've behaved very badly," she continues coldly. "And now you're trying to drag Andrei into your problems?"

"I'm not trying to drag Andrei into anything," I say angrily. "He put himself in the middle of this."

"Because he sent your wife a package?"

"Because someone looking for that package may have murdered my wife."

Mrs. Zhilina watches me imperturbably as I struggle to calm down. This isn't going the way I'd planned. The electric kettle whistles and she rises to attend it. She returns carrying two conical glass beakers of tea on a tray.

"Drink," she says, pushing one toward me. "It's good for you."

I pick the beaker up and take a tentative sniff—peppermint. I take a sip and set it down again.

"Now," she says, "explain yourself."

"There's a lot I don't know yet," I say, chafing at her tone. "The starting point is that Andrei stole money from Turndale—a lot of money."

"Ridiculous," she says crisply. "Katya would have told me."

"Katya doesn't know. But you must've realized something was wrong when Andrei disappeared."

"He told me he had personal difficulties and needed time to himself."

"Ridiculous," I say throwing her own word back at her. "Turndale fired him. Katya knows that. Or didn't she tell you?"

Mrs. Zhilina taps one finger on the table, the same gesture Katya makes when she's angry.

"Tell me," she says.

"About a year and a half ago, Andrei came into a chunk of money. I haven't figured out where it came from yet. He used the money to fund a foreign-exchange trade with a Swiss bank. He made a big bet that the dollar would rise against the euro just as it began falling. Within a month, he was down a million dollars. Instead of closing the position and taking his loss, he doubled up. The market moved against him again, and suddenly he was down two million dollars. The Swiss were ready to close him out. He needed more money to keep the position open. You with me so far?"

"Yes," she says quietly, blue-veined hands gripping her tea. "How do you know this?"

"I pulled records off his computer in Moscow. Andrei's

job with Turndale was to buy stock in Eastern European companies. His records indicate he put five million dollars of Turndale's money into a Russian company named Fetsov, but somehow the cash ended up in his personal account."

"I don't understand."

"My best guess is that he counterfeited the stock certificates. A guy in Hong Kong did the same thing a few years back. In America, stock certificates aren't issued much anymore—everything's kept track of electronically. Lots of second- and third-tier financial markets still use printed stock certificates, though. Andrei told Turndale he'd used their money to buy Fetsov stock and gave them the counterfeit certificates. Then he wired the five million to the Swiss and doubled his bet on the dollar again. He lost the five million in seventeen days. So he counterfeited more shares. And then things got ugly."

"How could a single individual have fooled a big company like Turndale?" she asks skeptically.

"Happens all the time," I say. "It's hard to spot a good fraud if you're not looking for it, and Andrei's smart. He pretended to sell the fake Fetsov certificates to another company for a profit and used the money he'd supposedly received to buy different fake certificates. He kept all his fake positions turning over constantly and he kept booking false profits. From Turndale's perspective, everything was great. They never realized their portfolio of Russian stock was slowly being transformed into a collection of worthless counterfeit paper."

"There must have been some safeguard," she protests.

"Of course. Eastern European companies keep registers listing the rightful owners of all the physical stock they issue. The clerk working for Andrei should have confirmed Turndale's positions with each company at least once a week by phone. Except Andrei's clerk was hanging out at his mamma's house in Salerno, with Andrei's blessing, and all the double-checking the clerk was supposed to do was being done—or not being done—by Andrei's secretary, a Russian woman he'd hired locally."

"How much?" she whispers.

"Over a billion," I reply, still shocked by the magnitude of the amount. Andrei's records had revealed an almost unbelievable string of desperate trading gambits and losing positions, the hole he'd sunk into becoming a near-bottomless pit with dizzying rapidity. It was incredible that he'd lost that much money that fast.

Mrs. Zhilina hunches over her tea, face averted. I can only imagine how she must feel. As for me, my friendship with Andrei died in the basement of Mr. Rozier's library, victim to a growing certitude that his panicked maneuvers must somehow have led to Jenna's murder. There are too many coincidences to draw any other conclusion.

"But why hasn't it come out?" Mrs. Zhilina asks plaintively. "Why doesn't Katya know?"

"That's the bit that puzzled me at first. And then I remembered Katya telling me that William Turndale was selling his shares in Turndale and Company. I think William eventually figured out what Andrei was doing, fired him, and came up with a plan to make good the loss. He hasn't told anyone about the theft because he intends to sell his shares in Turndale to an unwitting buyer and then use the proceeds to buy back the counterfeit stock. Fix the problem with his own money before anyone else learns the truth."

"Again," she says, "I don't understand. Why would he want to do that?"

"Two reasons. One, Turndale's worth a lot more as a going

concern than it is as a crippled hulk with regulators crawling all over it. William's shares will bring way more than a billion if no one knows there's any problem. So he could buy back the counterfeit securities and still have enough money to retire in style, maybe even stay on the board as a senior statesman."

"And the second reason?"

"Pride. Imagine what the press would say. William Turndale, one of the smartest and meanest guys on Wall Street, conned out of a billion dollars by a single employee, the company his father founded brought to its knees. Someone like William would probably rather kill himself."

A few moments pass in silence.

"What does this mean for Andrei?" she asks, her voice surprisingly well controlled.

"You already know the answer to that," I respond levelly. "There's nothing anyone can do to help him at this point. I'm worried about Katya."

"Why?" she asks sharply.

"If the truth comes out, the company's going down, and William's looking at jail time for his cover-up. Katya's the number-two person in the firm, and Andrei's her twin brother. She's going to have a lot of trouble persuading anyone that she didn't know what was going on. At an absolute minimum, the SEC will probably get her for failure to supervise and bar her from the securities industry."

"And at a maximum?"

"I don't want to speculate. Jail's a real possibility."

"I see," Mrs. Zhilina says softly. "Thank you for explaining so well. Assuming you're correct, can William succeed with his plan?"

"My opinion? Not in a million years. There's no way a

buyer's due diligence wouldn't turn up a billion dollars' worth of fake stock. He must be crazy."

She lifts her tea with steady hands and twirls the beaker, watching tiny flecks of tea spin like leaves in a high wind.

"You suggested that your wife was murdered by someone looking for Andrei," she says. "You think that person was William Turndale?"

"No," I reply, having considered the possibility at length earlier. "Angry as he must be, William's got to want Andrei to stay hidden. The last thing he needs right now is to attract any external scrutiny."

"Then who?"

I shrug, unwilling to share my thoughts any further. Lyman's still at the top of my list, but I've been thinking about Vladimir more and more. I'd bet the prior business he did with Andrei was forging stock certificates. If so, Andrei would have been dependent on Vladimir to keep his scam going, and Vladimir could have used that dependency to win a position at the clinic. It isn't hard to imagine Vladimir as a mercenary working for terrorists. Incredible as it seems, Davis might have been telling me the truth. Maybe Andrei discovered what Vladimir was doing and fled, in which case Vladimir would have been looking for him.

"So," Mrs. Zhilina says evenly. "What must I do?"

"Tell me where Andrei is. The more I can learn about what happened, the more I'll be able to help Katya."

Her eyes bore into me again.

"Your motivation is to help Katya?"

"One motivation," I reply, meeting her gaze. "I never meant to hurt her. I want to make amends."

"And what else do you want?"

"Vengeance. Whoever murdered my wife has to pay."

"An eye for an eye and a tooth for a tooth," she says, nodding slowly. "That's justice. I'll help you any way I can, but I don't know where Andrei is. He's been leaving messages on my home machine every few weeks, saying that he's well and that I shouldn't worry."

I'm disappointed, but not out of options yet.

"There's another thing you might be able to tell me," I say. "Has Andrei ever had a relative or family friend that he referred to as *bon papa*?"

Her mouth twitches, a tell so tiny that I would have missed it if I'd blinked. She knows something.

"Why do you ask?"

"Andrei's been using a debit card linked to a numbered bank account in Luxembourg to pay for his personal travel. If I can access the account on-line, I might be able to figure out where he is. The phrase *'bon papa'* is his personal security question. I think the answer might be a name—someone he knew as a boy, or when he was a student. It's important I figure this out to help Katya."

"There's no one I can think of," she replies stiffly.

I'm leaning forward to remonstrate with her when a thought catches me up short. Andrei once confided that the root cause of the tension between Katya and their mother was Mrs. Zhilina's refusal to tell them anything about the father who abandoned them. All Andrei and Katya ever knew was that he was an American she'd met in Europe. Maybe Andrei learned more. Maybe Andrei's *bon papa* isn't from Mrs. Zhilina's side of the family.

"I'm not trying to dredge up unpleasant memories," I say, deliberately oblique for the sake of her pride. "If you give me a name, I won't repeat it."

"I already told you," she says in the same stiff tone. "There's no one."

My phone rings before I can respond. I check the display reflexively and see Katya's office number.

"One second," I say to Mrs. Zhilina, lifting the phone to my mouth. "Hello?"

"Katya would like to see you in her office as soon as possible," Debra says.

"Fine. I'm on my way."

I hang up and get to my feet, debating whether or not to take another run at Mrs. Zhilina. Anything Andrei found out about his father, he likely shared with Katya, which means I'll learn it in a few minutes anyway.

"That was Katya's secretary," I say. "I've got to go meet Katya now. You're quite sure—"

"I am," she says coldly.

What was it Katya said to me the other day? That she'd been trying to persuade her mother to tell her things for years, and that she hadn't had any luck yet. I turn to go.

"Don't forget," Mrs. Zhilina says to my back. "You said you wanted to make amends. I expect you to look out for Katya."

It's a bit much for her to hector me, given that she's the one withholding information. I repress my instinctive sarcasm, mindful of all the bad news she's had to absorb.

"I will," I say, answering from the heart. "There's no one else more important to me now."

27

LOW CLOUDS HANG ominously in a darkened sky as I exit the museum. It smells like snow. Scanning the street for a cab, I notice a white step van double-parked across Fifth Avenue, in front of the old Stanhope Hotel. A man smoking a cigarette looks toward me through the open passenger window, features downlit by a streetlight. My heart races as I realize he looks like Vladimir. He flips his cigarette into the street as the truck begins moving, orange embers arcing through the night air. The truck turns left on Seventy-ninth Street before I think to get the plate number. I button my coat higher as I shiver, wondering if I'm imagining things. What would Vladimir be doing in America? Disappearing people, maybe, I realize, thinking of Lyman. Everything that's happened is somehow connected. It could be that Vladimir's tidying up. Permit or no, I should be carrying my dad's gun.

I flag a taxi and settle sideways in the rear seat, watching the traffic behind us for the white van as I try Tilling yet again, raging at her continued unavailability. My only new message is from Tigger.

"Peter. Where are you? Give me a call as soon as you can."

I hang up and dial him back, glad for the distraction. He answers on the first ring.

"It's Peter," I say.

"What number are you calling me from?" he demands.

"I got a new cell phone. It's a long story."

"Where are you now?"

"Manhattan. In a taxi."

"You're never gonna guess what happened," he says, laughing gleefully. "We gotta talk. When can we meet?"

I glance at my watch.

"Seven o'clock at the Harvard Club," I say. "What is it?"

"I'll tell you later," he says. "This is too good for the phone. You're gonna love it."

28

A CREW-CUT MAN who looks to be in his mid-thirties is waiting for me when I step off the elevator into Turndale's old-world reception area. He's a big guy, with a head that droops toward me on a long neck, dark eyes half-hidden beneath a protruding brow. He looks like a ferret. He's wearing a navy blazer, gray slacks, and a Secret Service–style earpiece and lapel pin. Probably an ex-cop of some sort hired as executive security.

"You're supposed to be wearing that on your suit jacket," he says, looking at the adhesive visitor's pass in my hand.

"Haven't got one," I reply, brushing past him.

"Wait a minute, wise guy," he says, catching hold of my sleeve.

I've been manhandled by enough guards for one week. Spinning toward him, I knock his hand away and slap the pass against his chest.

"Don't touch me. You got that?"

He peels the pass from his tie and folds it in half, not looking down.

"You already got one shiner," he says, jerking his chin

toward my bruise. "A smarter guy might have learned some-thing."

I can't afford to let petty rage get the better of me.

"I'm here to see Katya Zhilina," I say tersely.

"Boardroom," the ex-cop mutters, pointing with his chin again. "You're expected."

I walk down a corridor and through a pair of large open doors into the boardroom. A black-lacquered table thirty feet long sits on an enormous Oriental rug in the center of the room, the high-gloss surface reflecting a constellation of pink-ish halogen spots overhead. To my right, an ornately carved wooden fireplace surrounds a blazing gas fire that must have required an expensive exemption from the city's fire code. A large winter landscape hangs over the mantel, barren trees partially obscuring snow-covered wooden buildings, cloaked peasants hurrying about their business.

"Do you recognize the painting, Mr. Tyler?"

William Turndale's entered the room behind me, trailed by the weaselly character I met in the reception area. William's tall, at least my height, despite a slight stoop. Skin sags from his neck as if he's begun to erode internally, a big man starting to melt from within. Pale blue eyes gleam fiercely beneath a full head of snow-white hair. Aging or not, William's still for-midable.

"I don't know much about art," I say warily, surprised that he's stopped in to say hello. We've met only a handful of times, and never outside of Katya's presence. There's no rea-son for him to speak to me now that I'm persona non grata on the Street.

"There's a remarkable story behind that painting," William says, walking toward me. "Hitler was interested in art. He col-lected canvases from all over occupied Europe. He was planning a museum in Linz, his hometown, to display his most prized acquisitions. Are you familiar with any of this?"

"No," I say, wondering where Katya is. William's standing next to me now, staring up at the landscape.

"The core of the collection was a group of eighty paintings that were stored in Neuschwanstein, a nineteenth-century castle in the Bavarian Alps. There was a da Vinci, a Caravaggio, a Raphael, a Canaletto, and two Vermeers. Imagine that. There are only thirty-five known Vermeers in the entire world, and ten of those have doubtful provenance. The entire collection vanished at the end of the war. The Soviets accused the Americans of stealing it and the Americans accused the Soviets. No one's ever unraveled the mystery."

"Imagine that," I echo, beginning to get impatient.

"There's one painting from the collection that's unusual in two respects. *The Village in Winter,* by Pieter Brueghel the Younger. First, it's the only painting that Hitler acquired legitimately, a loan from an aristocratic German family. And second, it's the only painting of the group that's ever been seen again."

He tips his head toward the landscape and smiles, purplish lips drawn up to expose his canines.

"Fascinating," I say. "Will you excuse me? I was hoping to have a quick word with Katya."

"She's in Chicago," William says. "You told her you knew what Andrei had done. I thought perhaps we could chat."

I feel myself flush as I realize what's happened. Katya's worked for William for twenty years, and even though there's no reason she should be feeling loyal to me just now, it still hurts to realize she passed my message to William without speaking to me first.

"Don't fret," William says, apparently noticing my distress. "She didn't tell me. I've been monitoring her phones ever since her brother disappeared. I heard your voice mail."

"Katya's going to be pissed," I say, simultaneously relieved that Katya didn't give me up and incredulous at William's audacity.

"She's gotten over worse," he says indifferently. "I'm not an easy man to work for."

"Most people say you're a prick," I shoot back, wanting to wipe the complacent look off his face.

"Your language is a little rich for my taste," William says, smiling easily. "I just got off the phone with your old boss, Josh Kramer. He used the term *prima donna* when he described you, which is a more polite way of saying the same thing. And of course there's the small matter of your wife's murder, which the police seem to think you committed. Glass houses, Mr. Tyler." He winks as if we were chatting companionably.

Back when I worked for Josh, he related a story he'd heard William tell once. William did a tour with the army prior to joining his family firm, working as an intelligence officer in Berlin during the early sixties. One day, he questioned three brothers suspected of spying for the Soviets. Unable to persuade any of the three to talk, he fell back on an old interrogation trick, pointing at the eldest brother and telling a German guard to take him outside and shoot him. Moments later, William and the remaining brothers heard a shot. William pointed at the youngest brother and said he was next. Both men spilled their guts, confessing everything. The punch line of the story was that the unwitting guard, new to his job, actually had shot the eldest brother. Josh was reverential as he described the shout of laughter William finished the story with, thrilled by his callousness.

"You want to talk?" I say, looking him in the eye. "Talk."

"Why don't we sit down first," he says. "Earl?"

The security guard sidles around the table and pulls out a chair for William. I sit down next to him with my back to the fire, figuring I already know where this conversation is going.

"Would you like something to drink, Mr. Tyler?" he asks.

"Nothing, thanks."

"To business, then. A little bird told me that you took some files from a computer belonging to me."

It takes me a couple of seconds to put the pieces together. There's only one person connected to Turndale who might know I took Andrei's files.

"Dmitri called you."

"Excellent, Mr. Tyler. Very quick. Josh said you were smart."

"You didn't know that he had Andrei's computer?"

"Regretfully, Dmitri wasn't quite as forthcoming as he seemed when Earl and I conducted the postmortem on our Moscow office. It's disappointing how few people are. He's evidently gotten himself in some legal trouble over there. What was it again, Earl?"

"Pandering," Earl says. "Fags."

"Odd, don't you think?" William asks rhetorically. "Pandering's a stalwart of most Eastern European economies. At any rate, he thought he might be able to trade information in exchange for some assistance."

"You have a relationship with the Russian cops?" I ask suspiciously. "Perhaps you asked them to look for Andrei?"

"Heavens no," he says, sounding amused. "The last thing I want is a gang of Russian thugs asking Andrei questions. Dmitri requested monetary assistance."

"You called Josh back in September and asked about a

foundation that Andrei was involved with. You were looking for him then, weren't you?"

"I was interested in Andrei's financial affairs, not his person," William says, watching me closely. "Perhaps you know why?"

"I do," I reply. "And I can guess why you're interested in Andrei's files. But they won't help you find your money. It's gone. Andrei lost it all trading his personal account."

"Well," William says. "That answers my first question. You know about the theft."

"Andrei kept good records."

"Documentation was one of his strong suits," William says wryly, shaking his head as if over a child's foible. "He sent me his trading records with his confession. I know the money's gone. That's not why you and I are talking."

William's answered one of my outstanding questions: how he learned about Andrei's theft. Andrei must have owned up when his losses became too large to conceal.

"Then why?"

"You're the smart one," he says. "You tell me."

"You want me to keep quiet about the counterfeit securities so you can sell your shares in Turndale for a good price."

"Well done." He smiles at me patronizingly.

"Hushing this up is crazy. You can't hide something this big. You're going to destroy your company and cause big trouble for Katya and God only knows how many other people."

"You, Andrei, Earl, and I are the only people who know what's happened. Unless you've already told someone else?"

"This isn't a playground secret. You're holding a billion dollars of fake stock."

William cranes his neck like a bird, fixing me with a cold eye.

"You must realize I have a plan."

"Of course. I assume you intend to use the proceeds of your share sale to buy back the fake stock before anyone figures out what happened."

"Bravo, Mr. Tyler," he says, clapping softly.

"You're delusional. The buyer's bound to figure it out, and when he does, you're going to jail, and you may take Katya with you."

"In a public sale of my shares, you'd certainly be correct. In a very quiet, very carefully negotiated private sale, with a counterpart who's extremely apprehensive about spooking me and thinks he's getting a bargain price from a tired old man, you'd be surprised. I'm not about to let Andrei, the regulators, or anyone else destroy my company," he says fiercely, voice suddenly booming in the cavernous room. "Turndale will become an independent subsidiary of a larger financial firm, with Katya at the helm. That's not a bad outcome for anyone."

Not a bad outcome. I stand up and walk to the gas fire, extending my hands for warmth. The flames barely throw any heat. Being forced to sell your family firm is like losing custody of a child. William's not telling me the whole truth, but I haven't got the time or inclination to work at understanding why.

"Let's get to the point," I say. "You don't want me to tell Katya, or anyone else, what I've learned. You want me to bury my evidence. So here's the deal. Katya's a friend of mine. I have to make sure she's protected. You provide me with a handwritten note saying you take sole responsibility for the cover-up, and detailing the steps you've taken to keep Katya ignorant, and I'll keep my mouth shut. If everything goes according to your plan, no one will ever be the wiser. If the shit hits the fan, I'll give the note to Katya and testify to everything I know."

"Interesting," he says. "Please." He touches the arm of the chair I vacated. "Sit."

"There's nothing more to talk about."

"There's always something more to talk about. You're looking for Andrei, aren't you? Sit."

I step forward uncertainly, wondering if he actually knows anything about Andrei's whereabouts.

"Earl," he says. "Turn that damned fire off."

Earl passes behind me as I resume my seat.

"I'm not making any deal that doesn't protect Katya," I say.

"Please don't try to anticipate me, Mr. Tyler," he says, leaning forward to catch hold of my forearm. "It's insulting."

I start to jerk my arm back, catching a flash of movement behind me. My left shoulder explodes in pain, my lungs exhaling involuntarily in a keening moan. I hear William speak over the roar of blood in my ears.

"The elbow, Earl."

I try to jerk away again, provoking a fresh bolt of pain from my shoulder. My elbow explodes, white-hot anguish blinding me with tears and paralyzing my chest muscles. I vomit black coffee and bile onto the shiny table and hear William speak again.

"Put him on the floor."

Earl catches hold of my hair and drags me sideways out of the chair. I fall heavily on my left side, unable to catch myself, and shriek at the impact.

"Be quiet, Mr. Tyler," William says. "Unless you want Earl to work on the other shoulder."

Earl's still got me by the hair, one sharp knee pinning my head to the floor. I open my eyes and see a black leather sap dangling in front of my face.

"I'm going to throw up again," I say, choking on the words.

"I doubt it," William says. "Everything usually comes up in one big gush. One reason it's a good idea to keep prisoners on a light diet. Considerate of you to have skipped lunch. Hit him again, Earl. We don't have his full attention."

"No," I shout. "I'm paying attention."

Both men laugh. I blink furiously, sweat running into my eyes. My arm feels as if it's threaded with molten wire from the elbow to the shoulder, the pain unbelievable.

"The question I'd like answered," William says, "is who else have you told about this?"

"No one."

Earl presses his forearm against my right shoulder, grinding the left side of my body into the carpet with his weight. I scream, fresh tears pouring from my eyes.

"Shh," William says. "Try again."

I can barely breathe, tears and mucus clogging my windpipe. If they listened to Katya's voice mail, they already know I visited Mrs. Zhilina.

"Katya's mother," I say. "She's the only one."

"You told her everything?"

"No," I say, trying to protect her. "Just that Andrei stole from you. Not how much, or what it meant to Katya or the company."

"Earl."

The sap catches me on the right hip, agony traveling through my pelvis and up my spine.

"It's the truth," I manage to gasp.

"Why tell her only half the story?" William asks.

"It wasn't any of her business. I just wanted her help finding Andrei."

"The nose, Earl."

"No," I shout as Earl cocks his arm. "I'm telling the truth."

"Wait," William says. He looks down at me, hands folded calmly in his lap. "Nothing more to add, Mr. Tyler?"

"No," I say piteously.

"Well," William says, pushing off the table to get to his feet. "Then I suppose we'll have to leave it at that for the time being. You're fortunate that Earl and I have other engagements this evening, Mr. Tyler. Consider this a warning. Stay out of my business, or I'll arrange for us to have a more lengthy chat, and you'll discover just how much of a prick I can be. Understand?"

"I understand."

"Good," he says. "Earl, show Mr. Tyler out, please."

Earl lifts me up, catches hold of my bad arm, and twists it up into my back, frog-marching me across the room as I try not to moan. A rear door leads to a service corridor. He summons a freight elevator, holding my head tight to the side of the cab as we descend. It's all I can do to stand. My reflection's visible in the dull aluminum doors, blurred and misshapen. It's a relief not to see myself more clearly, shame beginning to penetrate my shock. Dragging me from the cab on the ground floor, Earl uses my body to slam open a fire door, then pushes me into a dank alley.

"I got something for you," he says, releasing his hold on my hair. He slaps my temple hard enough to make my head ring, the folded visitor's pass fluttering to the ground. Grabbing my shoulders, he heaves me into the brick wall opposite the door, then stands over me as I slump to the ground.

"Sorry I touched you," he says. "I hope you had a nice visit."

He kicks my injured shoulder, and I descend into darkness.

29

JENNA AND I went skiing for my thirtieth birthday. I'd never snowboarded, and wanted to learn, so I took a morning lesson on the bunny slope. Two hours later, I linked three turns without falling and the instructor declared me a natural. After lunch, I rode the gondola up and started down a gentle intermediate run with Jenna skiing beside me. A few hundred yards farther, the hill steepened and I caught my heel side edge, falling backward and snapping my head into the packed snow like the tail end of a whipped towel. When I opened my eyes Jenna was cradling me in her arms, her hot tears falling on my face.

"I think I'm okay," I said groggily. The azure sky framing her looked like a warm sea miles away, and I had a moment of vertigo, feeling I might fall up into the blue. I struggled onto my elbows and the world righted itself.

"Why are you crying?" I asked.

"You hit your head so hard. You were so pale."

"You thought I was dead," I said, too dazed to process how upset she was. I stuck my tongue out and let my head loll, clowning.

"Stop it," she shouted, slamming me hard on the chest with both fists, like a child having a tantrum.

"Knock it off," I said, sitting all the way up and raising an arm to protect myself.

She was on her knees, hair hanging loosely around her face as her shoulders heaved silently, skis standing in the snow behind her.

"Jenna?"

I tucked her hair behind her ear with one finger, touched her chin, and turned her tear-streaked face to me.

"I was so scared," she said, her voice thick with emotion. "I felt so alone."

Waking up in the alley behind Turndale's building, my face pressed to the cold pavement, I think for a moment I'm back on the mountain with Jenna kneeling over me. I raise my head, expecting to see her. She's not there, and I suddenly feel so scared and alone that I let my head drop down onto the pavement and weep. My phone rings. Rolling painfully onto my back, I fumble it out of my pocket with my good hand.

"Yeah," I croak.

"It's Rupert," Mr. Rozier says. "Did I catch you at a bad moment?"

"No."

"I learned something interesting about that deposit in your friend's account. You might want to stop by later. The children are gone by seven-thirty. I'll be here until eight."

I can't lift my left arm, so I take the phone from my ear and read the time off the display. It's six-forty.

"I'll see you at seven-thirty," I say.

He says good-bye. I hang up and dial Tigger.

"Hello?" He sounds like he's on a speaker phone.

"It's Peter. Where are you?"

"Drivin' around Times Square tryin' to find a garage that doesn't charge forty bucks for two hours. Why can't you join a club that's got parking?"

"I'm in a jam," I say. "You mind picking me up?"

"Where are you?"

I lift my head again and look around, trying to get oriented.

"Forty-seventh," I say. "Between Sixth and Seventh. The north side of the street."

"Five minutes."

I let my head drop and lie motionless on my back. A rectangular swath of night sky shines with reflected light above the alley, low clouds gleaming golden with rose-colored highlights. It would be nice to fall up and away. Not yet, I tell myself, rolling to my stomach and inching my way up to all fours. Not yet.

30

"YOU DON'T WANT TO TELL ME what's going on, that's your business," Tigger says, steering with one hand and jabbing at me accusingly with the other. "But you should be goin' to the hospital."

"I told you. Nothing's broken."

"You could barely get in the car."

"I didn't want to get in your car. It's freezing in here. Who drives around with a busted heater in the middle of the winter?"

"Maybe I should buy a new car because the vent fan's broken?"

"Maybe you should get the thing fixed, you cheap fuck."

"They had to order a part. And don't change the subject."

Bantering with Tigger makes me feel a little better, even if my teeth are chattering. It's not just the heater. Tigger insisted on stopping by a Korean grocery after he picked me up, where he bought a jumbo bottle of Advil and paid a teenage clerk to load ice bags through the passenger window, packing my arm, shoulder, and hip like fresh fish. The throbbing's just about tolerable if I sit still, although I may freeze to death. I'm trying hard not to think about Earl and William laughing at me as I lay on the floor writhing in pain. I've got other scores to even first, but I hope like hell I have a chance to get to them.

Tigger pulls the car up in front of the library and double-parks. We sit quietly for a moment, watching a heavy black woman in a transit uniform lead a small, sleepy-looking boy down the steps. It's seven-fifteen.

"Seriously, Petey," he says. "What the hell is going on?"

"I told you. I'm trying to figure out who murdered Jenna."

"And you can't let the cops deal with it?"

"I'm working with the police, but there are other people mixed up in it. It's complicated. I can't tell the cops everything yet."

"And you can't tell me why not."

There's nothing I'd like better than to tell Tigger everything, but I can't risk talking about what Andrei's done until I can speak with Katya and make sure she's protected herself.

"Right."

"And what you can tell me sounds like a lot of shit."

"We've been through this already," I say, sighing loudly.

"Remind me who gave you that black eye? Oh yeah, I forgot, you fell getting out of bed." He mutters in Yiddish, the intonation obviating any need for a translation.

"So tell me why you were so excited when we spoke earlier," I say, wanting to distract him before he can get himself going again. "What happened?"

"You got a lot on your mind already," he says dismissively, waving the subject away.

"I could use some good news."

He stares through the window sullenly, probably thinking

to punish me by withholding information, the same way I'm withholding it from him. A familiar grin begins to creep over his face after a few moments, though, his thumbs starting a tattoo on the steering wheel.

"You sure you want to hear?" he asks.

Mr. Rozier won't be free for another fifteen minutes.

"Absolutely," I say.

He slips sideways in the driver's seat and grins, rocking a little bit with pleasure.

"You're gonna love this. My lawyer—"

"Your daughter, Rachel."

"Yeah, but I like sayin' it the other way. My lawyer spent the whole weekend goin' through your e-mail. For a woman who's the head of Human Resources at Klein, and a lawyer herself, Lemonde screwed up big-time."

"Eve?" I ask, enjoying Tigger's excitement. "I would've bet she never put a comma wrong."

"That she knew about."

"What do you mean?"

"Rachel understands this computer shit. She said that Eve didn't just send you and the rest of the Human Resources Committee regular e-mails. She sent you document files with all sorts of spreadsheets and stuff attached to them."

"So what?"

"Plain e-mail, what you see is what you get. But somebody sends you a file, like a Microsoft Word document, you get a whole bunch more. There's somethin' called metadata that tells you who wrote it, when they wrote it, and how long they worked on it. If there are spreadsheets attached, sometimes you can unlock them and see hidden data. And sometimes," he says, rocking faster, "you can go back and see any changes the writer might have made, like if she was workin' late at night on her home machine and feelin' pissed off. Things she wrote and erased, never expectin' anyone would see."

"No shit," I say breathlessly, caught up in his story. "What'd Rachel find?"

"The quarterly personnel reviews Lemonde sent out were Word files with attached Excel spreadsheets. The spreadsheets had all sorts of data hidden in them—employee names and addresses, and each person's age, sex, race, compensation history, hire and fire date. Everything. Rachel says it's like a road map to a class-action suit." He pauses and makes a disapproving face. "Klein really has a crap record with women and minorities. I was kind of shocked."

"Everybody on Wall Street's got a crap record with women and minorities," I say, my laugh at his naïveté cut short by a stabbing pain in my shoulder. "We spent all kinds of money on the diversity seminars you never went to because we were scared to death of getting sued. Just so we'd have some good facts on our side."

"I guess," Tigger says. "I never realized the numbers were so bad."

"You knew. All you had to do was look around. You weren't thinking about it."

"True." He stares over my shoulder for a moment, one hand tapping restlessly on his knee as he frowns. "Anyway, that's not all. A couple of weeks before you left—"

"Before I got canned."

"Right. A couple of weeks before you got canned, you and Lemonde went back and forth on promoting Keisha, because Lemonde didn't think she'd gone to a good-enough school."

"Like that should make any difference. Lemonde told me we weren't going to start promoting community college graduates to professional positions just because they were *cheerful*. She said the word *cheerful* exactly like she meant because they have nice tits. Pissed me right off. I checked out Keisha's school on the Web and found out they specialize in minority arts."

"Minority arts?" Tigger asks, an expectant grin lighting his face. "What are minority arts?"

"Face painting maybe. Learning to dance the hora. What the fuck do I know?"

"Good point," he says, sounding disappointed. "What the fuck do you know? Anyway, you must have sent a note to legal."

"Right. I asked if we could get in trouble for discriminating against graduates of minority-oriented programs, and I copied Lemonde. I figured it would burn her ass a little and put some pressure on her."

"She went fuckin' crazy," Tigger says, shaking his head excitedly. "You're not gonna believe it. You know the note she sent you back, sayin' she was gonna review Keisha's case again?"

"This is going to be good, right?" I ask, helping him build the punch line. Much as I'm enjoying his story, Lemonde and Klein feel like ancient history. Seeing Tigger happy feels good, though.

"Oh yeah," he says. "According to the metadata, she wrote it at two a.m. Friday night on her home computer. There's a whole paragraph she cut out, a rant against sneaky line managers—"

"That would be me."

"Right. A rant against you for 'subverting personnel policy by protecting geriatric staff with Neanderthal attitudes'—"

"That would be you."

"Stop interrupting. A rant against sneaky line managers who subvert personnel policy by protectin' guys like me and trying to promote—are you ready for it?"

"Hit me."

"A high yellow slut in a low yellow dress."

"No," I say, laughing disbelievingly. "Who would have guessed Lemonde could turn a phrase?"

Tigger's rocking so hard that the car's shaking, a huge smile plastered across his face.

"Rachel says Klein's completely fuckin' dead if any of this ever gets to a jury. A racial slur in a company document is the sound of a cash register ringing. The documents prove they've been underpaying, underhiring, and overfiring women, minorities, and people over forty, and their head of Human Resources wrote a memo denigrating seniors, blacks, and women. Rachel says they're so fuckin' dead, it's unbelievable."

"I still can't believe Eve wrote that," I say, laughing again.

Tigger shrugs.

"Accordin' to Rachel, it's a well-known fact that people write all kinds of stuff they'd never say. There's been shrinks doin' studies about it."

"Is Rachel going to be able to get any of this into evidence?" I ask. "Klein's bound to fight like crazy."

"Now I'm comin' to the good part," he says.

"*Now* you're coming to the good part?"

"It just keeps gettin' better," Tigger says, giggling like a child. "Rachel filed a motion with the judge this mornin' saying you'd joined the lawsuit and waived your privilege, and demandin' the e-mail be admitted. Klein's lawyers called half an hour later and asked her for a meeting. Rachel says they must have been expectin' our motion. They rolled over on *everything.*"

"What do you mean, 'everything'?"

"We got a choice. We can get rehired with back pay and seniority, or they'll pay us off for our 'emotional distress.' The openin' bid was two million bucks each. Rachel figures they'll go five easy, maybe more."

"Wow," I say, struggling to process the options. "And the quid pro quo?"

"What you'd expect. Nondisclosure agreements, we both give up all rights to any information we've discovered, et cetera, et cetera. And one more thing," he says, suddenly sounding sheepish. "If you want to come back and then you're convicted of ah, you know, a felony, they can force you to quit and pay you off."

"Sounds fair," I say, not wanting him to feel uncomfortable. "What about Eve?"

"Dead woman walking. Good riddance."

"So what do you think?"

"What do I think about makin' Eve Lemonde and Josh Kramer eat a shit sandwich? Are you kiddin' me? I got a woody like I just ate a whole bottle of Viagra," he says, grabbing his crotch.

"So you want your old job back?"

"Only if you do."

I look away. I was distraught when Eve fired me, not knowing what I was going to do with myself. I still don't know, but somehow I can't imagine going back to Klein. That incarnation of myself seems as remote now as a character in a novel.

"I've got to figure out what happened to Jenna first," I say quietly.

"So fuck 'em," he says quickly. "We'll take the cash."

"Is that what you want to do?"

"I'd ask you the same question," he says, "but then we'd sound like a couple of teenage girls tryin' to decide whether or not to get our muffs waxed."

"Sitting here right now, Tigger, all I can say is that I just don't give a fuck. About the job or the money."

"You feelin' a kung fu Master Kan 'snatch the pebble from my hand' type of enlightenment, or a George Bailey pre-Clarence kind of disillusionment?"

"I'm feeling like I'd pop you in the head if I could throw a punch," I say, smiling weakly at him.

"You really don't care?"

"I don't think so. Not now. Not while Jenna's killers are still out there."

"We could stick it to them," he says tentatively. "Tell Klein we're not gonna settle and give Rachel the go-ahead to start signin' up anyone she can for a couple of monster class-action lawsuits. It might be the right thing to do."

"Klein gets the e-mail excluded and it could turn into the wrong thing real quick."

"They get the mail excluded, they get the mail excluded," he says with a shrug. "That's the breaks. I meant the right thing to do like the *right* thing to do. The ethical thing."

"Ethics on Wall Street is only eating half the other guy's lunch when he goes to the can. You taught me that."

"And not bangin' your secretary on your wife's birthday," Tigger responds automatically. "Right. But what we got on Klein affects a lot of people. Maybe we should be thinkin' like fiduciaries."

"Fiduciaries?" I say, laughing. "A fiduciary is a guy—"

"Who gets paid a fee for fuckin' people," Tigger finishes.

"Stop quotin' me to me. All I'm sayin' is, maybe we should give it a few days. Let Klein sweat while we figure things out. Stallin' them can't hurt."

"Agreed," I say, offering him my good hand. "Listen. I'm feeling like I've got a chance of figuring things out. I'm looking for a guy and the cops are looking for a guy. Either one turns up and I might learn what really happened to Jenna. Then maybe I'll be able to think more seriously about what happens next."

"No problem," Tigger says. "Do what you gotta do. Where you sleepin' tonight?"

"Harvard Club, I guess."

"Shit," Tigger says, glancing at his watch. "I forgot. I asked Rachel to meet with us. She must be hangin' around the lobby there, steamin'. Tell you what. I'll go meet her and tell her what we've been talkin' about. You call me when you're done here and I'll come back and get you. You can sleep at my place tonight. I got some homemade chicken soup that'll fix you right up."

"Done." I open the door and try to climb out.

"Hang on a second." Tigger climbs out the driver's door and comes around the car to give me a hand. "You're a real mess. You're not gonna be able to get out of bed tomorrow."

"Which is okay," I say, leaning against the car as he closes the door, "because getting me out of bed will give you something to do with yourself."

"Right," he says, taking my arm. "You'll be doin' me a favor."

31

I'M SITTING IN THE SHABBY ARMCHAIR next to Mr. Rozier's desk, my feet propped on an open drawer and a couple of ice bags from the Korean grocer tucked around my body. Mr. Rozier enters the room carrying two steaming mugs and hands me one. Hot chocolate. I take a long, grateful sip, careful not to move any part of my body save my good arm.

"Your friend Mr. Meyer is right," he says, sitting down facing me. "It's foolish not to go to the hospital." He picks up a pencil and points the sharp end at my shoulder. "A joint injury can lead to arthritis. You get a built-in barometer like us old folks, learn what it's like to be living on thirty-two hundred milligrams of ibuprofen every day and slugging Maalox from the bottle so you don't burn a hole in your stomach."

"I'm going to be fine," I say. "They're just bruises."

"You must have got the common sense knocked right out of you."

"Thanks for assuming I had some. You said you learned something interesting about that deposit."

He touches the eraser to his chin, frowning as though he'd been sassed.

"Don't get me wrong," I say hastily. "I'm grateful for everything you've done, and I know you and Tigger are right that I should see a doctor, but I'm really anxious to find this friend of mine."

"Tigger?" he asks, lifting his eyebrows.

"Mr. Meyer. Tigger's his nickname. Because he bounces up and down a lot."

"I see," he says in a tone that suggests I'm concussed. "Well, about that deposit. You were right that there's no bank matching up to GPICCARDAG, so I ran the name through a search engine a couple of different ways and found an outfit called Galerie Piccard AG."

"Which is what?"

"An old-line Swiss auction house. Like Sotheby's. Furniture, paintings, antiques."

"You think my friend sold something at auction?" I ask doubtfully.

"A painting," he says, lifting a catalog from a stack of periodicals on his desk. The cover's a glossy reproduction of a Madonna and Child, Galerie Piccard printed in gold at the top. "I'll show you."

"Where on earth did you get that?" I say, amazed.

He flips through the pages, smiling.

"A friend of mine works over in Room 300 at the main library. They collect auction catalogs and results, among other things. I gave him the date and the amount of the deposit and he was able to identify the painting right away. Said it was the only thing that matched. He dropped the catalog off for me on his way home. Here."

Mr. Rozier holds up the open catalog. There's text in four

languages on the left-hand page and a color photograph of a painting on the right. I suck my breath in abruptly, startled.

"What is it?" he asks.

"I saw that painting," I reply wonderingly. "Just a couple of hours ago. Something in winter, by a Dutch guy, right?"

"The Village in Winter," he says, turning the catalog around again so he can read the text. "By Pieter Brueghel the Younger. He was Flemish, which mainly means Belgian. Where'd you see it?"

"At the office of Turndale and Company. That's where I was before I came here."

"Huh." He flips to the back of the catalog and examines some pages paper-clipped to the rear cover. "The buyer isn't listed, only the sale amount. Four point one six million Swiss francs before premium. The exact amount deposited in your friend's account."

"William Turndale told me a strange story," I say, feeling bewildered. "He said the painting had been part of a collection put together by the Nazis for some museum Hitler was planning in Linz."

"Right," Mr. Rozier says, lifting another periodical from his desk and handing it to me. It's a eight-year-old copy of *Time,* the cover a painted portrait of a woman in a white cloth cap, the light from an unseen window catching her face. The headline reads THE LINZ COLLECTION.

"The Brueghel auction was big news in the art world," he continues, "because the rest of the collection's never been seen again. People suspected the seller might know where the other paintings were." He taps the cover of the magazine I'm holding. "This is one of the Vermeers. There were two in the collection."

"So William Turndale told me. Who sold the Brueghel?"

"No one knows. The seller was listed as the estate of Frederic von Stern—"

My phone rings, interrupting him.

"Sorry," I say, apprehensive of missing a call from any of the people I've left messages with. I put the handset to my mouth. "Peter Tyler."

"I'm at the Harvard Club," Tilling says. "Where the hell are you? I told you to stay put so I could find you."

"I've been calling you all day," I reply heatedly. "Have you learned anything about Lyman?"

"Not on a cell phone. Tell me where you are."

"Nearby," I say, unwilling to have Tilling meet Mr. Rozier. She might well ask him what I've been up to, and I haven't figured out how much I want to tell her about Andrei yet. "I'll meet you there. Fifteen minutes."

"Don't be late," she says, hanging up.

"Something's come up," I say to Mr. Rozier, gingerly working my way to my feet. Learning what happened to Lyman is more important right now than figuring out how Andrei got hold of a missing painting. "I've got to go. Will you be here tomorrow?"

"I'm here twelve to eight, Monday to Friday. But hold your horses a second."

"You have something else?" I ask, trying a little cautious stretching. My left elbow and shoulder are still too painful to move, but my hip seems to have recovered some. I'm mobile enough to catch a cab.

"I do." He reaches to his desk and picks up a single piece of paper printed with smudged text. "This is from microfiche," he says apologetically, adjusting his glasses. "The von Stern who owned the painting was a professor of art history at Humboldt University in Berlin before and after the war.

Quite the grand old man, evidently. The Museum Conservation Institute at the Smithsonian published a testimonial to him on the hundredth anniversary of his birth, written by the senior conservator at the Uffizi, in Florence. Apparently, von Stern taught an entire generation of Europeans modern techniques of conservation. He mentions that von Stern was like a father to his students, and that he was known to them by a nickname." Mr. Rozier looks up at me and grins. "You care to guess what it was?"

"*Bon papa?*" I say, scarcely believing it's possible.

"Bingo."

"You're amazing."

"I'm a librarian," he says modestly. "You want to try that Luxembourg bank account again?"

"Please."

Mr. Rozier navigates the antique Apple laptop on his desk to the correct Web page while I struggle to assimilate the new information he's given me. One thought clicks immediately. Mrs. Zhilina is a conservator at the Met. I'd be willing to bet that she was once a student of von Stern's at Humboldt University. I knew she was holding something back.

"You have that account number and password?" Mr. Rozier asks.

I read them to him while he types. The Web site demands the answer to the secondary security question and he enters the name von Stern. A screen we haven't seen before pops up, a hypertext menu in French, with the bank's logo in the top right corner.

"We're in," he says.

My phone rings again and Mr. Rozier flaps a hand toward me amiably.

"Answer that if you want," he says. "I'm not in any hurry."

"Peter Tyler," I say distractedly, putting the phone to my ear again.

"It's Tigger," he whispers.

"I can barely hear you."

"Listen," he replies. "I'm at the Harvard Club. You expectin' to meet some cops here?"

"Yeah. Detective Tilling, the woman who was with Rommy at the funeral, and her partner, a short black woman. Why?"

"They're here," Tigger says urgently. "And they brought along about six friends. There's a couple of cops hangin' around the lobby pretendin' to read the paper, and a bunch standin' out front actin' like tourists. The manager threw a hissy fit a minute ago, said they couldn't be using their radios in the lobby because the club has a no cell phone policy. Hang on."

I feel a cold hand clamping my guts as I wait.

"Sorry," Tigger says a minute later. "I'm sittin' in one of the phone booths over by the coat check and there was a cop standin' right outside. You better find out what's goin' on before you come over here."

"I'll check it out," I say numbly.

"Call me back. I'll be waitin' to hear from you."

I hang up and stare at the phone in my hand, wondering why Grace would be lying in wait for me with half a dozen plainclothes police.

"Can I ask you for another favor?" I say to Mr. Rozier.

"Sure."

"I've got to make an urgent call. You read French. Do you mind having a quick look through that account for me? I'm interested in any recent activity that might help me figure out where my friend is."

"No problem. You need some privacy?"

"If you don't mind."

"I'll take my computer downstairs and work there," he says, getting to his feet and giving me a wink. "I'm kind of enjoying myself."

32

I SIT DOWN IN MR. ROZIER'S DESK CHAIR and dial Tilling's number on my phone, staring blankly at the crowded bulletin board over his desk while I wait for her to answer. I wonder what it means that Mrs. Zhilina might have been trained by von Stern, and that Andrei ended up with a painting that belonged to him. I'm feeling tired, confused, and beat-up. The guys in the London office used to send us Magic Eye puzzles, pointillist illusions that looked like NASA photographs of colorful star clusters until you'd focused your eyes the correct distance in front of or behind the image, at which point the mysterious patterns fused fleetingly into a brilliant three-dimensional representation of a tree, or a water-fall, or a horse at full gallop. Every fact I've learned recently is like a spray of colored dots in one of those puzzles, the sum an image I can't seem to resolve. I'd like some simple answers for a change. Tilling picks up on the fifth ring.

"Where are you?" she demands, her voice harsh in my ear.

"Delayed. Maybe we can talk on the phone."

"Maybe you can get your butt over here right now."

"Can't."

She smothers her handset, and I hear muffled conversation in the background.

"I'll meet you," she says. "Tell me where."

"Just you? Or you and all your friends?"

Five seconds tick by while I listen to her breathing.

"Something happened," she says. "I can't talk about it on a cell phone."

"This is about Lyman?"

"No. The city cops are working on him. Something different."

"About Jenna's murder?"

"Yes."

"What?"

"Not on a cell phone."

"I'm in a bad mood, Grace," I say, pissed off by her intransigence. "Give me a hint."

I hear more muffled conversation on her end.

"Call me back in ten minutes at the Seventeenth Precinct," she says, reciting the number. "You got it?"

"Yeah," I say, writing on a piece of scrap paper.

"Ask for me by name, and don't use your cell phone."

She hangs up. I hunch forward in Mr. Rozier's chair, burying my face in one hand as I try to imagine why she'd have so many cops waiting for me at the Harvard Club. Something's very wrong. It doesn't make sense that she wouldn't tell me anything on my cell phone. I'm spent, almost too tired to care.

Looking up, I see a faded copy of the Serenity Prayer tacked to the bulletin board, a wrinkled black-and-white photograph partially visible beneath it. I lean forward carefully and untack the prayer, revealing the picture. It shows a youngish Mr. Rozier on the front steps of the library, surrounded by smiling children. The kids in the front row are holding up a banner: THE HELL'S KITCHEN LIBRARY CELEBRATES NEGRO HISTORY WEEK. Signatures are scrawled along the edges. I touch the picture with my finger, feeling the indentations made by the children's pens thirty or forty years ago. Jenna would have liked Mr. Rozier; I'm sorry they never met.

My phone rings.

"It's Tigger. Everybody took off except the two cops hangin' out front. What the fuck is goin' on?"

"I don't know yet. Tilling and I are going to talk in a few minutes. Where are you now?"

"Across the street, in a bar."

"I should be done here soon. You mind picking me up?"

"I gotta gas the car first," he says. "I'll be there as soon as I can."

I dial Tilling a few minutes later at the number she gave me, still seated in Mr. Rozier's chair.

"Seventeenth Precinct."

"Grace Tilling, please. It's Peter Tyler calling."

The phone clicks repeatedly, sixty seconds elapsing before she answers.

"You're on a landline?" she asks.

"Yes."

"Mr. Tyler. This call is being recorded. You've previously waived your right to an attorney. Can you confirm that you're willing to answer some questions for me voluntarily?"

"What kind of questions?" I ask apprehensively.

"Is that a yes?"

"Tell me about Lyman first."

"I told you. The city police are handling it. No news."

I wonder if she's lying.

"Tell me why you were waiting to ambush me at the Harvard Club."

"After you answer my questions. You're going to want to know about this thing that happened, I promise. And you have nothing to hide, right?"

"How stupid do you think I am, Grace?"

"You want to know who murdered your wife?"

"You're saying you know?" I ask, her words propelling me to my feet. My hip aches, protesting the sudden movement.

"Now's the time to hang up if you don't want to talk to me," she says evenly. "It's your choice."

She's manipulating me. I'd tell her to get fucked if I weren't so desperate for information. I settle slowly back into the chair, realizing I'm going to rise to her bait. I want to know who murdered Jenna. Nothing else matters.

"What do you want me to tell you?"

"Everything you've done since you left the Marriott last night," she says. "Where you've been, when you were there, and who you've seen."

"It was a busy day," I say, hoping to get a better handle on what she's driving at. "Give me a tighter time window."

"Six to ten this morning."

"I was in bed at the Harvard Club until eleven-thirty. Asleep."

"Can anyone confirm that?"

"No," I say, resenting her implication. "I was sleeping alone."

"You slept late. Maybe someone called? Or a maid knocked?"

"The maid tried to open the door," I say, wondering if

she's questioned the staff already. "That was what woke me up."

"Tell me."

I briefly describe the maid's entry and my stumble out of bed.

"So you're injured?"

"A bruise. On my face. Why?"

"Any other injuries?"

"Nothing I can't explain."

"Is that a yes?"

"Next question, Grace," I say edgily. It sounds like she's trying to paint me into some scenario.

"Hang on." Her phone goes dead for a few seconds. "You lied," she says accusingly. "You're on your cell phone. You just blocked the caller ID."

"Why were you tracing my call?" I ask. "Does this have something to do with all the cops you had waiting for me?"

More silence. I knew it wasn't right that she'd objected to my cell phone.

"You're a clever guy, aren't you, Mr. Tyler?" Tilling says softly, venom audible in her tone. "Always one step ahead."

Her words are a slap, making it clear that any relationship I thought we'd built in hunting for Lyman is gone. She's just a police officer, I remind myself. It's only important that she help me find Jenna's murderer.

"If I were a clever guy, I wouldn't be talking to you at all."

"A few more questions," she says. "Then I'll tell you what happened. Did you travel to Westchester today?"

"No," I say, puzzled by the question.

"Do you know a man named John Franco?"

"Not that I recall. Should I?"

"Do you own a handgun?"

"Pass," I say nervously, thinking she might've searched my home and found my dad's gun.

"What do you mean, 'pass'?" she demands.

"I mean I'm not going to answer that question. Ask another."

"You want the DA to draw her own inferences?"

"Next question, Grace."

"It's Detective Tilling," she says. "Have you loaded or fired a handgun recently?"

"Pass again, Detective Tilling," I say icily.

"Did you pistol-whip a man named John Franco in his trailer home in Croton this morning?"

"No," I say, relieved by the absurdity of the charge. "Absolutely not. Why would you think I was involved?"

"Let me finish," she says. "Did you shoot Mr. Franco?"

"No."

"Did you hire or otherwise engage anyone to harm Mr. Franco?"

"No to all questions involving Mr. Franco. I don't know him and don't have any reason to want to hurt him. I wasn't involved in any way with anything that happened in Croton this morning. Tell me what this is all about."

"Someone dialed nine one one from Mr. Franco's home this morning and left the phone off the hook. Local cops responded. The place was pretty torn up, suggesting there might have been a fight. Mr. Franco was dead on the kitchen floor, a bullet hole in his head."

"I'm sorry," I say, trying to catch up. "How does this involve me?"

"Your name and office number were in his address book. Can you explain that?"

"What did this guy do?" I ask, searching my memory.

"Croton's not far from my place. Maybe he raked leaves for us once or did some odd jobs."

"He was a guard at the juvie center up in Wingdale."

"No idea," I say, mystified.

"Well, here's another interesting fact. We finally got the phone records from that number you gave us, the one Pongo got from Lyman. There are six calls between Lyman's number and Franco's home within forty-eight hours of your wife's murder."

My heart begins racing.

"You think Franco was the guy with Lyman when Jenna was murdered?" I ask shakily.

"We found locksmith tools in his trailer, and an open box of latex gloves. He's got a pair of boots that match some of the prints we took at your house. We're working on hair and fiber now. There's a good chance he's one of the guys."

Lyman murdered Jenna and Franco was his accomplice. I feel numb. I should be relieved to finally know the truth, but if Lyman's dead also, I've been cheated of my vengeance. And I still don't know who they were working for.

"I hope Franco suffered," I say, gripping my phone tightly. "I wish I'd killed him."

"You'd have been happy to beat and shoot him?"

"Absolutely."

"We found Franco's bank records," Tilling says. "He made a deposit the day after Jennifer was murdered. Five thousand dollars, cash."

"Someone paid him," I say, choking on my hatred.

"Possible," she says. "But I keep wondering. Why was your work number in Franco's address book?"

"I told you that I never heard of the guy. Maybe he had my details because Lyman gave them to him."

"Perhaps. Hopefully, we'll have a chance to ask Mr. Lyman at some point. Right now though, we've got to arrest Mr. Franco's murderer."

"You know who did it?" I ask breathlessly.

"We do," she says. "You did. You've got an hour to turn yourself in, Mr. Tyler. If you don't come forward, you're going to be the lead item on the eleven o'clock news tonight."

"That's what this is all about?" I demand furiously. "That's why you were waiting for me at the Harvard Club? I thought you had some brains, Grace. My number in his book doesn't prove anything. This is a Rommy move. This is the DA trying to look good on television. We've got to stay focused on Lyman. We need to find him, and we need to figure out who he was working for."

"I forgot to mention one final thing," she says ominously. "The shooter used an automatic pistol, and he didn't collect his brass. We got a fingerprint off the shell casing. Our forensic guy made a clean match. It's your fingerprint. You got an explanation for that?"

"That's not possible," I say, feeling as if I've been hit with a sledgehammer.

"One hour. And then every police officer in the state is going to be looking for you. We're describing you as armed and dangerous, and authorizing all necessary force."

33

I OPEN THE DOOR to Mr. Rozier's office in a daze and start down the stairs, clutching the handrail for support. I feel simultaneously weightless and leaden—my head buzzing while my legs drag like cement columns. Reaching the bottom of the staircase, I see Mr. Rozier sitting at one end of a long table in the empty reading room. He glances up as I limp toward him.

"You're looking peaked," he says, sounding concerned. "When did you last eat?"

"I don't remember," I reply, collapsing into the wooden chair next to him.

"I'll get you a candy bar," he says, standing up. "The girl at the circulation desk has a sweet tooth."

I've got to focus. Somebody set me up. But who? And why? Lord knows, I've got all the motive in the world to have killed Franco, and no alibi. Tilling's turned against me. If the police arrest me now, I'm likely to spend the rest of my life in jail.

"Here," Mr. Rozier says a moment later, reappearing with a Snickers. "Eat this."

I try to imagine my father's advice, but I can't hear his voice. An overwhelming urge to flee grips me.

"I've got to leave," I say. I have no idea where I'm going to go, but Tigger should be out front soon.

"Eat first," Mr. Rozier says, peeling the candy wrapper down like a banana skin and peering at me over his glasses. "Are you all right?"

"Sure," I say, trying to muster some bravado as I take the Snickers and bite into it. My mouth is parched with fear and the chocolate adheres to my palate.

"I printed out your friend's debit-card records," he says, sitting down and sliding a few sheets of paper toward me. "He used his card twice yesterday. Once at a Hess station on the Montauk Highway and once at a place called the Ocean View Inn, in Montauk itself. Figure he bought gas and then either spent the night or had a heck of a nice meal."

I pry the lump of candy loose with my tongue and swallow it whole, feeling as if I'm going to choke. Montauk's only about three and a half hours away, on the extreme tip of the south fork of Long Island. Can Andrei possibly be so close?

"I also took a look at his wire transfers," Mr. Rozier says. "He's been making some regular monthly payments recently. One of them is to an outfit called Empire State Warehouses. The reference field lists an address in East Hampton, near the airport."

East Hampton's about an hour this side of Montauk. Jenna and I rented a summer house near there once. I lift the papers and examine them, the words and figures neatly aligned. Mr. Rozier's listed all the transfers, and printed out driving instructions to the gas station, the inn, and the warehouse.

"I have to leave," I say again.

"You sure you're feeling all right?" he presses, looking at me uncertainly.

"Absolutely," I reply. Andrei's my one hope. I've got to drive out to Long Island and find him right now, before the cops pick me up.

"I'll see you out," he says. "It's started snowing, and those steps get slippery."

34

WIND-DRIVEN SNOW SWIRLS in my headlights as I cruise cautiously eastward on the deserted Montauk Highway. Lifeless McMansions planted in former potato fields line the road on either side, spectral deer triggering automated security lights as they drift from yard to yard, feasting on designer shrubs. Tigger's car is freezing. My hands are numb on the steering wheel. If it weren't for the seat heater, I'd have hypothermia. Tigger gave me his keys reluctantly, arguing I wasn't in any condition to drive and insisting he'd be happy to come along. I was abrupt with him, too anxious to get out of the city to explain myself.

I've got the radio on low, tuned to an all-news station. An electronic chime strikes eleven o'clock and a breathless female anchor reads a press release from the Westchester DA, which describes me as an armed fugitive wanted in connection with two murders. Civic-minded citizens are given a number to call if they see anyone matching my description and are warned that I'm dangerous. The announcer promises a live interview with the DA at eight o'clock tomorrow morning. Adrenaline surges through my system, and it's an effort not to speed as my lower brain begins screeching danger like a tripped fire alarm. I switch the radio off shakily, overcome yet again by a sense of unreality. How did my life ever reach this point?

Tigger's car phone rings, making me jump. I turned my own phone off, fearing the cops might track my signal. The phone rings six times, falls silent, and then begins ringing again. It's got to be Tigger, calling for an explanation of the news report. I press the answer button on the steering wheel reluctantly, unable to bear the jangling any longer.

"I can't talk now, Tigger."

"Peter?"

I guessed wrong. It's Katya.

"How'd you get this number?" I ask, surprised to hear her voice. Much as I don't want to discuss Franco's murder, I'm glad she's called. I might not have the chance later to tell her what she needs to know.

"From Tigger."

"How'd you know to call him?"

"He's the only friend you ever talk about," she says tiredly. "Where are you?"

"In his car," I say.

"Funny. And where is that?"

"Long Island. Where are you?"

"Chicago. At the Four Seasons. The airport shut down with the weather, and I can't get home until tomorrow. Pick up the handset."

"Can't. I'm driving one-handed. I hurt my left arm earlier."

"Badly?"

"Just bruises."

"I've had kind of a rotten day, too," she says, slurring her words slightly. So far, it doesn't sound as if she knows I'm a fugitive.

"Did you get my voice mail?" I ask.

"No," she says. "Only an e-mail from Debra saying you'd called, and an urgent message from my mother. She wanted me to phone her before I spoke with you. Why?"

It makes me feel a little better that she called me before contacting her mother.

"I went to see her when I couldn't get through to you. I told her that I knew why Andrei had been fired."

She swears under her breath. "Tell me."

I start to speak and then hesitate. Katya's an executive officer of Turndale. The more she knows, the fewer degrees of freedom she'll have.

"It might be better if I did this as a hypothetical—with no names and no details."

"Is it that bad?" she asks, understanding instantly.

"Yes."

Ice chinks against glass on Katya's end of the phone as she steels herself.

"Go ahead, then," she says crisply.

"Suppose a senior manager at a publicly traded investment firm began using the company's money to purchase securities he'd counterfeited. Suppose the amounts became so big that it threatened to destroy the company's reputation and business."

"I can't believe a senior manager would do that," she protests.

"Suppose the senior manager had personal investments that weren't working out. He might have borrowed a little money and played the market, trying to get even. He might have gotten unlucky."

Katya's silent. The well-intentioned embezzler is an all too familiar figure in the financial world, a trusted employee who fiddles a few bucks to cover a pressing need, pays it back, and then fiddles some more, with every intention of making full amends even as the "borrowed" sums grow vastly beyond his means to repay.

"If the senior manager were fired, though," she says slowly, "say because the head of the company figured out what he'd done, then the head of the company would be legally obligated to call in the regulators and make a clean breast of it. The fraud would become public knowledge."

"Maybe the head of the company isn't willing to accept the consequences. Maybe he's decided to cover up the fraud, thinking that as long as no one else knows what's happened, he can sell his shares in the company for a premium price and then use the proceeds to make good the hidden loss."

There's another, longer silence.

"I'm hanging up," she says. "I have to get hold of William."

"Wait. I've already spoken to him."

"When?" she asks, sounding confused.

"Earlier today. He intercepted my voice mail to you and had Debra invite me to your office. We met in the Turndale boardroom and he confirmed everything."

"William's been monitoring my voice mail?"

"Since Andrei disappeared. You've got to be careful, Katya. He's dangerous."

"Don't exaggerate," she says sharply. "This is disastrous enough as is. Whatever William might have done, he's not a thug."

I don't want to upset her any more than I have to, but she has to appreciate what she's up against.

"William has a big guy named Earl working for him. A former cop?"

"Ex-FBI. Why?"

"William was keen to persuade me to keep quiet about what I'd learned. Earl helped. That's why I'm driving one-handed."

"You're saying Earl hit you?" she asks incredulously.

"At William's instruction."

"Jesus. Are you all right?"

"I'll live," I say, unwilling to admit how hurt I am.

"Give me a minute."

I hear the click of her handset being placed on a hard surface and then the sound of running water. The snow's falling more heavily now, and I fumble with the levers on the steering column, trying to make the wipers go faster.

"I'm back," she says.

"You okay?"

"How I feel isn't the issue," she says tersely. "What are you doing out on Long Island?"

"I got a lead on Andrei."

"Peter. Listen to me. I want you to go home."

"That's not an option any longer."

"Don't argue with me," she pleads. "It was wrong of me to get you involved. I've been a coward. I should have confronted William myself."

"I'm glad you didn't. Because if William or Earl hurt you, I'd have to do something about it, and that would really mess up my plans."

"Is that supposed to be funny?"

"Not in the least."

A silvery fox comes into view, trotting along the shoulder with something limp hanging from its mouth. I swing the wheel left, giving it a wide berth.

"Peter . . ." She sighs. "Take my word for it. You don't have to worry about William or anyone who works for him hurting me."

"But I do. Nobody's going to believe you weren't a part of this unless you're the one who blows the whistle. You've got to get a lawyer and open a line to the regulators. Tell them you don't know anything for sure but that what you do know has you concerned."

"It's not that simple."

"It is that simple," I insist. "Your only responsibility is to yourself."

"What about Andrei?"

"You can't cover for him. It isn't right for you to put yourself at risk."

"Is that really what you believe?"

Her question hangs in the ether between us. I don't know what I believe right now.

"I think this is all going to come out one way or another," I say, managing to avoid a direct answer. "It's only a question of whether or not you survive it."

"And Andrei?" she asks, not letting me off the hook.

"The best you can do is be there to help him pick up the pieces."

"But what if the head of our hypothetical company is right? What if he can make good the loss without the regulators or anyone else being the wiser?"

"Don't you get it, Katya? William has everything on the line here—his company, his wealth, his reputation, and his freedom. This is a desperation move: I wouldn't put anything past him at this point. You've got to protect yourself."

"I told you," she says. "He'd never hurt me."

"Are you fucking kidding me?" I demand, mystified by her certitude. "He's been listening to your voice mail. He . . ."

Headlights reflect in my rearview mirror. A cop's turned in behind me.

"Hang on," I say.

The police car follows me as I creep through the empty downtown district of Bridgehampton, trying not to go too fast or too slow. My heartbeat's at least 160, and the steering wheel feels alien in my grasp. The cop takes a right at an intersection and I exhale loudly in relief.

"Katya?"

"I'm still here. What was that about?"

"Nothing," I say, wiping my face on the sleeve of my coat.

"Why did you go see my mother?"

"Don't try to change the subject."

"I don't know that I am."

I pause for a second, not following her. A sign looms through the snow, indicating the Easthampton Airport a few miles ahead on the left.

"Just tell me," she says.

"Okay," I say, explaining to her about the Luxembourg bank account as succinctly as possible. "I visited your mother to ask if she knew who the *'bon papa'* Andrei's security question referred to was. She said no, but then later I figured out that it was a guy named Frederic von Stern. Have you ever heard of him?"

"He was my mother's professor when she was at university," she answers, her voice difficult to read. "Her mentor. How did you figure it out?"

I tell her about the painting, and Mr. Rozier's knack for research. "What I don't understand is why your mother would have lied to me."

"You've heard me talk about her over the years. Why did she ever lie?"

To conceal the identity of Andrei and Katya's father.

"You're not suggesting that von Stern was actually . . ."

"No," she says, laughing mirthlessly. "The little she told us about our father was true. He was an American she met when she was a student in East Berlin, studying under von Stern. Think. You're almost there."

One quadrant of the inscrutable puzzle I've been wrestling with abruptly resolves, the linkage between certain facts breathtakingly obvious.

"William Turndale," I say. "He was in Berlin with the army when your mother was there, and he was interested in art. He and your mother might have met."

"They did. And he helped her escape to the West, and he supported our family when I was little, and he arranged for my mother to be hired by the Metropolitan Museum. And then, when I was twenty-one, he sought me out and offered me a job."

"Because he's your father."

"He is."

Stunned as I am, it occurs to me that this may put an entirely new spin on things. Maybe Andrei wanted to wound the father who never acknowledged him, and William covered up the theft to protect his son. Imagining Andrei vengeful is as difficult as imagining William selfless, but people don't always think clearly when family's involved. Regardless, they've both put Katya in an impossible position.

"When did you figure it out?" I ask.

"I didn't." She pauses, ice rattling again on her end of the phone. "Ever since I was a teenager, I'd suspected that my mother was still in touch with my father. There were too many things that didn't add up. My mother worked for the Met as a conservator, but she raised us in a nice town house on the Upper West Side of Manhattan. She sent us to good private schools, and bought us expensive clothing, and took us to Europe on vacation. It was obvious that someone else had to be paying the bills, and who the most likely candidate was. I used to follow my mother around the house, shouting at her, demanding the truth. But I never considered William as a possibility until a few months ago. Andrei sent me a letter right before he vanished."

"That's incredible," I say, still trying to read her mood. "What did the letter say?"

"Just that William was our father, and that I should tell our mother I knew and ask her to explain the details."

"Did you?"

"Did I what?"

"Tell your mother you knew."

"You've got to be kidding me. I wouldn't give her the satisfaction. That's one reason I've been so keen to speak with Andrei, to learn the rest of the story."

"Then why did you tell your mother about us?" I ask, the question slipping out before I can catch it.

"I never," she responds vehemently. "Did she say something?"

"She referred to our 'liaison.'"

"The only person I ever mentioned anything to was Andrei," she says, sounding embarrassed. "I wrote him an e-mail late one night, when I was upset because I couldn't reach him. He shouldn't have told her."

"It doesn't matter," I say, wondering if Katya's e-mail

explains why Andrei never reached out to me after he fled. "And none of this changes anything. You've still got to look out for yourself."

"You're wrong, Peter. Don't you see? This is about my family. My brother embezzled from my father, and I'm the one who has to decide what to do about it."

"Katya—"

"Don't," she says, her voice breaking. "Everyone I love has betrayed me, Peter. Even you. But that doesn't mean I can turn my back on them."

"I'm sorry," I say helplessly.

"If you're really sorry," she says, "if you really want to do something for me, then please just go home and let me sort this out myself. At least I'll know you're safe."

"I wish I could," I say, not wanting to tell her there's nowhere safe for me now.

"I'm serious, Peter," she says pleadingly. "Please."

"I can't."

"There's a lesson here, isn't there?" she says, her voice fading. "I can always count on you to let me down."

The phone clicks and she's gone.

35

THE CAR'S TWICE AS COLD AND EMPTY after Katya hangs up. I'd give anything to be able to call her back and set things right, but it's not fair to burden her with my problems tonight, and I can't explain away what happened between us. Her accusations hit home. I hurt her, and I let her down.

It was less than a week after I raised my hand to Jenna in front of the shrink's office. One of the Gulf State embassies was hosting a reception for their finance minister, and Katya and I bumped into each other in a banquet room done up like a petro sheikh's tent, ivory silk panels draped from an ornate gilded frame and ice sculpture of oil tankers. We drank champagne and gossiped about the market and mutual acquaintances until a military band began playing a medley of Andrew Lloyd Webber, half a dozen silver flutes shrilling "Memory."

"I don't care how good the food is," Katya whispered, polishing off a caviar-laden blini. "We've got to get out of here."

We ended up at the Harvard Club. A solitary barman polished glassware and willed the clock toward midnight while

Katya and I sat at a corner table in the near-empty lounge, sipping whiskey and gambling at backgammon. Moth-eaten taxidermy and portraits of long-dead Fellows stared down from the walls as she twirled her dice cup pensively.

"I'm going to fall asleep—this game's too slow. What do you think about a little craps before we call it a night? Say a hundred bucks a pass?"

I laughed.

"What?" she demanded teasingly. "You don't know how to play?"

"I know how to play. It's just that I don't think of craps as a girl's game."

"'A girl's game,'" she repeated, mock sternly. "I hope you're trying to piss me off, because I'd be disappointed to learn you're so clueless."

"Forgive me," I said, laughing again. "It goes without saying that you'd play."

"Hmmm." She leaned back in her chair and folded her arms. "That felt kind of backhanded. You think of me as one of the guys?"

Katya was wearing a black linen dress scooped low at the neck, with an elaborately embroidered white shawl draped loosely over her shoulders. Her outfit probably cost more than my entire wardrobe, but it was still easy to picture her in the jeans and boots she'd worn the first time I'd seen her. Nothing about her had changed.

"Never." I nudged her knee with mine. "You're beautiful. I've always thought so."

"Ha. I'm just Andrei's sister to you."

"There goes your clairvoyant act," I said, alcohol and unhappiness making me reckless. "Even married guys have fantasies."

"Thanks, I guess," she said, giving me a small smile. She upended the dice cup on the board and tapped the bottom ruminatively, as if conjuring a combination from the dice hidden within. "I always wondered what would have happened if we'd met before you and Jenna."

I felt my perspective lurch as Katya's words settled. The last few days had been rough. Jenna had barely spoken since our fight, and I wasn't sure there was anything left to say. Maybe Jenna had been right all along. Maybe it had been a mistake for two people as different as we were to have gotten together.

"I'm sorry," Katya said, misinterpreting my silence. "I've said the wrong thing."

"You haven't."

"I have," she insisted. "I should go."

She stood, gathering her shawl around her as I wrestled with the implications of my thought: If Jenna and I really are done, if this is the end of my marriage . . .

"Stay," I said. "I can get a room here."

Katya was quiet for a long moment, her eyes lowered.

"I haven't got any use for pity."

I stood up and moved toward her until our bodies were almost touching. I could feel her breath on my neck as I bent forward to speak softly into her ear.

"I admit to being confused right now, but I know I want you. Pity doesn't enter into it."

"Confused about what?" she asked, barely audible.

"Confused about us. I've wanted you since the night we met," I said, hearing the truth as I spoke it. "I couldn't let myself own up to it before, but things are different now."

"Andrei told me that you and Jenna were having trouble," she said, looking up at me. "He said you were trying to work things out. You have to understand, Peter. I can't let myself get between you."

I wondered fleetingly how much Andrei had told her. It didn't matter. An instant's hesitation on my part and Katya would be gone.

"You won't be. It's over between me and Jenna. We're going to separate."

It didn't feel like a lie at that moment. My hands hung heavily as I waited for her response. I didn't dare reach for her. Katya dropped her eyes again and then leaned toward me very slowly, her head coming to rest on my shoulder.

"Then let's go upstairs," she said.

I woke to a dark bedroom. The shower was running, and enough light leaked through the blinds to see that it was morning. My first thought was of Jenna. I hadn't called to tell her not to expect me. Angry or not, she was bound to be worried.

A fuller realization of what I'd done crashed over me like a wave and I sat up, panicked. I knew how hurt and humiliated Jenna would be if she found out I'd spent the night with Katya, regardless of our estrangement. My infidelity would finally prove me exactly the selfish prick she'd never wanted to marry, all my promises false.

The shower fell silent, prompting a second surge of panic. I had no idea how to handle things with Katya. The bathroom door opened and a blaze of light dazzled me.

"Hey," Katya said. She had a white towel wrapped around her body, damp shoulders gleaming. I couldn't make out her expression. "When'd you wake up?"

"A few minutes ago."

"The amenity kit only had one toothbrush, and I used it. I hope you don't mind."

"Not at all," I said, attempting a smile.

There was an uncomfortable pause.

"I understand that you must be going through a difficult time," she said. "Last night doesn't have to be anything more than it was. No harm, no foul, okay?"

"I guess," I said, feeling a pang completely at odds with my guilt.

"You guess." She twisted her hair into a loose braid and tossed it over her shoulder. "I'm standing here in a towel, Peter, with wet hair and no makeup. Could you say a little more than 'I guess'?"

"You're beautiful," I replied, falling back on truths I felt confident of. "I meant what I said in the bar. I've always wanted you."

"I never doubted it," she said, shaking her head ruefully. "Self-esteem's not my problem. But if last night was just about you feeling lonely, then there can't be an encore."

Her voice quavered the tiniest bit as she finished, and she shifted nervously on bare feet. The logic of the previous evening reasserted itself: Jenna wasn't going to forgive me. My failings with her were no reason to wound Katya. I stood up naked and walked across the room, my hand rising to catch the top of her towel.

"Don't," she said, her gaze locked on mine.

"What if I want an encore?"

I backed toward the bed, gripping her towel tightly. She followed stiff-legged, as if ready to bolt. I kissed her as we reached the bed and she kissed me back, tentatively at first and then more firmly. She untwined my fingers from the towel and pressed my palm to her chest. Her heart beat furiously beneath the rough cloth.

"I trust you, Peter," she said. "You understand that, don't you?"

"I do," I said, consumed by desire.

She unwrapped the towel and let it drop.

The air-conditioning kicked on sometime later, the breeze cool on my exposed shoulders and chest. Katya lay snugged against me, one arm and one leg draped over my body. I shivered as perspiration evaporated from my skin.

"Are you okay?" she asked.

"I'm great," I said reassuringly. "How are you?"

"Kind of overwhelmed, but happy. I've got to get going, though."

My hand wandered below her waist.

"Stop." She laughed, squirming away from me. "I have a meeting." She sat up on the bed. Raven hair and dusky nipples contrasted with marble skin, fine blue veins chasing her breasts. "What about you? Are you busy this morning?"

"Nothing Tigger can't cover."

"You're lucky to have him."

"Most of the time. Tigger's like family, which is good and bad. He won't keep his nose out of my business, and he's always got an opinion."

"Are you going to tell him about us?"

"Not right away," I said carefully.

"Does he know that you and Jenna are splitting up?"

"I haven't had my coffee yet, Katya," I said, uneasy about where the conversation was heading. "Maybe we could meet for a drink later."

She hesitated a moment before nodding.

"I'll check my schedule and give you a call." She kissed me and got out of bed, lifting her towel from the floor. "I have to get cleaned up again."

Her hand was on the bathroom door when my cell phone rang. The phone was on top of the desk, immediately to her left. She picked it up and glanced at the display.

"It's Jenna," she said, looking stricken.

The ring was piercing in the quiet room. Katya tossed the phone to me underhand and I fumbled at the controls on the side, trying to mute it. The resulting silence seemed very loud.

"I'm sorry," I said finally.

"Don't be. I needed a wake-up call." She wound the towel around her body again and came back to sit down on the edge of the bed. "Later isn't good enough, Peter. I need to know exactly what's going on between you and Jenna."

"Irreconcilable differences," I said, pretending a composure I didn't feel. "Isn't that the phrase?"

She held my gaze for a long moment.

"You're moving out?"

"I'm not sure exactly."

"Why not?"

"Because we haven't got it all figured out yet." I sat up against the headboard, trying to tug the bedclothes high enough to cover myself. The blanket was pinned by her weight.

"You said you were separating."

"Give me a break here, Katya," I said edgily. "I told you last night that I was confused."

"Not about Jenna," she replied instantly. "You said it was over between you."

"It is," I said, trying to sound convincing. "We just haven't talked it all out yet."

I reached out to touch her leg. She caught my hand by the wrist and held it.

"Answer a question. What will you do if Jenna asks you to stay?"

"She won't."

Katya's grip tightened.

"But if she does?"

I didn't know the truth and couldn't brave a lie. Much as I wanted Katya, it was impossible to imagine turning my back on an appeal from Jenna. Long seconds ticked past. Katya lifted my hand from her leg and pushed it away.

"Let me tell you what I think," she said, her voice shaky. "Jenna's angry and you're hurt, so you took me to bed to punish her and to make yourself feel better."

"You're wrong," I insisted. "I'll figure things out with Jenna tonight and call you tomorrow."

"Don't bother."

"This is an argument about nothing," I said pleadingly, reaching toward her again. "Jenna isn't going to ask me to stay."

She slapped my hand away hard and stood up, her face contorted with anger.

"How flattering. You're desperate to be with me, but you need to check that your wife's done with you first. Well let me tell you something, Peter: I've never been anyone's second choice for anything, and I'm not about to start now. I trusted you, and you lied to me. I don't want you to call, and I don't want you to come around. You've hurt me enough already."

36

I TURN LEFT at a second sign for the East Hampton Airport and begin driving slowly north along a dark, winding, snow-covered lane. The road bumps over a railroad crossing and dead-ends opposite a service entrance to the airport. The gates to the airport are chained, the buildings beyond the fence dark. An ice-encrusted sign identifies the narrow perimeter street as Industrial Way. According to the directions Mr. Rozier printed for me, Andrei's rental property is just down the street to the right. Dimly lit low-rise structures are visible through sickly stands of scrub pines as I creep eastward, looking for street numbers. I spot Andrei's and pull to the curb.

This is a dangerous place for me to be. A wealthy, underpopulated resort town like East Hampton is bound to be overpoliced by bored cops, and simply being here at this hour makes me appear suspicious. I'd consider spending the night elsewhere and coming back in the morning if I could figure out where I'd be safe. Easing forward a few feet to get a better look down Andrei's driveway, I see fresh tire tracks in the snow. Indecision vanished, I pull into the parking lot in front of the building, leaving the car in a dark corner.

Trudging back to the driveway, I kneel to examine the tracks with the penlight I used in Andrei's apartment. I can't tell if they were made by a vehicle coming or leaving. Turning the light off, I move toward the building, a long, sparsely windowed sheet-metal structure, and pause fifty feet from a loading door on the far end to take stock. There's no sound save the wind whistling through the trees. I step forward tentatively. A bell clangs in the distance and I see red lights flashing a few hundred yards off. Heart in my throat, I spin toward the car, realizing even as I turn that it's only the railroad crossing gates signaling an oncoming train.

My relief is short-lived. There's a man standing right behind me. I jump backward, off balance, and lose my footing, falling heavily on my injured side. A hoarse groan escapes my lips. The figure above me is ghostly in gray-white camouflage, monocular night-vision goggles strapped to his face. He's holding an automatic rifle, which is pointed at my chest.

"Get up," he says in guttural, accented English, motioning with the gun.

"I'm a friend of Andrei's," I say, trying to sound calm as I struggle to a seated position.

"Get up," he says again, prodding me with his boot. "Now."

A train whistle sounds in the distance and he turns his head toward it. The penlight is still in my hand. There's a chance that this guy works for Andrei, but that's no reason to put myself at his mercy. I turn the light on as he looks back to me, pointing the beam directly into the lens of his goggles. He recoils immediately, blinded by the glare, and I roll to my right, simultaneously kicking out hard with my left leg. My instep connects solidly with his knee and he collapses sideways, shouting with pain. I lunge for his gun one-handed as he falls. A sharp blow makes impact at the base of my spine, sprawling me facedown in the snow. Another blow finds my kidney. Curled up in anguish, I see a second camouflage-clad man standing above me, an upended rifle in his hands. He lifts the gun again, the butt aimed toward my head, and it occurs to me that I might be about to die. Light spills from a door in the side of the warehouse before he can strike, and a voice shouts something incomprehensible. The man standing over me lowers his rifle with a furious expression and drags me to my feet. He manhandles me toward the warehouse, agony hunching me like a geriatric. Looking up as we approach the door, I see a big guy in blue coveralls framed by the light. Vladimir. Shit.

The train roars past just before we reach the door, a few warm, sleepy passengers visible through brightly lit windows. None looks my way. Vladimir grabs my shoulder and jerks me into the building, using my momentum to spin me face-first into the adjacent wall. The sound of the train fades in the distance as I lean heavily against the wall, wondering what I've gotten myself into.

"No moving," Vladimir says, reaching from behind to unbutton my coat and strip it off roughly. He searches my clothing and then grabs me by the collar, dragging me backward into a folding chair.

"Sit," he commands.

Two more big, impassive-looking guys with flat Slavic features are in the room with us. They're both wearing blue coveralls like Vladimir's, and they're both holding guns. I rest my good arm on my knees, attempting to catch my breath as Vladimir and the man who hit me head back out into the snow, most probably to attend to the guy I kicked. Looking around, I see that I'm in a small cinder-block office, the gray concrete floor littered with cigarette butts and the air heavy with smoke. A battered steel desk, a couple of folding chairs, and a small ceramic heater are the only furniture, and there's a cardboard panel duct-taped across the sole exterior window. The door opens again and Vladimir reenters alone.

"You're a big fucking difficulty," he says, shaking a cigarette loose from a pack on the desk. He strikes a match, the flame revealing indigo shadows under his eyes and several days' stubble on his face. "My opinion is to shoot you."

"Have you shot Andrei?" I ask, affecting a calm I don't feel.

"You understand nothing," he says dismissively.

"I understand that Andrei's missing and a couple of guys looking for him murdered my wife. Maybe you can tell me more."

"You know what this place is?" he asks. "What is to happen here?"

"All I know is that Andrei's paying the rent. Is he here?"

Vladimir turns his head to one of the other men in the room, repeating the word *rent*. The other man responds with a single word of Russian.

"Rent," Vladimir says. "Yes. How do you know this?"

"Go fuck yourself," I say, my voice shaking. "I want to talk to Andrei."

"E'b tvoju mat," he growls, sitting on the desk. He runs one hand over his shaved scalp. "Who is knowing you are here?"

"Where's Andrei?"

He takes a cell phone from his pocket and squints at the keypad, dialing with his thumb. I hear the faint tinny whisper of someone answering. He begins speaking in Russian, saying my name twice. My legs tremble as I wonder who he's talking to and, more urgently, whether he's seeking permission to act on his opinion and shoot me. He says *"da"* repeatedly and then hangs up.

"You stay here tonight," he says, dropping his cigarette on the floor and rising to crush it with a boot. "We are down one man because of you, so you will help with our doing. If you are a difficulty, you will be hurt. Tomorrow, I tell you where to go to see Andrei."

"Why should I trust you?" I ask suspiciously, relief at the prospect of living to see Andrei mixing with apprehension at the thought that Andrei and Vladimir might still be working together.

"Because I am not shooting you," he says irritably. "Which is a much easier doing."

I can't fault his logic.

"What do you want me to do?" I ask.

"Come," he says, moving to the door. "I show you."

37

THE DOOR OPENS into a vast hangarlike room with rust-streaked metal walls and blacked-out windows. Heat roars from exposed HVAC ducts overhead, making it difficult to hear. There are three step vans parked at the south end of the building, and four long A-frame racks constructed of light lumber extending toward the north. Each rack is at least fifty feet long, and all four are hung with paintings, like a low-budget art show at a National Guard armory. I have an oblique view of landscapes, still lifes, portraits, and religious scenes, some framed ornately, others frameless. A painting in the third rack from the left catches my eye. It's a moderate-size oil of a seated woman wearing a white cloth cap. The Vermeer that was on the cover of the *Time* magazine I saw in Mr. Rozier's office.

"These are the Linz paintings," I say wonderingly.

Vladimir puts two fingers in his mouth and whistles loudly toward the vans, not bothering to reply. I take a step toward the paintings and he jerks me back roughly by my good arm.

"No tourism," he says gruffly.

Yet another man in blue coveralls emerges from the back of a truck, and Vladimir shouts a few sentences of Russian at him.

"What's going to happen here tonight?" I ask.

"Something or nothing," Vladimir says peremptorily as the man from the truck walks toward us. "No more questions. This is Lev. You do what he says or you have big fucking trouble."

Lev's carrying two automatic weapons and a spare pair of coveralls. He hands the guns to Vladimir and then helps me slip the loose-fitting jumpsuit over my clothing, easing my bad arm through the sleeve with surprising gentleness after I wince. Vladimir removes the banana clip from one of the weapons and strips the bullets out, putting the loose shells in his pocket. He waits for Lev to zip me up before slinging the unloaded weapon over my head, lifting my bad arm to rest on the barrel.

"Good," Vladimir says. "Now you are looking like Rambo."

His cell phone rings. Glancing at his watch, he hands Lev the loaded weapon and walks off a couple of steps to take the call.

"Why the coveralls?" I ask Lev quietly. He looks at me with a baffled expression. I pinch the blue fabric at my chest and pull it away from my body. "Why?"

"Ah," he says. "To know who not to shoot."

"Will there be shooting?"

Lev smiles enigmatically, looking distinctly less gentle. Vladimir hangs up the phone, unclips a walkie-talkie from his belt, and begins barking urgently in Russian.

"Come," Lev says, beckoning to me. "It is time."

———

Vladimir stands alone and unarmed on the ground floor as the loading door lifts, cold air rushing into the building. Lev and I are on a black metal catwalk suspended from the ceiling, ten feet above the floor. There are five of us spread along the catwalk, all with weapons held at port arms. More than enough to massacre whoever comes through the garage door, if that's the intention. Lev's just behind me, his tension palpable. A tractor-trailer backs slowly into the building. Lev flips the safety off his weapon. My heart's pounding wildly and I realize I'm holding my breath. I gulp cold air as three men climb down from the truck's cab. No one's begun shooting yet. Vladimir touches a button on the wall and the loading door begins to close.

Two of the men walk quickly to the rear of the truck, the third joining Vladimir. The man speaking to Vladimir is a big guy wearing jeans and a black sweater, his face hidden by a blue baseball cap. The air rushing from the HVAC system drowns their words, but the body language seems civil enough, a quick handshake preceding a discussion that seems to be about logistics, both men gesturing to various points in the building. The man in the cap looks up at the catwalk, his face clearly visible. I recoil instinctively into Lev as I recognize Earl.

"What the hell's going on here?" I whisper to Lev.

"A trade," he says, shoving me away with his gun butt. "Be quiet."

The catwalk's well shadowed, and Earl's gaze drifts past me without any show of recognition. Despite Earl and Vladimir's outward amiability, Lev still has his weapon in a ready position, trigger finger extended and resting against the guard. Two more men emerge from the rear of the truck. All four begin unloading equipment—chairs, tables, tripod-mounted spotlights, computer monitors, and an assortment of other gear—and assembling it next to their vehicle with Earl's and Vladimir's help. Cables snake everywhere. Snatches of conversation are audible over the roar of air handlers as the men call to one another, speaking in French. Lev and I patrol silently overhead.

A Frenchman wearing a sleeveless sweater begins a slow tour of the racks, consulting a thick notebook as he examines individual canvases. He pauses in front of a large landscape, tucks his notebook under his arm, and claps loudly, attracting Earl's attention. Earl and Vladimir walk to where he's standing, unhook the landscape from the rack, and carry it to a table. Two of the other Frenchmen deftly remove the frame. One begins scraping delicately at an exposed edge of the canvas, collecting the shavings in a small dish, while the second maneuvers over a wheeled scanning device of some sort, taking direction from a third man seated in front of a computer monitor.

It looks like the men with Earl are vetting the paintings, checking to make sure they're genuine before they trade for them. I glance toward their truck. If this is a trade, I'm wondering what Earl's brought as payment.

Hours pass. The man with the notebook selects about one painting in ten for examination. Earl and Vladimir bubble-wrap the paintings he's passed over and the paintings his colleagues have already examined, stacking them against the far wall of the warehouse, near the tractor-trailer. I'm exhausted, mentally and physically, and my body aches all over. I've pissed in a bucket at the far end of the catwalk twice, my urine red with blood.

The racks are finally empty, all the paintings wrapped.

Earl and Vladimir wait awkwardly at a remove while the Frenchmen confer quietly. Lev watches hawklike, his trigger finger tapping restlessly against the gun's guard.

The man with the notebook turns to Earl and gives him a thumbs-up. Earl takes a phone from his pocket and makes a call. Three long minutes later, Vladimir's phone rings. He answers, listens, and hangs up. Earl and Vladimir shake hands as Lev flips the safety on his gun and lowers the barrel to the floor.

"That's it?" I ask. "What happened?"

"The trade," Lev says.

"What trade?" I ask. "What did you trade for?"

Lev frowns. "No questions."

The Frenchmen break down their gear while Vladimir and Earl load the paintings into Earl's truck. Half an hour later, the loading doors close behind the departed tractor-trailer, and the Russians break out in a ragged cheer. Lev and I join the others in the small office, where Vladimir produces a bottle of iced vodka and hands out cigarettes. Russian chatter and blue smoke surround me. Lev insists I drink a toast with him, the fiery liquor burning my throat. I wait for the merriment to subside and then approach Vladimir.

"Can I go now?" I ask anxiously.

"Soon," he says, looking at his watch. "We go first. You wait fifteen minutes and don't follow."

Following's the last thing on my mind.

"Where's Andrei?"

"You go to the Ocean View Inn," Vladimir says, stubbing his cigarette out on top of the desk. "In Montauk. Dr. Anderson is there."

"Emily's there?" I ask, surprised.

"*Da,*" he says. "She will take you to Andrei."

38

MY HEAD NODS and I jerk awake, checking my watch. Vladimir and the others left only ten minutes ago, but if I sit in this smoky office much longer, I'll fall asleep. I stagger out into the cold and see the morning sun hanging low on the horizon, the parking lot washed with plum-colored light. Teeth chattering and body protesting, I make my way to Tigger's car. The frozen metal burns my fingers as I unlock the door, but the engine starts instantly, a good omen. A crystalline rooster tail of snow flies from the trunk as I accelerate out of the lot. I haven't got many options at this point. If Andrei can't help me, my choices are to surrender to the cops and pin my hopes on Tilling to uncover the truth, or to finish the job I was too cowardly to complete at my breakfast table.

A flagman waves me to a stop as I approach the airport access road. Braking impatiently, I avert my face, pretending to search for something on the passenger seat. There's bound to be a picture of me in today's paper. Three hard taps sound against the passenger's window, startling me. I look up and see Earl smiling through the glass. He's still wearing his baseball cap and black sweater, but now he has a gun in his hand. He motions with the barrel for me to lower the window.

"You looked good in a jumpsuit," he says, smirking. "From what I hear, you'll be wearing one with a number on the back before too long."

"What do you want?" I ask, my brain racing. I ease up on the brake pedal, steeling myself to mow down the flagman. I might be able to race clear before Earl can get off an accurate shot.

"An hour of your time. To speak with Mr. Turndale. He's at his house in Southampton, about fifteen minutes from here."

"I can't do it right now," I say flatly, looking into the barrel of his gun. "I've got to be somewhere."

"I'm sorry," he says, lowering the gun. "I didn't realize you had another engagement. I'm sure Mr. Turndale will understand. Ralph, move away from the front of Mr. Tyler's car there."

The faux flagman steps aside, inviting me to proceed with a flourish.

"That's it?" I ask uncertainly.

"Sure," he says, shrugging. "Tell you what. I'll even wait a couple of minutes before I call the cops and give them your license plate. Just to make things sporting."

Earl grins while I think it over. There's no way I'll make it to Montauk if the police know I'm in Tigger's car.

"The cops might be interested in hearing what you and your boss have been up to," I say.

"Yesterday," he says dismissively, "you might have had some leverage. We're past that now. So make your choice."

It's clear he isn't going to negotiate.

"What does William want to talk about?" I ask.

"I'm sure he'll tell you. One hour. Yes or no?"

As with Vladimir, the strongest argument for Earl's sincerity is the fact that he hasn't shot me yet.

"An hour," I reply. I can call the Ocean View Inn on Tigger's car phone and tell Emily I've been delayed. "No more. I'll follow you over."

"That's very considerate of you," he says sarcastically. "Mr. Turndale will be grateful. It might be better, though, if I rode with you. Just to make sure you don't get lost."

I hesitate. Objecting will only make him more insistent, but I can't risk calling Emily with Earl in the car. William can't learn that I've found Andrei.

"Come on," Earl says, trying the door handle. "Open up. I'm freezing my ass off out here."

I touch the button to unlock the doors, accepting defeat.

"Why's it so cold in here?" Earl asks as he swings the door shut.

"I hadn't noticed," I say. "Feel free to turn on the heat."

Earl fools with the climate controls for a few minutes and then gives up, shivering violently all the way to Southampton. I don't tell him about the seat heaters. William's house is a shingled mansion on an oceanfront street, the drive secured by electronic gates and the front yard screened by high hedges. Earl shows me to a hexagonal room dominated by an elaborately carved wooden desk. Three glass walls front the ocean. The floor's bare, the half-height bookcases lining the remaining walls empty. Exposed picture hooks and rectangular patches of unbleached paneling suggest absent paintings.

"It looks like William's moving out," I say.

"Wait here," Earl says through bluish lips. "Mr. Turndale will be right in."

There's no phone on the desk, and I don't want to turn on my cell, for fear of being tracked by the signal. I sink into an upholstered armchair facing the sea, my legs aching. White-caps roil blue water beyond the surf line, early-morning sunlight reflecting off the spray. I wonder what William traded for the paintings and why he wants to talk to me. I'm too tired to be scared. My head lolls, the sun warm on my face. Closing my eyes, I drift into unconsciousness.

"Mr. Tyler," a voice says.

I start awake to see William seated behind the desk, the sun blazing over his right shoulder. He's wearing a navy turtleneck and a charcoal sweater, his sleeves pushed up to reveal surprisingly powerful forearms.

"Sorry to wake you," he says, lips curling up to reveal his long yellow teeth. "But I understand you're in a hurry. Would you like some coffee?"

Someone's put a serving tray on the desk between us. I lean forward, fill a china cup, and drain it in a single long pull.

"Help yourself to more," he says. He removes a bottle of aspirin from a desk drawer and sets it down next to the cof-feepot. "You might want a few of these also. I must say, you look terrible."

I refill my cup and then struggle with the childproof cap on the aspirin bottle. William's solicitude makes me uneasy, but I'm beyond affecting any kind of stoicism. I extract four aspirin and wash them down with the hot coffee.

"To business," he says. "I have three questions for you. Much as you may dislike me, you'll answer my questions,

because you don't want me to call the Southampton police.
Agreed?"

I tip my cup toward him, conserving my energy.

"Good," he says. "First. What were you doing with the
Russians last night?"

"I found the warehouse address in one of Andrei's files,"
I say, instinctively concealing my access to Andrei's bank
account. "I figured it was worth a look, so I drove by last
night, and that's when the Russians grabbed me. They didn't
want to take a chance on my telling anyone they were there."

"What do you mean, you found the address in one of
Andrei's files?" he asks, looking troubled. "What kind of file?"

"It looked like a 'to do' list. Call this person, call that person, go to the bank. And the address."

William ruminates for a second and then shakes his head,
as if clearing a dissonant thought.

"Something's not quite right about that story, Mr. Tyler,
but it isn't worth pursuing at this point. Consider that a warm-
up inquiry, more in the way of idle curiosity. Now I'd like the
truth. Katya phoned me late last night. She sounded distressed, and demanded we meet. I gather you spoke to her."

"She called me," I say warily.

"You told her what Andrei'd done?"

William warned me to stay out of his business. I look
toward the door, wondering where Earl is. Another beating
and I won't be able to drive.

"Circumstances have changed since we spoke yesterday,"
William says impatiently. "It doesn't matter to me if you told
her. I only want to know how she reacted."

"She was upset," I reply, not completely following. "What
do you mean?"

"Was Andrei's theft news to Katya? Or did she already know?"

His voice catches on her name, and everything suddenly becomes clear. The arrogant old prick can't bear the thought that Katya might've been involved in Andrei's betrayal.

"You'd know better than I," I reply disdainfully. "You've been spying on her, haven't you?"

"True. But she's very smart."

"A chip off the old block?" I ask, unable to resist the jab.

"Ah," he says, leaning back in his chair and looking at me shrewdly. "You have been busy, haven't you, Mr. Tyler? And where did you come by that particular bit of information?"

"What bit of information?" I ask lamely, belatedly realizing that I've revealed too much. The caffeine's worked through my empty stomach near instantaneously, loosening my tongue and making me incautious.

"Don't play the fool," William says, staring at me intently. "How did you learn that Katya's my daughter?"

"She told me," I reply, trapped by my own carelessness.

William gets up and walks to the windows, hands clasped behind his back as he stares out to sea.

"How long has she known?"

"Only a few months," I say. "Why didn't you ever tell her?"

"A détente," he says cryptically. "An arrangement I regret. And now I'd like the answer to my original question. Did Katya know that Andrei was stealing from me?"

"Of course not. You shouldn't have to ask that question."

"True again," he says quietly, surprising me with his agreement. "It was foolish of me to suspect her."

He's silent for a moment, the only sound the surf booming against the beach outside.

"Well," he says finally, turning from the windows and resuming his seat at the desk. "On to my last question, which is more in the way of a request, or a favor, if you will."

He must be kidding me. I wouldn't do him the favor of pissing on him if he were on fire.

"A favor that benefits Katya," he says, reading my face correctly. "The next couple of weeks are going to be very difficult for her. She's in for some rough water, and I won't be there to help her. I'd like you to explain some things to her on my behalf."

"The next couple of weeks are likely to be very difficult for me," I say, incredulous at his presumption. "Or haven't you read the papers?"

"I know all about your problems, Mr. Tyler. I also know you care for Katya. You made that clear yesterday when you insisted on her protection as the price of any deal with me. There's no one else I care to confide in right now, and you already know most of the story. I'm sure you'll find some way to communicate with her."

"What kind of rough water?" I ask, feeling a sense of trepidation on Katya's behalf.

"Several kinds, actually," he says calmly. "I transferred my shares in Turndale to a Swiss escrow agent yesterday afternoon, and then released them to the Russians last night, after the Linz paintings passed muster."

"You can't do that," I object immediately. "You're holding control stock. The minority shareholders are going to go crazy."

"There's nothing in the company charter or our governing law to prevent me," he says, waving a hand airily. "And the minority shareholders will have other things to worry about."

"Because you have no intention of making good Andrei's loss," I say, abruptly understanding his actions. "You're going to keep the paintings for yourself and let Turndale go bankrupt."

"Exactly." He bares his teeth again as he grins. "That's why it was so important to me to make sure you hadn't told anyone what Andrei did. I didn't want the Russians to learn the shares were worthless before the exchange."

39

ONE OF TIGGER'S FAVORITE TRADING PARABLES is a description of his first business trip to London. He woke up Monday morning raring to get to the office, looked left as he stepped off the curb in front of his hotel, and woke up three hours later in the emergency room at Charing Cross Hospital, a victim of the reversed traffic pattern. A passing truck's side-view mirror caught him squarely in the side of the head, and would have killed him if the mount hadn't been spring-loaded. "The more experience you get," he used to tell our trainees, "the more you're gonna start makin' assumptions about how things work. And the more assumptions you make, the more likely you are to wake up in a hospital with your clothes cut off and your wallet gone for a walk."

Gazing at William's smug smile, I realize I've been guilty of any number of assumptions recently, the most foolish being that William might have been acting to protect his son.

"It's hard for me to believe that you care very much about what happens to Katya."

"It's a surprise to me as well," he says genially. "But I do. She's been very loyal. So I've provided for her as best I can."

"Provided for her how?"

"In several ways," he says. "Our conversation today is one of them. I want her to understand what I've done. As to the rest, I've lodged certain exculpatory documents with Turndale's lawyers. Katya will have more than enough evidence at her disposal to exonerate herself of any involvement in Turndale's demise."

I slug down two more aspirin with the remains of my coffee. It occurs to me that Andrei's no worse off than I expected and Katya's likely in a better position.

"So you traded a bunch of worthless stock to the Russians for a priceless collection of stolen art," I say acerbically. "That's quite a coup. Of course, you won't just have the SEC trying to put you in jail for fraud now; you'll also have the Russians sizing you for a pine box."

"Great men leave their mark by performing great deeds," he says with satisfaction. "And great deeds are rarely achieved without risk."

"I wasn't aware fraud qualified as a great deed. Perhaps you've confused a mark with a stain," I reply evenly.

"You're here to listen," he says sharply, bonhomie vanished. "If it's talking you're interested in, I'll have Earl call the police."

I stare silently, wishing I were in a position to give him the kind of beating Earl gave me yesterday.

"As a young man, I decided that my life's work would be to accumulate an unparalleled collection of art, a collection that would enable me to endow a spectacular personal museum, on the order of the Frick, or the Gardner. I came close to achieving my objective once, but the opportunity slipped away. I eventually resigned myself to the notion that Turndale and Company would be my legacy. Andrei's theft came as a nasty shock. But then, just when things seemed darkest, fortune smiled on me, and the opportunity I'd missed in my youth reemerged. Turndale and Company will fail, but Turndale House—my museum—will survive."

"My recollection is that the Linz paintings were stolen," I say, beginning to wonder about his sanity. "Don't you think that might become an issue for Turndale House? Say about sixty seconds after you open the front doors?"

"An excellent point," he says, placing the tips of his fingers together. "Let's think about my situation logically, shall we? The American government will want to prosecute me for securities fraud, the Russians will be after my head, and—as you implied—any number of private individuals, not to mention Western European governments, will sue Turndale House for recovery of their art. And then there are the Israelis. They seem to get their noses into everything. I'll need protection from all of them. What would you do in my position?"

"Shoot myself."

"I despise flippancy," he says curtly. "Try again."

"I wasn't being flippant. That was my best idea."

"How disappointing. I might as well be talking to Earl, save that his suggestion would have been to shoot someone else. Name an interested country that isn't afraid to say *no* to America."

It only takes a second. "France," I say, intrigued despite myself.

"Exactly," William says, treating me to one of his lizardlike winks. "If you're forced to take a partner, it's important to make sure your interests are aligned. Imagine how enticing it was to the Gallic mind when I suggested they could simultaneously recover their own lost art, seize control of their neighbors', and thumb their nose at the United States. Altogether a trifecta, from their perspective. The negotiations were a snap. They even offered me a Légion d'honneur. Sub rosa, of course. As if I'd want a medal from a nation of greasy cowards."

"The international pressure is going to be tremendous," I say, caught up for the moment in his fantasy.

"I have a few tricks up my sleeve. Turndale House will be located in Saint Barths, in the Caribbean. It's technically part of France, but just separate enough so the French can play both sides of the street, simultaneously advocating adherence to international law and ensuring no judgments are ever enforced. There will be a thousand small, irresolvable points, endless discussions of jurisdiction, title, theories of owner-ship, and so forth—the kind of bureaucratic obstructionism the French really excel at. And all the while, they'll quietly promote the notion that, after all, the paintings are in a museum, they're being well looked after, and they're accessi-ble to scholars. I've even agreed to let the hoi polloi in from time to time, although I'd have preferred not to. Small accommodations will be made, token payments, concessions in unrelated areas, that sort of thing. My personal museum will endure."

"And your own deal?"

"Full immunity from extradition or seizure of assets, and round-the-clock protection. Security's much easier to manage on an island."

"You know the French will give you up in a heartbeat if it gets too hot for them, no matter what they've promised you."

"I've documented their complicity," he says casually. "They understand I won't go down quietly and know that I've taken steps to protect myself in the event of an unexplained accident."

"Congratulations. You've planned for everything. Too bad

Katya has to pay the price. She'll stay out of jail, but the scandal will end her career."

William closes his eyes and sighs, deflating like a rooster unpuffing, his shoulders sagging.

"I've done what I could for her."

"Done what you could?" I repeat scornfully. "You've ruined her."

William half-rises and slams one hand flat on the desk.

"You think I want my father's company bankrupted?" he says, spitting the words at me like stones. "My daughter tainted by scandal? Turndale will founder, and I'll be vilified, but Katya will escape any formal censure. It's the best result I could achieve."

"You're running away and leaving her in the lurch."

"Wrong, Mr. Tyler," he says, sinking back down into his seat and smoothing his sweater. "You're running away. I'm running toward something."

I don't respond, figuring I've already pushed him too far. I glance at my watch, wanting to go.

"We're almost done here," William says, in control of himself again. "I'll be leaving the country later today. I've written Katya a note, but certain things are better communicated face-to-face. Your role is to fill in the gaps."

"I don't think she's going to be very sympathetic," I say contemptuously.

"Katya's like me. She's smart and she's ambitious. When she thinks it all through, she'll appreciate why I took the steps I did. The only real mistake I've made was to hire Andrei. I fault myself for that. I should have known better."

"You should have known better why?"

"Because he was queer," William says, an expression of loathing on his face. "My son. I learned about his sexual

preferences when he was away at school. That's why I
recruited only Katya out of college. It was a rule in the intelligence community never to employ homosexuals. They can't
be trusted. When he came to me for a job a few years back,
though, I let sentiment sway my judgment. The moral here is
never to compromise your principles."

The moral is that egoism justifies anything.

"One final thing," he says, staring at his hands. "I've
reserved the right to name my successor as chairman of Turndale House. I'd be happy to name Katya in a few years time, if
she's interested."

"How sweet," I say, thoroughly sick of him. "You'd like to
buy back Katya's love with the directorship of your inter-
nationally reviled museum."

"Sarcasm's as tedious as flippancy," William says, his voice
assuming its previous hard tone. "Is there a point you'd like to
make?"

"Katya's never going to forgive you."

"It's a funny thing," he says, looking directly at me. "I've
never given a damn for people. Visit the Met some weekend—
hundreds of ignorant tourists coughing and sneezing all
over masterworks, each one imagining how many color
TVs they could buy if they owned a single painting. I despise
them. Blood's thicker than water, though, a commonplace I
began to understand only once Katya came into my life. It's
unexpectedly exhilarating to see yourself in another person.
Magical almost. Katya's free to disdain me, but I won't give up
on her."

My dad used to say that all the time, that blood was
thicker than water. He also used to say that blood will out,
that breeding tells. I stand up and feel faint, my vision narrowing tunnel-like, until I seem to be looking at the room

from a distance. I shake my head, trying to regain my perspective.

"There's nothing of you in Katya," I say.

"It's time for you to go," he replies, touching something on the underside of his desk. The door opens and Earl beckons, my coat over his arm. "Good-bye, Mr. Tyler. I don't expect we'll be meeting again."

40

I STAGGER LIKE A DRUNK on the short walk to Tigger's car, too exhausted to concentrate on anything more than placing one foot in front of the other. The caffeine buzz has given way to a thudding headache, and I've got an odd metallic taste in my mouth. It's all I can do to get the key in the ignition. Earl sees me off with an amused expression, his parting words a mocking admonishment to drive safely.

As soon as I've driven a few blocks, I pull over to dial the Ocean View Inn on Tigger's car phone, not trusting myself to attempt it while moving. The numbers on the keypad seem much too close together. Emily's checked in, but she's not answering the phone in her room. A mumbling front desk clerk refuses to look for her in the breakfast room, and makes me repeat my eight-word message three times. Christ.

The clerk's directions are to follow the Montauk Highway until it ends. My head's nodding again, and I open all the windows, hoping the cold air will keep me alert. Black road stretches interminably in front of Tigger's car—staying in the correct lane and maintaining a constant speed require complete concentration. I feel like I'm driving through a child's primary-colored nightmare: white earth, blue sky, yellow sun, and an unseen enemy lurking.

It's just before ten when I finally pull into the Ocean View's parking lot. The porch stairs leave me gasping, my feet seemingly far beneath me. I push the front door too hard and it slams against the wall. The clerk, three people at the desk, and a woman in a high-backed chair by the fire all turn to stare. The woman in the chair is Emily. I've never been so relieved to see anyone. She rises as I enter and takes my hand.

"You look terrible," she says. "You've got no color at all. What happened to you?"

I try to shrug, wincing as my bad shoulder protests.

"Come with me," she says. "I want to take a look at you."

She helps me up a flight of stairs and into a low-ceilinged bedroom with plank floors and faded brown wallpaper. A desk, a wardrobe, a nightstand, and a four-poster bed are the only furniture. I sit on the edge of the bed and assist passively as she strips off my clothing, too done in to feel embarrassed. Unloading medical equipment from a pink-and-orange shoulder bag, she takes my blood pressure, listens to my heart, and palpates my abdomen.

"You've got some nasty hematomas on your arm and shoulder," she says. "Did you get hit in your torso?"

"Kicked," I say.

"Have you vomited any blood? Or passed any blood in your urine or stool?"

"Urine."

"Have you taken any painkillers?"

"Aspirin, about an hour ago."

"How many?"

"A bunch."

"That's bad," she says. "Aspirin's an anticoagulant. You've

got some internal bleeding, and you're a little shocky. I'm going to call an ambulance."

"Don't," I say, grabbing her hand. "The police are looking for me."

"I'm a doctor," she says. "My first job is to look after your physical health. Shock's very tricky. You could even die."

"I'm just tired."

"Your fingernails are blue, your skin's pale and clammy, your pulse is elevated, and your blood pressure's low. Don't tell me how to diagnose."

"Please," I say. "The cops think I killed a guy named Franco. If they find me, I might never have the chance to clear myself. I need to speak to Andrei."

"You're hallucinating," she says, freeing her hand easily.

"I'm not. Read the papers. I just need some time with Andrei. Please."

Her face reels in and out of focus, eyes narrowed and skeptical beneath a furrowed brow. Her hair smelled sweet when she bent forward to listen to my heart, like a newly mown field. Jenna had a poster of a Wyeth painting in her room at college, the one of a young woman half-lying on a grassy hill, looking up at a house on the rise above her. I used to imagine myself on that hill with her, the two of us surrounded by tall grass, a warm breeze carrying the scent of the earth.

"Peter," Emily says sharply.

"What?" I ask, confused.

"Get in bed. Now. Go to sleep. I'll keep track of your vitals. If you take any turn for the worse, I'll have to call an ambulance. I can't take proper care of you here."

"I need to talk to Andrei first," I protest, my voice sounding far away.

Emily turns down the quilt on the bed and takes me firmly by the arm.

"Sleep," she says, guiding me into bed. "Andrei's nearby, and he's not going anywhere. You'll see him later."

There are any number of questions I want to ask her— about Vladimir, about Davis's accusations, about Lyman. She tucks the quilt around me and caresses my forehead gently. Her pillow smells like flowers. My eyes close of their own volition, and I spin down into the dark.

41

I HALF-WAKE to a banging on the door.

"Come back later," I shout, thinking I'm at the Harvard Club.

"Open up, Peter," a woman's voice demands. "It's Tilling."

I kick the covers away, panic-stricken, and move instinctively to the window. It's almost full dark and there's a Suffolk County Police SUV parked on the beach, red lights flashing. I'm fucked. Tilling knocks again.

"Come on, Peter," she says. "Don't make us kick the door down."

I undo the dead bolt. Tilling and Ellis are in the hallway, a tall policeman hovering behind them. I'm surprised they don't have their guns drawn.

"How'd you find me?" I ask, my desperation audible.

"The desk clerk said you lurched in this morning looking like a bum. He saw your picture in the afternoon paper. Running was stupid." Her eyes flick over my body. "Nice boxers. Ugly bruises."

"You mind if I get dressed?"

"You mind if we come in?"

"If you want." She's only asking to mock me.

"Wait here," she says to the tall policeman as she and Ellis enter. Ellis shuts the door and leans against it, glaring. Tilling takes the desk chair. They're both dressed as they were two nights ago, Ellis in her Patagonia outfit, Tilling in her army parka. The room's crowded with three of us in it. I open the wardrobe opposite the desk to look for my clothes, self-conscious about being watched. My left arm's still useless, and I have to sit on the bed to get my legs in my pants.

"Who beat you up?" Tilling asks.

"I'm not going to make any statement without my lawyer."

"There's a note here," Tilling says, lifting a sheet of paper from the desk. "Signed by someone named Emily."

"That's none of your business," I reply weakly, knowing they can go through my things at will now.

" 'Back at six,' " she says, reading. " 'Vitals stable. Don't exert yourself.' "

She holds the note up so Ellis can see it. Ellis pulls a compact digital camera from her pocket and photographs it, the flash blinding.

"Get a couple of his bruises also," Tilling says.

Ellis turns the camera to me and snaps some more photos. I'm not in a position to refuse.

"So," Tilling says, setting the note down. "Is Emily the one we've been looking for? The woman you were cheating on Jennifer with?"

"She's not involved," I say angrily. "I only just met her. She's a doctor, working in Moscow."

"Pretty quick work. You must have quite a way with the ladies."

"You enjoy taunting me?" I ask, standing to buckle my belt.

"I'll tell you what I'd *enjoy,* Peter," Tilling says vehemently. "I'd *enjoy* your answering some questions. Just once, I'd like to think a conversation with you isn't going to be a complete waste of time."

Her phrasing catches me up short. "What do you mean, 'conversation'?" I ask. "You're here to arrest me, aren't you?"

"Maybe," she replies evenly, glancing at Ellis.

"I don't understand."

"There's a chance you might be able to buy yourself some slack here. But you have to talk to me. Right now."

It's difficult to temper the sudden surge of hope I feel. I've got to be careful; I want to believe there's a way out, and Tilling's more than clever enough to take advantage of that vulnerability. I sit back down on the bed, slipping on my shirt, and try to look less fraught than I feel.

"You can ask a few questions," I say. "No promises, though."

She takes a tape recorder and a small notepad out of her pockets, turns the recorder on, and sets it on the bed between us.

"Detectives Tilling and Ellis questioning Peter Tyler at the Ocean View Inn in Montauk, New York. December tenth, five twenty-three p.m. Mr. Tyler, you've previously been read your rights. Do you remember those rights?"

"Yes."

"And do you waive counsel at this time?"

"For now."

"Do you know Anthony Rommy, formerly a detective with the Westchester County Police?"

"Yes. What's Rommy got to do with anything?" I ask, feeling wrong-footed.

"Just answer my questions, please. When did you last see Mr. Rommy?"

"I don't know. A month ago maybe. In a car outside my house."

"You didn't see him after that?"

"No."

"Do you know anything about Mr. Rommy's movements or activities during the last twenty-four hours?"

"No. He called me three or four days ago and said he was in Brunswick, Ohio, where I grew up. That's the last time I heard from him."

Tilling makes a note of Brunswick.

"Have you paid or otherwise encouraged anyone to surveil Mr. Rommy's movements or activities at any time in the last three months?"

"No. I had a private investigator check the guy out before my wife's funeral, but that was it."

"Do you know anyone interested in hurting Mr. Rommy?"

"Yes. Just about everybody who ever met him, including me and you. Why are you asking about Rommy?"

"Do you know anyone with a specific intention to harm Mr. Rommy?"

"No."

"Can you tell me where you were yesterday between the hours of eleven a.m. and seven p.m.?"

"Yes."

She waits expectantly and then sighs.

"*Will* you tell me where you were yesterday between the hours of eleven a.m. and seven p.m.?"

"No," I say, hope dissipating. Nothing good is going to come from this line of questioning. "Not right now. But I was with people. Different people. I've got a solid alibi for pretty much the entire time."

"Are you familiar with a rest area between exits fifty-one

and fifty-two on the Long Island Expressway, in the town of Huntington?"

"Maybe. I don't know. I don't spend much time on Long Island, but I'm sure I've driven past it."

"A trucker found Mr. Rommy in a cardboard box at that rest area last night, dead. Do you know anything about his death, or have any idea who might have killed him?"

I open my mouth to express shock and then close it. Tilling's been playing me. She's going to arrest me for both Franco's murder and Rommy's.

"Well?" Tilling says. "You want to make a statement?"

"I do," I say quietly. "And then I'm done talking. I had nothing to do with Rommy's death. I had nothing to do with Franco's death. And I didn't kill my wife. That's it. Now go ahead and arrest me."

"Don't be in such a hurry," Tilling says, turning off the tape recorder and pocketing it. "Officially, I'm done here. Unofficially, I thought you might like to know that Rommy cleared you of Franco's death."

"What do you mean?" I ask, certain she's still toying with me. "I thought you said he was dead when they found him."

"He was. But there was a videotape in the box with him. Whoever killed him interrogated him first. The whole thing's on tape."

"Jesus," I say. "Interrogated him how?"

"Stripped him naked, tied his hands behind his back, and hung him up by his ankles. Beat him with a metal bat until they broke most of his bones and turned his insides to jelly."

Bile rises in my throat, rending me speechless for a moment. "Even Rommy didn't deserve that," I manage to say.

"No one does," Tilling says flatly. "It's a tough tape to watch."

"What did Rommy say?"

"That one of his old buddies in the department has been copying him on our case notes. He got hold of the phone number that Lyman gave Pongo. We'd put in a request to the cellular provider for the call logs, but Rommy slipped a clerk some cash to make sure he got them first. Rommy saw the calls from Lyman to Franco and figured Franco might know something, so he took a ride up to Westchester and beat the truth out of Franco with a gun butt. Apparently, Lyman had a security gig for some Swiss pharmaceutical company a few years back and Franco worked for him as a guard. According to Rommy, Franco said Lyman called him out of the blue and hired him to help rob your house. They were looking for a FedEx package. Your wife came home unexpectedly and walked in on them in the kitchen. Lyman chased her into the garage and hit her with a crowbar."

"Jesus," I say again, the raw description of Jenna's murder bringing tears to my eyes. I drop my face into my hands, hoping to God no one else has killed Lyman yet. "Do you know who Lyman was working for?"

"Rommy said Franco didn't know. Franco dealt only with Lyman, and Lyman didn't tell him much."

Andrei's still the key: He must know who was looking for the package.

"What?" Tilling asks, looking at me closely.

"Sorry?"

"You were thinking about something. What?"

"You still haven't explained how Rommy cleared me of Franco's murder."

"Rommy cleared you by confessing that he killed Franco. He realized that Franco's story was more likely to get you off the hook than to implicate you, so he shot Franco in the back of the head and wrote your name and office number in his address book."

"He hated me that much?" I ask disbelievingly.

"You got him fired. And he was expecting big money from the book about you that he's been working on with that scumbag writer. Rommy was deep underwater—gambling debts, child support, a marker to a loan shark for twenty grand. If you were proved innocent, he was going down." Tilling shakes her head. "The poor sap even thought he might get to play himself in the movie."

"But what about the bullets? Last night, you said my fingerprints were on the shell casings."

"They are. Rommy broke into your house a few weeks back. He found your gun, pocketed the bullets, and replaced them with bullets from his own gun. They were the same caliber."

"Why on earth would he have done that? And how could he have known he'd want bullets with my fingerprints?"

"Evidently, Rommy was quite the throw-down artist as a cop," Tilling says contemptuously. "He saw an opportunity to grab some plantable evidence from your house and he took it. He said on the tape that he scattered a bunch of hair and fiber from your place at Franco's, but the lab hasn't had a chance to work on that yet. He also said he did something similar about five years ago to put some other sorry bastard in jail. The DA's completely freaking out. Every guy Rommy helped convict over his eighteen-year career has got a shot at getting out on appeal."

"So I'm cleared of everything?" I ask hopefully.

"Officially?" Tilling says. "No fucking way. You've gone from being the number-one suspect in two murders to being the number-one suspect in three. Rommy's entire confession was extracted by some guy in a ski mask working him over like a side of beef, and most of what he said is to your benefit."

"Unofficially?"

"No one seeing the tape would think he was lying. It rolls start to finish without a break, and Rommy spontaneously mentions a dozen or more verifiable details about Franco's murder. There's no way anybody could have prepped him for a performance like that, much less made him stick to his lines while being beaten bloody. Also, we grabbed your gun from your house in Westchester—which, by the way, you don't have a permit for. You've got a fifty-round box of Remington ammunition that's light seven rounds, but your gun's loaded with Winchesters. The gun that killed Franco? Rommy said he swiped it from the police property room, and we've already been able to track it back. There are way too many things pointing at Rommy for you ever to be indicted on Franco. And Franco's statements to Rommy provide a credible alternative motive for someone else to have murdered your wife. Hearsay maybe, but the DA's feeling pretty shy right now. Not to mention the fact that Rommy was the lead investigator on your wife's case, and everything he turned up is now suspect. So the only case you potentially look good for at this point is murdering Rommy, and, having been wrong twice, the DA's not in a big hurry to move against you on that one. Although it would be a good idea to get your alibi on the record."

"Just to be clear, I'm not under arrest?" I ask, scarcely able to believe it.

"No," Tilling says. "You're not."

I fall back on the bed, dizzy with relief.

"Peter," Tilling says. "Why do you think I'm telling you all this?"

"I don't know," I say, turning my head to look at her. She's hunched forward intently, elbows on her knees. Her hair's matted on one side, her eyes red and swollen, and she looks as tired as I felt this morning.

"Two reasons," she says. "One, it'll all be in the press within forty-eight hours. A lot of people watched that tape. There's no way to keep a lid on that kind of news. Two, I'd like you to know that I believe you're innocent. I want you to trust me."

"Why?" I ask, surprised by my lack of sarcasm.

"Because I need you to open up to me. I think you may know more than you realize."

"All I've got are questions, Grace."

"Tell me who beat you up," she coaxes. "That's got to be a good starting point."

I stare up at the ceiling, trying to sort through what I should reveal.

"I was at Turndale and Company's offices last night from around six to six-thirty," I say slowly. "That's part of my alibi. I signed in at the lobby desk and showed a guard my ID. I met with William Turndale and his bodyguard, a big ex-FBI guy named Earl, in Turndale's boardroom."

"Met to talk about what?"

"William fired Andrei. I wanted to know how come," I say, still figuring it's better not to mention Katya's name before I have to.

"What did Turndale say?"

"Not much. He told me to keep my nose out of his business and had Earl work me over with a blackjack."

"Shit," Tilling says, scribbling in her notebook. "Did anyone else see it?"

"No. But when William was done, he had Earl take me

down the service elevator and heave me into the alley out back. It might've been caught on a security camera."

"Find out where William Turndale lives," Tilling says to Ellis.

"Don't bother," I say. "I can tell you where he is, or at least where he was this morning. He and Earl are at his place in Southampton, on Gin Lane. They're planning to leave the country."

"Why?"

"Some kind of securities fraud," I say, unwilling to tell her anything that points to Andrei before I've had a chance to speak with him. "I don't know all the details."

"Shit," she says again. "This is all going too fast. Why the hell didn't you tell me this before?"

"Maybe I would've," I say. "Last night at the Harvard Club. But then I found out you were waiting with a gang of cops to arrest me for a murder I hadn't committed."

"Get on the phone," she says to Ellis. "Call Jackson at the Seventeenth Precinct. Ask him to get somebody over to Turndale to review last night's security tapes. Maybe we can pick this Earl character up on assault, see where it goes." Getting to her feet, she looks down at me. "You're coming with us."

"I'm not," I say, determined not to go anywhere until I've seen Andrei.

"You are," she insists. "You had an unlicensed firearm in your home. That's a felony. You come with me voluntarily or I'll arrest you."

"You arrest me and I'll refuse to press charges against Earl," I say, standing up. "You won't have any cause to hold him."

"What kind of bullshit is this?" she demands, stepping forward so we're nose-to-nose. She's as tall as I am in her boots, breath smelling of stale coffee. "William Turndale must have had a reason for firing Andrei and beating the crap out of you. Maybe he's the guy who sent Lyman to your house. He might be responsible for Jennifer's murder."

It's possible, but Lyman doesn't seem to fit into William's schemes. My gut still tells me that there's something else going on, something that only Andrei can explain.

"There are a lot of levels to this thing," I say, willing her to believe me. "I need time to ask some questions I don't think you could get answered. So if you want me to trust you, you've got to trust me."

Tilling's hand burrows beneath her coat and emerges with a pair of handcuffs. She holds them up between us.

"You do what you think is right, Grace," I say, keeping my eyes fixed on hers. "But if you think I'm innocent, you've got to know we're on the same side."

She turns her head, looking at Ellis.

"I'm at a fucking loss here," she says. "What do you think?"

"You might as well trust him," Ellis says. "You've believed him all along."

42

I THROW OPEN THE BEDROOM WINDOW after Tilling and Ellis leave and lean out into the cold salt air, relieved beyond measure. The ocean's calm, with ankle-high waves rolling rhythmically onshore, and a flickering path of silver light coming from the moon. A dog howls in the distance; I take a deep breath and howl back, carrying the note until my lungs burn and my throat feels ragged. The cop in the SUV below me rolls down his window and looks up.

"What the hell do you think you're doing?"

I give him a friendly wave and pull my head back in. The bedside clock says it's almost six. Emily should be back soon. Hunting through the nightstand, I find my wallet, keys, and phone. I turn the phone on, startled when it immediately rings.

"Hello?"

"Peter. Where are you?" It's Katya.

"Long Island," I say. "Montauk."

"Are you okay?" she asks, her voice hushed.

"I'm fine," I say, glad she called. I need to tell her I've found Andrei, and that William's fled after trading away his stock in Turndale.

"I've been calling all day," she says in an urgent undertone. "The police are looking for you."

"They aren't," I say, whispering back. "So we can talk as loud as we want."

"What do you mean?" she demands, speaking louder. "The story's been all over the news."

"Sorry," I say. "I'm still feeling kind of giddy. The police were just here. I'm off the hook."

"How's that possible?"

I relay my entire conversation with Tilling, omitting only the fact that I've set the cops on William and Earl.

"That's unbelievable," she says. "You're totally free and clear?"

"Pretty much. I'm still a suspect in Rommy's death, but I don't think it's going to be a problem."

"They were wrong about the first two murders so now they're investigating you for a third?" she demands hotly.

"It's not like they don't have a point. The videotape was an incredibly lucky break for me."

"Thank God. I can't tell you how worried I've been."

"No more than I've been about you," I say, moved by her concern. "I'm sorry I didn't tell you everything last night, but I wanted you to stay focused on taking care of yourself. Did you talk to a lawyer?"

A car door slams outside and I hear the sound of the police SUV pulling away. Katya clears her throat.

"We'll get to me in a minute," she says. "Who did kill Rommy?"

"No clue. Maybe the same person who sent Franco and Lyman to my house. They might have thought Rommy was getting too close to the truth."

"That doesn't explain the videotape."

"You're right, but I don't have time to think about it. I've found Andrei."

"Where?" she asks eagerly.

"Nearby. I'm going to see him later."

"Andrei's in Montauk?" She sounds surprised. "When we spoke this morning, I thought he was in Europe."

"You spoke?" I ask, surprised in turn. "He called you?"

"No. The head of our London office called as I was getting out of bed. He said Andrei was up on our internal text-messaging system and wanted to talk to me. I logged in on my laptop and we chatted."

"I don't get it. Why didn't he phone you? And how'd he get into your system?"

"He said he couldn't phone. I don't know why. And the system's open-platform, designed for client access. I asked him where he was and he made a joke, saying he didn't have enough consonants on his keyboard. That and the fact that it was so early made me think he was in Eastern Europe."

"That's kind of odd," I reply. Something's not right. "Are you sure it was him?"

"We used to sing a Russian nursery song together in the tub when we were little: 'Hush You Mice.' I asked him the name and he knew. It was Andrei."

"What did he have to say for himself?" I ask, still feeling uneasy.

"That he'd been traveling, that he was looking forward to seeing me soon, and," she says, slowing for emphasis, "that he'd found a buyer for Turndale's entire portfolio of Russian securities."

"There's nothing to sell," I say, angry at Andrei for deceiving Katya further. "The securities are bogus."

"Stop right there," she says heatedly. "First off, nobody's ever told *me* the securities are bogus."

She pauses, perhaps expecting an objection, but she's only employing the deniability I gave her last night by couching Andrei's theft as a hypothetical.

"True."

"And second, I had London check them out this morning. The entire portfolio was signed off recently by our external auditor as part of the year-end process. There's absolutely no reason for me to suspect that those securities aren't good."

"Who's the auditor?" I ask skeptically.

"A small Russian firm," she says too casually. "They're new. William hired them right after Andrei left."

"Jesus, Katya. Don't delude yourself. You know why William switched auditors. Andrei's just trying to stall you, so you won't expose him. He didn't phone because he knew you'd hear the lie in his voice. There's no buyer."

"Wrong. We dealt. Andrei wired a billion dollars of same-day sterling to our correspondent bank in London and I released the securities. The whole transaction took about thirty minutes."

"How could you have done that?" I ask, amazed by her recklessness.

"How could I not?" she replies combatively. "Andrei's the one who assembled the portfolio. He knew it better than anyone else. If he had a cash purchaser, why shouldn't I have sold it?"

I feel sick, certain she's made a terrible mistake.

"Who was the buyer?"

"A Luxembourg foundation Andrei brought in as a client about a year and a half ago. He did business with them regularly when he was still with Turndale, and he was listed as an authorized signatory for them in our records."

"He was a signatory for a client while he was working for you?"

"I'm looking into it," she says, sounding annoyed. "The important fact is that he had the authority."

This keeps getting worse: Andrei must have conned the Luxembourg foundation somehow, just as he conned Turndale. Katya's only deferred Turndale's inevitable collapse, at the same time putting herself in the middle of a suspicious transaction.

"And what are you going to do when the foundation calls next week, or next month, or next year, and says the securities are no good?"

"I asked Andrei if there was going to be a problem and he said no."

"You believed him?"

"He's my brother," she says simply.

I don't know what to say: There was a time I would have believed Andrei, too.

"The whole thing feels wrong."

"It's not like I don't have questions, Peter," she says. "How long will it take me to drive out there?"

"Figure three and a half hours. If you start now, you can get here before ten."

"I can't leave yet. The governor of the St. Louis Fed is in town, and we're having dinner. If I beg off early, I should be there by midnight. You'll keep your phone on?"

"Yes."

Emily's in the hall. I can hear her speaking to someone.

"There's something else I have to tell you," I say reluctantly.

"I spoke to William this morning. He sold all his shares in Turndale last night."

"He what?" she asks, her voice rising sharply. "To whom?"

"I don't know for sure."

"Don't hold out on me, Peter," she says imploringly. "Please."

"Russians. Probably dirty."

"You're kidding me, right?"

"I'm not."

"Christ." She sounds stunned. "How the hell did that happen? The minority shareholders will go berserk. There's bound to be a lawsuit."

"I think William's beyond caring about lawsuits," I say, watching Emily open the door. She has her pink-and-orange bag over her shoulder and looks worried. "He's planning to leave the country."

"Tell me everything you know," she implores.

"I can't right now. I've got to go see Andrei."

"Hang on a second. William told you he sold his stock to Russians. You think Andrei's involved in this somehow?"

"He might be."

"To hell with dinner," she says. "I'm getting in a car now."

43

"THERE WAS A POLICEMAN IN THE HALL," Emily says. "He wanted to see my ID. Is everything okay?"

"Everything's fine," I say, not surprised that Tilling left someone behind to check up on Emily's identity. Ellis's vote of confidence notwithstanding, I don't think of Tilling as the trusting kind.

"I thought the police wanted to arrest you for murder."

"I got lucky."

She gazes at me doubtfully for a second, her expression gradually giving way to one of concern.

"You look pale again," she says. "Sit on the bed. You can tell me what's happened while I check you over."

Emily examines me while I recount my conversation with Tilling. She seems distracted, not asking too many questions, which is just as well. There's a topic I need to cover with her before I see Andrei.

"One more thing," I say as she unwraps her pressure cuff from my arm. "I was stopped coming into the United States the other day. A federal agent named Davis made some bizarre allegations about Andrei and your clinic."

She touches a finger to my lips, shaking her head, and then points to the door.

"Our friend's place is just a few minutes down the beach." Rummaging in her shoulder bag, she pulls out a banana. "Eat this to get your blood sugar up and we can walk there. We'll talk on the way."

Gagging on the richness, I gulp a third in a single bite while she fetches my coat from the wardrobe. She takes the fruit from me so I can slip my good arm into one sleeve, holds it to my mouth for me to take another bite, and then moves closer to help guide my bad arm into the other sleeve. Her eyelashes are blond, and there's a spray of faded freckles across her nose. I feel awkward, shy in retrospect about her undressing me earlier.

"So tell me," I say, searching for small talk. "Do you usually keep fruit in your bag?"

"I grabbed the banana downstairs with you in mind," she says, smiling as she holds it up again for me to finish. "But since you ask, yes. The Gypsy children in Moscow are all undernourished, and the smaller ones never get to keep any of the money they beg. I buy what I can afford and scrounge the rest from tourist hotels. Bananas are the most nutritious."

"The hotel staff don't say anything?" I ask, amused by an image of Emily lurking in opulent lobbies, surreptitiously swiping fruit from silver bowls.

"It's not a problem," she says, dropping the peel in the trash and beginning to button my coat with deft fingers. "Everybody knows me. I'm the American doctor who collects bananas and hands out condoms. And no jokes, please. I've heard them all, in English and Russian. Although it is true the bananas sometimes do double duty—they're a useful teaching aid in my line of work."

"I met a couple of your Gypsy kids in an underpass," I say sourly. "One took my watch."

"You did well if you hung on to your wallet," she says sympathetically. "They're incredibly quick. One got my watch a few years back, and a ring I was partial to. I don't wear jewelry anymore."

"But you pack fruit for them."

"Never give up on children," she says, carefully lifting my bad arm and tucking the hand inside my coat, propping my wrist on a button. "My guiding principle. If there's a single thing that keeps me going, it's the fact that so many of my patients are children. Ready?"

I feel like I've been waiting an eternity.

"Absolutely," I say. "Lead on."

The policeman's gone from the hall, and there's no sign of the SUV on the beach. Emily and I walk toward the ocean until we reach the damp sand at the water's edge and turn left, the moon lighting our way. My fervor to see Andrei is rapidly devolving into uneasiness. I've been too busy looking for him to have given much thought to our meeting. The worst possibility is that he already knows Lyman's employers were responsible for Jenna's murder, and never communicated the truth to me for his own selfish or guilty reasons. If so, I can never forgive him. But if he didn't know about Lyman, I really can't understand why he never got in touch with me, regardless of what happened between me and Katya, or how shamed he felt by his theft.

"Andrei never told you that he was gay, did he?" Emily asks, interrupting my train of thought.

"No," I say, feeling embarrassed.

"And that makes you angry."

"I don't care who he sleeps with," I reply stiffly. "But we were friends for a long time. It's not right that he didn't say anything."

"Did he ever actually lie to you?" she demands. "Or did you just make the assumptions you wanted to make?"

I remember what Andrei said to me in Rome: that my worldview was so rigid that I didn't always see things or people the way they really were.

"It's not just that he didn't tell me he was gay," I say defensively. "There are other things he didn't tell me, more important things."

"And there's nothing you ever concealed from him?"

Only the fact that I betrayed Jenna, one of his close friends, by sleeping with his sister. I don't respond.

"Let me ask you a question," she says, skipping sideways as a rogue wave threatens her shoes. "You and Andrei were in the same business, right?"

"More or less," I reply, relieved at the change of subject.

"He told me that he'd call up people he never met, all over the world, and agree to exchange hundreds of millions of dollars' worth of stock or bonds just on the basis of a phone call."

"That's pretty much how the financial markets work at the institutional level."

"It's hard for me to understand. When the clinic bought a copying machine, I had to sign a thirty-page contract."

"The top end of the financial market is like an English men's club," I say, welcoming an opportunity to play the expert with her for a change. "Your word is your bond. The worst thing you could ever do would be to jeopardize your reputation."

"The very point I was driving at," she says. "Andrei didn't

think your men's club was very open to diversity. He was concerned about his reputation."

"He seems to have gotten over that," I say testily.

"I don't like your tone."

"And I don't like the fact that you're apologizing for him."

"I'm not apologizing. I'm trying to explain." She takes a deep breath and then exhales loudly. "There's something I need to tell you before we get to Andrei's house."

"What?"

"Andrei has AIDS."

"Christ," I say, feeling as if I've been kicked in the gut. "Is he okay?"

"No. I wouldn't be here if he were. I diagnosed him with Burkitt's lymphoma in August. That's a nasty lymphatic cancer that's associated with HIV/AIDS. Treatments in the United States are better than I could provide in Moscow, so I checked him into Stony Brook University Hospital here on Long Island. They've got a good AIDS oncology program, and I know some of the staff."

"Why's he out of the hospital, then?" I ask, a growing sense of dread suggesting the answer.

"He didn't respond to treatment," she says softly. "The doctors at Stony Brook discharged him as a kindness, so he could die in a more comfortable setting."

Tears start from my eyes. An image comes to me from our days at Klein, before business school: Andrei grinning at the top of the key after I'd dunked a no-look pass, his hair wet with sweat and his face flushed with pleasure. I don't know if I can face another loss at this point.

"There." Emily points to a glass house set back above the grassy dunes and takes my arm, guiding me toward it. I balk at the steps, fearful of seeing Andrei wasted and dying. She tugs my hand.

"Come on," she says. "It's important to say good-bye."

The stairs rise to a porch. I wipe my face with my sleeve as Emily opens a sliding door onto a cement-floored kitchen. A heavyset black man in green scrubs is sitting at a hexagonal metal table, drinking Diet Coke and reading a newspaper by the light of a bare hanging flood. There's a baby monitor on the table by his elbow. The sound's turned low, but I can hear a woman singing a simple tune unaccompanied. The man looks up as we enter.

"No change. I gave him his meds twenty minutes ago. He's been in and out."

Emily leads the way to a double-height living room, its cinder-block walls crisscrossed by sculpture made of rusting pipe, branches snaking crazily and interspersed with broken-faced gauges. We climb aluminum steps to a darkened balcony, where she taps softly on a door before opening it.

Andrei's lying in a hospital bed, an IV drip hanging from a pole and a gas cylinder affixed to the metal headboard. The clear plastic walls of an oxygen tent distort his features. He looks shrunken, eyes covered by bandages and a pale blue knit cap on his head. A partially opened window admits sea air, gauze curtains fluttering in the breeze. Votive candles flicker on the windowsill, on a marble mantel over a faux fireplace, and on the pickled-wood floor. Mrs. Zhilina sits on the far side of the bed, crooning to Andrei quietly as she clasps one of his hands in hers.

"I've warned you repeatedly," Emily whispers, squatting to lift two brilliantly guttering candles near the bed. "Oxygen's heavier than air. It puddles. You're going to start a fire."

"There's nothing to burn in this house," Mrs. Zhilina replies stonily. "Renting it was a mistake. It's ugly."

"Have you met?" Emily asks, looking from Mrs. Zhilina to me.

"We have," Mrs. Zhilina says, glancing at me expressionlessly.

I think to ask why she said she didn't know where Andrei was when we last spoke, but I realize it's not the right time. I'm here for Andrei, not to try to fathom her deceptions.

"I'm going to make some tea," she says, leaning on her cane as she rises from the chair. "Perhaps the two of you would be good enough to keep Andrei company until I return."

"Of course," Emily says. "Peter and I still have a lot to talk about."

44

"SIT THERE," Emily says, pointing to Mrs. Zhilina's seat. "I'll pull up a stool on this side."

I walk around the bed and sink down into the vacant chair, staring through the plastic walls of the oxygen tent. Andrei's face is a husk, his cheeks sunken and lips bloodless. Only the slightest movement of the crisp white sheet covering his chest hints that he's alive at all.

"Take his hand," Emily says. "Gently."

Andrei's near hand lies palm-up on the bed, fingers slightly curled. I hesitate, afraid to touch him.

"You won't hurt him," Emily says. "And he's not contagious."

His skin is hot and dry, as if a fire were burning within. I slip two fingers into his grasp, covering his hand with mine, and feel a slight pressure in response.

"Is he conscious?" I ask, startled.

"Not really. He drifts in and out. I'm trying to keep him under as much as possible because he's in so much pain."

"This is awful," I say, choking back a sob. I look at my

friend lying in bed, blind and drugged, death the only release. "Isn't there anything you can do?"

"It's not my decision," Emily says. "Mrs. Zhilina has his proxy. It's difficult to let go of a child. When she's ready, she'll tell me."

"That's not what I meant," I say despondently, realizing I don't know what I did mean. Sitting at Andrei's deathbed with his feverish hand clasped in mine, the only truth I'm sure of is that I'm about to lose one more of the very few people I ever cared about.

"I haven't got any miracles to offer," Emily says gently. "We all die. I've sat next to dozens of beds like this. It's a blessing that we have enough drugs to ease his way. That's not always the case."

"When Mrs. Zhilina is ready," I say, stumbling over the words, "will you . . ."

"Of course," she replies. "There aren't many doctors in my line of work who haven't crossed that bridge at some point."

Andrei's wearing a hospital gown, the neck loose, and I can see the edge of his rugby scar, a puckered line circling his shoulder. We fell out of the habit of playing basketball after business school, our schedules seemingly too difficult to coordinate. Looking back, my devotion to Klein seems a puzzling waste. I should have paid more attention to the people I loved.

"You have questions," Emily says. "I'm sorry Andrei can't answer them for you. I'll tell you what I can, though."

"A man named Lyman was looking for Andrei," I say, pulling myself together. "Do you know why? Or who he was working for? I think he's with the same people who were after me in Moscow."

"I don't recognize the name," she says. "All Andrei told me was that he had a problem, that some people were looking for him, and that I should be careful of phones and e-mail. He said they might be able to use the local cops to hassle his friends but that Vladimir could use the clinic's connections to protect me, and that I should let Vladimir or one of his boys escort me around Moscow."

So Andrei trusted Vladimir to the last. He wouldn't have recommended that Emily seek Vladimir's protection if he hadn't.

"When was this?"

"Early September."

"You must have asked him what was going on," I say insistently.

"I told you before," she replies, tucking loose hair behind her ears, "Andrei and I had an understanding. There were things I couldn't know without risking my professional standing."

"Things like what?" I ask, wondering if she's alluding to Andrei's theft from Turndale.

"You recall my telling you about the problems we're facing with multidrug-resistant TB and the fact that none of the pharmaceutical companies are willing to do work on it because there isn't a paying market?"

"Right," I say tentatively, wondering where she's going with this.

"A little over a year ago, I was talking to a colleague at a conference in Vienna. He'd heard rumors that a Swiss company had stumbled onto a treatment that attacked the bacilli from an entirely different angle."

Andrei shifts on the bed, mouth opening as he mumbles a few words. Emily lifts his other hand and strokes it. There's a network of plastic tubes taped to his forearm.

"How do you stumble onto a treatment?" I ask.

"It happens more often than you'd imagine. Genomics will change things eventually, but for the moment, drug development is pretty haphazard. The Swiss were working on acne. Like TB, severe acne is treated with antibiotics and, like TB, the use of antibiotics has encouraged resistant strains. The Swiss were experimenting with a drug that inhibited the synthesis of metabolic enzymes—in effect, starving the acne bacilli to death. It looked good in the lab, so they began clinical trials in Russia."

"Why Russia?"

"Please," she says. "The target market for acne products is teenagers. Would you let your teenager sign up for a drug trial if you could afford other treatments?"

"No," I concede.

"Russians can't afford other treatments, and the clinical standard there is pretty good, despite the lack of money. A researcher reviewing the posttrial work-ups noticed something unusual. Forty percent of the subjects had been infected with latent TB before the trial, which means they carried TB bacilli but didn't exhibit any symptoms. That's not unusual: As much as a third of the global population carries latent TB. After completing the Swiss acne protocol, though, every single clinical subject's TB load went to zero. The researcher reported his findings up the chain and the company commissioned a second acne trial, this time using a prison population. That was clever of them. By going into prisons, they got a subject group more likely to be infected by virulent TB strains without having to disclose to anyone external the real purpose of their study. The results were the same: The drug seemed to be a golden bullet for all strains of TB, with no significant adverse side effects."

"You heard all that as a rumor?" I ask, still trying to figure out why she's telling me this.

"The rumor was just that there was a new drug, and that the company had decided to sit on it. Everything else I learned later."

"But why would the company sit on it?"

"The Swiss were making a bet," Emily says bitterly. "If MDR-TB makes the leap to the developed world, the drug will be worth billions. They think it's going to happen, and I agree with them. Ten years ago, there was an outbreak of MDR-TB in Florida that took almost two and a half years to eradicate. Twenty-six out of eighty-one patients died, all with access to the best health care available. Imagine the demand if a more widespread outbreak occurred."

"You told Andrei about the rumor you'd heard," I say, suddenly understanding.

"I did," she replies. "A few months later, he gave me some CDs containing clinical trial data for a new antibiotic—raw results as well as the researcher's notes. The drug being tested inhibited synthesis of metabolic enzymes, and seemed particularly effective against TB. He asked for my opinion. I reanalyzed the results independently and told Andrei that the drug looked like the real thing."

He must have bribed someone at the company, I realize, not quite sure how I feel about that. The gauze curtains begin flapping loudly, and I get up to close the open window. The votives on the sill and mantel have all blown out.

"A couple of weeks after that," Emily continues, "Andrei told me he was on the board of a charitable foundation that had obtained the formula for a new TB drug and wanted to conduct a clinical study of the drug's efficacy against MDR-TB. He asked me to design it."

"Hang on," I say as I resume my seat, my brain going in too many different directions. "Drugs get patented, right?"

"They do. Sometimes just the underlying molecule, sometimes the molecule and the manufacturing process."

"And wouldn't a company patent a drug before they got to the point of doing clinical trials on it?"

"Undoubtedly."

"Then what you're telling me doesn't make any sense. If the Swiss had already patented the drug, why would Andrei's foundation want to conduct an independent trial on it?"

"I don't know that Andrei's drug was the Swiss drug," she says, reminding me that Andrei kept the particulars from her.

"Suppose it was."

"Then I'd imagine that Andrei's foundation intended to publish their results and let public opinion pressure the Swiss into manufacturing it."

"But you already had clinical results."

"Those studies were targeted at acne," she says patiently, "not full-blown TB. They were highly indicative, but not conclusive."

I'm feeling wired now, my brain humming the way it used to when I was working on a big trade.

"That rumor you heard," I say. "What was the name of the Swiss company?"

"Zeitz," she says. "They're huge. Part of a European conglomerate that does all sorts of things."

Tilling told me that Lyman had worked security for some big Swiss pharmaceutical company a few years back. More of the puzzle snaps into focus. I'd lay odds that the company he worked for was Zeitz.

"If Andrei's foundation had gotten hold of Zeitz's drug, could Zeitz have found out?"

"Clinical trials have to be approved," she says. "And, depending on where you apply, the process might or might not be transparent. Assuming Zeitz has a TB drug, they'd be particularly interested in monitoring any trial application targeted at TB. Even if Andrei's application wasn't supposed to be publicly available, they might have found out about it. It's hard to keep things secret when there's so much money involved. The application certainly would have contained my name, and it might have contained Andrei's."

If Zeitz found out Andrei was running a trial on their drug, they would have done anything to stop him. Once the drug's efficacy against MDR-TB was proved and made public, they'd have to release it, regardless of the fact that there wasn't a paying market. Zeitz stood to lose billions.

"Assume Zeitz were the people looking for Andrei," I say, circling back to the beginning of our conversation. "What would they have been hoping to achieve?"

She shrugs. "Maybe they wanted to persuade him that it was in his own best interest to cancel the trial and reveal how much of their data he had, and how he got it. One way to achieve that would be to intimidate him, to rough him up physically and threaten him with worse."

"Did Zeitz ever come after you or the clinic?"

"I don't know for sure, but someone tipped off the Ministry of Health that Chechen terrorists were using my clinic to test a virulent strain of MDR-TB stolen from a Swiss lab." She shakes her head in disgust. "I went directly to the minister and offered to open my records to any competent review board. That's the last I heard of that story. Then someone hacked into our computer system. Whoever broke in got by our primary firewall but wasn't able to penetrate the secondary security that protects our confidential data."

I get to my feet and begin pacing, too wound up to sit. Zeitz tried to pressure Emily with the same bullshit story about terrorism that Lyman peddled to Davis and De Nunzio. All the pieces tie together. I go to the window and stare out at the waves. Zeitz is responsible for Jenna's murder. I wonder how I can avenge myself on a conglomerate. Emily croons something softly behind me.

"What?" I say, turning to look at her.

"I'm sorry," she says, Andrei's hand pressed to her face. "The tune Mrs. Zhilina was singing got stuck in my head. It's a Russian children's song."

"'Hush You Mice,'" I say, guessing the name of the song Katya mentioned to me earlier without quite understanding why.

"That's right," Emily says, looking at me quizzically. "Do you know it?"

Pennies begin dropping in my brain. Seeing Andrei sick threw me for so much of a loop that I didn't think through the ramifications of his incapacity. He couldn't have been messaging Katya this morning. It must have been Mrs. Zhilina who repurchased the counterfeit securities, pretending to be Andrei.

"Andrei's sister said something about it. Tell me, when we spoke on the phone in Moscow, you said you'd made a call for me, and that you might be able to let me know more about the people who were after me later. Who did you call?"

"Mrs. Zhilina," Emily says. "She's on the board of Andrei's charitable foundation as well."

The bedroom door opens. Vladimir stands framed in the doorway, wearing the same green scrubs the nurse downstairs had on. He crooks a finger at me.

"Come," he says. "Mrs. Zhilina is wanting to talk to you."

I look toward Andrei and notice the transmitting half of the baby monitor plugged in under his bed. Mrs. Zhilina must have been listening; she doesn't miss a trick.

"Can I lift the edge of the oxygen tent?" I ask Emily.

"Yes," she says.

The noise of the ocean fades to a faint whisper as I duck my head beneath the plastic, all the doubts I've had about Andrei these past few days dispelled. Leaning forward, I kiss him gently on the cheek.

"I love you," I say. "Good-bye."

45

A DOOR OFF THE LIVING ROOM opens onto a darkened sunporch with a glass wall facing the ocean. Mrs. Zhilina sits in a rocking chair, her cane leaning against the wall behind her. Gray-blue shadows chase across her face as she rocks slowly, a steamer blanket draped over her legs. A red light glows from the baby monitor in her lap.

"Would you like some tea, Peter?" she asks, looking toward me and Vladimir.

"No," I say, filled with a sense of anticipation. If anyone knows the answers to my remaining questions, it's got to be her.

"Are you sure? This is the only room in this loathsome house I don't find oppressive, and it's impossible to heat. The tea's warming."

"I'm fine," I say. The room's a sauna compared to Tigger's car.

"Just the one cup, then, Vladimir," she says to him. "And please close the door behind you."

He obeys wordlessly, her tone suggesting a relationship I wouldn't have suspected.

"You met Vladimir through Andrei?" I ask.

"No. Vladimir's father and I used to work together. I introduced him to Andrei. Sit."

There's a second blanket draped over the rocker next to hers, and I wrap it around my shoulders as best I can, still clumsy with my injured arm. I hear the sound of pages rustling, and then Emily's voice, speaking a low, mellifluous Russian.

"She's reading Tolstoy to him," Mrs. Zhilina says, turning the baby monitor off. "I'm sick to death of Tolstoy."

"I've never read him."

"An idealist," she says dismissively. "I find religion and philosophy as tedious as modern art and architecture. Andrei and I disagree."

"You found some common ground."

"We did," she says. "And our actions had consequences we never intended. I'm deeply sorry about your wife."

"I need to know what happened," I say grimly. "Tell me about Zeitz."

"I will," she says. "Zeitz is the end of the story, though. Emily's told you the middle. Perhaps we should start at the beginning."

"I already know the beginning."

"Really?" she asks, lifting an eyebrow. "Then you tell me."

"Andrei got sick and it changed his perspective," I say impatiently, fitting together the pieces I've learned. "He wanted to do more, to help people who didn't have the same access to medical care that he had. He found Emily and started up the clinic, funding it out of his own pocket and with contributions he solicited locally. Sometime last year, Emily told him about the drug Zeitz was rumored to have. Suddenly, he needed a lot more cash—first, to pay off whoever sold him the drug and the data and, second, to fund the clinical trial he had to run. He began stealing money from Turndale."

"You think Andrei a thief?" she asks frostily.

"Misappropriated, then," I say, uninterested in splitting hairs. "He used the cash to play the market, thinking he would put his profits toward the clinic and return the principal before anyone figured out what he'd done. He made some bad bets, so he doubled up. By the time he stopped, he was down a billion dollars. He panicked. His reputation, Katya's job, and William's company were all at risk."

I pause, wondering if she'll react to William's name. I'm curious as to what really happened between them.

"Continue," Mrs. Zhilina says, her voice expressionless.

"I'd guess that's when he came to you. He confessed what he'd done, and together you figured out how to tidy everything up. The key was the Linz paintings. You must have learned where they were hidden when you were studying with von Stern. You negotiated with William to trade the collection for his stock, and then either sold the stock or borrowed against it to buy back the bogus securities. Problem solved, or so you imagined."

"What do you mean, or so I imagined?"

"William had control stock. Turndale's minority shareholders are almost certainly going to launch a monster lawsuit demanding to know exactly what William got for his shares, and insisting on their right to equivalent compensation. The whole deal could unravel. Andrei should have known better. He should have talked to a securities lawyer."

"And if William simply donated his shares to a charitable foundation?"

Her question derails my train of thought.

"You gave William the paintings," I say hesitantly. "And then you had the Swiss escrow agent assign his shares to this outfit that Andrei was on the board of, Fondation l'Etoile?"

She nods.

"And then L'Etoile bought back the counterfeit Russian shares," I continue, walking myself through the steps. "So, depending on how you think about it, William either received the paintings as compensation or he implicitly received the billion dollars and used it to buy the paintings."

"Or neither," she says. "Perhaps William was just generous. In which case, as the extremely expensive securities lawyer that Andrei hired explained it, there's no equivalent compensation for any minority shareholder to demand."

"You're out of my depth," I admit. "I'm not a lawyer. But I do know that you're playing awfully fast and loose with the rules. If the SEC figures out even half of what's gone on here, everyone involved is going to be in big trouble."

"L'Etoile is a private foundation. Andrei and I are the sole directors, and the only ones who know exactly what transpired. The SEC won't learn anything that I don't tell them. But this isn't really what you want to talk about, is it?"

"No," I reply, setting my curiosity aside. "Tell me about Zeitz."

The door to the porch opens and Vladimir appears, carrying a teacup on a saucer. He and Mrs. Zhilina converse in Russian while I fret, anxious to learn what she knows.

"So," she says as Vladimir exits. "We come to Zeitz. Emily's surmise was correct: They had obtained a copy of Andrei's trial application. Realizing Andrei had their drug, they sent Lyman to threaten him. Andrei was scheduled to enter the hospital, so he checked in under another name and effectively disappeared. Zeitz knew that Andrei's foundation was funding the trial, and they were able to learn that I was on the board as well. Lyman caught up with me one morning in the rain, as I was walking to work. He said things would be difficult for us if we proceeded with the trial. I tried to brush past him. He'd closed his umbrella as he spoke and, as I walked away, he tripped me with it."

"When did this happen?" I ask urgently.

"September twelfth."

Four days before Jenna was murdered.

"What did you do?"

"Andrei was hospitalized, and I was focused on working through the details of the trade with William. It wasn't the right time to confront Zeitz. I withdrew the trial application."

"Did you tell the police about Lyman?"

"No. He was insignificant."

"'Insignificant'?" I say, barely able to control myself. "Lyman and a man named Franco murdered my wife the next week."

She lays a hand gently on my bad arm.

"I'm sorry," she says. "You can't know how grieved I am."

"Zeitz has to pay," I say, my voice shaking.

"I've given it some thought," she says. "I know how to hurt them."

"What do you mean?" I ask, taken aback.

"We'll produce their drug," she says, her hand closing on my arm. "We'll make them grant us a license for unrestricted global distribution and not let them earn a cent from it."

"We don't have any leverage," I say, trying to free myself. She squeezes tighter, hurting me.

"You're wrong," she replies, a fierce smile twisting her lips. "We have Lyman."

I spring to my feet as she releases me. "How?"

"He flew into New York the morning after you arrived back from Moscow. Emily told me that Zeitz might be after you, so I set Vladimir to watch the hotel where Lyman had stayed before."

"How did you know where he'd stayed?" I ask breathlessly.

"The umbrella," she exults. "The one he tripped me with. It had the hotel's name on it."

She's got Lyman. Black joy swells my chest until a sudden thought catches me up short.

"Does Zeitz know you have him?"

"They do," she says. "We've already opened negotiations with them. Lyman admitted your wife's murder, and confirmed Zeitz's reasons for warehousing the drug. We have his confession on tape. Zeitz is being very cooperative."

"One thing," I say, pointing at her. "We're not giving Lyman back."

"What do you mean?"

"What I said. Lyman has to pay."

"Vladimir's men questioned him," she says. "The way the Soviets taught them to question people. Lyman's paid considerably already."

"Not enough. You said it yourself, yesterday. An eye for an eye, that's justice."

"And if Zeitz demands Lyman returned alive as the price of their TB drug?"

"You're not listening to me," I say, standing over her.

"You insist on Lyman's death," she says quietly. "Even if it means millions of innocents die needlessly?"

"It's not negotiable," I say, hate filling my heart. "Tell me where he is."

"An eye for an eye," she says, looking away from me. "Vladimir should be in the kitchen. He'll take you to Lyman."

46

VLADIMIR OPENS A SIDE DOOR onto a courtyard, a snow-capped hedge obscuring the street to my right, and a trellis tangled with leafless vines overhead. Ten yards away, a shadowed figure leans against a gray garage, smoking a cigarette. Vladimir calls out sharply in Russian and the man retreats inside.

"There?" I ask, scarcely believing Lyman is so near at hand.

"Yes," he says.

He touches my shoulder as I move forward. Glancing sideways, I see a gun in his hand, the grip extended toward me. I take the gun from him and heft it. It's an automatic, smaller than my father's gun, and lighter. I rack the slide and flip the safety up with my thumb. I start toward the garage and he touches my shoulder again.

"What?"

"Listen," he says gruffly, breath condensing cloudlike in the chill air. "English is a difficult making for me."

I nod impatiently.

"Mrs. Zhilina is saying things. Some," he says, smoothing

the surface of one hand with the other, "is truth. And some . . ." He turns one hand sideways and chops down into his flattened palm as if striking it with an ax, pretending to brush the severed portion away.

"Less than truth?" I guess, trying to understand him. "Half-truths?"

He nods and then grabs me by the upper arm, leaning forward to kiss both sides of my face. His eyes glisten. I can't even begin to imagine what this is all about.

"I'm sorry," he says. "You understand? She is saying and I am doing, but not knowing. I'm sorry. This is my only saying."

"Lyman killed my wife, right?" I ask, wanting to make sure there's no confusion.

"Yes."

"I'm going to kill him."

"Yes."

"So there's no problem, is there?"

"No," he says. "No problem. But I am saying my sorry. For not knowing."

"Don't worry about it," I say, turning back toward the garage. I haven't got time to figure out what's bothering him. "You're forgiven."

The interior of the garage smells of smoke, shit, and propane, a portable heater on full blast in one corner. Plastic sheets cover the floor, the ceiling, and three of the four walls; all the windows are masked. Two wooden chairs face each other in the middle of the room, a tall lamp without a shade standing between them. The Russian who was smoking outside is seated in the nearer chair, a pornographic magazine open in his lap and a cigarette dangling from his lips. There's a metal bat leaning against the wall behind him, and a video camera on a tripod, pointed toward the second chair.

Lyman's duct-taped to the second chair, cigarette butts littering the floor around him. He's naked and gagged, sitting in a pool of blood and urine with his eyes closed and his head slumped. Heavy blue bruises cover most of his body; his face and chest are dotted with small round blisters. Vladimir says something to the seated Russian, who stands and catches Lyman by the hair, holding his head up and slapping him repeatedly across the face. Lyman doesn't react. The man takes the lit cigarette from his mouth and threads it into one of Lyman's nostrils. Lyman jerks awake with a shriek, his limbs flexing spasmodically.

"Now," Vladimir says as the Russian turns Lyman's face to me. "Shoot."

I step forward and press the gun to Lyman's forehead, just the way I've imagined it a thousand times before. His eyes cross beneath slitted lids and he moans loudly, a fresh stream of urine trickling down the chair leg.

"For Jenna," I say.

This isn't right. I hear Jenna's voice in my ear and suddenly see the room as if from her perspective—me with the gun extended, Lyman lowing fearfully into his gag, and the Russians waiting expectantly. Pushing her words away, I draw a deep breath and command myself to shoot. My finger tightens on the trigger as a bloody tear leaks from Lyman's eye and tracks slowly down his cheek. This isn't what Jenna would want. It isn't right. I step backward and point the gun to the ceiling, realizing I'm covered in sweat.

"I'm not going to do this," I say to Vladimir, my voice choked. "I'm not going to kill him in cold blood. You take your people and get out of here. I'll wait a couple of hours and then call the police."

"Is better," Vladimir says, taking the gun from me. He raises his arm in a fluid motion, touches the gun to Lyman's head, and fires. The noise is no louder than a hand clap. Lyman's body spasms, smoke rising from a hole behind his ear as the air fills with the smell of burnt hair. I double over, vomiting, and hear the other Russian laugh.

Vladimir pats my back with one hand.

"Is better," he repeats. "You are not a man to be killing."

47

"I DON'T UNDERSTAND," I say weakly.

I'm back in my chair on the sunporch, my stomach still roiling. Mrs. Zhilina rocks ever so slightly beside me as she gazes out at the ocean.

"There's a cup of tea for you," she says, nodding to a small table between us.

I pick the cup up and slurp from it, trying to wash the taste of bile from my mouth.

"Vladimir killed him."

"Yes," she says calmly. "We sent Zeitz a videotape of Lyman's confession yesterday morning and gave them twenty-four hours either to sign over the TB drug or suffer the consequences. They came back with one condition: that Lyman and his accomplice be silenced. Vladimir wanted to dispose of Lyman earlier, but I saved him for you."

Her words make me even queasier. She kept Lyman for me the way she might have kept dinner for Katya or Andrei when they arrived home late as children.

"You said Zeitz wanted Lyman back alive."

"I asked what you would do if that were their condition. Was that why you didn't kill him?"

"No," I say, the conversation too surreal for me to feel indignant.

"You surprised me by not acting. In your place, I wouldn't have hesitated."

My father would have done it, I realize. In a heartbeat.

"I don't know," I say, confused as to how I feel. "Maybe there are some things I won't do."

She turns her head to fix me with a hard stare.

"Lyman and his accomplice were small, vicious men. They've paid for their crimes. Now it's time to take revenge on Zeitz. L'Etoile is holding all of William's stock free and clear, plus two hundred million in cash and the rights to Zeitz's TB drug. The stock and cash together give you well more than a billion dollars to see the drug into production."

"Me?"

"Of course you," she says insistently. "Who else is there? I'm too old, Andrei's near death, neither Emily nor Vladimir are business people, and Katya will be busy with Turndale. That leaves you."

"No," I say. Who does she think she is?

"Why?" she demands.

I take another sip from my cup, trying to marshal my thoughts. The tea tastes bitter.

"Two reasons. First, I don't know where the money came from, and I don't trust you to tell me the truth. L'Etoile just spent a billion dollars to buy back the securities Andrei forged, so how can you still have more than a billion of value? And second, because I don't want to be involved with you, or

Vladimir, or anyone else who might be working with you. I don't like you, and I don't like the things you've done."

"Because I had Vladimir shoot the man who murdered your wife? A man you were insistent on killing?"

"It's more than that. You mentioned Lyman's accomplice. His name was Franco, and he was killed by a former cop named Rommy. Someone grabbed Rommy and beat him to death."

"Lyman gave us Franco's name," she says coolly. "Vladimir was watching the house when Mr. Rommy arrived, and he heard gunshots. If Vladimir hadn't acted as he did, you'd likely be in a jail cell right now. The gracious thing would be to say thank you."

She sounds as if she were discussing the weather. I remember the look on Tilling's face as she described the damage done to Rommy. The cup and saucer slide from my lap as I stand, smashing on the floor.

"Let me make it simple," I say. "I don't want anything to do with you or your foundation."

"You feel competent to judge me," she says acidly. "Despite your wanting to kill Lyman half an hour ago, the consequences to the rest of the world be damned."

"I was wrong. I made a mistake. I don't want to make another."

I walk toward the door.

"I was innocent," Mrs. Zhilina says as my hand touches the knob.

"Of what?" I ask, knowing that I should leave now and never look back.

"Of everything. I was only nineteen when I first met William Turndale."

I turn my head. Mrs. Zhilina's face is bright in the moonlight. Nothing can change my opinion of her now, but I'd like to know what happened between her and William for Katya's benefit, if for no other reason.

"Please," Mrs. Zhilina says, touching the chair I just vacated with her hand. "If you're going to judge me, you should know the whole truth."

48

"I HADN'T EXPECTED to hear Professor von Stern's name from you earlier," she says. "How did you learn it?"

I settle back into the rocking chair beside her, not surprised she's started with von Stern. Whatever happened between her and William began in Berlin, forty-some years ago, when she was von Stern's student.

"The bank records I found on Andrei's computer showed a deposit from a Swiss auction house. A friend of mine was able to tie the deposit back to the sale of the Brueghel that von Stern had lent to Hitler's collection."

"How very enterprising," she says. "And what did you learn about the Professor, other than his name?"

"Nothing really. That he was an expert in art conservation, and that his students called him Bon Papa."

"The professor was a great Francophile," she says, not troubling herself to apologize for having feigned ignorance of the nickname yesterday. "The war pained him greatly. He loathed the Nazis."

"Which is why he was doing favors for Hitler."

"Your generation knows nothing of life under a totalitarian government," she says dismissively. "Everyone makes the accommodations they have to make."

"You're suggesting he was a good German?"

"I'm suggesting that he cared about art," she snaps. "The Nazis formed a committee to purge their museums of *entartete kunst,* degenerate art. They were burning canvases. Professor von Stern did his best to save what he could."

I can't help wondering if she learned more than just technique from von Stern—maybe she picked up her ethics from him, as well. Perhaps his higher purpose justified his actions, just as she believes her higher purpose justifies hers.

"So how did von Stern end up with the Linz paintings?" I ask, steering clear of an argument with her.

"The paintings had been transported from all over Europe. A number were handled quite roughly. In late 1944, the entire collection was moved from Neuschwanstein Castle to a special workroom at the Old National Gallery in Berlin, so the professor could clean and restore them."

"There must have been records. Why didn't anyone ever figure it out?"

"A cosmic joke," she says dryly. "Everyone assumes that the Nazis were infallible when it came to paperwork. But the clerk at Neuschwanstein who prepared the movement order was careless. He filled it out backward, writing the origin as the destination and vice versa. It never occurred to the Americans or the Soviets that German paperwork could be wrong, and that the paintings had actually been taken from Neuschwanstein to Berlin rather than the reverse. The Americans spent years drilling holes in the masonry of the castle, confident the paintings were hidden behind a wall or beneath a floor. William Turndale was the only one clever enough to consider the possibility of an error in the records. And, more clever yet, he was the only one to guess why the paintings might have been sent to Berlin in the first place."

The loathing in her voice when she speaks William's name is unmistakable. I'm increasingly curious as to the truth of what happened between them.

"William knew that Professor von Stern was the pre-eminent conservator in Germany," I say. "He sought von Stern out."

"He did. The professor had been captured by the Soviets when Berlin fell. The Russians gave him the choice of working for them or being sent to a labor camp. The art was still his priority. He spent the postwar years conserving and cataloging paintings that the Russians had seized from the Nazis. By the time William turned up, in the spring of 1960, Professor von Stern was back in his former post at Humboldt University in East Berlin. It was still possible to move between the eastern and western sectors of the city at the time. William began visiting the professor covertly. He flattered him with questions and admiration. Eventually, he mentioned the Linz paintings. He told the professor that he was an American intelligence officer, and he proposed a deal on behalf of the American government. If the professor were to help the Americans gain control of the missing paintings, the Americans would resettle him in the United States. William swore that the American government would make every effort to restore the paintings to their rightful owners, and only keep those canvases that proved unreturnable."

"Was there actually a deal with the American government?"

"Of course not," she says, looking over at me incredulously. "William wanted the paintings for himself. But he was smart to approach the professor as he did. The professor had withheld his information from the Soviets because he wanted to see the paintings returned to their owners."

"So von Stern agreed."

"With a single condition. Bon Papa was seventy at the time. The war years had taken a toll on him physically, and he lacked the stamina necessary for the fine work demanded by his craft. I'd been sent to him from the Academy of Arts in Leningrad two years previously, when I was seventeen. Increasingly, it was my hands that he relied on to touch the canvases for him. We'd become very close, like a father and daughter. Bon Papa told William that any deal had to include me, and he took the precaution of insisting that he wouldn't reveal the location of the paintings until we'd both traveled safely out of East Germany."

She's stopped rocking, her face a mask of pain as she stares through the glass window into the past.

"William moved quickly. He provided us with identity papers and flew us to Lisbon, where we checked into a hotel. He came to Bon Papa's room the evening that we arrived. He had tickets to New York for us, on a boat that was leaving the next morning. William had fulfilled his end of the bargain, so Bon Papa told him where the paintings were hidden. William flew into a rage."

"Why?"

"He'd assumed the paintings were concealed in Berlin. In the final days of the war, though, when the city was threatened by Soviet artillery, the professor had secretly transported the collection to Potsdam, where he hid it in the basement of his family's former hunting lodge. Potsdam isn't far from Berlin, but it was securely within East German territory in 1960. The

American government might have been able to unearth eighty paintings from a basement in East Germany and smuggle them across the border undetected, but William alone hadn't a chance. He'd failed."

Mrs. Zhilina pauses, and I have a terrible premonition about what she's going to tell me next. I know enough about William to imagine how he would have reacted to failure.

"William slapped the professor. Bon Papa fell backward and hit his head on a bedpost. He was bleeding. I tried to go to him, but William caught me by the arm and threw me on the bed. He pushed my face down into the bedclothes, smothering me, and began tearing at my dress. . . ."

Tears trickle down Mrs. Zhilina's cheeks. She blots her face with a handkerchief drawn from her sleeve. There's nothing for me to say.

"Bon Papa's skin was cool by the time William left, and the blood beneath his head had begun to congeal. I didn't know what to do. I was all alone, in a strange country. I managed to get myself on the boat to New York the next morning. I tried to overcome my grief, and to persuade myself that things would somehow be better in America. Within a few weeks of arriving, though, I realized I was pregnant."

She takes a deep breath to steady herself.

"I had no money. I looked for work in a museum or a gallery, but I was unemployable because of my accent and where I'd been trained. Americans weren't interested in students with Eastern European credentials, and Bon Papa's name had been stained by his affiliation with the Nazis and the Soviets. It would be years before Germans of his generation were rehabilitated by the art community. A priest at the Orthodox church that had been sheltering me found me a job as a cleaning woman, and helped me locate a place to live.

Andrei and Katya were born. I scraped on for four years, working at night while they slept at a neighbor's. It was too much. I fell asleep one day while they were playing, and Katya burned her arm badly on the stove. I was at my wit's end. I knew I couldn't keep on alone."

"I'm sorry," I say, torn as much by the image of Katya and Andrei vulnerable as children as by her story.

"I'd kept up with the art press," she continues, as if she hadn't heard me. "I knew that William had returned from Europe and been appointed to the board of the Metropolitan Museum. I went to see him. I told him about Katya and Andrei, and said that if he didn't help us, I'd go to the newspapers. He replied that the authorities would deport me, that my documents were forgeries. I said I didn't care. I had nothing more to lose. We reached an understanding."

"He supported you."

"No," she says vehemently. "He got me my job at the Met, a job I was more than qualified for. And he gave me enough money to establish a proper household. I insisted it be a loan. My job at the Met didn't pay much, but once I had access to proper materials, I began making *lubok* to earn extra money."

"*Lubok?*"

"Painted prints. Traditional Russian folk art. I distressed my work so the dealers could represent it as prerevolutionary. Older *lubok* sold for a premium. As my skill progressed, I moved on to icons."

She grips the handkerchief tightly in one fist, sounding more assured.

"That's how I came to know Vladimir's father. He was a diplomatic courier who sold *lubok* and icons, genuine pieces that he smuggled out of Russia. We developed a partnership.

He sold my reproductions to collectors in Zurich and London, representing them as originals. A number of my pieces ended up in museums, both here and in Europe. I made more than enough to pay William back, and to look after Katya and Andrei properly. Everything was going as well as I could have hoped. The children grew up. And then one day, Katya phoned me from university, telling me she'd been offered a job at Turndale, and that she'd accepted."

Her voice trembles with rage.

"Why didn't you tell Katya the truth?" I ask.

"I was afraid that she might despise me, or worse, that she might form an attachment to William."

"That doesn't make any sense."

"You've never been raped," she says angrily. "You've never raised a child so desperate to know her father that she withheld her love from you. Losing Katya to William was the worst thing I could imagine."

There's too much pain in her voice for me to doubt her.

"You called William?"

"I did," she says. "He mocked me, saying he'd take good care of her. I'd made sure Katya and Andrei wouldn't know him, or how they'd come into the world. I didn't want them to be burdened. And now he was using that against me. I swore that day to make him pay for everything he'd done. I had one weapon left—I still knew where the Linz art was. The East Germans were using von Stern's former family lodge as a government dacha, making it impossible to try for the art. I bided my time. In the fall of 1989, the East German government collapsed. Vladimir was working with me by then, and he was able to take advantage of the confusion to recover the paintings before William could act. I waited for the right moment and then sold the Brueghel at auction, hoping to attract William's attention. He bought the painting and then made inquiries after the seller, sniffing at my bait."

"You waited what, almost thirteen years before selling the Brueghel," I say, confused by the time line. "Why then? Because Andrei was in financial trouble?"

"Andrei's clever," she says reproachfully. "He took money from Turndale, but he never lost anything. The trading records you saw were falsified for William's benefit."

"Which is why the foundation still has more than a billion in assets," I say, the truth suddenly obvious.

"Exactly," she says. "Andrei invested Turndale's money. Contrary to what you and William believed, he did well. So much so that we were able to pay all the foundation's expenses, repurchase the counterfeit shares, and still have several hundred million in cash left over."

I was a fool. I should have doubted Andrei's trading records when I first saw them: He lost too much money too quickly. There's an old trading desk saw that says a great trader's right just more than half the time, and a terrible trader's right just less than half. No one could have been as consistently wrong as Andrei's records indicated he was. My accounting professor was right: All fraud is obvious once you admit the possibility.

"We wanted William to think Turndale was going to fail," she says. "He had to be desperate when he negotiated for the art."

"So you could get a better price?"

"That was part of it. The foundation needed sufficient resources to carry out Andrei's vision. And I had to wrest control of Turndale from William, so I could put Katya in charge. Those are my gifts to them. But more important than the price was that William agree to our conditions for the trade."

"What conditions?" I demand, frustrated again at not understanding her.

"Fifteen years is a long time to wait," she says. "But eighty paintings by almost as many different artists was a huge undertaking for me. I couldn't allow William and his experts more than a single night to examine my forgeries."

49

"YOU'VE RUINED WILLIAM," I say, amazed at the cunning of her revenge.

"Worse," she says calmly, beginning to rock again. "I've humiliated him. He prided himself on his artistic and financial acumen. I've made him a fool."

"Where are the real paintings?"

"They were delivered to the Metropolitan Museum this afternoon, along with all Professor von Stern's original notes regarding their provenances. The majority should prove returnable. I only wish I could see William's face when he reads about it in the press. I pray God grants him a long enough life for him to suffer properly with his shame, the way I've suffered with mine."

The more she tells me, the more frightening she reveals herself to be.

"You've been planning this since Katya first went to work for William?" I ask, still grappling with the extent of her duplicity.

"You misunderstand. It took years to prepare the bait, but the exact nature of the trap only suggested itself at the last moment. Much of what I've done was improvisation. I hadn't intended to involve Katya or Andrei. Only after Andrei told me he was sick, and explained what he wanted to accomplish before he died, did I see the possibility."

"Andrei wouldn't have approved of murder," I say, feeling a need to speak for him.

"Certainly not," she admits. "It was difficult enough to persuade him to take the steps that he did. Andrei was always reluctant to let the ends justify the means. I encouraged him to think of William's money as his rightful inheritance—an inheritance better spent on the sick and impoverished than on a new wing for the Metropolitan Museum. The one blessing of his illness is that he never learned of your wife's death. The guilt would have crushed him."

"You subverted his good intentions to serve your revenge."

"No," she says emphatically. "I've served us both faithfully."

"Would Andrei agree?"

"Tolstoy or someone of his ilk could probably write a great fat book on the morality of my behavior. I've done what I thought best for my children and for Professor von Stern's legacy. I've done terrible things—worse even than you know—to promote their interests, and to revenge Bon Papa. I lost my innocence the evening that William raped me, and compromised my scruples the day that I begged him for his help. He and I may spend eternity together in hell, but I regret nothing."

I regret nothing: "Je Ne Regrette Rien," the title of an old Edith Piaf song my father used to sing when my mother reproached him for his absences or his infidelities as we ate dinner. He'd begin softly, singing in an exaggerated accent while tapping time on the table, gradually increasing in volume until his voice drowned out her accusations, and the thumping of his fist sent dishes crashing to the floor. I knew he was wrong to taunt her, but I never had the courage to say so. She'd flee to their bedroom, weeping, and he'd tell me to put the telescope in the car. Those were the nights we'd stay out till dawn, my father sipping whiskey from his flask and offering me the occasional pull as we took turns howling at the sky. I'm thankful that it was Jenna's voice and not his that came to me when I was standing over Lyman. For the first time ever, I'm glad I'm not like him.

"You regret nothing," I say, feeling a renewed determination to hold Mrs. Zhilina accountable. "Not even hiding Andrei from Katya while he's been dying?"

"I've accepted that God will punish me," Mrs. Zhilina says levelly.

"That's not an answer."

"Katya had to work with William. I couldn't risk making her party to a conspiracy against him. I had no choice but to keep Andrei and Katya apart."

"The ends justifying the means again. Your revenge was more important to you than their need for each other, and their peace of mind."

"I chose between evils," she says angrily. "Everything I did was for their benefit."

"Katya won't think so. She'll never forgive you for keeping Andrei from her."

"Love demands sacrifice. A conviction you don't seem to share."

"Meaning?"

"Fondation l'Etoile is the means to both Andrei's legacy and Katya's professional happiness. If Andrei and Katya are your friends—if you love them—you'll accept the role I'm offering you, regardless of your feelings about what I've done. I'm prepared to resign from the board. You and Emily will become l'Etoile's codirectors."

"Tell me something," I say, my mind whirling. "How did you know about me and Katya?"

"I saw an e-mail that she wrote to Andrei," Mrs. Zhilina says, no hint of remorse in her voice. "He was already in hospital, and I'd begun looking after his affairs. Katya was distraught at your treatment of her, and racked with guilt for betraying your wife."

"And yet you want me to take on this responsibility, despite knowing how much I hurt her."

"What I *want* isn't achievable. My son is dying, and my daughter despises me. We've established my willingness to compromise. I'll settle for your cooperation."

"I'm sorry," I say slowly. "The answer's still no. I don't want to be part of this."

"You don't believe that I'll give you a free hand," she says shrewdly.

"Not for a second."

"Discuss it with Emily," she suggests. "You might see things differently in a few days."

I shrug, unwilling to indulge her with an answer.

"One more thing," she says, reaching over to touch a cold finger to the back of my hand. "The package Andrei sent your wife. Vladimir recovered it. Would you like it?"

"What is it?" I ask, trembling.

"A book," she says.

A book. My eyes tear at this final confirmation that Jenna died for nothing.

"I'll get it for you," Mrs. Zhilina says. "It's upstairs."

"I'll go with you."

"No," she says, getting to her feet. "I need to have a private word with Emily. Vladimir will help me on the stairs. I'll be down in a few minutes. You can wait here, or in the kitchen, as you prefer."

I rock quietly on the cold porch after Mrs. Zhilina leaves, worn-out from grief and shock. The moon's higher now, and the surf rougher, a diaphanous spray shimmering over the breakers. Katya will be here soon. I lean my head back against the chair and close my eyes, trying to pull myself together. Tonight's going to be terrible for her.

The kitchen door opens sometime later, startling me from a light doze. It's Emily, Vladimir standing behind her.

"Do you mind coming in here, Peter?" she says, her voice strangely muted.

"What is it?" I ask, stepping into the kitchen.

Emily takes my hands. There are tears shining in her eyes. "Andrei's gone. Just now. Peacefully."

"Did Mrs. Zhilina . . ."

"Yes," she says, embracing me. "It was time."

Anger overwhelms my grief: Mrs. Zhilina's deprived Katya of the opportunity to see her brother one last time, to make her farewell.

"I want to talk to her," I say.

"Who?" Emily asks, leaning back to look up at me.

"Mrs. Zhilina."

"She is leaving this for you," Vladimir says, holding out a book.

I release Emily and take the slim volume from him. It's an English translation of Tolstoy's "Confession." A sheet of paper is tucked between the pages. I unfold it and see a note written in an antique copperplate:

> *Peter:*
>   *I am an old woman, and the time has come for me to make my final sacrifice. Yesterday, after we spoke at the museum, I signed away control of Fondation l'Etoile to you and Emily. Vladimir has the papers. I pray you'll honor Andrei's wishes. If nothing else, please be kind to Katya.*
>   *Oksana Zhilina*

"Where is she?" I ask, looking up at Vladimir. I'm damned if I'll let her present me with a fait accompli.

"Come," he says. He opens the sliding door to the deck and leads me outside, pointing over the dunes. "There."

"Where?" I ask. There's no one on the beach. He gestures again, and I shift my gaze higher. There's someone in the water, fifty yards offshore, swimming toward the horizon. I start forward instinctively, but Vladimir checks me.

"No," he says. "Is better."

We watch together as the figure becomes more distant. For the life of me, I don't know how I feel. An outsize swell rolls over the swimmer, moonlight rippling from the crest. It passes and the ocean's empty.

SPRING

50

THE ADDRESS I'M LOOKING FOR turns out to be a moldering brick apartment building on the outskirts of White Plains, overlooking the Bronx River Parkway. There's a faded sign out front advertising studios and one-bedroom apartments for rent, and a pair of battered wooden planters on either side of the door, sporting a few lonely daffodils. The street's deserted at 6:30 on a Sunday morning, the newly risen sun glinting off the rough concrete sidewalk. I take my phone out, dial a number, and hesitate with my thumb over the send button, wondering if I'm asking for trouble. Maybe, but it's the right thing to do. Pressing the button, I put the phone to my ear. It's answered on the fourth ring.

"Grace Tilling," she says, sounding half-awake.

"Peter Tyler."

She clears her throat and coughs, the phone turned away from her mouth.

"As I live and breathe," she says. "To what do I owe this honor?"

"You've been trying to get hold of me."

"Only for about three fucking months."

"I've been thinking. I want to talk."

"When?"

"Now."

"Where?" she asks. I can hear the bed groan as she sits up.

"You decide. I'm downstairs, in front of your building."

"I don't like this," she says more alertly. "How'd you get my address?"

"Does it matter?" I ask, half-hoping she'll tell me to get lost.

"There's a park at the end of the block," she says. "Wait there. I'll meet you in ten minutes."

"I'm not interested in Ellis or anyone else joining us."

"You and me," she says. "Ten minutes."

The park's a patch of concrete with a rusted swing set, the ground littered with green and brown shards of glass. I wait on the one bench that hasn't been vandalized. Grace walks toward me wearing gray sweatpants that say FORDHAM LAW on the leg, and a blue nylon windbreaker with a police badge silk-screened on the breast. She has a Yankees cap pulled low on her forehead. Her eyes flick over my body as she stops in front of me, taking in my new jeans and blue blazer. I've put some weight back on, but I'm still a lot lighter than I was six months ago.

"You look good," she says. "You're tan. Keisha told me you were in Brazil."

"Business. We're working on a proposal to build a pharmaceutical plant down there in partnership with the government."

"Your buddy, Robert Meyer . . ."

"Tigger."

"Right. Tigger and I spent some time together. He told me all about this foundation you guys are running. No wonder you had trouble getting back to me. You're a busy outfit. You're doing all kinds of good stuff."

"Thanks," I say, ignoring the tinge of sarcasm in her voice.

"Personally," she says, putting one foot up on the bench next to me and leaning forward, "I don't give a fuck how many good deeds you do. If it had been up to me, I would have arrested you on the gun charge and threatened you with a couple of years upstate unless you cooperated with us. You promised to help us nail the guys who hired Lyman and Franco, and whoever murdered Rommy. You said there were a lot of levels to this thing, and that you were still asking questions. Only instead of telling us what you learned, you let someone buy you off with this fancy foundation job. Ellis and I trusted you, and you fucked us."

"That's not what happened."

"Bullshit."

"I'm here now," I say. "To keep my promise."

She tips the brim of her cap up, crow's-feet surrounding her eyes. A cynical smile spreads across her face as she looks at me.

"Let me guess," she says. "You want to talk off the record. That's why you showed up unannounced and said it had to be just you and me."

"I'm not going to testify to anything, if that's what you're asking."

"But you'll tell me what happened," she says, nodding slowly. "Why?"

"I made a promise," I say, shrugging.

"That's it?"

"That's half of it," I say, looking up into her careworn face. "When we spoke in the parking lot at Jenna's funeral, I got the feeling that you weren't just doing a job."

"I made a promise also," Grace says. "The same promise I make to every victim. I'm still working for Jennifer and I don't give a damn about anything else."

"That's what I thought. That's why I've decided to tell you the truth."

The deli across the street opens while we're talking, a sleepy-looking girl hand-cranking an old-fashioned metal security gate open. Grace buys coffee for both of us, and I reciprocate when our cups are empty. We sit side by side on the bench as I tell her about Katya, Andrei, Emily, William, and Zeitz, and about Mrs. Zhilina. She interrupts repeatedly, pressing for details. The only fact I withhold is that Vladimir and his gang used to work at Emily's clinic.

"So you don't know this Vladimir character's last name, or anything else about him?" she asks.

"No."

"I'm sorry, Peter," she says, shaking her head. "I'd keep you out of it if I could, but you're the one who saw Vladimir murder Lyman. You're going to have to testify to the grand jury so I can get a warrant."

"I won't."

"I'll subpoena you."

"I'll perjure myself."

"Don't you understand?" she demands angrily. "There isn't any other way to break this thing open."

"I realize that."

She stares at me incredulously.

"This Vladimir guy brutally murdered two people. One of those people used to be my partner."

"I'm sorry. I don't condone what Vladimir did, but seeing him punished is less important to me than the work I'm doing now. I won't jeopardize Fondation l'Etoile's reputation or anything else by spouting wild stories about Russian killers who won't ever be caught or convicted."

"Zeitz is guilty of conspiracy, at a minimum. You're willing to let them buy you off with this drug?"

"If you want to look at it that way. I prefer to think of the lives we're saving. I've given it a lot of thought, Grace. This is what Jenna would have wanted. I'm content to let things lie."

"You're content," she says furiously, flinging her empty coffee cup at a nearby trash can. "You're content because everything's worked out for you. Hasn't it?"

"My wife and my best friend are dead," I say, touching her arm to soften the reproach.

"Don't try to guilt me," she snaps, jerking away. "You know what I mean."

Her hat's pulled low again, concealing her face, but she's clearly livid. I'd leave now if I weren't going to have to recount this entire conversation to Tigger later.

"There's something else I wanted to talk to you about."

"Pray tell," she says sarcastically.

"I got your address from the same private investigator who dug up the dirt on Rommy before Jenna's funeral. He's an ex-cop, a guy who's still pretty plugged in to your department. He told me that things haven't been going so well for you at work."

"There's a hot news flash. What would you expect? My former partner and I caught a high-profile murder. The DA put out a warrant on the wrong guy, we didn't find the right guys until one of them turned up dead, the dead guy was murdered by my ex-partner, and then persons unknown took out my ex-partner and the other killer. The only arrest I made was an ex-FBI agent who was driving around Long Island with a couple of machine guns in the trunk of his car, and that was in another county."

"I don't see why you took the heat."

"Don't you?" she asks, shaking her head. "Shit flows downhill. The DA's political and the chief's superstitious. She thinks I've got a bad smell and he thinks I'm unlucky. It works out to the same thing."

"That first time we met, in my office, Rommy mentioned that you were going to law school," I say. "I hear you're almost done."

She tilts her head sideways to make eye contact and extends a hand to touch my arm, mirroring the gesture I made a moment ago.

"Stay the fuck out of my life," she says softly. "You got that?"

What was it Tigger'd said? "The worst she can do is walk away." I take a deep breath.

"L'Etoile's going to do business in some dicey places. We could use a lawyer with a strong public-safety background."

She laughs, her eyes never wavering from mine.

"One of the bad things about being a cop is that I can't punch some asshole like you in the side of the head without feeling like I'm hiding behind my badge."

"It's just an offer," I say, not having expected anything different.

She reaches toward me, not quite touching my chest with her finger.

"It sounded like something different."

"It was Tigger's idea," I say, shrugging. "He likes you. So does Keisha. I'm sorry if I offended you."

"I suppose I should say thanks, but etiquette's never been my strong suit."

"The offer's open," I say, getting up. "Call me if you want to talk."

"Wait," she says. "We're not done yet."

I sink back down onto the bench, tucking a leg beneath me so I can face her. She's got one hand covering her face. I wonder what she's thinking.

"I saw a picture of you on the back page of the *New York Sun*," she says. "At the opening of that kids' center in Hell's Kitchen you sponsored. Katya Zhilina was standing next to you. Are the two of you spending much time together these days?"

"Some," I say, surprised by the change of topic. "We're trying to figure things out."

She drops her hand to her lap and stares off toward the Bronx River Parkway below us. Traffic's heavier now, the discrete rush of solitary cars having built to an unalleviated background whine.

"Years ago," she says, "my father taught me that the right way to treat other people is to imagine myself in their shoes, and then decide how I'd want to be treated. You think that's good advice?"

"I do," I say, trying to work out what she's driving at.

"If I were you," she says, "I'd want to know the whole story."

"What do you mean?" I ask, a funny fluttering in my chest.

"Let me tell you about being a homicide cop," she says. "Most murders are easy to solve. A guy gets drunk and smacks his wife in the head with a bottle. A woman gets pissed about her husband cheating and shoots him. Simple stuff. The cases that aren't easy are the ones where the motive isn't obvious. The way you solve a hard case is to collect as much information as possible and look for contradictions or coincidences. Usually, you realize after the fact that there were any number of things that could have broken it for you, things you forgot to ask about, or didn't check up on, or just didn't put together."

"So?"

"I didn't know Mrs. Zhilina worked at the Metropolitan Museum until I read her obituary," she says. "Ellis and I visited her at home when we spoke to her about Andrei, and we didn't think to ask if she worked, or where she worked."

"So?" I repeat.

"Jennifer told the priest how she found out you were having an affair. She said the other woman's mother called her, and that they met. That would have been Mrs. Zhilina, wouldn't it?"

Nothing about Mrs. Zhilina should surprise me at this point, but I can't help being shocked.

"Yes."

"Why would Mrs. Zhilina tell Jennifer about your affair with Katya?"

"I don't know. To punish me for hurting Katya, maybe. What are you implying?"

"Patience," she says. "Let's talk about Lyman for a minute. Mrs. Zhilina didn't know his name, but she figured out where he was staying. Vladimir must have staked out the hotel lobby and followed Lyman upstairs, grabbing him as he entered his room. Right?"

"I guess."

"It's a big hotel, though. Lots of people walking through the lobby. How was Vladimir able to pick Lyman out of the crowd?"

"I don't know," I say, my sense of uneasiness growing.

"Another point," she says. "If Andrei was already in the hospital on Long Island when he supposedly sent the book to your house, who mailed it, and how did Zeitz know it had been sent?"

"Goddamn it," I say, getting to my feet again. "I'm not going to play games with you, Grace. Tell me what you're saying."

She tips her head back, looking up at me.

"We found an e-mail from Andrei to Jennifer in her in-box, sent the day before she was murdered. The message told her to look out for an important package from him."

"That doesn't make sense," I say uncertainly. "Andrei suspected Zeitz was reading his e-mail, and he knew they were looking for him. He'd warned Emily about it."

"Which brings me to the phone call," Grace says. "The one Jennifer got at work the day she was murdered, just before she left the office. We subpoenaed all the phone companies serving the tristate area to see if we could identify the source. It took a while, but we got a hit. The call was made from a pay phone in the lobby of the Metropolitan Museum."

"Here," Grace says, nudging my hand with a wad of napkins from the deli.

I don't know how much time's gone by. I feel disembodied, as if I were lying in the street after being hit by a car.

"You want me to tell you what I think happened?" she asks.

I nod, wiping my face.

"I figure it like this. After Lyman tripped Mrs. Zhilina in the street, she realized that Zeitz meant to play rough. She needed leverage to make them back off. She decided to entice Lyman into committing a crime that Zeitz would feel compelled to cover up."

"She couldn't have known that Lyman would kill Jenna," I say, my voice quavering like an old man's. "That's impossible."

"True. But I'd bet Mrs. Zhilina had Vladimir watching your house. If Lyman never showed, she wouldn't have lost anything. When he did, Vladimir got a good look at him and then phoned her. She hung up and called Jennifer from the pay phone. It would have been okay if Lyman had only roughed up Jennifer. That alone would have given Mrs. Zhilina enough to negotiate with. But the result she really wanted was the one she got. Jennifer surprised Lyman and he murdered her."

"How could Mrs. Zhilina have tricked Jenna into going home?" I ask, still in denial.

"Your guess is as good as mine," Tilling says. "I'm more interested in why Vladimir didn't just grab Lyman and Franco when they left your house. It would have saved him a lot of trouble. Here."

She taps my hand again, this time with a bottle of water. I open it and take a drink, remembering Vladimir's apology to me the night he killed Lyman.

"Vladimir didn't know what Mrs. Zhilina had planned," I say, a horrified comprehension dawning. "He let Lyman and Franco leave because he wanted to check on Jenna. He's the one . . ." My voice breaks. "He's the one who smoothed her hair."

"Possible," Tilling says. "Lyman hightailed it out of the United States later that same day."

"Mrs. Zhilina deliberately enticed Lyman to harm Jenna," I say, fresh tears streaming down my cheeks. "Why? Just to punish me?"

"If she wanted to punish you, she would have let you take the fall for Franco's murder."

"Then what?"

"Peter."

I wipe my face again and look at Tilling. She's wearing a pained expression.

"You remember what I said before, about the advice my father gave me."

"Yes."

"If it were me, I'd want to get it all straight. No matter how bad it was."

"Tell me," I say.

"Think about it. You told me that everything Mrs. Zhilina did was to protect Andrei's and Katya's interests. She tried to break up your marriage, she put your wife in harm's way, and she maneuvered you into a role where you'd be responsible for Katya's well-being."

"No," I say, beginning to understand her. "That's not possible."

"How long has Katya been in love with you? Do you know?"

I can still remember the look on Katya's face as she held my hand at the TriBeCa bar, pretending to tell my fortune. I'm too overwrought to answer.

"Mrs. Zhilina wanted to make Katya happy," Tilling says. "She did what she thought she had to do."

"I can't believe that," I say, burying my face in my hands. "It can't be true."

"Look," Tilling says, putting a hand on my shoulder. "I'm just a cop. You need a friend. Someone like Tigger. Tell him about it and see what he thinks." She pats my back gently and then stands. "You're not a bad guy. I'll make you the same offer you made me: Call me if you want to talk."

51

LATE-AFTERNOON sun filters through budding trees, making a pattern on the metal café table where Tigger and I sit. We're in Bryant Park, behind the main branch of the New York Public Library, surrounded by foraging pigeons and a sea of yellow crocuses. He listens silently as I relate the conversation I had with Grace earlier today.

"I'm sorry, Petey," he says when I've choked to a conclusion. "Mrs. Zhilina was evil. The sad truth is that the world's full of evil."

"I don't know what to do."

He reaches across the table and takes my hand.

"There was this guy I used to know who survived the concentration camp. Had a number tattooed on his arm, lost his whole family, everything bad you could imagine. He was married when I met him, had a couple of good kids and a nice business. He used to give talks at the temple on Yom Hashoah, the Holocaust Remembrance Day. I asked him one time how he did it, how he could get up every day and live his life after all the evil he'd experienced. He asked me how could he not?

He was livin' for his family and friends and neighbors who'd been murdered, and he wouldn't let himself be defeated. He was a brave man."

"I hear you, Tigger, but I don't know what to do."

"Rupert lent me an English copy of that book you found in Andrei's apartment. The one by Tolstoy. There's a sentence in it that kinda summed things up for me: 'The changes in our life must come from the impossibility to live otherwise than according to the demands of our conscience.'"

"Which means what?"

"You went to Emily's clinic with me. You met those people. We got no choice about what we're gonna do."

Touring Emily's clinic, I'd felt Jenna at my shoulder. The children were the most heartrending, listless and wasted. Tigger's correct. There's no way I can turn my back on them.

"And what about Katya?"

"I only have two things to say. You can't blame her, and you can't tell her what Mrs. Zhilina did. It wouldn't be fair. Other than that, it has to be about how you feel. There's nothin' wrong if you want to be with her, and there's nothin' wrong if you don't."

I remember walking Katya through the cemetery after the funeral for Andrei and Mrs. Zhilina, listening to her vent her sorrow and rage, holding her as she wept. A week later, I exercised my authority as Turndale's controlling shareholder to order her back to work, telling her she was needed to see the company through the SEC investigation and reminding her of her responsibility to her shareholders and employees.

"What would you do?" I ask Tigger.

"It doesn't matter," he says, shaking his head. "This isn't about me or anybody else. It's about what you feel."

I watch a couple of kids play Frisbee on the lawn at the center of the park, thinking about Tigger's words. He glances at his watch.

"You need to be somewhere?" I ask.

"I'm supposed to meet Rachel at the hospital. She's havin' an ultrasound, and she invited me along to get a first look at my grandchild. Why don't you come with? You can hang out in the waitin' room and then have dinner with us after. She'd enjoy bringin' you up to speed on our class action suit against Klein. She's kickin' their butts."

"No thanks. You go. I'm going to sit here for a while."

"You sure? I could go with Rachel another time."

"Don't worry. I'll be fine."

"I'll call you later," he says, giving my shoulder a squeeze.

The shadows lengthen as the sun sinks, the park slowly emptying. I plumb my heart, trying to understand how I feel. My phone rings.

"It's Katya," she says, sounding exultant. "One of our lawyers just got a call at home from the SEC's lead investigator. They've decided to hang everything on William and give the company a clean bill of health. The announcement will be made tomorrow morning, before the exchange opens. Our stock's going to take off like a rocket."

"That's terrific," I reply automatically.

"You in the city?"

"Yes."

"I want to go out and celebrate. How about dinner at Le Bernardin?"

A monarch butterfly touches down on a crocus by my knee, a lingering shaft of sunlight firing its orange-and-black wings like stained glass. It explores the flower briefly before launching itself skyward again, clearing the treetops and beating its way north, up Sixth Avenue.

"Peter?" Katya says. "What do you think? Are you free?"

"Yes," I reply, watching the monarch disappear into the twilight. "I suppose I am."

Author's Note

SOME READERS MAY IMAGINE that my description of bad behavior in the financial community is a veiled jab at my former firm, Goldman Sachs Group. Nothing could be further from the truth. In an industry renowned for its bad behavior, Goldman is notable for consistently adhering to a higher standard. I can't imagine a more ethical or meritocratic organization, and I'm very, very proud to be an alumnus.

Acknowledgments

A GREGARIOUS former colleague of mine at Goldman Sachs once told me that his notion of hell was having to work in a small room all by himself. There were any number of occasions during the writing of this novel when I sat alone in my office, plot snarled and characters recalcitrant, silently agreeing with him.

Fortunately, I always seemed to get support when I needed it. My wife, Cynthia, was encouraging from my first mention of this project, and her confidence sustained me during several difficult periods. My brother, Terry, generously consented to be one of my first readers, and managed to tactfully highlight the myriad deficiencies of my initial efforts without ever discouraging me. When I felt ready for more experienced guidance, I hired four then graduate students from Columbia's MFA program to work with me—Mike Harvkey, Jane Ratcliffe, Scott Wolven, and Jennie Yabroff. All were terrific. Mike had a felicitous interest in the darker elements of my plot and a knack for identifying where I'd gone wrong in a scene. Jane aggressively challenged me to know my characters better, insisting on greater self-awareness and clarity of motivation. Scott—whose criticism tended toward the philosophical—earned my eternal gratitude by insisting I purchase *The Friends of Eddie Coyle* by George V. Higgins and read the introduction by Elmore Leonard. I strongly recommend that any struggling writer reading these words do the same.

All of which brings me to Jennie. Almost everything good in this book is there because she challenged me to write it. She served as critic, taskmaster, grammarian, therapist, and muse, and it's no exaggeration to say that I never could have completed this project without her.

When I thought the manuscript was finished—or, more precisely, when Jennie threatened to brain me with a copy if I didn't stop tinkering with it—I gave it to select friends to read. Ashley Dartnell was kind enough to return her copy replete with scribbled insights that I drew on heavily in subsequent rewrites. Larry Kramer gave me a brisk professional rundown of what was working and what wasn't and offered a wealth of tips on the process of getting published. The astute and knowledgeable Maria Campbell thoughtfully suggested a number of agents, eventually steering me to her good friend Kathy Robbins, of The Robbins Office.

Kathy was a godsend. She's the best imaginable agent, radiating a reassuring mixture of competence and moxie. She polished the rough edges of my manuscript with her trademark green pen and then led me by the hand through the bruising process of selecting—and being selected by—a publisher. David Halpern, Kate Rizzo, and Coralie Hunter also helped with matters great and small. I'd particularly like to express my gratitude to Rachelle Bergstein, who weighed in throughout the editing process with discerning observations.

Lastly, I'm grateful to the people at Knopf. Peter Gethers

and Claudia Herr, my editors, suggested any number of subtle cuts, adds, and changes that dramatically streamlined and enhanced the story, and Peter Mendelsund designed a fabulous jacket. I couldn't have been happier with the process, or the result.

To all the above, my sincerest thanks.

An Excerpt from

THE GARDEN OF BETRAYAL

Coming soon from Alfred A. Knopf

I WOKE EARLY and listened to Claire breathe. She had her back to me, but she didn't sound like she was sleeping, so I rolled onto my side and used one hand to gently massage her neck and shoulders. Some mornings she ignored me, some mornings we made love, and some mornings she wept. After a few minutes of no response, I got up.

Frank, the night doorman, had a taxi waiting by the time I got downstairs. He said good morning and solemnly handed me a few pieces of mail addressed to my son. It was a shock when I first received mail for Kyle about a year after he disappeared—a solicitation from a preteen magazine called *Tiger Beat*. He would have been thirteen at the time. I spent the day thinking about it and then knocked on the building super's door. Tears in his eyes, he admitted that he'd been intercepting junk mail addressed to Kyle for the past twelve months and turned over a full cardboard box. I made myself go through it—Reggie Kinnard, the detective working with us, had mentioned that the psychopaths who kidnap children will occasionally amuse themselves by sending the victim's family mail. There wasn't anything unusual in the box. A friendly representative of the Direct Marketing Association who I spoke to on the phone suggested I simply scrawl the word 'deceased' on everything and return it to the post office. Instead, I had the super continue intercepting it, so Claire and Kate wouldn't see it, and arranged for Frank to pass it along. These days, it's all solicitations for acne products and CD clubs and summer job programs and magazines like *Maxim* and *Outside*. The kind of stuff any nineteen-year-old might receive. The kind of stuff Kyle might actually be interested in, if he's still alive somewhere.

I stopped to pick up the papers at an all-night newsstand on Seventy-second Street and then went to work. There's always someone at the office when I arrive, no matter the time—the hedge fund I rent space from trades twenty-four hours a day. There are only about sixty employees, but they occupy an entire floor of a midtown office building, the northern half of which is a single, large, unpartitioned trading room. One corner of the room is taken up by the fund's namesake, a midnight blue 1966 Ford Shelby AC Cobra that sits on a low dais, halogen spotlights reflecting off its mirrorlike finish. The car had proved too large for the elevators, so Andrew Coleman, the fund's founder, had arranged to have it hoisted by a crane, after workers cut a garage door–sized opening into the side of the building.

When Andrew and his son Alex first suggested setting me up as an independent analyst five years ago, I was hesitant. My entire career had been on the sell side, peddling research on oil companies to clients of the investment bank I worked for. The notion of trying to market myself as a freelance energy pundit was intimidating. Two years out of the market and lacking the institutional connections that had made people want to talk to me, I was afraid I wouldn't be able to deliver anything of value. Save one or two old friends, I was right to think that my former sources would abandon me, but wrong to worry that it would matter. Cobra was the grand-daddy of the hedge-fund community, progenitor of multiple generations of firms that gossiped and fought and generally behaved like an extended family. Andrew and Alex made a few calls on my behalf and suddenly I had a dozen clients, all funds that Wall Street was desperate to do business with. These days, there isn't a sell-side guy on the Street who won't drop everything to answer my call.

I grabbed some coffee from the pantry and settled in at my desk. I was reading an industry rag half an hour later when my news screen suddenly began to beep. Glancing up, I saw the headline, "Explosion Reported at Nord Stream Pipeline Terminus," the keywords "Nord Stream" and "pipeline" highlighted in yellow. The terminus was in Russia, near St. Petersburg. I picked up my phone and called Dieter Thybold, a friend at Reuters in London.

"It's Mark," I said when he answered. "What's up with this pipeline explosion?"

"No idea yet," he replied tersely. "I can't even confirm that there was an explosion. But something strange is going on."

"Strange how?"

"Today's the day they're holding the construction comple-tion ceremony for the terminus. A lot of reporters and digni-taries are visiting. The whole site went quiet twenty minutes ago. Nobody can get hold of their people. And we just got word a moment ago that the Russians have closed their air-space between St. Petersburg and the Finnish border, and that there's been a huge increase in encrypted radio traffic out of their military bases at Pribilovo and Kronshtadt."

"So how do your people know there was an explosion?" I asked, my adrenaline beginning to pump.

"There was a camera crew shooting the ceremony. The footage should be on air any minute. You can see the tiniest hint of a flash in the last frame of the video before it goes dark."

"Satellite views?"

"Too cloudy. I've got to go."

"Wait. You're thinking terrorism?"

"It's hard not to, isn't it? But we haven't got many facts yet. I'll e-mail you a partial list of the attendees that we cobbled together. That's about it right now."

"Thanks. I appreciate it. Stay in touch."

I hung up and turned on CNN, watching the screen out of the corner of one eye while I speed-typed an e-mail to my clients. The gas pipeline the terminus was supposed to serve wouldn't be finished for three years yet, but the market impact of any kind of incident there—much less a terrorist attack—would be instantaneous. The immediate risks were a knee-jerk spike in energy prices, weakening global equity markets, a steeping yield curve, and a declining euro. Dieter's e-mail arrived. I copied the list of names at the bottom of my own e-mail, wrote *URGENT* in the subject line and hit the send button. Alex Coleman, Andrew's son, was in my office thirty seconds later.

"You think this is serious?" he demanded.

Alex looked terrible, rough patches of psoriasis visible in his hairline and bluish circles beneath his eyes. He'd been having a bad time with the market for months. In truth, he'd been having a bad time with the market for years. I could guess what his positions were today from the sweat soaking his shirt beneath his arms.

"I don't know anything more than what I wrote."

"You have a hunch?"

"Half the countries that used to make up the Soviet Union are furious about this pipeline, and they'd all like to see Russia take it in the neck. I think this is bad."

"Shit."

He rushed out just as CNN cut to a special report. They had obtained the footage Dieter referred to. It opened with an establishing shot: frozen marshes, snow, and the bleak gray waters of the Bay of Finland. The shot tightened as it panned to the terminus. It was nothing much to look at—squat scrubbing and absorption towers, low brown buildings to house the compressor equipment, an antennae-festooned central control station on tall stilts, and endless miles of dull blue pipe and valves. There was no housing—according to the CNN commentator, the workers commuted from Vyborg, thirty miles to the east, or from Hamina, in Finland, thirty miles to the west. The shot tightened further as a group of heavily bundled dignitaries began emerging from a building that was probably a dining hall. I recognized Jacques Pripaud, the head of Banque BNP Paribas, as the first out the door. His expression seemed consistent with a meal at a Russian cafeteria. He was closely followed by his counterpart at Deutsche Bank. I pulled a copy of Dieter's list closer and turned the volume up a little, hoping the commentator might identify more of the faces I didn't know. Dieter had sent me twenty-two names, including the chairmen of four of the largest banks in Europe, a Russian deputy prime minister, the mayor of St. Petersburg, and the German foreign minister. The pipeline had been hugely controversial in Europe, implying an energy dependence on Russia that made people old enough to remember the cold war queasy. All the businessmen and politicians who'd supported it had turned out to wave the flag.

The camera followed closely as the men trooped across an icy parking lot to a white canvas tent. Inside was a gang of valves, one of which had a gilded control wheel attached to it. The diameter of the attached pipe was way too small to be anything other than some kind of secondary line, but then the entire act of turning a valve by hand was pure theater—everything in the facility was automated. A microphone on a stand stood to the left of the pipe gang. The Russian deputy prime minister tapped on the microphone a few times to settle the crowd, took a sheaf of folded papers from his pocket, and opened his mouth. The screen flared orange for a tenth of a second and then went black.

"Shoot." I drummed my fingers on my head, trying to think of who else I could call. CNN had frozen the last frame of the footage on the screen, and my attention drifted to a small yellow credit on the bottom right corner that read *Courtesy of EuroNews.* Someone I knew had gone to work at EuroNews a few years back. I willed my mind blank and the name suddenly popped into my head: Gavin Metcalfe. He was a Brit who'd worked at the *Economist,* but he'd left London to take a job as a producer with EuroNews because they were headquartered near the French Alps. He and his wife were big skiers. I punched the intercom button on my phone.

"Amy, have we got a number on Gavin Metcalfe? M-e-t-c-a-l-f-e."

"Two," she answered a second later. "A work and a cell. Both U.K."

"No good. He's in France now. Or at least I think he is. Call the main switchboard at EuroNews in Lyons and ask for him please. And give me the cell number," I added as an after-thought. There was some chance he'd kept it.

The cell kicked directly into voicemail, a generic prompt suggesting I leave a message. Hoping the number hadn't been reassigned, I explained why I was calling and then followed up with a text from my own cell. My intercom flashed as I pressed the send button.

"It's weird," Amy said. "No one's answering . . ."

"Hang on," I interrupted. My cell was ringing. I picked it up and checked the display, seeing the London number I'd just dialed. "Gotta hop. This might be him."

I lifted the cell to my ear.

"Mark Wallace."

"Open a browser window on your computer," a voice answered. There was a rushing sound in the background that I couldn't identify.

"Gavin?"

"Don't interrupt. I'm in a car, and I haven't got much time. You're interested in Nord Stream, right?"

"Right," I said, my excitement building.

"So do what I tell you. Open a browser window and type this in the menu bar: F-T-P-colon-backslash-backslash-euronews-dot-net-backslash . . ."

I pecked carefully at the keyboard as he dictated a URL that was about fifty characters long, interrupting several times when I wasn't sure what he'd said. Gavin had some kind of impenetrable northern accent that made all his vowels sound the same. He told me to press enter and I did.

"It wants a username and password," I said.

"The username is 'batailledepatay,' one word, all lowercase.

Password 18061429. Bloody frogs having a go at me every time I turn around."

I could hear someone speaking in the background. It sounded like a child.

"I see a bunch of folders. You're with your family?"

"On our way to the airport. Click the folder labeled archive, and then click the one inside that with today's date, and then click the one inside that named NordStream."

"Done."

"You'll see two files—EsatIIB135542 and EsatIIC141346. Click on either to download it to your desktop. They're big files, but the server's hooked directly into the Internet backbone, so the limitation will likely be on your side."

"What are they?"

"Video. The first is the raw footage you've been seeing on television. The second is something else entirely."

I clicked the second. We were connected to a dedicated fiber optic cable as well. A dialogue box indicated that I had ten minutes to wait, the file transfer speed a number I'd never seen before.

"Give me a hint," I said, wondering what the hell was going on. "I'm under a lot of pressure here."

"You?" he sneered. "I've had the effing DGSE in my face all afternoon."

"Remind me who the DGSE are?"

"Bloody French foreign intelligence creeps. Jackbooters. They turned up just after we released the first footage and put a lid on us. I went out for a cigarette and kept going. If I wanted to work for fascists I would have taken a job with Murdoch."

"So what's the second file?"

"It's what it isn't that bears thinking about. It isn't our footage. We had one cameraman and one reporter on the ground, and we lost them both in the initial blast. I'm inside the airport now, on the ring road. I'm going to have to hang up in a moment."

I scribbled the words "initial blast" on a yellow pad. I had to stay focused.

"Who shot the footage, then?"

"Our satellite truck kept running after our lads went off the air. Someone pirated one of our frequencies and the feed was automatically uploaded. We didn't even realize we'd received it until an hour ago."

"Does it show what happened?"

"Yes."

"Is it bad?"

"It makes the guys who did 9/11 look like a bunch of shit-arsed teenagers. Make sure you watch the whole thing."

"Will do," I said, wondering fearfully what I was about to see. There was just one more question I had to ask. "Has anyone else got this yet?"

"No. I hadn't figured out who to give it to. I want it distributed, but I don't want my name mentioned. You understand?"

"You're fleeing the country, Gavin," I said, feeling obliged to point out the obvious. "It's not like they aren't going to figure it out."

"There's a difference between suspecting and knowing. I have your word?"

"Of course."

He hung up without saying good-bye. The dialogue box indicated that I had seven minutes to wait. I typed another urgent email, alerting my clients that I had tentative confirmation of a major terrorist action and that full details would follow shortly. The Dow was down 100 points when I hit the send key. By the time Andrew and Alex showed up in my office, it was down 250, and my phone turret was pulsing like it was going to explode.

"What the hell is going on?" Andrew demanded. He had a raptor's profile—an aquiline nose, deep-set eyes, and short-cropped white hair. Part of his legend was that pressure only ever made him meaner. Alex looked as if he'd been run over by a car.

I rotated my screen sideways and touched the download box with a finger.

"We'll know in a minute. I have video."

Andrew paced irritably as Alex slumped into a chair. The file completed downloading and I clicked on it. My media player opened and a second later the screen filled with an image I couldn't identify, the lower half shiny gray metal and the upper a blurry blue tube. The field of view began shifting smoothly upward and suddenly I got oriented.

"The camera's mounted on one of the scrubbing towers," I said. "It was pointing straight down, maybe so nobody would notice it."

"Whose camera?" Andrew demanded.

"My contact didn't know. Pirates, he said."

The picture scrolled higher until the Bay of Finland was just visible at the top of the screen, and then began tracking to the right.

"What's that?" Alex said, pointing at the screen.

Four metal struts reached skyward, the ends blackened and twisted. Dark smoke was spewing up between them.

"The control tower," I replied, horrified. Even with the

terminus only performing minimal duty, there would have been at least three or four guys in the control tower.

The camera kept panning and the white marquee where I'd last seen the Russian deputy prime minister about to speak—or what was left of it—came into view.

"Jesus Christ," Alex said.

Flaming scraps of canvas surrounded a charred, rectangular area that looked like an airplane crash site. Burned corpses and scattered body parts became distinguishable as the camera zoomed in. A few survivors crawled on the ground, blood seeping from appalling wounds. Alex grabbed hold of my garbage can and threw up. I felt that I wouldn't be far behind him. Andrew started to leave.

"Wait," I managed to say. "My contact said I should watch until the end."

"Why?"

"I don't know."

"Can you speed it up?" Andrew asked impatiently.

"I think so."

I clicked my mouse on the appropriate button and the video began playing at ten times speed. Andrew lifted my phone and entered a handful of crisp orders while I tapped out yet another urgent email with trembling fingers. Six minutes later—an hour of elapsed real time—the Russians had four military helicopters and fifteen or twenty fire trucks and ambulances on the ground, and another couple of helicopters circling overhead. The parking lot I'd seen earlier had been converted into an emergency triage zone, with dozens of coveralled medics working on the injured.

"Stop," Andrew said.

I pressed the pause button. A pale red X had suddenly

appeared in the center of the screen, a column of similarly colored numbers superimposed to the far left.

"Play," Andrew said. "Half speed."

I fumbled with the mouse. The camera swung slowly toward the helicopters and the emergency vehicles. Andrew touched the changing column of numbers on the left with one finger.

"Distance and azimuth," he said. Andrew had been an army officer in Vietnam. I hadn't, but I had a sudden dread of what to expect. "Speed it up again."

The camera lingered fractionally on each of the landed helicopters and on the larger pieces of emergency equipment, the central X blinking repeatedly. Each time the X blinked, it left behind a red dot. The camera pulled back for a wide view and I felt my heart in my throat. The blow wasn't long coming.

Every one of the emergency vehicles and helicopters exploded simultaneously. A fraction of a second later a rolling wave of synchronized explosions took out the triage zone. No one on the ground had a chance. Alex retched again.

"Mortars," Andrew announced softly. "Some targeted, some pre-positioned. Probably on the roof of one of the buildings. They must've anticipated where the emergency workers would set up. Who the hell are these guys?"

I shook my head numbly as the camera rose higher, pointing at the sky. The pale red X changed to blue, as did the column of numbers on the left. It panned left until it located a hovering helicopter and then zoomed in. The blue X began flashing.

"I don't believe it," Andrew said.

A white streak appeared on the lower right of the screen. The helicopter burst into flames, heeled over onto its side, and fell from the sky. The camera swung left again with the same terrible mechanical precision. A second helicopter came into view, fleeing to the east. A second later, it too fell out of the sky in flames, taken down by a second missile. The camera did a final slow pan. The horizon was empty save for bellowing plumes of black smoke, and the ground was a sea of fire.